W9-AQT-834

A Deadly Wilderness

A Deadly Wilderness

THE TIES THAT KILL

Kelly Irvin

THORNDIKE PRESS
A part of Gale, Cengage Learning

GALE
CENGAGE Learning™

Detroit • New York • San Francisco • New Haven, Conn • Waterville, Maine • London

GALE
CENGAGE Learning™

LIBRARY OF CONGRESS CATALOGING-IN-PUBLICATION DATA

Irvin, Kelly.
    A deadly wilderness / The Ties That Kill.
      p. cm. — (Thorndike Press large print Christian mystery)
    ISBN-13: 978-1-4104-2930-8
    ISBN-10: 1-4104-2930-X
    1. Detectives—Texas—San Antonio—Fiction. 2.
Murder—Investigation—Fiction. 3. Drug dealers—Fiction. 4.
Inner cities—Texas—San Antonio—Fiction. 5. Large type books.
    I. Title.
PS3609.R82D43 2010b
813'.6—dc22   2010015550

Published in 2010 by arrangement with Tekno Books.

Printed in the United States of America
1 2 3 4 5 6 7 14 13 12 11 10

To Tim, Erin, and Nicholas for putting up with me.
You are the reason I look forward to getting up every morning.

ACKNOWLEDGMENTS

It's important to state for the record that the events in this novel are complete and utter fiction. San Antonio parks are incredibly safe, beautiful places for families to share wonderful times together, in large part because of the San Antonio Park Police. The crimes that occur in parks in this novel are figments of a feverish, overactive imagination.

As much as people talk about writing being a solitary pursuit, most people don't write a book alone. In my case, I needed a lot of help to get here. My thanks to the Writing Girls, my critique group, the women who have nudged, urged, cheered, and "discussed" with me for six years on this road to publication. Peg Brantley, Susan Lohrer, and Angela Mills, the snoopy dances we've shared have spanned the continent. Our cyberspace chats are among the highlights of my fiction writing career.

The support of my fellow writing junkies of the Alamo City Christian Writers group has helped me through the pain of rejection and given me the strength to persevere. It helps to know I'm not the only one who has strange people conversing in my head at two in the morning. Thanks to my Sunday school class at Northwest Hills United Methodist Church for years of support and prayers. You really are a Class Act.

And then there's my husband, Tim, my number one supporter, who had confidence in me before I even had it in myself. And to my children, Erin and Nicholas, for all those years of putting up with me hunched over my laptop, completely and totally oblivious to the real world around me, for all the times you had to yell "Kelly!" instead of Mom, just to get my attention, for all the meals you fixed for yourselves and all the cheering you did, thank you seems hardly sufficient. Love you guys.

It just goes to show God wasn't kidding when He said he would forgive and forget. By His grace, we all get a second chance.

PROLOGUE

The hunt had been good.

Lalo Hernandez veered from the trail, scooted through a stand of trees, and crouched behind thick bushes, enjoying the warm noon time sun on his back. It was a beautiful day, making the job all the more enjoyable. He fingered the hilt of the long knife strapped to his waist as he leaned in and peeked between branches laden with leaves that scratched his face.

His prey sat on a flat rock in a small clearing several yards from the main trail, gulping water from a bottle. He wasn't alone, a fact that filled Lalo with a certain excitement. He liked a challenge. Another man sat cross-legged in the grass, a bottle of Dos Equis in one hand and a half-smoked joint in the other.

The possibility of taking them both out crossed Lalo's mind, but his employer had only paid for one hit and disposing of two bodies would be problematic. He shifted slightly as his knees began to ache — the price he paid for longevity in a business where most guys got out, got killed, or went to prison before the aches and pains of old age hampered their ability to get the job done.

He caressed the knife's hilt again, forcing himself to focus. A nice kill before a lunch of gorditas and a margarita would anesthetize his pain quite nicely. Perhaps a siesta with *su mujer*. The two men seemed to be discussing some sort of business deal. He was too far away to hear the details. It didn't matter. Lalo had no interest in their lives, their business, their families. None of it would matter in a few minutes.

Men in his occupation learned to be patient. To pick the right moment.

The crackling of leaves to his right made the skin on the back of Lalo's neck prickle. He sucked in his breath and held it as he slithered deeper into the brush and tugged his black stocking down over his face. He suspected his victims might see it as a death mask, but really it simply gave him the necessary anonymity.

A woman ducked into the clearing. Tall with the leathery skin of someone who spent a great deal of time in the sun. She marched, arms swinging, head back, straight to the rock. Lalo's prey stood. The other man remained on the ground, sucking on his joint.

The woman got in the prey's face, hands gesticulating. A fight. Lalo swore very softly. He hadn't banked on a crowd at his little party. He slipped the knife from its sheath, the carved handle a nice fit in his hand. The desire to control its power as it plunged into soft tissue and muscle almost overcame him. But not quite.

Another minute. Give it another minute. Patience.

His good luck held. The man whirled and stalked away from the woman, even as her large mouth continued to flap. He walked straight at the brushy area where Lalo had concealed himself. Distaste and anger colored the gringo's face as he picked his way through the thorny underbrush. Lalo curled up tight in his hiding place, the knife ready.

The man picked a spindly live oak and relieved himself. Lalo allowed him the dignity of zipping up his pants before he crept forward. The prey gaped at him, his eyes huge in his white face. Lalo thrust the knife up and up — straight into the prey's chest.

The sensation was everything he'd hoped for. The surprise on his prey's face only added to the intense rush of power that fueled the pumping of blood through his body and accelerated the beat of his heart. The man sagged forward, his hands up as if to ward off an attack. Too late.

"You can't do this — you won't get away . . ." He stumbled, fell to his knees. "My father will . . . my father will get you . . ."

Lalo heard pounding feet and glanced away long enough to see the man and woman fleeing. They'd seen, or they'd heard, or both. He would deal with them later. Right now, he wanted to capture every fleeting second of this kill.

His prey crumpled to the ground, gasping, a wet, gurgling sound. "You won't . . ."

His mouth worked, but the sound petered out. Lalo jerked the knife out and squatted to peer at his prey. The fight drained from the man's face, his mouth went slack, and the fear in his eyes dissipated. His features went flat.

Lalo nodded in satisfaction. His breathing began to return to normal. Time to find a nice out-of-the-way resting spot for the newly deceased. One where he wouldn't be found any time soon, just as Lalo had promised his boss.

But first he needed to do one more thing. He picked up a hand and contemplated the man's wedding ring. Nice, simple, gold band. Neat, clean fingernails, too.

The sharp blade worked its magic. Lalo had his trophy.

CHAPTER ONE

"Mom worries about everything."

The irritation in Marco Acosta's voice made Ray Johnson hide his smile. The boy sounded like an irritable old man, not an eight-year-old. Ray's amusement faded as he contemplated the reasons Marco had grown up too fast. He edged his way up a narrow spot in the rocky trail and glanced back at Benny Garza. Marco's foster cousin showed no sign he saw irony in Marco's complaint. Benny's mother was in prison, doing time on a drug charge. Marco was lucky to have a mother who cared so much.

"Your mother worries because she loves you." Ray eased back and adjusted his sunglasses as a cluster of juniper gave way to an open space lit by the early morning sun. "It's been a rough year for everyone."

"She's not going to let me go camping in Big Bend with you." Marco's breaths came in puffs between the words. The terrain became more tortuous and the path meandered along a deep ravine. "She doesn't want me to spend the night away from home."

Sweat rolled down Ray's neck and soaked the back of his T-shirt. Susana's reluctance to let Marco out of her sight was understandable. She'd lost so much already. "I'll talk to her when we get back. I promise."

Eying the ground to make sure he stayed on the trail, Ray tightened his stride to allow for the boys' shorter legs. Marco raised a water bottle to his mouth and drank. His tennis shoe was untied. "You need to tie your shoe, Marco." The police-officer-slash-Boy-Scout in Ray sprang to attention. His nerves hummed with the realization Marco wasn't paying attention — to his shoe or the sudden jagged swerve in the path. "Watch where you're going!"

Marco tripped over the shoelace and stumbled toward the ravine. The water bottle flew. His arms flapped.

Ray flung himself forward. His fingertips brushed the strap of Marco's backpack. The boy glanced back, face startled, eyes wide, his lips a tight O. Then, he disappeared from sight. Ray teetered. The toe of his boot caught in the root of a cedar tree, halting his momentum a split second before gravity

16

kicked in and the weight of his six-foot-four frame dragged him forward. He pitched headfirst into the narrow fissure.

He thrust his hands at bushes and branches but clutched only air. Tumbling, he smacked into rocks. Prickly pear and yucca scratched his face; branches punctured skin.

His head bounced like a soccer ball against the ground. Pain ping-ponged through his skull. He finally landed on his back, arms flung wide, his left foot twisted under his right leg. Noise still rang in his ears.

So much for a relaxing break from an endless parade of murder investigations.

He turned his head, fighting pain. "Marco? Marco, you okay?" He peered through half-open eyelids, sure he could see a hand on the ground a few feet away. It was too big to be Marco's. Flies swarmed where the ring finger should've been.

Ray strained to raise his arm. He reached toward the hand. Purple spots danced in front of his eyes. The light squeezed into narrow pinpoints, then faded to a murky black.

A panicked voice penetrated the pain. "Mr. Ray! Mr. Ray!"

Small hands patted Ray's face. He opened

17

his eyes to a soft, blue sky dotted with tufts of popcorn clouds. Benny's dirty face filled his vision. He sucked in air and immediately regretted it. The rank odor of decaying flesh made his eyes water and bile burn in the back of his throat.

"What the — " He tried to rise. Pain dug a trench from one ear to the other. He sank back. "What is it?"

Benny leaned in close. Ray heard his agitated breathing and smelled his little boy sweat. The dirt and leaves on his clothes told Ray he'd come down the side of the ravine in a slip-and-slide fashion. "Marco fell on a — a body. You gotta get up. He's dead. It stinks. It stinks bad!"

"Whoa! Easy, Benny, easy." Ray grabbed his hand. "Are you hurt?"

"No! We gotta get out of here!" Thin features contorted with fear, Benny tugged from Ray's grasp and darted toward Marco, who knelt a few feet away, his back to Ray. "Come on, let's just go!"

"Marco, are you hurt?" Ray struggled to get up. A sharp pain in his ankle, coupled with the fierce pounding in his head, made the ground rise and fall. He sank back again. "Marco? Are you okay?"

Marco swiveled around. Tears streaked his face, but Ray saw no blood. His amber eyes wide, his gaze swung back-and-forth from the ground to Ray. He'd lost his cap; leaves clung to his shorts and T-shirt. "I landed on him. I touched him. Somebody cut his finger off!"

Marco's voice cracked. He pointed. Ray followed the line of his trembling fingers. Three outstretched fingers pointed back, a bloody stub where the fourth should have been. The hand Ray had seen before he passed out belonged to a body, spread-eagle and half-covered by brush.

The man hadn't been dead long — his features were recognizable — but birds and other animals had begun their work of tearing soft flesh from bone as San Antonio's early summer heat baked the body. "Move away." Ray schooled his voice to stay cool and calm. He hated that Benny and Marco had seen this — they'd both had enough tragedy in their lives. First things first: he wanted them away from the scene, then he'd shift from off-duty friend to on-duty police officer once they were calm. "Come over here so I can take a look at you."

Gaze still on the body, Marco stumbled to Ray, one arm dangling awkwardly at his side. Ray grabbed his thin frame in a hug. "Look at me, Marco. Does your arm hurt?"

Marco buried his head in Ray's chest. Ray

felt a shudder rip through him. "Where does it hurt?"

"My wrist." Marco held out his swollen arm.

"Can you bend it?"

Marco's sharp intake of breath answered that question.

"You have to watch where you're going on these trails." Ray kept his tone soft. Marco had enough problems without this.

"I was thinking." Marco's tone mixed anger and shame. "About stuff."

"Yeah, about Mr. Ray and your mom." Benny piped up. Thin face pinched, he'd squatted next to Ray.

"Huh-uh! I was not." Marco gave Benny a look that said hush up. Benny ducked his head, showing his foster cousin his usual deference.

"Don't worry about it. We're gonna be fine." Ray understood Marco's preoccupation. Susana was never far from Ray's mind, either — not since the day the previous year when he'd helped his former partner move his sister from Corpus Christi to San Antonio. "Just give me a minute."

He touched the back of his head where pain pounded like a jackhammer. His fingers came back bloody. His stomach rocked and ears buzzed. He considered his options.

20

With his ankle injured, it seemed unlikely he could hike out. And there was the body to consider.

If his cell phone had survived, and he could get a signal, he'd call Samuel, his boss and Susana's brother. It wouldn't be a pleasant conversation. Samuel was almost as protective of his nephew as Susana was of her son. "We'll have to wait for your Uncle Samuel to get the medical examiner and the evidence guys out here, and then we'll get you to the ER so they can fix up that arm."

"No!" Marco stopped, his lips pressed together. His skin had turned sickly gray. "Don't call *Tío* Samuel. He'll worry. I could hike back to the trailhead and get somebody. Benny can stay here and take care of you."

"No." Benny looked offended. "You fell down. I'll hike. You stay here."

Red spots flamed on Marco's pale cheeks. "I'm the oldest — "

"Just hang on, guys, no one's hiking anywhere alone." The scene was already contaminated. The medical examiner's investigator and the evidence techs wouldn't be happy. He needed to move the boys as far back as possible. "Go sit by that tree over there. Benny, why don't you look around, see if you can find our caps? And my sunglasses. Who knows where they ended up."

Marco stumbled over to the Ashe juniper on the edge of the strip where they'd landed. Benny, hands on his hips in an unconscious imitation of an angry adult, started up the incline in search of Ray's San Antonio Police Department cap.

After glancing back to make sure they weren't looking, Ray let his head drop, jaw clenched, and tried to stand. Sweat beaded on his forehead. Giving up, he sucked in a breath through his mouth to avoid the smell and scooted close enough to get a good look at the body.

Blue shirt, jeans, hiking boots. Dried red stains cascaded down the front of the shirt and jeans. Blood. Too much blood for a simple tumble down a hill. The ring finger on the left hand was missing. Theft of a ring or a trophy? A breeze ruffled the man's sleeve. Ray had the sudden sensation the corpse might raise its injured hand in a macabre wave.

No. This guy would never move again. Ray slid off his backpack and rummaged for his cell phone. It had survived intact, and he had a signal.

Samuel sounded preoccupied. "What's

up? I thought you were hiking with the boys."

"I am — was." Ray explained the situation. "The guy's missing a finger and he's covered with blood. It wasn't an accident."

"We'll get paramedics up there for you and Marco." Always the problem-solver, Samuel's voice bounced around as if he were already moving. "Salvador is next on the rotation — I'll bring him with me."

"I can handle the investigation. Just send out Deborah." Deborah Smith would love telling her colleagues that her new partner had walked off a cliff.

"You're on vacation — and you're injured."

The vacation hadn't been Ray's idea. Samuel had insisted. "So? As soon as the paramedics get me fixed up, I want the case. I'm bored with this vacation thing."

"We'll talk when I get there." When Samuel used his boss voice, there was no sense arguing. "I'm on the way. I'll call Susana after I assess the situation."

"I should call her — " Ray could already hear that conversation in his head.

"She's at the hotline center. She won't answer her personal phone on shift." Samuel's voice held a hint of pity. "Besides, I'm her older brother. She'll just snap at me.

23

You, she'll chew up and spit out."

Ray dropped his cell phone into the backpack and stared at the body. He'd tumbled head over heels several hundred yards, injured his ankle, and blacked out in order to find this guy. No matter what Samuel said, that made it his job to find out how the man had ended up at the bottom of a cliff. Dead and missing a finger.

CHAPTER TWO

Sergeant Samuel Martinez stopped at the edge of a ravine and peered down. "Ouch."

Marco had picked a bad place to go over the side. Rocky, steep terrain featured an array of prickly plants. Ray sat on the ground below. A park police officer squatted near him.

"Don't touch anything down there!" Samuel started down, not waiting for the paramedics and evidence crew to catch up.

Detective Deborah Smith, Ray's partner, was the only one who'd kept up the park naturalist's pace in the twenty minutes it had taken to find this spot. Deborah's long-legged gait had matched Samuel's perfectly, something he tried not to dwell on too much.

He slipped and slid, twice landing on his behind as he fought to stay upright. Deborah grabbed his arm for a second. "Easy, Sarge."

She flashed Samuel a high-wattage smile and let go. Samuel gritted his teeth and righted himself.

"Nice biceps." Deborah murmured the words as she tromped past him.

He caught a whiff of her light, familiar scent. Even in this breathless heat, she smelled good. Not as good as his wife did, of course. The effect of her smile lingered longer than it should have, leaving him with the disconcerting sense he'd done something wrong.

"*Tío* Samuel, over here." Marco's voice. "We're over here."

He wiped his dirty hands on his dress pants, glanced at Ray, but headed toward the boys. The ME would take the lead on the body.

"You guys okay?" He squatted next to his nephew and touched Marco's arm with one finger. "This the arm that hurts?"

Marco nodded, his eyes huge in his dirty face. "There's a dead guy over there. Somebody cut off his finger."

"I know. We'll take care of him. In the meantime, the paramedic will look at your arm, and then we'll get you out of here."

"Mr. Ray fell, and he can't get up." Benny's solemn expression gave no indication he'd know why people would find this state-

26

ment funny.

"Yeah, he's a big lazy bum, isn't he?" Samuel plastered on a smile. "He probably thinks I'll carry him out of here piggyback. Hah! I'm gonna make him carry me."

Benny grinned, relief written all over his face. "No, Mr. Samuel." He danced a little jig. "Carry me. Carry me!"

"Well, since you don't weigh any more than a gnat, I probably could just stick you in my back pocket." Samuel glanced up to see one of the paramedics approaching. "This guy will fix you up while I talk to Ray. You two just hang tight, and we'll be ready in a while."

He left the boys in the man's capable hands and picked his way over the rough ground to where the other paramedic, a guy named Greg Miller who played on his church's softball team, examined the back of Ray's head. Samuel gave his former partner a good once-over, trying to gauge his mental, as well as physical, state. Sweat soaked Ray's T-shirt. His skin tone had gone gray under his tan. He crossed his arms and grimaced.

Samuel squatted next to him. "Well, Grace, how're you doing?"

"That's Mr. Grace to you." Ray laughed, the sound strained.

"You got two left feet or what, Bible Boy?" Deborah nudged Ray's leg with a dusty loafer.

A bright red blush crept up Ray's neck. He glanced at Samuel, then away. Things were not going well between Ray and his new partner — a development Ray hadn't bothered to mention to his boss. Anger surged through Samuel.

His voice gruff, Ray introduced the Park Police officer. "Officer Saenz hikes out here a lot and knows these trails. We may need her expertise."

"Good to meet you." Samuel shook hands with Saenz. "Which parks do you patrol? How often do you get over here?"

"We cover the northwest division parks. Even though this is a gated wilderness area, it's treated pretty much like the rest of the parks," she said. "I patrol by a couple times each shift."

Samuel nodded, but his gaze traveled to the paramedic's hands on Ray's foot. "Is it broken?"

Greg tugged on the hiking boot, trying to get it off a swollen foot. The ankle looked purple.

"Naw, I don't think so, but his noggin could be." The paramedic grinned. "It looks kind of big."

Ray rolled his eyes, making Samuel want to smack him. "My head is fine. I just need a little help getting up and out of here."

"Let me be the judge of that. You may need stitches. With any luck, they'll have to shave some of that hair. Anything else hurt?"

"Ribs," Ray admitted, "but it's not bad, I just need to walk it off. Marco's the one who needs help. He's pretty freaked out."

"Relax, Ray." The irony of that instruction was not lost on Samuel. Normally he held the title of uptight boss. "Marco will be fine."

"I tried to call Susana. I got voicemail."

"Her shift's not over yet." Samuel glanced at his watch. "I told you, I'll call her."

A look of relief flitted across Ray's face. "I should do it. It's my fault."

"Just let me get a handle on the DB, and then we'll get you out of here."

Trying to ignore the stench, Samuel stood and surveyed the scene. The combination of heat and vegetation made the question of footprints moot. It seemed unlikely that the man had been carried down here. More likely he'd come the same way Ray had, head over heels. Samuel immediately framed the next question: had the victim been alive and fallen into that rough-and-tumble flight, or had he been thrown over the edge

29

already dead?

One of the EU techs snapped photos with a thirty-five millimeter while the other pulled a video camera from a bag. They also needed to do a rough sketch of the scene before any evidence was collected. Details from the sketch would later be inputted into a computer program to produce the diagram. Samuel tried to be patient. The wait would be worth it when it came time to nail a suspect with a guilty conviction.

A hand over his nose, he knelt next to Tito Sanchez, the ME investigator who'd caught the call. "What's the deal?"

"Well, the most obvious thing is the wound in the chest," Tito said, not taking his gaze from the corpse. He chewed a wad of gum as he worked, his way of avoiding the cigars he used to favor. Samuel had always hated the smell of the cigars, but the odor would've been preferable to this smell.

"And the missing digit, or course. The victim's a white male, mid-thirties. No ID that I can find. Looks like a stab wound to the heart. Those tend to be immediately fatal." Tito stowed the bubble gum in his cheek while he talked, making him look like a cherubic Hispanic chipmunk. "Somebody gutted him like a deer. Big knife. Like a hunter would use."

He lifted the head and shoulders. "Not much blood. With a wound like that there should've been a lot of blood."

"So he bled out elsewhere, and his body was dumped here." Deborah scribbled in a small notebook she'd pulled from the bag slung over her shoulder. Samuel decided that her presence at the scene — brought on by her partner's tumble — would make her the lead on the case. "Was the finger chopped off before or after he died?"

"After." Tito said. "I'll know more when I get him back to the morgue."

"How long do you think he's been here?" Deborah used her pen to slide damp, blonde bangs from her face.

"Your guess is as good as mine." The investigator shrugged. "Rigor mortis sets in eight to twelve hours after death and lasts two to three days, but the heat accelerates decomp. You want to get Mr. Grace out of here, I can handle this end."

Samuel grinned to himself. It looked as if Ray was stuck with a new nickname. "Detective Smith will be the lead on this one." Angry flies dive-bombed him. He swatted at them in self defense. "Let her know when you schedule the autopsy, please. Smith, when we get back to the top, ask the naturalist to show you around. This had to have happened nearby. We need the primary crime scene. Interview all the park staff. Find out where they were every minute for the last two days. Give me what you've got back at the station before end of shift."

The detective nodded, her pen clamped between her teeth as she stared at something on the ground. A tech dropped a tent next to whatever it was and moved on. Samuel could trust Smith to do her job, but he was accustomed to running investigations, not observing from the sidelines. "You want to interview these guys first?" she asked.

"I'll handle the preliminary stuff." Samuel glanced at his notebook, searching for the park naturalist's name. Diane Brickman. He strode back to where the group clustered around Ray.

"This is your park, you're the most familiar with it. Do you have any suggestions on how a body would end up in this ravine? It looks like he was killed elsewhere, and his body dumped."

Officer Saenz brushed her hands together as she got to her feet. "He must've been killed in the immediate vicinity and during daylight hours. It would be extremely difficult to get up here in the dark, lugging a body. The chances of getting lost or falling would be phenomenal."

"Ms. Brickman, think back over the past two days. Did anything out of the ordinary happen? Anyone acting suspicious? Any difficult guests?"

The park naturalist shook her head. "We had Boy Scout and Girl Scout troops out here this week. We do presentations for them in the outdoor classroom so we've been really busy."

"I understand. I'm just trying to find out if anything unusual happened in the last few days. How many people work here?"

"Myself and the other park naturalist, a horticulturist."

"How big is this place?"

"About six hundred acres. At night, it's pitch dark out here."

Three people and six hundred acres. "Thanks for our help. Detective Smith probably will have more questions for you later. Right now, I'd like to get my officer out of here."

"We need to get him to the hospital." The paramedic nodded in agreement. "The doctor will want x-rays. We're looking at a possible concussion. Sprained or fractured ankle. Maybe some broken ribs."

"Don't talk about me like I'm not here." Ray sounded as if his age matched that of his hiking companions.

Samuel gave him the benefit of the doubt. The guy's day had been tough. "Can he walk out?"

"He lost consciousness, and he's got a laceration on the back of his head that'll probably take five or six stitches. Multiple abrasions. It might be better to take him out on a stretcher."

"I don't need — "

"Shut up, Ray." The paramedic cut off his patient's protest. "I'm most concerned about the blow to the head. The ankle looks like a bad sprain, but we'll want to x-ray that, too."

"I'm walking out of here. It was just a stupid fall. I'm supposed to teach Bible study tonight." Ray rolled to one side and pulled himself to his knees.

"So get a sub. Doctor's orders. I'm not giving you a lollipop, if you don't behave." Greg grinned and put a hand on Ray's shoulder. "Just sit tight for a second. Don't be so bullheaded."

"You're not a doctor, and I don't want a lollipop." Ray shrugged off his hand. "We need to get the boys out of here, now."

Samuel followed Ray's gaze. Benny sat cross-legged on the ground, while the other paramedic talked to Marco. "Okay, Ray. If you want to try to make it under your own steam, fine, let's go."

Ray nodded, his face grim. Greg grabbed one arm and Samuel the other so they could heave him to his feet. Ray kept his left foot in the air, not putting weight on the injured ankle. Samuel let his hand drop. "You all right?"

"Yeah, yeah I'm fine." Ray shrugged off Greg's hand and straightened up.

"You're gonna need help." The paramedic started forward, one hand outstretched.

Ray half hopped, half limped two steps forward, then put one hand to his temple, his body weaving. "I'm fine — "

He pitched forward and landed flat on his face.

"Oye, they found the body." Lalo squeezed the phone between his shoulder and ear as he took one hand from the steering wheel long enough to bring the slim brown cigarillo to his lips. He sucked on it and blew a series of perfect smoke rings, savoring the taste and aroma of excellent tobacco while he waited for the string of Spanish expletives to end.

"Already? You sure?" *El señor* did not sound happy.

Lalo flicked the cigarette out the window and focused on staying two car lengths back from the woman's dirty green Trailblazer. He'd been following her since she left the park. She seemed totally oblivious, as well she should. He was good at this.

He'd been keeping an eye on her since the day before, waiting for his chance. Her argument with his mark had been fortuitous — for Lalo. Not so much for the woman. She now played a pivotal role in their scenario.

The arrival of the police and emergency personnel had been cause for concern, however. Lalo had been forced to shift the focus of his surveillance to see what business they had at the park. Now he was glad he had.

"The ME and the evidence people went up the trail with the police. Now they bring out a man on a stretcher. They found it, *señor*." Lalo maneuvered the silver BMW, his sweet baby, onto the highway exit ramp. Yes, it belonged to *el señor,* but possession was nine-tenths of the law. And he always followed the law. Almost always. Sometimes. When it suited him.

"How'd they find him so fast — I thought you said you dumped him a long way from the trails?"

Lalo had asked himself the same question. He'd lugged that body a long way in order to ensure its resting spot would be undetected for days, maybe even months. "Dumb luck, *señor,* it had to have been dumb luck."

"You didn't leave any ID on him, did you? You didn't leave anything they can trace back to us, right?"

A Mustang cut him off on Hildebrand Avenue. Lalo slammed on the brake. He didn't respond to the driver's single-digit salute. He never drew attention to himself. "Trust me, they won't find the place where I took him out. It was pure chance his body was found at all."

More cuss words. "What about the woman?"

"I am tracking her now. She will tell me who the other man was. Do not worry. And we may be able to use her to shift the focus in another direction. Leave that to me, *señor.* This is what you pay me for."

"Pay you way too much, considering the mistake you made. You better fix it. You messed up big time, sticking our guy with them around. When you do her, make sure you don't leave nothing behind this time. Nothing. Or so help me, you'll live to regret it."

"Piece of cake."

"You screw this up, you'll be choking on that piece of cake." The sound of ice cubes clinking against glass was loud in Lalo's ear. A slurp and swallow followed. "Come by the house later this afternoon. I want your reports in person from now on."

"Sí, señor." Lalo glanced at the gold Rolex that peeked from under the sleeve of his white dress shirt. He would interrogate and dispose of the park lady and still have time for a lovely afternoon siesta with Sylvia. "I will be there at four."

He disconnected and tucked the phone in his pocket, contemplating his future. He didn't possess an endless supply of patience. The boss wore on him. In Lalo's business he ran into men like *el señor* all the time. Lots of business savvy, but no people skills. Himself, he'd had the benefit of the best education Mexican pesos could buy. His parents had wanted him to be an accountant. He'd decided he'd rather have his own money than count someone else's. And the boss paid well. So Lalo put up with the tirades and watched his bank balance skyrocket.

He glanced at the small ice chest on the seat. The gentleman had good taste in wedding rings. A simple gold band. Lalo decided to overrule the boss. He could leave something with the park lady after she expired. A lovely red herring.

38

The woman in the Trailblazer turned into the driveway in front of a small bungalow that needed a paint job. Lalo *tsk'd* to himself as he pulled over to the curb two houses down. Her yard was overgrown, the trees needed trimming. The new owner would most likely take more pride. He ran his hand over the weapon lying next to the ice chest on the seat. He'd change the MO as usual. A .357 Sig-Sauer P229 this time. He stuck the two-tone weapon in his waistband and reached for the handle on the door.

No. He swore and eased back on the seat. A man dressed in sweats and running shoes jogged up to the steps where the lady stood fumbling with her keys. They chatted. Her hands flailed as she talked. The man nodded, stepped forward, touched her arm. She opened the door. They disappeared inside.

Lalo drummed his hands on the steering wheel. He could do them both. But then the boss would be unhappy. He sighed again. Glanced at the Rolex again.

So much for the siesta. He would have to leave the finger on ice.

CHAPTER THREE

Susana Martinez-Acosta grabbed her purse from under the desk and shoved back her chair, grateful her five-hour shift at the crisis hotline center had ended. Her ears hurt from the headset. She was hot, tired, and depressed. Dozens of high-octane emotional calls did that to a person. "I'm out of here, Autumn." She waved at the center director and started to walk away.

The phone rang.

Susana bit her lip and tried to ignore the jangle. Surely another volunteer would get it. She glanced around the former schoolroom-turned-crisis-center. Everyone already had a call. One more wouldn't hurt her. She stifled a sigh and slipped on the headset. "Bexar County Crisis Hotline."

"My husband's cheating on me."

The woman at the other end of the line gave a sob that wrenched Susana's heart. She dropped her purse on the desk and sat back down. "Ma'am, do you want to tell me why you think that?"

The woman's sobs died. Her voice filled with a hysteria-edged anger. "He told me he'd never do it again. But he is. I know he is. I wanna die, I just wanna die."

"Let's calm down for a second." Susana sat up straight, both feet flat on the floor, blocking out the sound of telephones ringing and the incessant buzz of other volunteers talking. "What makes you think he's unfaithful?"

"It wouldn't be the first time. I don't know why it upsets me so much. He's been doing it for years. I think he did it when I was in the hospital having our first baby." Pain bloomed in the woman's voice, her sobbing louder.

"Ma'am. Ma'am. My name's Susana. What's yours?"

"Oh, I can't tell you my name."

Usually callers didn't mind giving their first names. Fright seemed to overtake hysteria.

Susana tried again. "This call is completely anonymous. I'll never know who you are or where you're calling from. It's easier to talk if we're on a first-name basis."

"No. They can't ever know I called you.

They'll find out. I can't. I shouldn't have called."

"Who, ma'am? Who can't find out?" Susana focused on keeping her voice kind, but firm. She glanced toward the back of the room. Autumn, her thick black-rimmed glasses sliding down her nose, thumbed through a report. Susana could rely on her for help, if she needed it. "Your husband? I promise, he won't know unless you tell him."

"Not him. Them. My husband would never hurt me. Not that way."

The woman seemed to swing from emotion to emotion, angry, indignant, hurt, not usual for people calling a crisis hotline. And this much naked fear was odd, at least for Susana.

"Tell me about your husband. What makes you think he's having an affair?"

"He leaves and never says when he's coming back, then he's gone for a long time, and never says where he's been."

"Did you ask him?"

"Yes, I asked him. He says it's work. Or he says he needs time to think. He says he goes hiking — without me and the kids." The woman gave a short, angry bark of a laugh. "When I call his cell phone, there's no answer. Why doesn't he answer? He knows it's me. The ring-tone is mine."

Jerk. Susana pushed away her reaction. Her biggest failing so far had been her inability to separate her own emotions from those of her callers. "Have you tried talking to him about how you feel?"

"He's not big on talking about feelings. It wouldn't help. He doesn't care how I feel. If he did, he wouldn't leave me here with them all day long. I could kill him for that." The hot anger in her voice made the threat seem very real.

"Ma'am. Think about the impact that would have on your children. You need to be here for your children. So does your husband." Like Susana needed to be there for Marco. With his dad gone, being there for Marco and keeping him safe were her responsibilities. Hers alone. She searched for the right words. "Try letting him know how upset you are at his attitude. How much you and the kids need him. But in a calm way. Have a quiet conversation."

"It's hard to be calm when he smells like Estee Lauder Youth Dew and has hot pink lipstick on his collar." The woman yelled the words into the phone. Susana waited, sweat soaking her blouse under her arms. The old air conditioner must have gone out again.

When the woman spoke again, she sounded resigned. "He's a jerk."

Like a lot of men. Except for Susana's brothers. And Ray. Steady strength, soft touch. Susana shoved away the memory. Focus.

"It sounds like you have a right to be angry. Your feelings and your needs are important, too. You need to be able to talk about them. Especially in a marriage." Yeah. Ms. Counselor. The image of her husband's face loomed in front of her, hurt, eyes sad at her refusal to forgive, wanting one last kiss before he went to work. The next time she'd seen him, he was dead, his body mangled in a car accident.

"I know. I know. But these people are different."

"What people are those?"

"His family." More sobbing.

Did she live with her in-laws? Susana wrapped the fingers of one hand around a curl in her hair to keep from biting her nails. She'd broken that habit — most of the time. "Have you considered marriage counseling?"

"Nobody is allowed to know. We don't air our dirty laundry in public. That's what he says." Sobbing. Noise in the background. The caller's voice became muffled, as if she'd put her hand over the receiver. "I'll be right there."

"Ma'am?"

"I have to go. If he doesn't show up pretty soon, I'll track him down myself. I'm gonna kill him."

Dial tone.

Susana considered laying her head down on her desk.

"Well, how did that one go?" Autumn plopped a bottle of water on Susana's desk and slid behind the next desk over. "You look frustrated."

"Thank you." Susana twisted the lid from the bottle and gulped, then briefly relayed details of the call. "I don't think I helped her at all."

Autumn wiped the thick lenses of her glasses on her "Got Jesus?" T-shirt. Her gray eyes shone with intelligence against the whitest skin Susana had ever seen. "You're doing it again. What did I tell you?"

"Sometimes they just need to vent." Susana parroted Autumn, mimicking her mentor's English accent. "It's not what I say, it's how well I listen."

"Exactly — except for the atrocious accent." Autumn stuck her glasses back on her face and smiled.

"I don't know. Sometimes I don't think

I'm very good at this." The doubts that crept into Susana's mind late at night reared their ugly heads in the light of day. Instead of getting a job as a firefighter and easing the financial situation for her and Marco, she spent her days getting her master's degree in counseling and volunteering at the hotline in order to get the experience she needed to get a paying job after she graduated. Maybe thirty-eight was too old to change careers.

"You're doing fine." Autumn stretched across the aisle to pat Susana's shoulder. "I promise. Now get out of here. Go have fun. Invite Ray to stay for dinner when he brings Marco home."

"Autumn!"

"You want to, you know you do."

Easy for her to say. Autumn had been married to a dentist for ten years. The worst thing that ever happened to him was pulling the wrong tooth. Or getting cut by dental floss.

Or . . . she entertained herself with the possibilities all the way to her Camry. Long enough to block out Autumn's well-meant advice.

Autumn didn't have feelings for a man who got shot at for a living.

As Susana opened her car door, her cell

phone rang. Samuel's name popped up on the Caller ID. She answered, one hand still on the door. *"Hola, big brother, que pasó?"*

"Sis, I'm on my way to the hospital. Marco and Ray took a fall at the park. It's not serious, but Marco's wrist might be broken." Samuel's words ran together as if he were in a hurry. Or, more likely, so she couldn't get a word in edgewise. "Meet me at Santa Rosa Northwest."

Ray didn't even have to be working to put Marco in jeopardy. "How bad is it? Is it bad? What about Benny?" Susana slid into her car and tried to jam the key in the ignition. The keys dropped into the foot well. Grabbing for them, she conked her head on the steering wheel. "Ouch. Ouch!"

"Are you all right? It's just Marco's wrist, and Benny's fine. I'm more concerned about Ray. He passed out. They're taking him to the hospital by ambulance. Meet me there. Oh, and Susana . . ."

"What?" Susana stopped moving, waiting.

"They found a body — "

"A human body — a dead body? Marco found a body?"

"Well, Ray and Benny were there, too. But Marco got there first."

"And you wonder why I worry so much." Susana didn't wait to hear her brother's response. She disconnected, mashed the key in the ignition. She should never have trusted Ray. Keeping Marco safe was her job and her job alone. Even if that meant she had to stay away from Ray.

Twisting the steering wheel, Susana shot forward. A horn blared. She rammed her foot down on the accelerator. She was on her own.

CHAPTER FOUR

Ray jerked from a half doze. Whatever the ER doctor had given him to dull the headache wasn't working.

"Ray?" A voice called his name from somewhere outside the cubicle curtains. Susana's voice.

He wanted to open his eyes, but he couldn't. If he did, he'd vomit. The bright lights in the ER made his stomach heave.

"Where is he?" Susana again.

Usually he loved her husky voice. Now it was full of angry fear. The curtain slid open with a squeak that made him wince.

"Where's Marco?"

Ray forced his eyes open a crack, squinting against the light. Susana whipped the curtain shut behind her.

"He's okay." Ray tried to sit up. He needed to get out of here, back to the crime scene. The pounding in his head escalated. Despite his protests, they were preparing to admit him for observation. He lay back, tried again. "He's in one of the other cubicles. They're putting a cast on his wrist. It's a clean break. Six weeks and he's good as new."

She started to back out, stopped. The hard anger seemed to leak away, leaving her oval face soft beneath a cascade of curly, brown hair. "Are you . . . your head . . . are you okay?"

"I'm fine. Just . . . don't go. Stay and let me explain."

A veil came down over the concern in her eyes.

Ray rushed to say the words. "I'm sorry. It was an accident. He wasn't paying attention to where he — "

"You're blaming him? He's eight." Incredulous anger laced her words. "You're the adult. You're supposed to take care of him. I trusted you to keep him safe."

A wave of anger blew away the painkillers and fatigue. "Whoa. Just hold your horses. You've never trusted me — ever. It was an accident." He pressed palms to his temples in a futile attempt to make the pain stop.

"Well, there won't be any more accidents." Susana jerked the curtain open and looked back at him, her amber eyes smoky with anger, fear, and something that looked like regret. "Because there won't be any more hiking."

His stomach dropped in a sick free fall. She couldn't mean that. More likely, she did. "Tell them to send me the bill. I don't want you paying for my — "

She disappeared from sight.

" — mistakes." Ray peered at the ceiling from under half-closed eyelids. "That went well, don't you think?"

Samuel's entrance into the cubicle some time later was much less spectacular. He dropped onto the stool next to Ray's bed, a weary look on his face. "You awake?"

"She leave?" Ray knew the answer, but he had to ask.

"Yep. Chewed me out for a while first, then took the boys and left."

At least Samuel wasn't mad. "Did you tell her about the body?"

"Yep." Samuel tilted his head back as if resting, his tone sardonic.

"What'd she say?"

"I believe her exact words were 'And you wonder why I worry all the time.' "

"Has she been able to get medical insurance? I offered to pay the bill, but I don't think she was listening."

Samuel's eyebrows rose over dark eyes.

"She won't let you pay her bills, and you know it. If she needs help, she's got family for that." His thumb jabbed his chest. "Besides, she managed to get a plan. The premium's killing her, but she's keeping up with it."

Samuel was right. Susana would never let Ray help.

"Get me out of here. I'm not spending the night." His Bronco was still at the park, or he'd have driven himself home.

"Ray, you have a concussion and a severely sprained ankle. They put five stitches in the back of your head. You've fallen enough for one day. You're staying." Samuel pulled a notebook from his hip pocket and opened it.

"It's not necessary."

"Let the doctors be the judge of that."

Doctors. They couldn't always help. The smell of Betadine and the sounds of gurneys being pushed through the ER reminded Ray of another hospital stay. The ticking of the clock as it measured the last minutes of his wife's life. Her face had been ethereal in its whiteness, and the tawny fuzz that had grown on her head after they stopped the chemo had been soft. He could feel the weak grasp of her fingers as they curled around his — and then loosened when she finally let go.

"Did they find the primary scene?" He forced away the memories by focusing on work, a skill he'd perfected in the last five years.

"Not that I know of. I called Smith for an update, but she didn't answer." Samuel glanced at his wristwatch. "She's your partner. I would've thought she would have checked on you by now. I left her a message to come by here to brief us."

"She's probably still tied up at the scene." Ray let his glance slid away from Samuel's. He was a friend, but he was also the boss now, and the one responsible for assigning Ray a new partner. Detective Deborah Smith. Any number of clichés applied. Bane of his existence and thorn in his side came to mind. A never-ending source of irritation coupled with aggravation. The words pounded inside his head to the same beat as the throbbing pain.

Ray hid his expression as he reached for a glass of water on the stand next to his bed. Samuel had enough on his plate as a newly-promoted sergeant. He didn't need Ray's whining, too. So, that left his personal life. Better not to go there, either, but he couldn't help himself. "Susana was really angry."

"She's upset. She'll get over it." Samuel's tone said he was getting the abridged version. "You know how protective she is of Marco."

"She made it sound like she wasn't going to let me see him at all."

"I wouldn't worry about seeing Marco. If he wants to see you, he will."

Deborah's sudden entrance interrupted the uncomfortable exchange. "How's it going, Bible Boy? They stitch you up?"

Ray's fingers tightened around the glass. He ignored the irritated glance Samuel sent his way. Deborah's shots at his faith were nothing new. "I'm fine. Did you find the primary scene — it's obvious the guy was killed some place else and dumped. I didn't see any blood under him."

"Naw. It's like looking for a needle in a haystack. The park is six-hundred acres. It has six miles of hiking trails. Three staff people. Fifty, sixty visitors a day." Deborah set a water bottle down on a supply table and pulled a notebook from her purse. "What I can tell you, though, is the guy's clothes are expensive: Eddie Bauer jeans, shirt from Dillard's. He was wearing a Rolex, a UT class ring, and his hiking boots were very worn. No ring finger on his left hand, so we don't know if he was wearing a wedding ring. Nothing in his pockets. Obviously someone didn't want him identified immediately."

"If it were theft, the killer would've taken the watch and the UT ring. If it's a trophy, it puts this in a whole new category."

Samuel smoothed his mustache. "Taking a trophy suggests someone who kills for the pleasure of it and wants to relive that pleasure later. Or is it that particular finger, that ring? Someone who's angry over wedding vows that have been violated. A crime of passion — act of violence symbolizing a sense of betrayal."

"We don't have enough information to theorize." Ray twitched with impatience. He wanted out of the bed. He had work to do.

"Deborah, if we don't get a hit on the databases, start going through a UT yearbook for the year on the class ring." A look of pain flitted across Samuel's face. He leaned forward, rubbing his shoulder. "We need to — "

The curtains flew open and the tall, skinny ER intern who had poked and prodded Ray earlier stepped in. "What's this? A cop convention? Out! Mr. Johnson's room is ready, and we're moving him now."

"This really isn't necessary. I'm fine. My

partner can give me a lift." Ray's voice trailed away as he squinted at the doctor's face. Stony. Unflinching. Maybe later Ray could slip out, take a taxi. Right. Fifty bucks or more to get to the ranch. He might have a couple dollars in his wallet. Surely they took debit cards. Of course, he was fuzzy on exactly where his wallet was. "Come on, Samuel, do something. Tell him I'll be fine."

"Thanks for taking care of him, Doctor." Samuel shook the young man's hand. "Ray, don't worry about anything. We're headed back to the scene. We'll get your Bronco back to your place later. I'll call Maddy, ask her to feed the animals. She's gonna want to see you anyway. I'll check in with you later."

"Don't call Maddy, she's got enough to worry about." His friend and neighbor's husband was in hospice care, his health failing rapidly.

"Yeah, well, she'll kill me if I don't." Samuel left, Deborah trailing behind him, leaving Ray at the mercy of the ER doctor. He'd rather pull a dozen all-nighters at the station than face this.

"Can I do something for you?" A nurse he hadn't even realized had entered adjusted the IV attached to his arm.

"Could you turn out the lights?" First

thing in the morning, he'd leave. A killer roamed free while a mutilated John Doe awaited dissection. A headache wouldn't stop him from bringing a murderer to justice. If they'd just give back his pants, he could get on with it.

CHAPTER FIVE

Splotches of bubblegum. Pink sticky stuff all over canvas. Susana didn't pretend to be a judge of abstract art, but that's what the acrylic mess hanging on the wall looked like. She leaned forward and peered at the placard. The artist had named his piece "Childhood." Because he stuck the gum on a board when he was ten? She almost smiled at the thought.

"Thanks for being my date." Her sister-in-law, Piper Martinez, turned her back on the painting, obviously equally impressed. Piper had talked her into coming to this lunchtime fundraiser. From the look on her face when she'd picked up Susana, she'd talked to Samuel about the previous day's events. She was obviously waiting for an opportunity to barrel her way into Susana's business. "I hate coming to these fundraisers by myself. With my kids doing their own thing this summer, it's nice to do something

I want to do."

"I really should get back to the house. I've a got a research paper to finish, and I'm redoing my resume — I'm thinking about getting a part-time job." Susana's gaze swept the gallery. She didn't have time to think about artwork, much less money to buy it. Sure, it was a good cause. The proceeds would benefit the Bexar County Women's Shelter, but no way she could swing even one small print.

"When would you sleep? Give yourself a break, for goodness' sake." Piper nudged her toward the next painting. "It won't hurt you to stop and smell the roses once in a while — or look at art."

Yes. It would. Every time she stopped for even a second, the image of Ray's scratched and bruised face floated through her mind. Sleep was highly overrated.

"You want to get something to eat?" She wasn't really hungry, but maybe it would deter Piper from further lecturing.

"Sure."

Dodging clusters of people, they made their way toward the refreshments. When Piper stopped to talk to someone, Susana forged ahead. She hadn't eaten breakfast, and she couldn't remember if she'd eaten the night before. Her gaze on the array of sandwiches and relish trays, she didn't notice the two women standing nearby until she heard a familiar voice.

"I want to go home. Now. Please."

Susana glanced up. The woman who had spoken was young, beautiful, with a voluptuous figure accented by an expensive-looking Donna Karan skirt and matching blouse in a deep emerald color.

"Don't be ridiculous. We just got here." The other woman, much older and dressed in a cool lime green suit with white-and pink-accents, jabbed the other woman in the shoulder with a manicured nail. "Paint a smile on that face, and keep it there while we announce this donation. Then you can go home."

Susana tried not to stare. She began filling her plate with finger sandwiches and fruit. The older woman stalked off. The younger one grabbed a glass of punch and took a long swallow. Shoulders shaking, she slapped the cup down on the tablecloth. Pink liquid sloshed over the sides.

"Are you all right?" Susana dabbed with her napkin to soak up the liquid.

The woman stared at her with red-rimmed eyes. "Do I know you? You sound familiar."

"I don't think we've met." Susana searched the woman's face, scrambling for words of comfort. Counselors were supposed to help people in distress. Yet the right words always seemed to escape her. "I'm Susana Martinez-Acosta. Do you need to sit? You look a little unsteady."

"Melody Doyle." The woman accepted Susana's hand in a brief, limp shake. "I'm fine. You really shouldn't butt into other people's business."

Feeling like she'd been slapped, Susana stepped back. "I'm sorry, I just thought — "

"Melody, get over here. Now." The older woman stood next to the podium, her carefully-drawn lips turned down. She motioned for Susana's new acquaintance to join her.

"Dragon lady calls." Melody hiccupped. Susana got a whiff of alcohol as the woman leaned in. "Word of advice. Don't ever live with your in-laws. It's murder."

With that, she turned and sashayed on three-inch-high sandals to the podium.

Her face still burning, Susana inched forward to watch. Where had she met this woman? At UTSA maybe? No. PTA? Church? No, that wasn't it.

Muriel Waverly, director of the women's shelter, tapped the microphone and it squawked. "Attention, please. We are just thrilled to share our good news. The Milton

Doyle family has decided to make an enormously generous donation to the shelter. Here today to announce the donation is Cynthia Doyle — Mrs. Milton Doyle — and her daughter-in-law, Melody Doyle."

"You ready to go?" Piper touched her elbow. "I want to run an errand before I drop you off, okay?"

Dragging her gaze away from Cynthia Doyle, who had replaced her annoyed tone with the tinkling voice of a Junior League veteran, Susana nodded. "If it doesn't take long. I've got a pile of books waiting."

"I know. I know." Ray sorted the mail as he talked on the phone. An oversized envelope on the bottom of the stack caught his gaze. He shoved the credit card pitches and bills aside. The return address was from the theology program. His application had arrived. He tried to concentrate on getting Deborah to tell him what was happening with the John Doe. "I feel fine. Do we have an ID?"

"We're working on it. You're supposed to rest."

"I don't want to rest. I want to figure out who he is and notify his family." Ray weighed the envelope in his hand, then turned it facedown on the counter. "Somebody out there is waiting for a son or spouse or dad to come home."

"Oh, Bible Boy, you're such a sentimental softy."

He disconnected and hobbled into the living room where he sank on to the couch and stretched out, the pain in his head a steady throb. D-dog sidled up, his pungent puppy breath in Ray's face, and gave a sharp woof.

"I agree." The puppy hopped up on the couch and plopped down. "Make yourself at home."

Filled with the need to occupy his mind with thoughts that didn't involve his job or his personal life, he switched on the TV and flipped through channels looking for an old movie. A familiar face made him pause. Carl Reinhardt, the parks department director, stood in front of City Hall, a half dozen mikes stuck in his face.

"I reiterate: the parks are perfectly safe. As you know, the park police have been moved from the parks department to the police department recently, but they're still on the job in our parks." Reinhardt wiped perspiration from his cheek. "And SAPD's homicide division is working hard to apprehend the perpetrator of this horrific crime. He or she will be caught."

The sound bite ended and a reporter, live from City Hall, filled the screen. "Reinhardt indicated that he's in close contact with the chief of police. However, park police would not be stationed in the parks until the murderer is caught, citing insufficient personnel. About one hundred officers cover more than two hundred parks."

The anchor on the set tossed the question to the reporter. "Joe, did the parks director say citizens should stay away from the parks until the murderer is caught? Is he guaranteeing their safety?"

"Chris, he says park police officers are out there twenty-four seven, making their presence known. But he also dodged the question of whether they are adequately trained. Park Police's training academy lasts only eighteen weeks before they go into the field. Many believe they are glorified park rangers, better-suited for giving directions and helping lost children. As we said in our initial report yesterday, what really makes this case ironic is that a homicide detective found the body while hiking. It seems park police really can't do the job their counterparts at PD can. This is Joe Reyes, reporting live from City Hall. Back to you, Chris."

Ray slapped the coffee table. Great. As if there wasn't enough animosity between

SAPD and the park police, who were now apart of the department, but still without parity in pay or training. Scaring citizens into thinking the parks were unsafe, murderers lurking in every corner, would just create hysteria and make his job — and Samuel's — even harder. The city manager and the mayor were probably on the phone to the police chief right now.

He considered calling Samuel to see if he'd seen the report. The phone rang before he had a chance to punch in his boss's number. Deborah's cell phone number appeared on the Caller ID.

"Raymond, Bible Boy, it's me again." From the sounds of Bob Seger in the background, his partner wasn't at work anymore. It was hard to hear her. "I thought you might want me to come out and rub your back for you — make it all better."

"The name's Ray." He sat up and hit the mute button on the remote. "Where are you?"

"Me and some of the guys decided to grab supper at La Cantina. You wanna come over? I could come get you."

His partner preferred liquid fuel to actual food at mealtime. Ray transferred the phone to his other ear and eased back on the couch, glancing at his watch. Deborah had left work early. That wouldn't earn points with Samuel. "Call a taxi. I'll see you in the morning."

"Hey, wait a minute. You're not coming in tomorrow." Her voice got louder. He heard someone say something, guffaws followed. Deborah laughed and called out to someone else. "Naw, he's a Bible boy, man, he doesn't drink. Might look bad on his application for saint."

"I'm hanging up now." Ray disconnected. The phone immediately rang again.

He grabbed the receiver. "Go home, already!"

"Detective Johnson?"

Ray blew out a breath. "Yes, this is Detective Johnson. Who's this?"

"My, how quickly we forget!"

"Janet Hutchens." Newspaper reporter and royal pain in the neck on a number of old cases. "How'd you get this number?"

"Detective, you don't want to know. Besides, I know where you live. I could've paid you a visit instead. In fact, if you like, I can run out there right now."

"What do you want?"

"Heard you found a body. How 'bout giving me the inside scoop. Do you have an ID?"

"Look, you want a story, go through chan-

nels. Call PIO. I'm off duty." Ray disconnected. After a second, he turned the ringer
off. If the station needed him, the dispatcher
would call him on his cell. He lay back, careful not to squash the puppy, and closed his
eyes.

He had no doubt he'd hear from Janet
again. She was a bulldog. But he had bigger
issues than a nosy reporter. Hung over or
absent tomorrow, Deborah wouldn't be
much help with this murder. How long
would it be before he'd have to tell Samuel
about her problem? He should have done it
by now, but he had entertained the illusion
he would somehow miraculously find a way
to help her. So far, the solution hadn't
presented itself.

"God, help me. Help her." Not particu-
larly eloquent, but succinct. The words
echoed in the silence. The puppy raised his
head, then dropped it again with a tiny
growl in the back of his throat.

"You're right." Ray had to do his job and
find a way to help Deborah. His own problems would have to wait. For however long
it took.

CHAPTER SIX

"You look deep in thought. What's up?"

Startled by Deborah's sudden intrusion into his office, Samuel jerked back, sending a full mug of coffee careening. Liquid soaked the reports spread across his desk.

"Chihuahua!" Ignoring the burn as hot coffee seeped through his shirtsleeve, Samuel snatched napkins from a paper bag holding a cold breakfast taco he had forgotten to eat and sopped up the liquid.

"Let me help." Deborah leaned over his desk, her face close to his, and shoved stacks of files away from the disaster area. Her hands shook.

"I've got it." Samuel glanced at the detective's face. Her cheeks were scarlet. Dark purple stained the skin under her bloodshot eyes. He pushed her hand away, surprised to find it icy. "I'll print a new set."

As he swept the sodden mess into the trash, Samuel tried to gather his thoughts.

She'd better have some good news. The early morning meeting in the lieutenant's office hadn't gone well. The city manager was calling the chief every half hour wanting to know whether they'd made progress on the John Doe case. The parks department director wanted PD to augment park police with regular officers in the city's two-hundred-plus parks.

"Where were you earlier?" He dried his hands with the last clean napkin. "I tried to call you for an update this morning. I didn't get an answer."

The detective didn't hold his gaze. "The ME finally got to the autopsy this morning. Man, are they backed up, bodies stacked everywhere. I went straight there from home. Guess I forgot to turn my phone on."

As she eased around the corner of his desk, he got a whiff of cigarette smoke mixed with that perfume he liked. Deborah dropped a blue folder on his desk and leaned over him to open it. Her long blonde hair swept forward baring the white skin of her neck.

He eased away, forcing himself to stay out of her space. "You get something?"

"Yep. I got an ID. The guy was in AFIS. You're not going to like this. Joseph Doyle. Known as Joey to his friends." Deborah rattled the information off, reading from a notebook. She'd made detective at thirty because she threw herself at every case with absolute abandonment like a heat-seeking missile that never wavered from the target. Strangely enough, she still seemed to have a need to impress him, despite the fact that he'd pushed for her promotion. "He had a brush with the law at age eighteen when he and some friends stole a car and went joy riding in Brackenridge Park. Got a fine, community service, probation."

"Tell me he isn't Milton Doyle's son." The temperature of the political hot potato had just tripled. "San Antonio's number one philanthropist."

"He is — was — Milt's youngest son." She sounded almost cheerful.

"Had they reported him missing?"

"Nope. We have no report filed by Milton Doyle or anyone else."

"So we'll have to go to King's Row Estates and tell Milton Doyle that his youngest son was murdered?"

Doyle was the biggest car dealer in the San Antonio area, with new and used dealerships in foreign and American-made cars, ranging from pickup trucks to luxury vehicles and even Hummers. His empire spread across Texas, with dealerships in

70

Dallas and Houston supplementing the older ones in Brownsville and McAllen.

"Looks that way. You want to go with me? We can grab lunch first." Her tone was playful, her expression an invitation.

"Have lunch?" Samuel suddenly felt like a high school boy who'd been invited to dance by the head cheerleader. He had two left feet, but *sure* teetered on his tongue. He bit it back.

"Come on, you don't get out in the field much anymore. And I'm sure you have more experience with this sort of thing than I do. I'll buy."

"Thanks for the offer but I — "

"What's going on?" Ray stood in the doorway, leaning on a wooden cane with a ram's head handle. Samuel couldn't tell from the look on his face how much his friend had heard.

Annoyance darkened Deborah's face. "Don't you know it's rude to interrupt a private conversation?"

"Private conversation?" Samuel spoke first, acutely aware of the dismay on Ray's face. "Smith, we'll go out to the Doyles' in thirty minutes. I'll meet you at my car. In the meantime, get all the background you can on Joey Doyle, Milton Doyle, and the family business."

"Yes, sir." Her tone was cool. "Excuse me."

She brushed past Ray. He came in and sat down across from Samuel. Samuel closed the Doyle folder Deborah had left, and then opened it again. "What are you doing here?"

"Was she hitting on you?"

The question rammed Samuel like an eighteen-wheeler. "No. Yes. I don't know."

"Well, that clears that up." Irritation tinged Ray's voice. He used the cane to tap the door shut. "I know it's been a while, but surely you can tell when a woman other than Piper is interested in you."

"She just suggested lunch. She even offered to buy." Samuel tried to stave off the guilt hemorrhaging inside him. He hadn't encouraged her in any way. She couldn't read his mind. She didn't know how much he'd been tempted to say yes to lunch and a lot more. "There's nothing wrong with that. You guys eat lunch together, don't you?"

Ray had a dangerous look in his eyes. "Yes, but we're partners, and I'm not her boss. It's strictly professional. Besides, I'm single. You're not."

"I'm well aware of that. Don't go blowing this out of proportion. We got a lead on the John Doe, and she came to tell me. I have to go with her to tell the parents, and she figured we could eat on the way. That's all."

"It's all in the way she asked. It's obvious from the way you're acting she makes you uncomfortable."

"Maybe you're overreacting because the two of you haven't exactly hit it off." Samuel tried to steer the conversation toward Ray. "Thanks for mentioning that, by the way."

"She just enjoys pushing my buttons."

"Well, you'll just have to tangle with her after we get back. Don't you want to know who he was?"

"Yes, but don't change the subject. I know you outrank me, but you are so clueless sometimes." Ray shifted in his chair. "You're not getting in that car alone with Smith. I'm going."

"What are you talking about? I'm the sergeant. I can handle Deborah."

"This is about perception. Either you're oblivious, or you just don't want to hear what people are saying around the station."

"What do you mean? What's being said?"

"Don't shoot the messenger."

Samuel waited, watching his friend's face turn a deep shade of red.

"I've heard it insinuated Smith got the promotion because there's something between you two." Ray shifted in his chair again, but plowed forward. "She may be a pain in my side when it comes to her lifestyle, but her work is top of the line. She doesn't need to barter her way up the ladder."

Samuel clenched the pencil in his hands so hard it snapped. He hadn't done or said anything to give anyone that idea . . . had he? "That's so ridiculous, I don't even know where to start."

"Samuel, I can see you doing it." Ray fiddled with the cane.

"Doing what?" Samuel dumped the pencil in the trash and stood up. He didn't have to do anything. People still thought the worst. He pulled his suit jacket from the rack, ignoring the twinge of pain in his shoulder when he pushed his left arm through the sleeve. Six months of therapy and weight lifting, and his shoulder still wasn't a hundred percent after getting shot on a task force protection detail.

"Blaming yourself. This isn't your fault. You can't control what other people think. I only told you so you could understand the situation better. Stay clear of her. She's my partner. I promise to get my act together. No more distractions."

"Sure. Have you tried calling Susana yet?"

"Let me handle the John Doe case." Ray

sidestepped the question.

Fine. Maybe it would take Ray's mind off his own situation. It couldn't make it any worse. "Are you up to it?"

"I'm fine. The ankle swelling's down already."

"And your head?" He'd let Ray decide whether he was talking about the concussion or his personal problems.

"I can handle it."

"Fine. The ME is still working on his autopsy report, but we know that the victim is Joseph 'Joey' Doyle. Son of Milton Doyle."

"You're kidding." Ray smacked the cane on the floor. "This'll be fun."

"Tell me about it." Samuel headed for the door.

"Where are you going? I'm handling Smith."

"I know. I'm going home."

"Home?" Ray's surprise showed on his face. "Alvarez will be all over you on this one."

"Piper woke up with a fever during the night. The kids went to church camp this morning, so she's alone. I'm just going to check on her." Samuel put a hand on the doorknob. He owed his wife an apology. One he didn't dare give her. "Alvarez is a micromanager. Maybe this will be the case that makes him trust me to do my job. I'll tell him about it when I get back — after I make lunch for my wife."

Ray leaned back, his expression perplexed. "Piper knows you'd never cheat on her."

"That has nothing to do with this." He prayed Ray was right. Samuel was a forty-eight-year-old father of three, not a teenager with raging hormones. "She's got the flu. I'm checking on her. I'll tell Alvarez about Joey Doyle after lunch."

Ray stood, leaning on the cane. "That'll work. As long as somebody else doesn't tell him first."

CHAPTER SEVEN

"Hey, Susana, there's a lady on the line asking for you." Chad Lowenstein held out the headset, with a questioning look.

Chad had been in two of Susana's classes last semester. He was a nice guy. And good looking. The stray thought startled her.

"You want to take the call?"

Glad her colleague couldn't read her mind, Susana dropped her purse on his desk and held out her hand. Chad laid the headset in it, his fingers brushing hers. Her early morning hotline shift was supposed to be over. She had errands to run and homework to do and a son whom she hadn't seen since yesterday. This had to be the last call. "This is Susana."

The silence stretched. The caller must have hung up. Susana started to do the same. Then she heard a strangled sob. "I think my husband was murdered."

The woman's voice was familiar. Susana

pushed her hair from her face and sat in the chair Chad had vacated. Maybe this time the woman would trust her enough to share her first name. "Ma'am, why don't you tell me your name, and we'll try to sort this out."

"It doesn't matter who I am. I just need to talk to someone." Another sob seeped across the line. "I can't stand it anymore. I'm so scared."

"Are you afraid for your life, ma'am, because if you are, you sh— "

"Don't tell me to call the police. I can't. And it's not my life. It's his. I'm afraid for my husband's life." The sobs got louder.

"What makes you think he's been murdered?" Susana cranked around and waved a hand at Autumn. The hotline director pushed up her glasses and picked up her own receiver to listen in. "Last time you said you were worried that he was having an affair."

"He is. I know he is. But he always comes home. This time, he didn't come home." Rising hysteria forced the woman's voice into a tight, upward spiral. "I think they've done something to him."

"Who?"

"I told you."

"I don't understand," Susana shook her

78

head at Autumn. Autumn shrugged, her eyebrows raised. "Is it your family?"

"His family. Oh, I don't know anymore. I just don't know. It's all so confusing. And he's not here. He didn't come home last night or the night before. Where is he? Why doesn't he call?"

"Please try to stay calm, ma'am. If you think something bad has happened to your husband, it would be a good idea to call the police."

"No. No. Oh, no. I should never have called you. What was I thinking?"

A crash followed by a dial tone resounded in Susana's ear. Once again, she'd been inadequate. "Ouch."

"Well, what do you think?" Autumn dropped her headset on the desk and walked over to Susana.

"That's what I was going to ask you." The sound of ringing phones and one-sided conversations grated on her nerves. The old private school converted into the hotline hub was too small.

"You took the call. What was her state of mind?"

"Upset. Fearful. Angry. Hurt. Worried. Suspicious. Shall I go on?"

Autumn smiled. "No need. What is your job at that point?"

"To help her calm down. Help her sort through her feelings. Suggest ways she can get help."

"Exactly."

"She thinks her husband might have been murdered. Shouldn't we call the police?"

"And tell them an anonymous caller thinks her husband might have been murdered?" Autumn leaned against the wall, her arms loose at her sides. How could she look so completely at ease when Susana was obviously blowing these calls? "He's had an affair and hasn't come home for a day or two?"

"Well, when you put it that way . . ." Susana took a long breath. Being a firefighter had been easy compared to this. Firefighters knew the enemy. They went to the scene, assessed the situation, doused the fire, and went on to the next one. Fighting unseen fears, anguish, and paranoia was much harder.

"Let it go, Susana. You did what you could. Your shift is over. Go home, take a bubble bath, and read a good book."

"Can't." Bubble bath and a book — it sounded so good. "Benny has a basketball game tonight. Marco can't play because of his wrist, so he's in a huge funk. But we have to go to support Benny — especially

80

since Daniel will miss his first game."

"Why won't Daniel be there?"

"He's out of town on a case — again. Benny was so disappointed."

"Not as disappointed as Nicole, I would imagine." Autumn knew Susana's brother was fighting to save a marriage teetering on the brink of divorce.

"His bosses don't give him a choice. He has a job to do." Susana waited for Autumn to point out the irony in her defense of her brother's work priorities. She already had her argument ready. She didn't get to choose his career. Why make her life more difficult by choosing a cop as a spouse, too? Autumn didn't rise to the bait. She just nodded, a knowing look on her face that made Susana want to crawl under the desk.

Under normal circumstances, she would consider a basketball game a great distraction from her problems. She loved watching the kids play. During the winter season, Ray had shown up with Samuel for all of Marco's games. They'd had a blast, cheering from the sidelines until they were hoarse.

"Is something wrong?" Autumn pulled up a chair and sat down next to Susana.

"No. Just the usual stuff. I'm tired."

"Still not sleeping at night, are you?"

Autumn leaned back, her expression an open invitation to confidences. "Would you like to talk about it?"

Susana tapped her pen on the desk, staring at it. As much as she appreciated Autumn's friendship, she didn't need a counselor. The silence stretched until she wanted to scream. "Ray took Marco and Benny hiking. They fell into a ravine, Marco broke his wrist, Ray has a sprained ankle. Instead of being concerned about Ray, I kind of yelled at him at the hospital. I told him he couldn't take Marco hiking any more."

"The mother bear defending her cub." Autumn patted Susana's hand. "Ray knows why you're so protective. He'll get over it. Especially if you call him and apologize."

"I need to get going. I've got to go to the library and do some research, and I need to get some groceries before I pick up Marco. He's practically living at my sister's these days." Susana stood, grabbed her purse from the desk, and brushed past the hotline director. "I'll see you later."

"Having a blowup isn't all bad," Autumn called after her. "You get to make up afterward."

The memory of Ray's hurt, angry face loomed. They definitely had the fight part down. Susana slowed her pace, thinking of the caller. She'd sounded so scared, so worried about her husband. Susana knew that feeling. She longed for those days when she had gone home at the end of the day to make supper and eat with her husband and child. She prayed the man was all right, and he had a good excuse for putting his wife through this, that, unlike Javier, he would come home. That thought brought her full circle to Ray. With his job, she could never be certain he would.

"Susana, wait. Wait!"

She looked back at the old school building.

Chad loped down the sidewalk toward her. "Wait a second."

He stopped in front of her, panting slightly. He was a few inches taller than her, and he had the lean build of a runner. "Hey, I meant to ask you. Are you going to the reception at St. Cecile's tomorrow night?"

Susana had received the invitation earlier in the week and had tossed it into the junk mail pile with mild regret. Just not enough time. She had enjoyed the project that had included interviewing pregnant teenagers staying at the home for unwed mothers. Collaborating with Chad had been fun, too. He had both a quick mind and a quick wit.

"I hadn't planned to. I just don't have

time." Susana studied Chad's face. It was open and honest.

"Come on, Susana. All work and no play, you know what that makes." He grinned at her, the skin crinkling around friendly blue eyes. "We haven't been back since we finished the project, and we really owe Barbara Pritchard a big thanks for letting us talk to those girls. We got that A with her help. Look, I'll even drive. I'll pick you up, chauffer you home. It'll be fun. We can dish dirt on all the professors we'll have in the fall."

"I'm really busy, Chad."

"I won't take no for an answer. As friends, okay. Not as a date." The cherubic look on his face reminded her of Marco begging for a second helping of ice cream.

"As friends?" She wavered, seeing Ray's face in her head. Ray, the cop. Chad was studying social work and psychology. "Thirty minutes."

"Thirty minutes. I promise. In and out." Chad squeezed her arm, his hand warm on her skin. "Pick you up at seven tomorrow night. You won't regret it."

Susana tried to smile. She already regretted it.

"You know, Susana, you can't let the phone calls upset you." His hand dropped back to his side. "You gotta leave it behind when you walk out the door. That's part of being a counselor."

"I know that, but it's hard to do when a woman thinks her husband has been murdered, and I can't even find the words to begin to help her."

"Ripping yourself up about it won't help." He gave her a speculative look. "You know, what you need is to have some fun. And I know just the person to help you have it."

Susana watched as he turned and trotted way. He was lucky, and he didn't even know it. Violent death had never touched his life. At least that was experience she could draw from to help this woman, if she ever called back. Susana knew about sudden, violent death, and she never wanted to get close to it again.

"You see this?" The boss slapped a folded newspaper down on the desk that separated Lalo from him. A fat finger sporting a gold nugget ring stabbed the front page.

"Yes, I have seen it and read it." Lalo picked up the paper and shook it out flat. The headline screamed OFF DUTY COP FINDS MURDER VICTIM IN PARK. The reporter's name was Janet Hutchens. A woman. Covering murders. He would never allow his Sylvia to do such a thing.

"The guy who found Doyle's body is a cop, Hernandez. *¿Entiendes?*" His fat face shook with anger. "I know this guy — he ran me in a few years ago when he was still on patrol. He thinks he's a tough guy."

"*Sí, señor, entiendo.* This will make it interesting." A worthy opponent for a change. Lalo could only hope. "You should not worry. I have dealt with police before."

"Then do it now. It's gonna be personal with this guy."

"You want me to eliminate him?" Lalo smiled. It would be so nice to have a challenge.

"No, *idiota.* I want to know what he knows." The boss skated on thin ice again. Lalo's trigger finger squeezed in and out. "Follow him. See if he leads you to the other guy. Use him, if you can. But don't touch him."

"I give you reduced rate for a cop. Getting him out of the way will make the rest easier."

"No. I pay you. I give the orders. Leave the cop alone — for now."

"*Está bien.* Unless he gets in my way and leaves me no choice."

Lalo locked gazes with the man. *El señor's* face became still, the anger draining away.

"You're the only guy I know who's more cold-blooded than I am, Hernandez. I can't see drawing attention to our operation by doing a cop."

Lalo touched the Sig-Sauer tucked under his jacket.

Maybe the boss couldn't, but he could.

CHAPTER EIGHT

Deborah sucked in a deep breath, trying to calm the white-hot anger surging through her. She twisted the lock on the door to the women's restroom, wrinkling her nose at the mingled odor of mildew and cinnamon air freshener. She splashed water on her cheeks and patted them dry with a paper towel before looking at herself in the mirror. The flickering fluorescent lights gave her skin a sickly yellow pallor that reminded her of a terminal cancer patient.

Stupid, stupid *chica,* how could she be so stupid? Samuel Martinez might seem like a decent human being, but he was just like the rest of them. Even Ray "I'm a Christian and don't you forget it" Johnson treated her like all the rest of them.

Flipping the lid on the toilet in the first stall, she sat down and dug her cigarettes and lighter from the bag she'd retrieved from her locker. Her hand caressed the silver flask. No. Not at work. Her hands shook with anger as she lit the cigarette. Shook with anger, not from the tequila she'd drank at the bar the night before. She'd had every intention of just having one beer. One beer for the road. But one had led to two, then to three. The guys had all been looking at her, wanting her. It felt good, even if she had no intention of giving them what they wanted. She shuddered at the thought. Tried to back away from old memories.

Her hand went back into the purse and pulled out the flask. She turned the lid with trembling fingers. Just one swallow. No one would ever know. The fiery liquid burned her mouth and throat before it warmed her from the inside out. She took a deep breath.

Ray talked a good talk, but what was so Christian about making sure his buddy rebuffed a simple, friendly overture. She hadn't set foot in a church in years, but she still remembered the stories. Jesus with the tax collectors, Jesus with the woman at the well. Guess they didn't teach that anymore. Well, fine. She would show these guys she could solve this murder. She hadn't been one of the youngest women to make detective in the history of this department for no reason. She'd worked her butt off for an opportunity like this. She'd figure out who killed Joey Doyle and flaunt her police work in their smug faces.

A rap on the bathroom door made her jump. One more swallow. She slapped the lid on the flask and tightened it before hiding it back in the bottom of her purse. After one deep drag on the cigarette she tossed it in the toilet and flushed. As she sprayed perfume in the air, she took one last glance at herself in the mirror. No telltale tear tracks on her face, no red eyes. Just the face of a good detective. She unlocked the door and shoved it open, keeping her face neutral.

Narcotics Detective Kayla Wallace leaned against the wall outside the door, her arms crossed. "This isn't your private office, Smith, and it's not the smoking lounge. By the way, your partner is looking for you."

Deborah angled past her without meeting her gaze. "What'd he want?"

"He said if you didn't meet him at the car in three minutes, he'd make the Doyle notification by himself." Wallace grinned and straightened. "You better watch out. That cowboy might solve the case without you. Steal your thunder."

"Fat chance." Out of the corner of her eye, Deborah saw the unladylike hand signal her fellow officer threw at her. "And bite me, okay?"

"If you're done with him, I'll take him." Wallace's voice wafted down the hall. "I've seen him in Wranglers. Yee-haw!"

Making notifications was the least favorite part of Ray's job. Pain did a drum solo in his head as he barreled through the station lobby, ignoring the civilians streaming around him. He just wanted to get it over with. Deborah had chosen a really poor time to do her disappearing act.

"Detective! Detective Johnson!"

He glanced up in time to keep from smacking into Park Police Officer Teresa Saenz. She had his backpack slung over one shoulder and his hiking boot in her hand.

"Officer Saenz. I'd completely forgotten about my stuff." Fighting with Susana, his hospital stay, the Doyle case, his partner's behavior — he'd been a little preoccupied since he'd been at the bottom of the ravine with Teresa Saenz.

"I was in the neighborhood so I thought I'd drop them off."

"Thanks." Ray took his boot, embarrassed to realize it smelled like his sweaty feet. "You could've called. I'd have come by the substation."

A fleeting emotion danced across her face — just long enough to make Ray pause and take a good look. She wore the usual dark navy uniform, but her straight, brown hair hung loose to her waist. Pink lipstick brightened her face. She looked a lot better than she had at the bottom of the ravine. "I thought with your bum ankle it'd be easier for me to do it. Did you see Joe Reyes's report on channel five last night?"

"Yep. The guy's a jerk. He doesn't know what he's talking about."

"Sure, he does. We know people don't respect us. Most people don't realize we can give traffic tickets, let alone make arrests." Teresa slapped her hand on her holster. "I'd really like to catch this guy, make Reyes eat his words. I want in on this investigation. Let me help."

So that's why she was here. Ray hesitated. Park Police always handed these things over to PD officers. The reorganization hadn't changed that, but Teresa knew the park. Of course, she had no experience with a murder investigation. "Thanks, but we've got a handle on it. We got an ID on the body, and I'm on my way to make the notification."

"You got an ID?" Her voice rose with excitement. "Come on, at least tell me who it is."

92

"I'm kind of in a hurry."

"I'll walk with you."

Ray pushed through the double doors into the June heat billowing from the asphalt parking lot and headed toward the car, Teresa dogged his steps as he shared the information.

"Joey Doyle!" She emitted a wolf whistle. "Wow, you guys have your hands full."

"Yeah. We need to find the primary scene where he was killed fast."

"I'll find it long before you homicide hot-shots do." She sounded very sure of herself. "There's a lot of ground to cover in that park, and you city cops couldn't find your way out of a tin cup."

"I've hiked out there plenty." His words sounded defensive, even to him.

"Yeah. And walked off a cliff. And passed out."

"I've hiked in every state park from here to the Grand Canyon." A long time ago with his wife, but Teresa didn't need to know that. They had reached the car, but she showed no signs of leaving. "You don't have to go for the jugular."

"Sorry." Her grin was sheepish. "It's just frustrating. If you weren't so stuck-up, I could help."

"I'm not — look, it's your park. There's

93

nothing to prevent you from looking around. Find the primary crime scene. Do that, and you're in my debt forever." He stuck his hand in his pocket before remembering Deborah had the keys to the Crown Vic. "I promise to give you credit for it, if you do."

"Deal." Her grinned stretched across her face.

"And thanks for bringing me the backpack — and the stinky boot."

"Don't mention it. I wasn't going to." The smile disappeared, leaving behind a more tentative look. "Uh, I saw in the PD newsletter that you were on the team that built those cottages for St. Cecile's Home for Unwed Mothers. I worked on the interior stuff. They're doing a big grand reopening reception tomorrow night. Are you going?"

Ray hated receptions. Standing around, drinking too sweet punch from dainty glasses. Making small talk. "I doubt it. They really aren't my thing."

"I thought maybe we could go together." Her cheeks reddened, but her lips curled into a smile. "We could chat about the case. Get to know each other."

Her warm brown eyes were hopeful. The image of Susana's angry face as she stomped away from his hospital bed floated through his mind. "I don't know — I'm busy with this case. It's nice of you to ask, though."

"Why don't you just meet me there? We can talk shop the whole time." She turned up the wattage of her smile. "I don't bite, I promise. Consider it business if it makes you feel more comfortable."

"Well, when you put it that way — "

"Great. I'll be waiting in front of the home at seven. If you don't show up, it'll be your loss."

She walked away, leaving him standing there, staring at the boot in his hand. Teresa Saenz was a law enforcement officer. She understood his job, shared the same interests, accepted the risks. She'd asked him. So why'd he feel like a traitor?

"Where's Sarge?"

Ray glanced up. Deborah strode across the parking lot. The look on her face didn't bode well for the long drive out to King's Row Estates.

"He went home. His wife is sick."

"Chicken."

Ray held out his hand, and she dropped the keys on his palm. The odor of cigarette smoke hung in the air, mingling with the scent of spearmint breath mints. Ray tried to ignore the pain that made it feel like his brain was about to implode. Telling a family

95

their loved one was dead was enough. He didn't need Deborah's issues on top of it.

"So what were you trying to accomplish?" He kept his tone noncommittal as he threw the boot and backpack into the backseat. "You caught him off guard."

"Martinez is a nice guy in a station full of jerks who spend half their time hitting on me and half their time telling each other that I must not like men because I won't go out with them." She jerked open her door, her face defiant. "Food, decent conversation. Is that, like, totally out of the question with you guys?"

Ray could feel the color rising in his face as he eased in behind the steering wheel. "Sorry. I didn't realize it was that bad."

"Don't feel sorry for me, Jesus freak. I like the fact that men like the way I look." She pulled a pack of gum from her pants pocket and began unwrapping a piece. "Martinez needs to loosen up."

"Why do you do that?" Ray waved away the pack of gum.

"Do what?" She stuck three slices of gum in her mouth. The wad in her cheek grew as she chomped. The snapping sound irritated him.

"I'm trying to apologize to you, and you insult me. And Sergeant Martinez."

"I just calls 'em like I sees 'em." She attempted to blow a bubble. Gum settled over her lips. She grinned and started peeling it off. "Oops."

"I *am* a Jesus freak. I'd like to talk to you about it when you're ready." Ray wondered if he could set his anger aside long enough to share his beliefs with his partner. His shortcomings were as bad as hers. The thought didn't improve his mood. "And Samuel's married. His wife is a friend of mine, so I'd appreciate it if you'd back off."

The whish of the air conditioner and the crackle from the radio filled the ensuing silence. Ray glanced sideways at Deborah. Her face had gone a deep burnt red. She stared straight ahead.

"What did you get on the Doyles?" Somehow, they had to work together. He missed the days when he and Samuel were a team. Half the time they didn't even have to talk.

"The Doyles are a classy bunch." Deborah opened the folder on her lap. Relieved, Ray studied the road. "Our victim, Joseph Doyle, was thirty-two years old, married, two children, ages four and five. He was the fourth of the four Doyle children. Worked at the San Antonio Cadillac dealership, shared in the business like the other kids. He'd been in trouble with the law a couple times, but the only one on his record was the stolen car incident. That's it."

"What about the wife?"

"Melody Doyle née Erickson. Age thirty. Married Doyle the year before their first child was born. She's a UTSA graduate, degree in business administration. They met when she went to work for his dad. No record. They live with the in-laws. Must be quite cozy."

"You got a lot fast."

"A little Internet, a few calls, all in a day's work."

"And you planned to impress the boss with your handiwork." Talk about throwing the first stone. Ray's face burned.

"It's the more likely scenario." He deserved the irritation in her voice. "Just doesn't make good copy for the tabloids, does it?"

"Look, Deborah, we got off on the wrong foot. Maybe we could — "

"The Doyles live on Crestway." Her stony gaze dropped to the file.

They made the rest of the drive in silence.

The Doyle residence turned out to be a monstrosity of a Spanish-style whitewash structure with a red tile roof. The maid who answered the door disappeared into the interior, leaving them standing in a spacious foyer of rustic Saltillo tile. The house was built around the traditional courtyard. Ray could see a huge swimming pool through floor-to-ceiling windows.

"What a way to live." Deborah's tone was wry.

"I guess." The trappings didn't fool Ray. This family had problems like any other. Maybe more. After all, when the police came to tell a family a loved one had been murdered, social or economic status didn't matter. The gaping wound ran just as deep.

"Did you find him? Did you find Joey?" A dark-haired woman, all curves in a skimpy bikini and a flimsy wrap, rushed into the foyer, followed by an older woman, better covered by pants and a polo shirt. "Are you here about Joey?" the younger woman asked.

"Melody, calm down. Give the officers a chance to tell us why they're here, please." The older woman brushed past her and stopped in front of Ray. "I'm Cynthia Doyle, and this is my daughter-in-law, Melody Doyle. My husband isn't here at the moment. What can we do for you?"

"Could I ask where your husband is?" Telling a father was hard enough, but to tell a victim's mother and his wife at the same time was the stuff of nightmares. "Would it be possible to get him home?"

"Yes, I suppose. Why?"

Mrs. Doyle's face took on a blank, stoic look Ray had seen before. "Is there someplace we could sit down? I'm afraid I do have some bad news."

"Just tell us." Melody's face contorted in anguish, her valley girl cadence exaggerated by tears. "It's Joey, isn't it? Tell us. Just tell us."

"Come into the living room." Mrs. Doyle ignored her daughter-in-law's outburst. "I'll call Milt from there."

Wondering if she did that a lot, Ray followed them into the living room. Mrs. Doyle went to an old-fashioned rotary phone and dialed with a finger adorned with a diamond and sapphire ring worth more than Ray earned in a year. Her murmured conversation was brief.

"He's on his way." She dropped the receiver into its cradle and waved a hand at the chairs. "Now tell me, what's this all about?"

Ray eased onto a leather chair. "I'm so sorry to have to tell you this, ma'am. Both of you. We found Joseph Doyle's body at the wilderness park on Wednesday morning. I'm terribly sorry for your loss. He didn't have any ID on him so it took some time to

100

identify him."

The words hung in the air, the silence like a preamble for the words of denial and cries of anguish that would follow. It always took time for the words to sink in, the shock to blossom, the confusion to fade into angry denial. Deborah shifted on the couch, her eyes questioning. He waited. He knew better than to plunge in. He gave them a chance to digest the fact that their lives had taken a horrible, irrevocable, downward turn.

Cynthia Doyle spoke first, her face white, her hands clenched. "How? Did he fall? Was he attacked by an animal? It's a wilderness park, isn't it?"

Melody Doyle began to keen. "I knew something was wrong. I knew it. You wouldn't believe me, but I knew something had happened to my Joey."

"Melody, get a grip. Please!" Cynthia Doyle's hands went to her face in a fluttering motion.

"It wasn't that kind of attack." Ray kept his tone soft. Every word now would rip another hole in a mother's heart. "Not a wild animal, but one of the human variety. Your son was murdered."

"Murdered? He was murdered? Do you know who did it? Did you catch the murderer?" Cynthia Doyle's gaze darted around the room as if she might see the perpetrator of this horrendous crime.

"Not yet, ma'am. We're working on it. We need your help."

"We didn't even know Joey was in trouble. We've been sitting around drinking coffee and playing golf while he was out there ... . out there lying on the ground . . . dead. How can we help?" She sounded as if she were envisioning the condition of her son's body. Ray wondered how good her imagination was.

"We did know he was in trouble." Melody stopped sobbing long enough to throw those quavering words out like a gauntlet. "Yes, we did."

"How?" Deborah spoke for the first time. She took an afghan from the back of the couch and wrapped it around Melody's shoulders.

Melody fixed her gaze on Deborah as if she had discovered her last friend on earth. "I told them when he didn't come home Tuesday night that something was wrong." She clutched the blanket to her body, rocking back and forth. "He called me from work and told me he was taking off at noon. He said he had a lunch meeting and then he was going hiking. He was a big hiker."

"Mrs. Doyle — Melody — did he say who he was meeting for lunch?"

"No. Just business. But when he didn't come home, I knew something was up. She wouldn't let me call anybody. Kept saying it wasn't unusual. That he used to do it all the time. But he hasn't done it since we had the kids. He wouldn't worry me like this. Leave me alone like this."

A fresh assault of tears followed, even as Cynthia Doyle protested, her voice too weak to give her words much meaning. "He didn't leave you alone. You have all of us here."

Before Melody could respond, Ray jumped in. "I think it's better if we arrange individual interviews with family members. Is there some place private that we could use?"

"Why privacy? You don't think we're somehow involved in Joey's death, do you?" Bewilderment showed in the older Mrs. Doyle's words, but Ray also detected hostility.

"It's nothing like that, Mrs. Doyle." Access to the people in this house was vital. He needed to know what was going on in the man's life, at home and at a work. In this case, the two locations were intimately related. "We have to establish every detail

103

we can about what your son was doing during the time leading up to his death. We need to know who he saw, who he talked to, what his frame of mind was, were there any problems, anything that can help us figure out what happened to him."

At his words, Melody's weeping began again, the sound more subdued, more desperate.

"Melody, please control yourself. I can't concentrate with you wailing like that." Cynthia Doyle's voice rasped with unshed tears. "Officer Johnson, I think we'll wait until my husband gets here to decide about these interviews, if you don't mind."

The minutes seemed to stretch forever until a flurry of activity in the foyer told Ray that Milton Doyle had arrived. A second later he strode in, a short, balding man with a red complexion that spoke of time in the sun mixed with liberal amounts of alcohol. He was followed closely by a younger, taller man in a polo shirt, khaki slacks and golf shoes. Ray's first impression was bluster.

"What's going on here?" The voice boomed. "What do these officers want, Cindy? What couldn't wait until I got off the back nine?"

"I'm afraid it couldn't wait, Milt. Joey's

104

dead." Cynthia Doyle could have been telling her husband they were out of milk.

"What?" The word was soft, all the boom gone. Ray would have sworn the surprise on Milton Doyle's face was genuine. His features crumpled. "Joey, dead? That can't be right. He was just, he just, I just . . ."

The words trailed away as the man who had entered the room behind him grasped the older man's arm. "You better sit down, Dad. Mom, what are you thinking, dropping a bombshell on him like that? Get him a glass of water. Dad, sit down."

The younger man took charge, forcing Milton Doyle into a chair before turning to Ray. "I take it you're the cops. What exactly happened to my brother?"

Ray repeated the barebones recitation he'd given the two women. The older Mr. Doyle seemed to shrivel to nothing as the words sank in. Kevin Doyle's face, in contrast, swelled with misdirected anger. "You've delivered your bad news, now get out. We need some privacy. We have to make arrangements."

"Wait, Kevin. We don't even know where Joey is. We need . . . his body." Cynthia Doyle's voice strangled on the last word.

A tear rolled down her cheek, and the elder Mr. Doyle stumbled from his chair.

The two embraced for a second in the center of the room.

Ray waited to speak until they broke apart and sat down on the second couch. Neither of the men had asked what had happened to Joey Doyle. "I'm afraid we can't leave until we've interviewed each person who lives here."

"Why?" Kevin Doyle looked peeved.

"Because he was murdered, and you probably did it." In a sudden windmill of motion, Melody launched herself at her brother-in-law. She pummeled and scratched, kicked and shrieked.

Deborah reacted first, throwing herself forward, trying to grab Melody from behind. An elbow connected with Deborah's face. She staggered back holding her nose, blood flowing. "A little help, Johnson?"

Ray waded into the fray, trying to avoid flying fists and feet. Kevin Doyle didn't retreat. Instead, he pushed forward, grabbing his sister-in-law's neck. "What is wrong with you? You're psychotic," he yelled. "I've been telling Joey that for years. You're nothing but trailer trash."

"Stop it! Both of you, stop it." Cynthia Doyle's voice climbed, but she didn't moved from her husband's side. "Stop it, this instant!"

Neither responded. Ray corralled Melody from behind, grabbed both wrists, and whipped them back. She struggled, doubling over at the waist, sobbed, and screamed obscenities.

Milton dragged his son back. "What's wrong with you? Your brother is laying on some slab in a morgue, and you're in a cat-fight with his wife?"

"She started it. The witch started it." Kevin gasped for breath. His hand went to his face, touching a scratch. He started forward again, his face contorted in anger. "Trailer trash."

"Enough." Ray thrust himself between them. Melody had dropped to the floor. "Back off, Mr. Doyle, or I'll be forced to arrest you."

"What? She assaulted me! I want to press charges."

"Kevin." Ray heard the warning note in Mrs. Doyle's voice. "We don't air our dirty laundry in public."

The man, his face still flushed with anger, took a step back. "No, we deal with it in private, don't we?"

The threat in his sardonic tone sent a chill through Ray. "Mrs. Doyle, why don't you change into some clothes and meet me in the dining room?" He squatted next to

Melody. "Can you do that?"

Tugging her swim cover tight around her heaving chest, Melody nodded.

"I'll meet you there in five minutes. Deborah, you okay?"

Deborah had a wad of tissues stuck to her face, her head tilted back. "Yeah." The word was muffled. "I'll take the gentleman."

The sarcasm told Ray she was referring to Kevin Doyle.

"Don't believe a word that witch says. She's psychotic." Doyle snarled as Ray walked toward the door. "You're an idiot if you don't see it. All my dad has to do is pick up the phone and you're off this case. Watch yourself, mister."

"Kevin, shut up!" Cynthia Doyle's eyes glittered with anger.

Ray shut the door gently, not giving into the desire to slam it. Kevin Doyle would find threats usually gave Ray all the incentive he needed to nail a guy to the wall. Melody Doyle had said her brother-in-law probably killed Joey Doyle. Ray intended to find out what would make her say that.

The younger Mr. Doyle now topped the suspect list.

CHAPTER NINE

Samuel tossed his suit coat on the loveseat in the living room, stepped over two cats, bent over, and planted a kiss on his wife's forehead. "Feeling any better?"

Piper sat up and pulled her housecoat tight. Her face bright with curiosity and fever, she nodded. "What are you doing here in the middle of the day?"

"Checking on my sick wife." He held out his hand. She took it and he pulled her to her feet. "Keep me company while I make you soup."

"So. Did you ID the victim?" Her voice sounded like a stranger's; she was so congested and hoarse. Samuel let her words trail after him as he headed for the kitchen.

"Don't worry about it, do you want some tea?" He pulled a chair out and motioned for her to sit.

"I'm cold. Tea would be nice. Is there some reason you can't tell me who it is?"

She tugged at her tattered robe again and sat. A steamy ninety-degree wind blowing across South Texas made it impossible for the air conditioner to cool their two-story house, yet she was cold.

Samuel hated it when she was sick, because it wasn't something he could fix. He stuck a mug of water in the microwave. At least he could try to make her more comfortable. "Joseph Doyle."

Piper sighed. "That's going to make it difficult for you, isn't it? Shouldn't you be at work?"

Ignoring her concern, Samuel opened the refrigerator and stacked the items he needed on the counter. Shredded chicken. Corn tortillas, fresh onion and tomato, cilantro, slices of *aguacate*. He lined up the ingredients as he tried to line up his response. He couldn't tell her why he was really there. Deborah Smith understood his work in a way that only another law enforcement officer could. She was everything he was not. Nonconformist, fluid, a wild child. She fought dirty. She was young, green, full of potential. Yet she had a pain in her eyes that looked familiar, a tantalizing reflection of himself. He'd never been unfaithful to his wife. Not physically. "You know who he is?"

"Everyone does." Piper had to raise her

110

voice over Tinkerbell's yowling. The cat had been circling the kitchen ever since Samuel had started cooking. Piper corralled her and hugged the skinny Siamese as if warming herself.

"Yes, it'll make it tough."

"Have you told the family?"

"Ray's out there now." With Deborah Smith. He shoved the thought back down as he dumped a tea bag into the hot water and carried the mug to Piper. Samuel had done his share of formal notifications. They sucked. He felt a wave of sympathy for Milton and Cynthia Doyle.

"Any idea who did this to their son?"

Samuel stacked the corn tortillas and began chopping them in strips while the oil heated. "No. Now can we talk about something else?"

"Maybe it was a random act. Maybe the killer didn't know Joey Doyle was the son of a millionaire."

"It doesn't really matter." Either way, it would be a media circus. He dropped the strips in the hot oil and was instantly engulfed in an aroma that took him back to his mother's kitchen. She would make tortillas from *masa,* her practiced hands moving ceaselessly as she interrogated him about school. Simple days before his dad

111

had died, and he became the head of the family. "Drink your tea. Does that cat need food?"

"She's got food. She's just spoiled. Stop changing the subject. The scrutiny will be intense from the media and the family and the mayor. Maybe you should be at work. I'm a big girl. I'll be fine."

Almost afraid she'd read his thoughts, he stepped over Rambo, an overgrown German shepherd sprawled across the rug in front of the sink, and went to Piper. He leaned over her and inhaled the scent of cough drops and Vick's VapoRub. Tinkerbell leaped from Piper's lap and trotted off, apparently not interested in sharing Piper with Samuel. "*Mi amor,* there will always be another murder." He kissed her cheek and rubbed her shoulders. "*Te amo. Siempre.* Remember that."

Piper slid around in the chair and looked up, face startled. Shame rolled over him. He should be man enough to tell her he loved her more often.

She put her arms around his neck and snuggled against his chest. "Hmmm. You'll get my germs."

"I suspect it'll be worth it." *God, I love her.* He could never find the prayer he needed. Fumbling for words, he pushed

112

Piper's hair back and kissed her neck, wanting to pick her up, carry her to the couch, and hold her. *God, only Piper.*

Before he could move, the cell phone stuck in his pocket rang in her ear. She jerked back.

"Sorry." He eased back toward the stove and hit the button. Lieutenant Alvarez's gravelly bass filled his ear.

"Where are you, Martinez? All hell's breaking loose over here."

"I'm sorry, Lieutenant. What's the problem?" Somehow Alvarez had gotten wind of the murder victim's identity. Someone had a big mouth.

"The problem is we've got the dead body of the son of a leading citizen and contributor to the mayor's campaign in our morgue and someone forgot to tell me."

"Word gets around fast."

"The ME is a friend of mine. He called to confirm dinner plans. He thought I knew. Whatever would make him think that, Sergeant?"

"I'm handling it, sir."

"Uh-huh. I was just in your office. You weren't there."

Samuel glanced at Piper. Eyes worried, her gaze was fastened on his face. She stood and moved toward him. He tried to muster a smile, but couldn't even come close. "I'll be back in half an hour."

"The media's gonna be all over this, Martinez."

The click of a lighter and a puff. Alvarez's heavy breathing filled the silence. Samuel could almost smell the cigarette at the other end of the line. "I'll coordinate with the Public Information Office."

"We need to be on top of this every step of the way."

"I understand. I'm on it." Sticking the phone in the crook of his shoulder, Samuel used tongs to drag the tortilla strips from the oil and lay them on a paper towel to drain. He didn't need the house stinking of burnt tortillas, reminding him of another failure.

"Who's the lead detective?"

"Ray Johnson."

"I thought he banged himself up stumbling over his own feet."

Samuel grabbed a knife and started chopping onion and garlic, letting the familiar pungent aroma steady him. "He's fine."

"Stay on top of it personally, Martinez."

Alvarez hung up, the dial tone beeping in Samuel's ear. "Nice talking to you, too."

"Lieutenant Alvarez." Piper had a bemused look. She leaned against the counter and wiped her nose with a tissue.

"Yep."

"He knows who the victim is?"

"Yep."

"Do you have to go now?"

"No."

"I don't want you to get in trouble with your boss so soon after your promotion." Piper touched his arm.

"Don't worry about it."

"Samuel, stop what you're doing, turn around, and look at me. In twenty years of marriage, you've never come home in the middle of the day to make soup for me. What is going on?"

"Sí, mi general." Samuel let the knife clatter onto the cutting board and faced her. She planted her hands on his chest. *"Nada.* Nothing is going on."

Her glare deepened. For a second, he was one of her seventh graders. He grabbed her hands and pulled her against him, wrapping his arms around her shoulders. "Ray will inform the family and handle the interviews. It's called delegating. Sit down. Finish your tea. All that's left is for the soup to simmer."

"Samuel, solving murders is what you do. I know what that requires. I live with it, and I've learned to accept it." She tilted her head back, her gaze all too knowing. "Talk to me. Please. Tell me what's wrong."

"Nothing. I just wanted to make *caldo* for you." Samuel shrugged away from her and snatched a towel. He wiped his hands with more force than necessary, then slapped it on the counter. "Why do you have to analyze everything? It's just soup."

He stomped from the kitchen and slammed the front door behind him. Before he could reach the truck, the garage door came up. Piper marched down the driveway.

"Piper, you're in your robe. Go in the house."

"No." Her breathing sounded labored. From the flu or from anger, he couldn't decide. He grabbed the door handle, but her hand slapped down on his arm before he could jerk it open. "I want you to know something, mister."

He stared at her crimson face. Her blue eyes brimmed with unshed tears. "And what is that?"

"This isn't about soup, you coward."

"*¿Perdóname?*" The air seemed to quiver between them. His gaze dropped from her accusing eyes to the soft hollow of her throat where he liked to plant kisses. She swallowed convulsively as he schooled his voice into a whisper. "You're mistaken."

116

"An emotional coward." He could hear the tears in her voice, but she refused to let them fall. It was as if she wanted to be like him, hiding her hurt. He would never wish that on his worst enemy, let alone his wife. "I want you to understand this, and then I'll leave you alone. When you shut me out, it hurts me far worse than when you let me in."

She whirled around and flounced off.

He stood there, face burning, for a long time. He couldn't take that chance. If she saw what was inside him, she might never want in again.

"*¿Donde estás?*"

"Sitting at the table eating lunch *con mi mujer.*" Lalo dabbed at his lips with the linen napkin. It irritated him to be interrupted during mealtime. Only for the boss did he answer his cell phone. Sylvia made a *tsk-tsk* sound as she took the plate of flautas, rice, and beans away. She'd keep it warm until the conversation ended. She took good care of him. He patted her ample behind. A soft giggle followed. She would disappear into the kitchen of their small temporary quarters until summoned again.

"They're at the house. The cops are at the house."

He contemplated the boss's level of anxiety. Sounded relatively high. Threaded with irritation. Aggravated, possibly.

"What house?"

"The Doyles, *idiota*."

His boss now tread on dangerous ground. Lalo picked up his glass of *jugo de tamarindo,* sipped, gently returned the glass to the table, and dabbed his lips again. "And?"

"I pay you to keep an eye on these things. Pay you quite well. You're at home feeling up the wife, instead of out there finding that woman. Instead of watching the cops."

"*Señor,* perhaps we should sever our relationship." The tendons in Lalo's neck hurt as he gritted his teeth, but he didn't allow his anger to seep into his voice. "It appears my usefulness to you has come to an end."

Ice clinked over the telephone line, punctuating the pause. The boss should lay off the strong stuff. It clouded his judgment. "No. No. Take it easy. I need your services. I need you to finish this."

Much better. "The police will have a number of statements to take at the Doyle residence. They will be there for quite some time. As soon as I finish my meal, I will proceed to the location, begin surveillance. You'll deal with security?"

"Done. Let me know what's going on, *ese.*"

"Of course." Lalo laid the phone down. *"Querida."* Sylvia appeared a few seconds later with his plate, the food hot.

"Where were we?" He smiled up at her, letting his hand trail down her arm as she set down the plate.

"The pros and cons of Vallarta as opposed to Cancun." Her plain face became animated. "Perhaps villas at both."

Lalo smiled. Why not? He ate a few more bites of flauta, chewing methodically, thinking. One more drink of *jugo.* Unable to stall any longer, he dropped the napkin, stood, and kissed her soft cheek. "I must go now."

"So soon?" Her expression begged him to stay. She was bored. Knew no one. Missed her *familia.* He had a few relatives in San Antonio, but her family had settled in Juarez. He'd tried to get her to go out on her own, but she was too afraid of strangers.

He couldn't stay. The boss wanted him at the house, and he had unfinished business with the park lady. She'd left her house the previous day with her gentleman friend on a motorcycle. He had attempted to follow them, but had lost them in the thick rush hour traffic. The boss hadn't been happy,

119

but Lalo had convinced him that haste did make waste. He would continue to bide his time, looking for the perfect opportunity.

"I'll be back early tonight. My business will be brief."

Depending on how he felt, of course. Quick and painless. Or endlessly and exquisitely painful.

CHAPTER TEN

Ray looked up from his notebook to see Melody Doyle stumble into the dining room like a sleep walker who suddenly awakes and finds herself in unfamiliar surroundings. He shot from his chair, took her arm, and guided her to a seat at the mahogany table. She didn't make eye contact, just sniffed hard.

He'd interviewed the maid and Kevin's wife while waiting for Melody. The maid's broken English hadn't prevented Ray from gathering she thought Joey was the best thing since sliced bread. Kevin's wife had been tightlipped, claiming she and Joey had never talked — not in the twenty years she'd been married to his brother. Deborah was questioning Kevin, Elaine, and Milton Doyle — in that order — in the elder Doyle's study.

Ray wanted to get his interview with Melody over quickly so the young widow could get on with the arduous process of grieving. He understood where she was in that journey — that mind-numbing, head-shaking, unbelieving stage. It didn't last long. The next stage was furious, head-banging anger. Followed by months of agonizing emptiness, before an unwilling acceptance settled in as a constant companion.

The skin on her arm felt icy. She jerked away from his touch and hunched forward, her fingers clutching a wad of tissues. She'd changed into jeans and a lacy undershirt that left nothing to his imagination. He averted his eyes, dropped into his chair, and studied the questions he'd jotted down.

"Who found him? How did someone find him if he was in a ravine?" She threw out the first question before he had a chance to take charge. Something in her voice told him only part of her wanted an answer, the other part wanted to believe it was just a horrible misunderstanding. "How long had he been there? Was he . . . was he . . . did animals . . ."

Ray forced himself to meet her gaze. "I found him."

She shook her head in disbelief. Her dark bangs fell over hazel eyes, making him want to brush her hair back from her face as if she were a child. "How? Were you looking for him?"

"No. I went hiking."

"Oh, oh." She put one hand over her mouth, the muscles in her throat quivering in a violent effort to swallow. The color of her face reminded Ray of a freshly fallen snow. She lowered a shaking hand. "Was he . . . how did he look?"

Ray's mind conjured up the image of Joey Doyle's body: the rusty bloodstains, the tattered blue shirt, the mangled hand. For a second, he could smell the stench of decaying flesh again. He cleared his throat. "The wilderness park is a beautiful place, ma'am, peaceful. It was like he was just resting."

She breathed in and out, the sound echoing noisily. "Good, that's good, isn't it? Thank you. Thank you for finding him."

"Yes, ma'am." It had been purely accidental and totally unwelcome, but Ray understood and accepted what she offered. At least her husband wasn't still lying out there, exposed to the elements and creatures who would tear his flesh from his body. At least she could bury him. "I hate to ask you these kind of questions right now, but we really need your help to find out who did this."

"You want to know why I said what I said

123

about the Doyles doing it?" Suddenly, she sounded nervous. Ray studied her swollen red eyes and trembling lips. "I was just overcome with emotion, I-I-I didn't mean it. I was distraught." Her voice rose with each word.

Not nerves, fear. He heard fear in the tortured stutter.

"Mrs. Doyle, tell me about your husband's relationship with his family." Ray kept his voice soft, trying to make her feel more at ease.

"Milt has had a couple heart attacks. They know it won't be long before he's gone." Melody shredded the tissues with shaking fingers and threw them on the table, avoiding his gaze. "They're sharks. Milt loves it. He plays with them. One day, he's leaving controlling interest to Kevin; the next day, it's Elaine. But never Joey. He just teases Joey because everyone knows Joey is — was — cute and sweet, but not much of a businessman. He had all these schemes to create more business, but nothing ever panned out."

"What kind of schemes, specifically?"

"I don't know. He just said it was going to be big, very big, that they would see and start taking him more seriously."

"When was the last time you talked to

your husband?"

"Face-to-face? When he left for work after breakfast Tuesday morning." She looked as if she were replaying that last scene in her mind. Ray hated to make her go through it. She would look back at that shared moment and come to the mind-boggling realization that it would never be repeated. "We ate blueberry muffins and drank orange juice."

Her voice trailed away, forcing Ray to prompt her again. "What did he talk about? Did he have anything on his mind?"

"Well, he did seem kind of happy, which was unusual, but he didn't say too much."

So he was happy. Happy about something that made someone else furious enough to kill him? Ray grasped at straws. "You don't care for Kevin, do you?"

"Are you kidding? Kevin never stopped riding him. Kevin isn't very nice." Melody's face twisted in a bitter smile. "He never let Joey forget his mistakes."

"Like the joy riding and the car theft in high school."

"Exactly. It was fifteen years ago, for crying out loud."

Since he had been eighteen and considered an adult, his mistake stayed on his record, but Ray didn't linger on that thought. "What about Elaine?"

125

"Elaine is Ms. Money Bags. She's also a bitter old biddy."

No hard feelings there. "So you don't care for her?"

"She lives here with her three kids. She's at the dealership all day, comes home, has a martini or two, and then calls me a freeloader. Who does she think entertains her kids all day?"

"And the other sister." Ray glanced at his notebook. "Sarah?"

"Sarah's the only one of the whole bunch worth knowing, and Kevin and Elaine despise her."

"Why?"

"Because she's smarter than they are. She's getting her masters in philosophy. She's going to teach at some university, and she's already writing a book."

"Going back to Tuesday, you said the last time you talked to him face-to-face was at breakfast. Did you talk to him again after that?"

"On my cell. He called me about eleven thirty, I guess. I was on my way to the Junior League luncheon."

"What did he say, exactly?"

"Well . . ." She hesitated, as if trying to remember — exactly. "He said things were coming together."

"What things?"

"I don't know what things. He didn't say what things. Just things." Her tone took on a hysterical edge. "He didn't tell me about business stuff. I was just the wife. I'm supposed to look pretty at cocktail parties, produce offspring, and be ready to perform when he comes home at night."

Ray kept his opinion of that statement to himself. "What else did he say?"

"That he was going to a lunch meeting, then to do some hiking. He said he would probably be a little late."

"I need to know something else, Mrs. Doyle." The question had to be asked. He'd put it off long enough. "Did your husband wear a wedding ring?"

"Yes, why?" She looked puzzled, then anger bloomed. "Are you telling me he didn't have it on? He took it off for some reason — to mess around, maybe."

She'd immediately gone there. What that did that say about her relationship with her husband? If she knew for a fact he was cheating, maybe murder had crossed her mind. Maybe she'd even done something about it. "We don't know."

"What do you mean, you don't know? He either had it on, or he didn't."

"The ring finger on his left hand was missing."

"The killer mutilated my husband's body?" She whispered the question.

"Yes." He'd gutted the man, but Ray didn't elaborate. He needed to keep her moving, not let her dwell on the image. "So what did you do all afternoon on Tuesday?"

Her face white with horror, she stared into space for a minute as if reliving the day. "After the luncheon, I had an appointment for a manicure and pedicure. I did some shopping at North Star. It was about four when I got home. I sat around waiting for Joey to come home. He never did."

Tears trickled down her face. She covered her mouth with her hands. Her eyes squeezed shut as a strangled sob escaped, a tiny sound that made Ray stare at the floor. She stood up, teetering for a second, then stumbled away. She stopped at the door, her back to him. Her shoulders shook.

"Just one more question, Mrs. Doyle, and we're done." Ray wanted to let her walk away. He wanted this to be over, but he couldn't let her go until he knew everything she knew. "Who was here when you got home?"

"You think one of them did it?" She looked back at him, her eyes dark with emotion. Wrapping her bare arms around her middle, she shuffled back and slid into her chair again. The emotion shimmering in her eyes wasn't grief. It was fear. Something or somebody scared Melody Doyle.

"You said they did. Why?" He wanted to probe, but lightly, not scaring her away.

"I said they *probably* did it. I was just lashing out. They're such creeps. I don't have any proof. And they would never cut his fing — they're not monsters." Was she trying to convince him or herself?

"If you could, please just tell me who was here when you got home."

"Elaine wasn't here. I don't know where she was. Maybe a date or something. Sarah was in Austin. I didn't see her boyfriend. He was probably working. Kevin came in about six, six thirty. I remember because he and Milt were in the living room, watching something on the big-screen."

"Mrs. Doyle, here's my card." He wrote his home number on the back and handed it to her. "Call me if you think of anything that might help us find your husband's killer."

She turned the card over and over between her hands, not looking at it. "I have to make some arrangements, don't I? Do I make arrangements for the . . . for his . . . for Joey?"

"I'm sure your in-laws will help. It may be a few days before we can release your husband's body."

Her face crumpled. Ray rose. She did the same, then her legs gave out, and she sank back into her chair. "How will I tell the children? Do you think a five-year-old understands death?"

"I'm sure you'll find the words. Just take your time."

"Mommy?" Melody turned at the same time as Ray. A small, blond boy clad in Superman pajamas stood in the doorway.

"Ethan, what are you doing down here? Why haven't you gotten dressed?" Melody darted across the room. The boy buried his head in her stomach as she clutched him to her body.

"Grandma was crying. Why am I a poor boy, Mommy?"

Cynthia Doyle had aged ten years in the hour it took Ray to do his other interviews. When he walked into an enormous kitchen filled with shiny stainless steel appliances and the faint aroma of fresh bread, she was standing at the stove, pouring hot water from a teakettle into a cup. She stared at him for a second as if trying to figure out how he'd gotten into her house.

130

"Care for some green tea?" She looked vaguely out of place, like someone unaccustomed to serving herself — or others. "The cook is distraught. I told her to lie down, but I'm sure I can manage to fix you a cup of tea."

"No, thank you, ma'am."

"Sit down, Detective. We might as well talk here. No one will bother us. My children can't find the kitchen, let alone cook."

Ray took a seat on one of the bar stools around a rectangular island. Mrs. Doyle took another one. An acre of blue, purple and white checkered tile separated them.

"Were you proud of your son?" He lobbed the first volley.

"Joey?" She stared into a fragile china cup, as if she didn't know which son he meant. "Yes, Joey was my problem child, I admit, but I loved him. He needed me more than the others. I had to watch out for him. Then I turn my back for a second, and look what happens." The timbre of her voice reminded him of a thin sheet of glass. Tap too hard, and it would shatter into a million fragments.

"Did your son have any enemies? Anyone who might hold a grudge against him?"

"How should I know? You're the detective. My tax dollars pay your salary so you

can solve murders like this one." The grieving mother metamorphosed into an aristo-
crat accustomed to servants doing her bid-
ding. "You're wasting time — mine and
yours."

Ray couldn't tell whether she was just irritated at being questioned by a minion or
if she had something to hide. "I need to ask
you a few questions to establish Joey's state
of mind and his normal routine. If we can
figure out if he deviated from that, it'll help."

"His state of mind? Did you ask Melody
about his state of mind? She contributed
plenty to his state of turmoil. I heard them
in their suite, arguing all the time. My poor
grandchildren were growing up in the
middle of a war."

Now there was a different take on things.
"Do you know what they argued about?"

"The woman's paranoid. She's convinced
Joey was cheating. She harangued him if he
was five minutes late, sure he'd been with
some other woman."

"You don't believe he cheated?"

"He may have, early in their marriage, but
not since he had children to think about.
She's delusional." Mrs. Doyle smacked the
cup down on the saucer. A diamond tennis
bracelet clinked against the china. "I never
understood what he saw in her. When he

brought her home the first time, I told him it was a mistake. It's always a mistake to marry out of your class."

Ray kept his face neutral. "Are you telling me you think your daughter-in-law is capable of murder?"

Mrs. Doyle gave a short, mirthless laugh. "You saw her performance in the living room. From the screaming fury I heard when I passed their room at night, she sounded perfectly capable of killing."

"Joey never mentioned any problems at work or outside the house to you?"

Something — fear maybe — flitted across her face, but it was gone before Ray could analyze it. "Nothing out of the ordinary. The usual, harmless sibling rivalry. Joey got frustrated with Kevin and Elaine because they didn't give him more responsibility. But he couldn't handle more. I told him as much."

Nice. "Did he ever mention a big business deal?"

"Joey?" This time the laugh was outright. "He was always coming up with these whoppers. Kept his dad and me in stitches. Llamas. Ostriches. Soybean sprout farming. Some invention that was supposed to keep facial hair from growing on women's upper lips. Ridiculous ventures."

"Nothing related to the car dealerships?"

Her smile died and her answer seemed too long in coming. "No. Joey sold cars. He was a good salesman. Very charming. And he had good manners. People like that when they're spending thirty or forty thousand on a car."

"Where were you Tuesday afternoon?"

Her eyebrows popped up. Then her features froze in outrage. "What are you implying, Detective?"

"Nothing, ma'am. It's just a routine question to establish everyone's whereabouts."

"There's nothing routine about losing a son to a murder. Get out there and find the monster who did this now before I call Phil Whittaker. I have his number on speed dial. He's Sarah's godfather."

Phil Whittaker was a banker and owner of two sports team franchises. He was also the mayor.

"I plan to, ma'am, but I still need an answer."

She slid from her stool and stalked to the door, pausing with her hand on the frame. "Here, Detective. I was here all day with my grandchildren. I had my interior decorator come in. I'm redoing the living room. Now get out."

"Yes, ma'am." He slid past her, taking the

time to meet her gaze directly before turning his back.

"Detective."

"Yes, ma'am?" He glanced back. Stark anger distorted her features, giving her face a horror-flick visage. Too much mascara and botox.

"Don't mess this up. I don't want this criminal walking away on some technicality. I'd rip his heart out myself, if I could. I expect nothing less from you."

"Yes, ma'am." Ray went in search of his partner.

Grieving mother or liar? Grieving wife or liar? One of them was lying.

The question was, which one? And more importantly, why?

CHAPTER ELEVEN

"Mom. Mom!"

Susana looked up from the stack of bills she was sorting to see Marco standing in the kitchen doorway. With what was left of the insurance money, Javier's Social Security, and the firefighters' fund, she was keeping their heads above water. Barely. She should pay bills when she was more rested, but when would that be?

From Marco's tone, he'd been trying to get her attention for a while. He'd retreated to his bedroom to play video games the second they'd arrived home from Benny's basketball game. Taxi, a Jack Russell terrier who adored her son, nuzzled at his leg before giving her a mournful stare. Neither dog nor boy looked happy.

"Sorry, sweetie, you know how it is when I'm doing high math." She tried for a comical grin. Marco had been morose at the game, not bothering to cheer for Benny even when he made his first basket of the season. She didn't know whether to be angry at Marco's lack of support for his foster cousin or worried about her son's state of mind — or both. "Need something? Some Tylenol for your wrist?"

"How come Ray wasn't at the game?"

So that was it. "He's working the case — you know the body y'all found in the ravine."

"He came to all my games last season." Taxi whined and Marco stroked the dog's head. "He knew Benny was playing his first game, and he didn't show up. Benny felt bad. Did you tell Ray he couldn't come because you were mad about me falling?"

"No. No, I didn't tell him that." Not in so many words.

"How come he hasn't called me? To ask if I'm okay?"

"He's just busy, Marco. I'm sure he'll call soon. Why don't you get out the ice cream — I think we both could use a bowl of chocolate chip." It was his favorite. Maybe she'd get a smile out of him yet. "We can sit out on the step and watch for fireflies while we eat. Taxi can even have a treat."

Marco didn't budge from the doorway. "I have to ask you something." His tone had gone from accusing to belligerent, the one he used when he knew she would say no to something he wanted.

"Sure, go ahead." She dropped her pen and rubbed her forehead, hoping her headache would kick back a notch.

"Do you think maybe we could go home — just for a visit?"

"Honey, we are home." She pretended to misunderstand.

"To Corpus. I wanna go to the beach and Jet Ski and go fishing like me and dad used to." Marco's face brightened. "It'd be fun."

For once, Susana didn't have the heart to correct his grammar. Her pain was almost physical as she contemplated how much an eight-year-old boy must miss his daddy. The longing in his voice wrapped itself around her heart so tight her pulse pounded in her ears. She had her memories, too. Clear blue skies, the smell of saltwater, gulls cackling as they soared overhead, the rough sand caught between her toes.

Except she'd sold the Jet Ski to the couple who had bought the house. "I'm sorry, but we don't have a house there anymore, so we'd have to stay in a hotel and rent the Jet Ski. We can't afford it right now. Maybe when I finish school."

"Why? Are we poor?" Worry darkened her son's face. "Because we don't have Dad anymore?"

"We're not poor. Things will straighten out when I start working again." Susana glanced at the gas, water, phone, and electric bills in front of her. Scrimping on clothes, passing up fresh shrimp and buying canned tuna, skipping movies and fast food, those things didn't keep her awake at night. The therapy bills, the health insurance, the house payments, and Marco's future education — those were the things that sat like barbells on her chest. "Besides, money's not everything. We've got each other. We're good."

"And we've got Taxi." Marco seemed to want to go along with her. "And Ray."

She'd walked right into that one. "Why don't you get out the ice cream, before it gets too late. It'll be time for bed soon."

Marco slipped across the room and stood in front of her, his fingertips gripping the edge of the pine table. Taxi stayed close to him. "Could we just drive down to Corpus?" Tears crept into her son's voice. "We could just sit in the car and look at the water. Please."

Susana couldn't look at him or she would be crying, too. "After I start working again, we'll go. I promise."

"Mom, I can't remember what our house looked like anymore. We could just drive by, and then come back."

Round-trip it would take at least six hours. She didn't want to see the old house that had new people living in it. "We'll see."

"That always means no!" Marco whirled as if to shoot from the room and stepped on one of Taxi's paws. The dog yelped and skittered under the table.

Susana grabbed Marco's arm. "Sweetie, the phone works both ways. You want to talk to Ray. Talk." She held out the phone. He looked at it, then glared at her, his face the spitting image of his dad's when Javier had argued with her.

He took the phone, then jerked away. "Come on, Taxi, come on, boy. I'm sorry, I didn't mean to step on you."

A second later the two were gone, Taxi's single, vociferous bark a sign the tension was getting to them all.

Susana gave into a bone-deep weariness and laid her head on the table, imagining Javier across the table from her. What would he say? Would he think she doing a good job with Marco? The image faded, giving way to another. Ray. His sweet brown eyes and long fingers as he handed her an ice cream cone after a ball game. Mocha mint. He'd chosen the flavor. When some of it dribbled down her chin, he'd wiped it away with one finger, his eyes tracing her features. Sudden heat washed over her at the memory.

He was so different from the mercurial, outgoing man she'd married. Susana jerked her head up from the table, shattering the image. She wanted to stop grieving for the close-knit family circle that had been ripped apart by a reckless driver. She wanted to bury, once and for all, the aching need to slide under the covers at night and snuggle up against a husband with whom she could share her joys and her burdens.

Mostly, she wanted to stop asking herself it she'd ever have the courage to reach for that dream again. If she didn't, that was all it would ever be. A dream.

"I think we interviewed a killer today."

Taking his gaze from the windshield, Ray glanced at his partner. Deborah stuck a french fry, drenched in catsup, in her mouth. She held a takeout bag under her chin to keep the red stuff from dripping on her shirt. Not that it would matter. It was already stained with blood from her encounter with Melody Doyle's elbow.

"Let's see. We interviewed twelve people, including the maids, a cook, a handyman, and a gardener. Care to narrow it down for

141

me?" Ray pulled from the restaurant parking lot and onto the access road to the highway. It had taken all afternoon and early evening to finish the interviews. His head and his hand hurt. Somewhere in his notes lurked a clue to Joey Doyle's killer.

"Well, the sister Elaine has ice water running through her veins, but she claims to have an alibi. She isn't big enough to stab him and throw him in a ravine, but she's cold-blooded enough to hire someone to do it."

"What makes you think she did it? And what was she doing all day Tuesday?" Ray's mind wandered back to Wednesday morning, conjuring up the heat of the sun on his face as he'd lain on his back next to Joey Doyle's decaying body.

"Because he annoyed her. She claims she was at the main dealership all day, doing paperwork and reviewing sales stats. She had dinner at Boudro's downtown, about seven, with a gentleman named Joel Wallace, a businessman who lives in King's Row."

Ray rolled his head, trying to pop a stiff neck. The aroma of Deborah's hamburger and greasy fries made his stomach rock. He should be hungry, but he wasn't. "Personally, I'd put Kevin Doyle at the top of my list."

"Kevin was definitely upset about his brother being dead, but he didn't seem all that surprised." Deborah slurped from a straw stuck in a large Dr. Pepper, the sound irritating Ray's already-taut nerves. "He said Joey always ran with the wrong crowd, even in high school. Smoked pot, talked trash, until the parents threatened to send him to military school. Kevin claims that in college, Joey just graduated to a better class of drugs and druggie friends. He also said Melody is in denial if she thinks he wasn't still using. According to Kevin, Joey wasn't hiking to commune with nature. He liked to get high out there."

"What did he say about Melody's theory that they were all jockeying to take over the family business because Milton won't be around much longer?" The woman's take on the situation gave Kevin some semblance of motive.

"He claims his dad's health isn't that bad. He said the only reason they fight over the business is because they all care so much about it."

"Yeah." They both snorted at the same time. Ray glanced in the rearview mirror. A silver BMW eased into the lane behind him. Strange, it had been behind him when he pulled into the burger joint. At least he

143

thought it was the same one. BMWs were the car of choice for San Antonio's upper middle class, but he couldn't shake a sudden sense of unease.

"Anyway, he also said Joey was unfaithful to Melody on and off during their entire marriage." Deborah went on. "He intimated things got pretty heated between them. She threatened to leave Joey, and he threatened to never let her see the kids again if she did."

"Cynthia Doyle said Melody accused Joey of having affairs, but she claimed it was all in her daughter-in-law's head. It would be motive, if it were true." Ray glanced in his side mirror. The BMW changed lanes and passed him. "You see that BMW? I think it followed us to the restaurant."

"How could you tell? They're a dime a dozen in this town." Deborah's tone said she had the same opinion of this phenomenon that he did. "Don't you want to know who Kevin says little brother was seeing on the side?"

Ray dragged his gaze from the BMW. "Sure. You got a name?"

"For a guy who claimed not to keep track of his brother's personal life, Kevin was quick with an answer. Candy Romano. She's the receptionist at the Ford dealership."

Ray loosened his grip on the steering wheel. Either he was tired or suffering from paranoid delusions. The BMW outdistanced an eighteen-wheeler and disappeared. He felt relieved for no apparent reason. "So did big brother have an alibi?"

"At the main dealership all day. With Elaine. Home watching TV with his dad in the evening."

"So they alibi each other. Convenient." Ray changed lanes, heading for the next exit. "Maybe they're all in it together."

"Or maybe they had nothing to do with it, and it was some psycho in the park who grabbed the first poor unsuspecting hiker who came along."

"Maybe."

"I thought we were going back to the station." Deborah sounded surprised — and disappointed.

"Thought I'd go shopping for a nice Ford pickup. Call and make sure Romano is still there. The showroom should still be open. Tell them she stays until we get there."

Deborah groaned as she grabbed her phone from the dash. "It's Friday night, don't you have a life? You know, like a date?"

"It won't take long." They might find a way to be real partners, but she didn't need access to his personal life. 'We'll work on getting warrants for the financials on Monday. Tonight, let's have a talk with the alleged mistress."

Sighing, Deborah stuffed the remains of her supper in the bag, tossed it in the foot well, and pulled a cigarette from a crumpled package.

"Light that, and I'll slow down to fifty and dump you beside the road." Ray took one hand from the wheel to rub a spot over his right eye. "I've already got a headache."

"Poor baby. I may have a busted nose, and you don't hear me complaining." She sniffed and stuck the cigarette back in the package. "It's no wonder you have a headache. You didn't eat. I still have some fries I can dig out of that bag."

She actually sounded concerned. "No thanks. I'll grab something after work."

Five minutes later, they pulled into the Ford dealership that served as one of the satellite locations in the Doyle empire. A young man and his pregnant wife wandered about, stopping at one shiny vehicle after another, deep in conversation about the pros and cons of ABS brakes and passenger-side air bags. Ray allowed himself to peruse the selection of pickups for a couple seconds, setting aside the questions he was formulating for Candy Romano. He'd never owned a brand new truck in his life.

"You can't afford one of these on what you make." Deborah leaned into a dark blue F350's window for a second and inhaled, a look of pure pleasure on her face. "Don't you love that new vehicle smell?"

"You have a truck that's only a couple of years old." He'd been a little envious when he'd first seen his partner's ride. And surprised. He'd taken her for more of a Stealth or Mustang type.

"Not like that one — mine was preowned. I live frugally. The truck is my only frivolous expense."

"Trucks are never frivolous." He laid on the drawl a bit thicker than usual. "This is Texas, after all."

Deborah laughed, the sound contagious. "Maybe, but can you imagine what the insurance would — "

Before she could finish the sentence, Ray's cell phone chirped. He glanced at the caller ID. Private caller. Susana's phone was unlisted. Maybe she . . . naw. She'd never call him. He answered on the second ring.

"Hi, Ray, Mom said it was okay if I called you. Is it okay, or are you busy?"

If it couldn't be Susana, Marco was a great second choice. Ray turned his back on Deborah's curiosity, and pretended to peruse the four-by-four diesel pickup's mammoth tires. "Hey, slugger, this is fine. I told you, you can call me whenever. What's up? How's your wrist?"

"Benny scored six points at the game tonight."

The game. He'd promised Benny he'd be at that game. Ray rubbed his forehead. "Wow, that's great. I bet he was excited. Did they win? I'm really sorry I had to miss it."

"Yeah. *Tío* Joaquin was there, but *Tío* Daniel didn't come. Or *Tío* Samuel either."

And no Ray. "I'll call him, Marco. As soon as I get a chance. It's just this case with the body we found — "

"That's what Mom said. She said you were busy working."

Susana was delivering a message to him through Marco. If he didn't have time now, nothing said he'd have time for Marco if things ever got serious between Susana and him. He wanted to pound the hood of the truck. Deborah had moved over so she could lean against the bumper, not bothering to hide her interest.

"I'll call Benny. How about you? Are you feeling all right?"

"I gotta go. We're gonna eat chocolate chip ice cream and look for fireflies."

"Hmm, chocolate chip. That's your favorite." Marco hadn't answered his question.

"There's some mocha mint, too, if you want to come over and have some." Mocha mint. Susana had bought Ray's favorite. "I can ask Mom if it's okay."

"I'm sorry, kiddo, but I'm working." Sitting on the front step, eating ice cream with Susana and Marco. The picture of the family he wanted was so perfect, his throat hurt with the effort to keep his tone light. "Thanks for the invite, though. Maybe this weekend we can try to catch a movie."

"I gotta go. See ya." Marco disconnected without responding to Ray's offer.

"That's nice. You're like a Big Brother or something." Deborah sounded wistful.

"Or something."

Ray caught a glimpse of sadness in his partner's face before it shuttered again. He wanted to probe, but Deborah was already headed for the office, her long-legged gait swift. She reminded him of a nervous thoroughbred. "Let's get this over."

Candy Romano turned out to be a chubby woman somewhere between twenty and twenty-five. Her hair was short and red, and her lipstick matched. This evening, her eyes were also red. She took one look at his badge and burst into tears. Ray wavered, looked at Deborah, and saw that she'd be no help. It was his day for grieving women. He took Candy's arm and led her back to her swivel chair before grabbing a box of tissues from her desk and handing them to her.

"This is about Joseph, isn't it?" Candy blew her nose so hard she squeaked. "You're here about Joseph."

"Yes, ma'am, we are." Ray eased onto the couch across from her. Deborah remained standing, leaning against the wall, studying Candy Romano as if she were a new specimen for her bug collection. "How well did you know Mr. Doyle?"

"Me?" The woman's eyes opened wide as if in disbelief. Real or a good actress? "I started working here as a telephone operator about two years ago. Now I help out with tag pickup, paperwork, stuff like that, too. I saw him everyday. We worked closely together."

"How close?"

"I got to know him pretty well." A blush stained her face beginning at the base of her jaw and spreading all the way to her hairline above green eyes. "Well enough to know how misunderstood and mistreated he was."

The last words were said with great indignation. Ray glanced at Deborah, sending her a mental high five. She waggled her eyebrows, her nod smug.

"Mistreated? How so, Miss Romano?"

She glanced toward the door. "I need this job, Detective. I live with my mom and three younger brothers and sisters. You can't tell anybody I said anything."

"It depends on what you tell us, Miss Romano. If it's just background information, then it could have come from anyone, right?"

She didn't seem to recognize he had sidestepped the issue. "Joseph was a good man. He was an honest person who tried to be nice. He was nice to me when the rest of the Doyles treated me like I was nothing."

"How was he nice to you?"

"He helped me out." She fiddled with files, straightening already neatly-stacked folders. "He caught me crying in my car one day, and he insisted I tell him what was wrong. My mom lost her job a couple months ago, and we couldn't make the payments on her car. He gave me money. Just like that. I told him I would pay him back, but he laughed and told me not to worry about it."

"He didn't ask you for anything in return?" Altruism was too rare a quality to assume a man like Joey Doyle possessed it.

"Well, he asked me to go to dinner with him a few times, and I went. I felt I owed it to him even though he never brought up the money. We shared a few moments." The defiant gleam in her eyes matched her tone. "He said he needed to bounce ideas off someone. I was honored he chose me. I'm taking night classes to get my degree in business, and I figured he really wanted my input. And he was such a nice guy. Things just sort of happened after that."

"Things?"

"Yes. Things. We would have made a good team in business and in life. Except — " she stopped, her gaze dropping to the letter opener she'd picked up from the desk. "Except he was married and had two really cute kids. He loved those kids. He talked about them all the time. He wanted to take them camping this summer . . ."

Her voice trailed off and tears rolled down both cheeks.

Ray pictured another woman crying earlier that day, her life shattered by her husband's murder. Now her worst suspicions about his fidelity would be confirmed. This scenario was wrong in so many ways he couldn't even begin to count them. "So what exactly did he tell you about business?"

"He said he had looked at the books. He thought Elaine had expanded too rapidly into the valley after opening the dealership in Dallas. They were stretched too thin. He said if the trend continued we'd have cash flow problems. He wanted to shut down the lower-performing dealership here in San Antonio and possibly the one in Brownsville."

"Which one would that be here in San Antonio?"

"The pre-owned cars on Broadway." Her tone said that should be obvious. "People think highway when they think of dealerships these days."

"And he spoke to Elaine and Kevin about this?"

"Yes. He even spoke to Mr. Doyle, Senior about it. Elaine said Joseph was too impatient. That he didn't know anything about business. That it takes a while to establish a new business, build it up. Joseph thought she was full of it. The dealerships were losing money."

Would someone kill over used cars? Doubtful. Over money, yes. "Miss Romano, when was the last time you talked to Mr. Doyle?"

"Tuesday. We had lunch together."

"How did he seem?"

"Wired."

"Like he'd been doing drugs?" Deborah spoke up.

"No. Joseph said he'd put that all behind him." Candy's voice rose in anger. "He was excited about something. He said he was going to stick it to his brother and sister. That he knew what they were up to, and he'd reveal it to the world."

"Reveal what? What were they doing?"

"He said he didn't want to tell me too much, it might be dangerous. That's exactly the word he used, *dangerous*."

"And then, what did you do?"

"Went back to work. What do you think we did?" Her defiant gaze dared him to tell her.

"And what did Joseph tell you he was going to do next?"

"Go hiking. Whatever he was planning, he was going to do it after hiking."

"You may have been the last one to talk to him before he died, Miss Romano. Think hard. Is there anything else you can tell us?"

She was silent, except for a soft hiccup of a sob. "No. And I wasn't," she said finally.

"You weren't what?"

"The last one to talk to him. I imagine his

killer said something before he murdered him."

She was probably right about that. "Did Joey have an office?"

"Do you have a warrant?" Another voice came from the doorway.

Candy looked startled as her gaze swung over Ray's shoulder. He glanced back. Kevin Doyle stood there. Ray rose as Deborah pushed away from the wall. "Why would we need one? We just want to look around, see if your brother was working on anything in particular."

Doyle thrust himself forward, his hands clenched in fists. "Candy, your shift is over. Go home."

Candy stood, her face uncertain. She grabbed a purse from a desk drawer and stumbled toward the door. She looked back at Ray, a question in her eyes.

He nodded at her. "We'll be in touch, Ms. Romano, if we have any further questions."

"Why question the hired help?" Doyle gave Candy a cold smile as she brushed past, her gaze pinned to her shoes. "She doesn't know anything, except how to seduce a married man."

Candy's half-stifled sob trailed after her. Ray didn't condone her relationship with Joey Doyle, but treating a hurting woman

155

badly wasn't right either. He wanted to wipe the sneer from Kevin Doyle's face with a two-by-four. He inhaled and exhaled. "We need access to your brother's files. He may have been working on something that led to his murder."

"Joey was killed at the park. His office had nothing to do with that. He had a lot of proprietary information at his disposal, and it would be a disaster if that information ever got into the hands of our competitors. Get out to that park and comb it for clues. You won't find anything here."

"Did you stop to think that something that happened here could have followed your brother out to that park?" Ray met the man's gaze head-on. "Or someone?"

"Are you accusing me of something?"

"I'm exploring all the options."

"Get out." Kevin took a step toward him. Ray didn't move. He towered over the other man.

"Let's go, Ray." Deborah inched her way into the space between Ray and Doyle. "All this testosterone is giving me a headache. We'll see you soon."

"We'll come back, Mr. Doyle, sooner or later. Just remember that tampering with evidence is a crime." Ray lingered, staring at Kevin.

Deborah jerked her head toward the door and started moving.

It was a bluff, of course, and Kevin knew it. By the time they got a search warrant, critical evidence could be long gone. Especially if the Doyles made a few well-placed phone calls.

Kevin already had his cell phone in his hand. "Get out! Get off my property!"

Ray couldn't resist a parting shot. "Actually, it's your father's property, isn't it?"

Kevin didn't answer. A satisfied smirk on his face, he was already punching in a number. Round one to the Doyles.

A rematch seemed inevitable, and Ray couldn't wait to wipe that smirk from the man's face.

CHAPTER TWELVE

In bright sunlight, Ray dragged himself up the side of the hill, sweat rolling down his forehead and into his eyes. Pain shot through his bum ankle.

When Teresa Saenz had called with the news she'd found an illegal camping spot at the wilderness park, Ray had been at his desk trying to decipher his notes. The weekend guys were at a scene, leaving the criminal investigation division quiet. It didn't matter that it was his day off. He wanted progress on this case. The judge had denied his request for a search warrant for Joey Doyle's office. If Teresa had found the crime scene where Joey had been stabbed before being dumped in the ravine, this might be their first real break. In the adrenaline high of the moment, he hadn't given a single thought to how difficult hiking with one good ankle would be.

"You're holding up the show." Deborah

shoved past him.

She'd been downright unpleasant when she'd answered her phone the third time he'd dialed her home number — after paging her and calling her cell phone. Her pasty white complexion, eyes crisscrossed with red lines, and sour expression spoke volumes. Whatever she'd done after they'd parted in front of the station the previous evening had involved large amounts of alcohol. She knocked back a swig from a twenty-four-ounce Ozarka as if there weren't enough water in the great state of Texas to slake her thirst.

"Unless you're offering to carry me up this hill, I don't see how that observation is helpful." Ray tried to keep his tone civil. After all, she carried the camera bag, leaving him free to use the cane to take the weight off his ankle. Two EU guys brought up the rear, lugging the rest of their stuff.

Teresa, her face glowing with excitement, didn't seem to notice the heat or Ray's discomfort. "Come on, you guys, we're almost there," she said as she surged forward.

"We're right behind you."

Finally she stopped, a grin plastered across her face. She stood in a small clearing. Smashed soda cans and empty Dos Equis bottles littered the ground, along with cigarette butts and junk food wrappers. The clearing was wide enough for two or three people to gather. A huge flat rock might serve as a seat. Scrub and bushes surrounded the area, making it invisible unless you were standing in it.

Teresa squatted a couple yards from the debris. "Look at this."

"Blood." Jim Mayes, the evidence unit lead investigator, began snapping photos of the long, dried stains on the vegetation before Ray could hobble over to them. The EU technician set a video camera bag on the ground and unzipped it. "A lot of blood."

"All the branches are disturbed and broken off in this area." Teresa motioned with one arm. "It's kind of set apart from the main spot where they were hanging out. It's almost like someone came over to look at something."

"Probably to take a leak," Deborah said. "Smells like it."

"How far are we from the ravine where I found the body?" Ray mopped his forehead with his shirtsleeve as he squatted next to Mayes to get a better look.

"Quarter of a mile, maybe." Teresa jerked one thumb toward the trail. "It's off the

160

beaten track. You're not supposed to get off the trail, and most people don't. They're afraid of getting lost."

"Let's spread out and comb the area. Teresa, if you find anything, don't touch it. Just point it out, and the EU guys will drop the tents."

"I know the drill." She flashed him a look. "Don't worry about me."

Ray ignored her pique. Procedure was critical, and he doubted Teresa had ever been this close to a murder scene.

Thirty minutes later, he was using the end of a ballpoint pen to sift through debris that had yielded what looked like a roach clip, the remnants of a joint, and dirty potato chips overrun by ants when Deborah let out a whoop.

"Ray, Jim. I've got it."

Following the sound of her voice, he reached her about the same time the evidence investigator did. Teresa was close behind.

"I've got it. The murder weapon." She pointed to a Bowie knife resting under a Cenizas bush about a hundred yards from the clearing. The blade, except for the part covered with a dried rust-colored substance, glittered in the late morning sun. Poor Doyle. Not a chance of surviving that.

"Ouch." Teresa's gleeful tone belied the word.

"It's all yours, Jim." Ray felt a surge of optimism. They had a weapon, bottles, and cigarette butts, which meant they might get a print or DNA, or both. The handle of the knife had probably been wiped clean, but still, a good day's work, all in all. "Okay. We'll leave you guys to finish up here. Let us know when you have a report. Teresa, can you get us started in the right direction? Once I get down to the main trail, I can find my way out."

"Before you take off, I'd like to fill you in on the interviews I did." Teresa pulled the rubber band from her sagging ponytail, letting her long hair swing loose in a ripple for a second before twisting it back up in a bun.

Ray tried not to stare. "What interviews?"

"I went back and talked to all the staff here. Found out some pretty interesting things."

"Like what?" He sat down on the nearest stony ridge. She shouldn't be doing interviews.

"One of the horticulturists knew Joey Doyle."

"Which one?" Deborah flipped open her notebook, her tone a blend of uncertainty and irritation. "You talking about Vicky Bar-rera?"

"That's the one. She and Joey Doyle had a thing going on."

"I interviewed her the day we found his body." The irritation in Deborah's tone deepened. "She said she had a doctor's appointment the previous day and was out all afternoon. After that she clammed up, wouldn't say another word."

"You didn't know who the victim was when you interviewed her. I did." Teresa sounded almost triumphant. "At first, she gave me the same story. Only thing is, one of the field maintenance workers told me he saw her here on Wednesday afternoon. He remembered because he thought it was weird she took the afternoon off and then showed up on the trails. So, I asked her if, by any chance, she knew Joey Doyle."

Ray accepted the water bottle Teresa offered him. She squatted next to him, sweat glistening on her forehead. He took a drink and handed it back. "So she admitted knowing him."

"Not at first. I kept pushing until she finally admitted that they'd had a few 'dates,' as she put it. She claimed she came here looking for him, but couldn't find him, so she went home. Never saw him again."

"So, he was having an affair with two women. That's motive for murder if either one found out." Deborah's irritation had disappeared, replaced with the ferocity that always accompanied a leap forward in an investigation.

"Not to mention the wife." Ray pictured Melody Doyle's devastation. It seemed impossible that her grief had been an act, but he had seen enough over the years to know it could have been. "None of them has the strength to stab a man, cart him a quarter of a mile, and then dump him in a ravine. Maybe we're talking about some kind of murder-for-hire scheme."

Deborah nodded. "We need to know if Joey Doyle had life insurance, and who the beneficiary is."

"Vicky Barrera is a big woman who works outdoors, and she knows these trails as well as anyone in town." Teresa seemed to be following her own thread. "And the field maintenance worker said he overheard her talking on her cell phone one day. Really mad. Screaming and carrying on. Sounded like she got dumped, the guy said."

"When was this?" Ray could have guessed.

"Last week."

Deborah said one word. Ray ignored it. A red hawk soared overhead, its screech filling the air. He admired its tremendous wing-span and effortless flight. Sure would be nice.

"We need to talk to Ms. Barrera." Ray stood, trying to keep his weight off the bad ankle. "You have the info?"

"I've got her home address. I'll transcribe my notes and e-mail them to you, too, so you can compare the statement she gives you to the one she gave me."

"Thanks, Teresa, you've been a great help, but do me a favor, leave the rest of the investigating to us."

The smile on her face dimmed and her chin jutted out. "I — "

"Could you get us down to the main trail? I can take it from there." He cut her off, hoping she'd read the regret in his face. She couldn't be messing in their investigation, reception or no reception. Agreeing to meet her there had been a mistake if it were going to keep him from doing his job.

She nodded, but didn't smile as she turned and led the way.

Deborah gave him a curious look. He ignored it and started down the trail, glad momentum would carry him to the bottom of the hill. An electronic chirping broke the silence. Deborah pulled her cell phone from her hip pocket.

Ray leaned against an ash tree, gritting his teeth while she talked, nodding as if the caller could see her. He could use a shower. And a glass of cold water.

"Let's go, Bible Boy." Deborah disconnected. "Looks like we're interviewing Sarah Doyle before we worry about our horticulturist."

Joey's sister. Sarah had been out of town the day of Joey's death. It seemed unlikely she knew anything, but thoroughness demanded the interview. "As long as there's ice water and air conditioning, that's fine."

A few minutes later, they were on the main trail. Ray thanked Teresa again. She ducked her head and nodded, but didn't say anything. Feeling like a jerk, he touched her arm. "See you this evening?"

Her dark eyes studied his face. "If you've changed your mind — "

"I'll be there."

She nodded, then disappeared back up the trail.

"Ray's got a day-ate. Ray's got a day-ate."

Deborah's singsong reminded Ray of the third grade. "Grow up, Smith."

She scrambled after him to the parking lot, still singing.

"Will you shut up, please?" He unlocked the car door and got in.

166

"Mighty grumpy, aren't we? Is that because Sarge's sister wouldn't go out with you? Had to settle for Miss Park Police?" Deborah slid in the other side, still grinning.

Ray flipped on the radio, found his favorite country station, and turned up the volume, filling the car with a Toby Keith tune he'd never understood. Nobody in his right mind fed beer to horses — not if they loved animals. He'd like to spend more time with his horses and less with people who stuck their noses where they didn't belong. Cops were like old ladies, sitting around yapping all the time about stuff that was none of their business. Susana was nobody's business — not even his.

Fortunately King's Estate was a quick five-minute drive from the park. Neither of them spoke again until Sarah Doyle met them at the door. She turned out to be an average-looking, twenty-something woman who hid a pair of gorgeous blue eyes behind thick-rimmed glasses. Her blonde hair swung to her shoulders and her face had that scrubbed-clean look of someone who didn't use makeup.

When she led them into a small sitting room off the main living room, a scruffy looking man with hair in a pony tail sat on the couch. "My boyfriend, Tommy Wheeler." Sarah waved one hand in his direction. "I hope you don't mind. He was a friend of my brother's and he's here to give me moral support."

"Sure." Ray shook the man's hand and gave him the once over. A case of opposites attract? He appeared to be slightly older than Sarah. His hair looked dirty and he sported a five o'clock shadow that had been allowed to linger past seven. He wore a Rolling Stones T-shirt, cut-off jean shorts, and thick rubber sandals. Of course, poor taste didn't make him a murderer.

After Sarah offered them seats on a settee that forced Ray's knees up into his chest, he plunged in. "Sarah when was the last time you saw your brother?"

The young woman's eyes filled with tears, and her voice quivered. "Sunday. I had brunch with him before I drove to Austin. I'm taking summer classes up there, and I needed to get back to study for an exam."

"How did he seem?"

"He was Joey, Detective. I don't know how to describe him. You had to know him." She got up from her chair and wandered over to a bookshelf where she picked up a framed photograph and brought it to Ray. The photo was old. Two children, one obviously Sarah when she was ten or twelve, and the other a boy a few years older. They were high in a tree, hanging upside down, legs hooked over a long branch, waving at the camera with both hands. "That's Joey and me. We used to do stuff like that all the time. He liked adventure."

"So he got in trouble a lot — gave your parents a hard time?" Sarah's story meshed with what Melody had told Ray.

"More than the rest of us, I guess. My dad wanted his children to be high performers. Joey could never measure up."

"So you were still in Austin on Tuesday?"

"Yes, taking an exam with about six other doctoral students. I'm sure that they would be glad to confirm my whereabouts."

Her tone was acerbic, but she had just lost a brother.

"What about you, Mr. Wheeler? Sarah says y'all were friends. Did you spend a lot of time with Joey?"

"Tommy and Joey were good friends," Sarah cut in before her boyfriend could respond.

Ray noticed he didn't look happy about it, either.

"Sarah, I can speak for myself." His tone was hard. "Joey and I spent some time together. I wouldn't say we were good friends, but we got along fine. I figured the rest of Sarah's family despised me so it wouldn't hurt to have one of them on my side."

"They don't like you?" Ray couldn't imagine why. The guy exuded a chip-on-the-shoulder mentality, and Ray was sure that the smell of sweat in the air was emanating from the vicinity of his dirty sandals.

"Not *GQ* enough. No pedigree."

"So, you ever do any hiking with him?"

"Sure, we hiked. We also shot pool, drank beer, and talked about getting real lives."

"Real lives?"

"I plan to make movies. I'm a cinematographer."

Ray's notes showed Wheeler took classes at UTSA and worked part-time in a camera accessory store. "What about Joey? What did he say his plan was?"

"Ah, I didn't listen much. He always had some grandiose moneymaking plan. Like he needed to get rich — he had that silver spoon stuck so far back in his mouth, it's a wonder he didn't choke. I, on the other hand, could really use the money."

"Tommy!" Sarah's fair skin stained red with anger. The tears that had threatened to fall earlier were now making tracks down her face. "That's my brother you're talking about, and we both have — had — the same silver spoon in our mouths."

"Yeah, well nobody would know you're loaded. You hide it well with Target clothes and Payless shoes. Joey liked to flaunt it. Like he had something to do with earning all those millions. It just got to me sometimes, the way he acted. Like the big shot."

Deborah shifted on the couch next to him. "So Mr. Wheeler, when was the last time you hiked with Joey Doyle?" she asked, beating Ray to the punch.

"It's been a while." Wheeler squirmed, his gaze dropping. "I guess I really don't remember the last time we hiked."

"In that case, where were you Tuesday afternoon?"

The look of discomfort on the man's face deepened. He squirmed some more. "I met a couple of friends for lunch. We had a couple of beers, and I must have taken a nap."

"Taken a nap?"

"Yeah, I was wiped out from studying and working so much. I'm taking graduate courses at UTSA and holding down a full-time job. It's a bear."

"So you were here at the Doyles', taking a nap?" Deborah seemed to be pointing out that this was the Doyles' home, and Wheeler was a guest.

"No. I fell asleep at a friend's house. On the couch."

"This friend have a name?"

"Sure. Patty. Patty Wheeler." Wheeler said the name quickly, his gaze darting from Deborah to Sarah and back. He looked poised for flight, his feet shifting and his hands coming off the arms of the chair.

Sarah's sharp intake of breath told the rest of the story. Ray watched as the angry red blush blossomed and spread. "You snake." She shot from her chair and slapped Wheeler across the face. The sharp whack echoed through the sitting room.

"Ouch! What did you do that for? I told you, I just took a nap. Nothing happened."

"A nap on your ex-wife's couch. Yeah, right."

"Okay," Ray intervened. "We'll need her telephone number and address to verify your story."

"She left for California yesterday. I don't know when she'll be back."

How convenient. "Where in California? We'll need a way to contact her out there, as well as the local telephone number and address."

"Yeah, Tommy, give them her address. In fact, you might as well show them where

172

she lives, because that's where you'll be staying. Get your stuff, and get out." Sarah was a blur of motion as she grabbed books, magazines, and CDs from a coffee table, from shelves, and from stacks on the floor. She flung them at Wheeler. "Let me help you."

"Could we just ask one more question?" Ray stood and angled for the door, ready to duck if an errant object came his way. Deborah stayed behind him. Good plan — his big body would give her some cover.

Sarah focused on them, but she didn't stop tossing CDs like hand grenades. "If you must." The words dripped hostility. She needed someone to blame, and they had forced Wheeler's hand in front of her.

"Mr. Wheeler, what time did you wake up and where did you go after you took the nap?"

Wheeler was on his knees, trying to pick up the stuff Sarah was throwing at him, ducking when a CD sailed past his head. "I don't know what time I got up, but I was at work at the store by six o'clock. I stayed there until closing at ten."

"We'll see ourselves out." Ray doubted Sarah heard him. The cacophonous noise of a relationship ending was deafening.

As they walked to the car, Ray's jaw hurt

from clenching his teeth.

"He's lying about something, isn't he?" Deborah asked, opening the car door.

"Absolutely, and he's afraid. He had to be petrified to admit he was at his ex-wife's house in front of Sarah. He wants us to know he cheats, because it gives him an alibi for Joey Doyle's murder. But there's more to it. He knows something."

"Definitely. I'm going to do some digging. Something's not right with that guy."

Ray agreed. Wheeler was scared, and he was hiding something. Another lead to follow. He eased the Crown Victoria through the gated entrance of King's Row Estates onto the access road. As he maneuvered around a green Mercedes, a flash of silver gleamed in the side mirror. A silver BMW. Same or different? Imported cars all looked alike to him.

"There it is again."

"What?" Deborah covered a yawn with the back of her hand and slumped in her seat. "There's what?"

"The BMW."

"What BMW?"

"The one that was behind us after we left the restaurant last night. I'm positive." Ray studied his rearview mirror. Four doors, a lot of tinted windows, same wheel covers. "I saw it on the road when we left the Doyles' house. It pulled into the restaurant the same time we did and left the same time."

"You think we're being followed?" Her tone was doubtful, but she glanced back.

"Maybe."

"So, let's find out."

It sounded like a taunt. In response, Ray jerked the wheel and made the turnaround before turning right again into a partially-completed subdivision on the other side of the highway. The BMW held back, but made the same turn seconds later. Ray slowed the vehicle to a crawl. The silver car did the same, backing off several paces. The subdivision had long, narrow streets, some filled with new houses, others with empty lots and half-completed structures. Traffic was light, with only two cars between them. Ray sped up and took a quick left, this time pulling into the driveway of a house that looked occupied. The silver car sped past. "Sit tight."

Deborah nodded and pawed at a cigarette pack. Ray gave her his most fierce frown. She dropped the pack. Time dragged by. "Maybe you're dreaming."

"Maybe." Ray started to put the car in reverse. As he did, the flash of silver re-appeared. The BMW drove by again, this time more slowly, and then pulled over against the curb half a block down.

"Now what?" Deborah had her hand on her Glock.

"Time to reverse the tables."

Ray backed from the driveway and hit the gas. The Crown Vic shot forward. He wanted to block the BMW, but the driver reacted too quickly. His dark face visible in the side mirror for a split second, the man whipped from the parking space, tires squealing. Ray jabbed the accelerator, trying to keep close.

"He's going back to the highway. Stay with him." Deborah had one hand on the dashboard and the other on the radio mike. They zigzagged around slower-moving cars, steadily losing ground, as Ray tried to avoid an accident. Nobody needed to get hurt, it wasn't worth it. Deborah notified dispatch of the pursuit, but before she could put the mike down the BMW fishtailed around a corner, slid past a moving van, and disappeared as the semi rumbled to a stop in the middle of a block. "You're losing him. Get around the van, Ray. Come on, pass the guy."

Ray swerved into the left lane and gunned the engine. A second later, he caught a flash of red and yellow in his peripheral vision.

He stopped breathing. A Big Wheel. His foot went from the gas to brake, even as he knew there was no way to stop in time. The Crown Vic skidded in an arc of burning rubber and smoke. His seat belt clinched his chest in a painful hug as he fought to maintain control. The car rocked crazily and spun to his left. A crunch and grind told him he'd hit something. The front of the car smashed up and over the curb and came to rest in a lawn of newly-laid sod.

"No, no, no." He shoved open his door, fumbled with the seatbelt, and scrambled out. "Did I hit a kid? Did I hit him?"

Deborah didn't answer. She was already out her door. He darted around the car. The mangled three-wheeler — the kind little kids conquer before they venture on to their first bicycles — smashed under the rear wheel of the Crown Vic, still resting on the street. Ray dropped to his knees, peering under the car. No blood, he didn't see blood.

"You hurt my Big Wheel!" He glanced back at the sound of a small, angry voice. A little boy, maybe five or six, stood in the middle of the street, hands on his chubby hips, his face an angry scowl under a mop of unruly, blond hair. "My mom's gonna be mad."

Ray put both hands on his knees and let

his head drop forward. He needed air.

"Your momma's gonna want to know what you were doing in the street, little buddy." The driver of the moving van trotted over to where the boy stood. "Best move to the sidewalk, son. Like to give me a heart attack when I seen that bike roll out in the street. I knew some little guy was gonna be right behind it. That's why I stopped. You guys were breaking all kinds of rules there. You coulda killed the kid. This is a residential area."

Deborah flashed her badge, and the van driver shrugged.

"I hate high-speed chases. I really hate them." Ray forced himself to stand and move toward the boy. "Let's go talk to your mom."

"I want to know who was following us and why!" Ray smacked the steering wheel. His hand hurt, but it was worth it. The boy's mother had been suitably severe with her child and not too worried about the totaled Big Wheel. Ray had written her a check for a replacement. The city might reimburse him, it might not. In the bigger scheme of things, it didn't matter. The vivid image of what little Riker Jefferson Junior's chubby body could have looked like bloodied and broken on the ground next to that flattened three-wheeler would stay with him for a long time.

"Calm down." Deborah seemed a little too blasé about the whole thing. "It's no big deal."

"Yes, it is!"

"I got the license plate, Ray." Deborah waved a napkin.

"Oh. Good job."

"Great job, you mean."

"Yeah. Great job."

Deborah tapped the number into the laptop, while Ray maneuvered the Crown Vic out of the yard. He needed to breathe for a few minutes. Deeply.

Deborah's next words told him the news wasn't good. Ray didn't want to know. "Do you mind? Cussing is a sign of a small vocabulary."

"Whatever. The plates come back to a 1999 Dodge Caravan belonging to Anita and Marvin Stroud of Leakey, Texas."

"Stolen plates."

"Yep."

Ray contemplated the white knuckles of his fingers gripping the wheel. Who cared enough to follow them? And why? Were they getting close to something?

He didn't know who or what it was, but

he did know one thing. He was going to find out.

CHAPTER THIRTEEN

Vicky Barrera lived in a bungalow in a quiet, older neighborhood between Brackenridge Park and the Botanical Garden. Made sense for a horticulturist. A green Chevy Trailblazer sat in the driveway. After ringing the doorbell brought no response, Ray pounded on the door while Deborah tried to peer in a front window. It had been a long day, and his quota of patience had evaporated. If this conversation resulted in a suspect who had to be escorted downtown for a full-scale interrogation, his day wasn't even close to being over. "Police. Vicky Barrera, open up."

"Okay. Okay. Hold your horses."

The door opened, and a woman Ray surmised to be Barrera glared out at them, one hand shading her eyes. She was a tall, heavyset woman with cropped, blond hair and skin dark and leathery from the sun. Her eyes were so red and swollen, he couldn't tell what color they were.

181

"What do you want?" She tightened the belt of a faded robe that didn't quite close over her gray sweats. She looked from Ray to Deborah and back. "If this is about Joey Doyle, I already gave my statement — twice. Once to this lady here."

"But not to me." Ray flashed his badge and stuck one boot over the frame before she could shut the door. "We just have a few more questions. It won't take long. My partner was missing some critical information the first time she interviewed you — like the fact that you knew the victim."

Naked emotion flitted across the woman's face. Grief. Fear. "I'm not feeling well, and I've told you everything I know." A paroxysm of coughing shook her.

Ray waited until she stopped hacking. "Could we come in?"

"Make it quick. I'm really sick." Barrera backed away from the door and wrapped her arms around her chest.

"How long had you been seeing Joey Doyle?" Ray slipped past her and headed into the living room. A thin, black cat rose from the back of the couch, leaped to the floor, and stalked from the room.

"I wasn't seeing Joey Doyle. I just knew him from the park."

The response reeked of defiance almost as

bad as her place reeked of Vicks and soiled cat litter. Two kinds of cold medicine and an open bottle of Jack Daniels sat on a coffee table decorated with used tissues. Cold medicine and alcohol. Dangerous. Maybe she didn't care.

"Are you sure, Ms. Barrera?" He kept his tone neutral as he sat in an overstuffed chair. Not calling her a liar. Yet. "The park police officer tells a different story."

"So I had a few dates with the guy. What does that have to do with his murder?" Barrera sank onto the couch, grabbed a tissue and blew her nose, making the honking noise of a large goose.

Deborah, still standing, shook her head. "Technically, I don't think you can date a married man. I believe that's called cheating." Her sharp tone surprised Ray.

"Well. Yes. But, but, but it was just a fling." Barrera crumpled up the tissue and threw it at the table with such force it bounced onto the floor. She reached for another. "Just because I fooled around with him doesn't mean I know anything about his death. I didn't even know he was dead until you guys found his body."

Barrera talked fast, her gaze fastened on a spot somewhere over Ray's shoulder. He glanced at Deborah. She gave an almost imperceptible shrug.

"When was the last time you saw him?"

"I don't know. I don't remember."

"Ms. Barrera, you were having an affair with Joey Doyle and you don't remember the last time you saw him?" Incredulity tinged Deborah's voice. "Give us some credit, please."

"I'm telling you it wasn't that big a deal. We met at the park. He was cute and charming. He liked to hike. We hiked together a few times. Had a few drinks together. I — " Barrera stopped, swallowing hard, the effort to hold back tears obvious in her face. "I liked him, but he was married, so I broke it off."

"You were at the park the day he died — after you took the afternoon off for a doctor's appointment. Why? Was it to see Joey Doyle?" Deborah didn't let up. Working with someone new had a certain learning curve. Deborah's style was interesting, kind of like a ballerina driving a bulldozer.

"I forgot something in the office . . . I had to pick something up." Barrera looked as if she might vomit.

"Like what?"

"Just a check stub I needed for my records."

"That's a long drive for a check stub. You

184

sure you didn't have a date with your honey?" Deborah made *honey* sound like a dirty word.

"No. I didn't see him. I never saw him." The words were right, but the tone was all wrong. It bordered on hysterical.

"I don't believe you."

"So don't believe me. It's the truth. I swear it."

Deborah lapsed into silence. Ray let it ride and then picked up the thread. "So why haven't you been at work since his death?"

"I have the flu. Maybe I should call my lawyer. Maybe this interview should be over."

Ray ignored the suggestion. She hadn't actually asked for a lawyer. They hadn't arrested her or Mirandized her. They didn't have enough — not yet. That put her in the person-of-interest category, not quite a suspect. "You didn't ask him to leave his wife and then kill him in a fit of anger when he refused?"

"Absolutely not. You, you can't believe . . ." Barrera's face turned white. "I loved — I liked him. I would never have hurt him. I — "

"I thought it was just a fling." Deborah interrupted, her half smile not reaching her eyes. "If you didn't see him Tuesday, when

185

was the last time you saw him?"

Barrera took another swipe at her nose. "Last week. A few days before he died. I told you. We broke up. He was married, so I broke it off."

"Uh-huh." Deborah slapped shut her notebook and turned as if to leave. Following her lead, Ray stood. They needed something to tie the woman to the crime scene. Or a witness who had seen Barrera with Doyle on Tuesday afternoon. If either existed, they would find out. In the meantime, they'd let her sweat.

"We're going to check you out, Ms. Barrera. If we find out you lied to us, we'll be back. With an arrest warrant. If you killed Joey Doyle, we'll find that out, too."

Barrera's face crumpled, but she didn't fold. "Investigate all you want."

Lalo eased his head back against the seat, enjoying the smooth touch of fine leather cooled by the frigid air pouring from the BMW's vents. Once the cops had left the park lady's house without her, his sense of urgency had trickled away. After the close call on the chase, he'd backed off and taken great pains not to be seen. He would not underestimate *Señor* Johnson again.

The park lady hadn't told them anything,

186

or they would have taken her in. The messages he had left on her recorder apparently had been effective. And it had been rather amusing, imagining her horror each time she pushed the button, and his voice filled the room. If she talked, she would be dead. Simple as that.

Of course, she would be dead, anyway, when he was through playing with her, but she wasn't smart enough to figure that out. She hadn't gone to the police. Now, he would give her a chance to get settled. The long, summer evening ahead would give them plenty of time to get acquainted face-to-face.

In the meantime, he needed to review what had gone wrong with his tail. The cop was a worthy opponent. Lalo warmed to the idea. Perhaps the boss would rescind his restriction on executing cops once the Doyle situation was resolved. He allowed himself a small smile. A good hunt would go a long way toward relieving a strange boredom that soaked to his very bones. It'd all become too easy. He needed a challenge.

The smell of industrial strength soap brought him out of his reverie. The AC repair uniform covering his body was snug, and he found the scent distasteful. To take his mind from his discomfort, he fingered

187

the gun, lying on the seat next to a small ice chest. He'd rather use his own weapons, but the boss insisted on giving him this one. Belonged to the dead guy. *El señor* called it a red herring. Lalo called it a sissy gun. The thing in the ice chest — now that was a true red herring.

Los Tigres del Norte sang on the radio. He imagined himself dancing with Sylvia. *Qué chula*. A nice plate of *mole*. *Qué padre*. First things first. He glanced up and down the street. *Nadie.*

It was time. Tugging a cap down over his hair, so it shielded his face, he strolled down the block, carrying a toolbox, made a quick turn into her side yard, opened the gate, and slipped around to her back door. Sliding glass doors. Lalo loved sliding glass doors. He peeked in. She was lying on the couch, eyes closed, a box of tissues on her chest. He tugged at his gloves. Nice tight fit. He went to work on the door.

She never moved. Not even when he padded into her living room. A bottle of cough syrup, cold medicine, and a half-empty bottle of whiskey sat on her coffee table. It was amazing how many people self-medicated with perfectly legal drugs. And yet they scorned the drug users on the street.

188

The lady snored loudly, her chest rising and falling. He sat down in the chair and gave himself a second to study his prey. He frowned. No challenge in this. He pulled out the weapon, tightened the silencer, and knelt next to her. *"Señora? Señora!"* He shook her arm gently.

She flopped, knocking the tissues to the floor. Her eyes opened and filled with confusion. "What? What?"

Lalo shoved the silencer up against her forehead and smashed a hand over her mouth. "Scream and you're dead, *señorita. ¿Me entiende?*" She nodded, and her teeth dug into his palm. He saw a flash of recognition and horror in her eyes. She had seen him that day. Pity. "You have some information I need. Who was the man with *Señor* Doyle the day of our most unfortunate encounter in the park? *¿Recuerdas?*"

She shook her head. He dropped his hand. A tear ran down her face, and she breathed noisily through her mouth. Snot slid from one nostril to her upper lip. He could smell the funk of her breath. It irritated him. He lowered the gun until the silencer was snuggled in her chest and handed her a tissue.

"Try again." Holding her gaze, he caressed her cheek. "This can be nice or *muy difícil.*

The choice is yours, *señorita.*"

"If I tell you, you'll let me go?" She gave a ragged sob. *Aye, pobrecita,* she was so afraid. He could feel her fear, like silk shimmering against the skin of his hand, the one that held the gun. Goose bumps marched up his arms at the thought. Perhaps, he wasn't so bored after all. "I didn't tell the police what happened up there. I promise I won't. You have my word."

He nodded and eased his weapon away from her chest, allowing the distance between them to grow to just the right space, letting her relax. "I believe you." He smiled.

"His name is Tommy Wheeler. He was a friend of Joey's." She whispered the words, the sick look on her face telling him she knew she was weak and a coward.

"Thank you, *señorita,* so much."

He raised the pistol and fired. One shot in the middle of her forehead. He was just far enough away to avoid the spatter. She jerked once, and her body fell back against the couch, the pillow cradling what was left of the back of her head. *Es todo.*

Now came the hard part. The boss wanted her body found in a park. *Keep the theme going,* he'd said. *Make the mayor and the city manager sweat. If people think this is some kind of sicko killing people in city parks, that*

190

will keep them off the right track. An interesting plan. Every job was different. Some bosses liked straightforward. Some, like the current *señor,* liked twists and turns. Lalo excelled at twists and turns.

He peered out the front window. Again, quiet. Such a lovely, quiet neighborhood. Sylvia wouldn't like it, though. Too lonely. He turned to grab the woman's car keys from the table. A thin, black cat wound itself around his feet, meowing loudly. Lalo leaned down and picked him up. That accounted for the smell in the lady's house. Poor *gatito* had a dirty litter box.

"Aye, pobrecito gatito, are you hungry?" Lalo slipped into the kitchen and searched the cabinets until he found a can of cat food. Whistling softly, he scooped the contents into the cat's bowl.

"¿Está mejor?" He stroked the cat's head before adding water to the second bowl. No need to leave a defenseless animal to fend for itself. "That will keep you until someone finds you."

He'd lingered a bit too long. Quickly, he checked her answering machine to make sure his messages had been deleted, then trotted out to her Trailblazer for a garage door opener. A few minutes later, he pulled the BMW in and put down the door.

The woman was heavy, especially wrapped in three blankets. He heaved her into the trunk, careful to keep the body on top of the drop cloths he'd placed in the bottom. He peeled off his overalls and laid them on top of the cargo. Backing out of the driveway, he wondered if the cops would notice the missing remote. Didn't matter. It would be at the bottom of an illegal dump in Bexar County by that time. As would all the other items used in the commission of this crime — except the sissy gun, of course.

He turned up the radio and sang along with *Los Chamacos.* He usually didn't sing in front of an audience. But the dead park lady wouldn't mind. He drove past a sign on Broadway that advertised a botanical garden. That was it. He'd wait until it was dark, then slip into the garden for a late night rendezvous. It'd almost be romantic if she weren't so dead.

Chapter Fourteen

Samuel wiped his face with a faded red bandana, tasting salt as sweat dripped from his mustache onto his lips. He hated mowing the lawn, which was why he had let it go too long. That and the fact that he'd worked too many Saturdays on too many cases. But mowing the lawn was better than thinking about the Doyle case. Lieutenant Alvarez wanted a progress report twice a day now.

"Samuel, telephone." Piper trudged barefoot across the yard. Her nose was still red, but her fever had dissipated. She'd been asleep — or pretending to be — when he'd returned home the previous evening. The pan of *caldo* still sat on the stove, grease congealed on the top. He'd dumped it in the disposal, letting the water run too long, taking his time washing and drying the pan.

When he'd slipped under the sheets and molded himself around her warm body, she hadn't moved away, but she hadn't responded, either, not even when he tugged at the strap of her nightgown and let his lips trail across her shoulder. She didn't look much different now than she had when he'd married her more than twenty years earlier. Only better curves. Why would he ever look anywhere else?

"Do you like what you see?" A smile flitted across her pale face and disappeared. "Stop giving me the once-over and take the phone. My hands are wet."

Yes, he liked it and never wanted to lose it. He took the phone, trying to ignore the gentle slap she aimed at his rear.

"Martinez." He tried to focus on the caller and not the way his wife looked strolling across their backyard, her arms swinging, head tilted back as if enjoying the sun on her face.

"I tried to call you at the station. They said you didn't come in today." Alvarez's voice managed to grate on his nerves more than it had the previous day.

"Not yet."

"The Doyle case isn't going to solve itself."

"Detectives Johnson and Smith have been on it all day. They have backup from a couple other detectives. They've found the

194

primary crime scene. The EU is processing it. We're on it."

"I just spent fifteen minutes assuring the chief that we're doing everything we can to find the guy who killed Milt Doyle's son. Milt was a big supporter of the mayor's campaign. They went to school at St. Anthony's together, where Chief Mendez went, by the way. The mayor is godfather to one of the Doyle kids. You get my drift?"

"I've talked to Detective Johnson several times today. They've got a potential murder weapon. It's being processed. They've got another suspect — a woman who worked at the park and was having a relationship with Joseph Doyle."

"Doyle was having an affair. Great." Alvarez sounded as if Samuel had just informed him a close relative had died.

"More than one."

"We need to keep that quiet. Tell your detectives to be discreet. And get in there and run the show, Martinez."

Samuel silently counted to ten. "Detective Johnson doesn't need me breathing down his neck. He's got the best solve rate in the unit."

"Apparently, he lacks diplomacy. He made the Doyles royally angry last night."

Only because they thought they were

195

royalty. Samuel studied his numbers some more. "He's one of the most diplomatic guys I've ever met."

"The Doyles aren't just any family. They're one of the wealthiest in town. They don't like some city employee giving them the third degree, treating them like criminals — their words, not mine."

"I assure you, Detective Johnson is nothing if not compassionate. He's that kind of guy." Sometimes Ray was too nice, too sympathetic. He took the families' pain home with him every night.

"The Doyles like to spread the wealth around. The mayor would like to make sure they keep doing that. Understand me?"

"Yes sir." Samuel understood the politics all too well, something he'd never counted on when he'd taken the promotion. He should have stayed on the street.

"I suggest you get your sorry butt back to the station and find out what's going on with this case. You read me?"

"Yes sir."

The phone line went dead. Samuel stood still, inhaling in the clean smell of fresh cut grass. Think about mowing. Don't think about the job.

The phone rang again, startling him into dropping it. He was tempted to leave it in the grass and mow over it, but he forced himself to pick it up. It was Carl Reinhardt, the director of parks and recreation. Samuel moved over to the picnic table bench to get out of the sun. No point in getting a reaming and sunstroke at the same time.

"I need to know when I can reopen the wilderness park. I've got a Friends of the Parks group screaming because they have Saturday morning classes scheduled at the outdoor classroom, and they've had to cancel everything." The park director sounded defensive. "I've got hiking groups standing at the gate. The newspaper is running an editorial tomorrow asking what the city is doing to make sure the parks are safe. It's a mess."

"Believe me, our first priority is to solve the murder. Right now, the best thing to do is to keep the park closed to protect the crime scene and the public."

A frustrated growl reverberated in Samuel's ear. "What if I hire private security, could we open the park then?"

"Unless you can guarantee that they can cover all six hundred acres on foot, at night, I don't see how that will help."

"Fine." His tone belied the word. "Keep me posted, will you?"

"Absolutely. My best guys are working it

right now."

"Thanks, Sergeant. I appreciate it."

Samuel dropped the phone on the table and leaned forward, elbows on his knees, head down.

"You all right?"

He lifted his head. Piper stood there, a tall glass of iced tea in one hand. Her face held only concern, all traces of the previous day's angry frustration gone.

"I'm fine." He took the glass and rolled it across his forehead. "Just fine."

She dropped down onto a lawn chair across from him. "You sure? You look gloomy."

"Gloomy?"

"Yes, Gloomy Gus. What did Lieutenant Alvarez want?"

"The usual. Don't worry about it, *corazón.*"

"You need to go into the station?"

"In a while, but I'll finish mowing first, if it kills me."

Piper nodded, but he could see the worry in her eyes. He set the glass on the picnic table, stood, leaned down, and kissed her hard on the lips, tasting cherry lip balm. *"Lo siento, mi amor,"* he whispered close to her ear, hoping she'd understand he wasn't talking about the work.

"I'm sorry, too." Her hand came up as if to touch him.

He jerked back and headed toward the mower. "I'm sweaty."

"I'm not averse to a little sweat."

Samuel looked back.

Her smile didn't reach her eyes. "It's not the mowing that will kill you. It's the job — unless I do it first."

Samuel ripped the mower cord, letting the noise swallow the need for an answer. She might be right, but if they didn't make some progress on this case, it wouldn't matter. At the very least, they'd yank the case. Worst-case scenario, they'd yank his job.

"You like playing the tough guy?" Ray pulled the Crown Victoria into the parking lot next to the station and glanced over at his partner.

"When someone is lying through her teeth like that, yeah." Deborah popped her seat belt, but didn't get out. "If Barrera didn't do it, why's she lying?"

"She had an affair with a married guy, and now he's dead. My guess is she knows something, even if she didn't do it." Vicky Barrera had looked petrified. And guilty. Just like Tommy Wheeler. Apparently more than one person had something to hide.

"Maybe she's lying because she did do it. Did you see the size of her biceps? She's almost as big as you."

"You think she could have dumped a man's body into that ravine?"

"Maybe. And she probably wouldn't hesitate to chop off that finger either. She didn't like being reminded that he was a married man."

Ray beat a rhythm on the wheel with two fingers and tried to think. "Can you see what you can dig up on her?"

"Sure. What're you going to do?"

"I have an appointment."

"Wahoo!" Deborah's shriek reverberated through the car. "I knew it. You do have a date."

"No — none of your business." Ray's face burned. Several homicide detectives had worked on the cottage project. By tomorrow, everyone would know he'd gone to the reception with Teresa. Word would get back to Samuel, and he was just a phone call away from Susana. Would she even care? Somehow, Ray doubted it, but Samuel would eat his liver for lunch if there were even the possibility that Ray might hurt his sister. "Just check out Barrera and Tommy Wheeler. We'll re-group tomorrow."

"Tomorrow? I thought on the seventh day,

Bible Boy rested."

"I do. I'll be in after church. I want to stay on top of this one. Samuel's getting heat. The longer we mess around, the harder it'll be."

"Tell me about it."

Right now, they had more suspects than they knew what to do with. Vicky Barrera. Melody Doyle. Kevin Doyle. Elaine Doyle. Tommy Wheeler. The list went on and on. Somehow, he had to narrow it down. People who watched TV thought crimes were solved quickly. Usually it was careful, methodical research that resulted in the information that broke a case. Too bad he didn't have time to be methodical. Murders not solved in the first few days often turned into cold cases.

So why had he agreed to meet Teresa at the reception? He contemplated that question as he took a quick shower in the PD gym and put on the clean change of clothes he'd stowed in his locker that morning. Desperation. Stupidity. Weakness. Several possibilities presented themselves. None made him look good.

Whatever it was, it was too late to back out now. He tried to call Teresa's cell to tell her he was running late, but her voicemail picked up. Maybe she'd changed her mind

201

after their powwow on the hill. He rushed to the Bronco and made the quick trip to the home a few blocks south of downtown in less than five minutes. Teresa was waiting, leaning on the white picket fence in front of a Victorian-style mansion that had been turned into administrative offices to serve the ministry for teenage mothers.

She looked deep in thought, giving Ray a chance to study her. Red silk blouse. Black fitted slacks. Black ballerina slippers. She had her hair French-braided. Nice. She looked up at him before he could say anything.

"Hey, there you are." Her smile seemed tentative. "I was almost afraid you wouldn't come. You seemed miffed at me this afternoon."

"Sorry I'm late." He leaned next to her. "I wasn't mad. I'm just used to doing things a certain way."

"And you don't want me interfering." She tossed her braid back over her shoulder. "I understand."

"No, you don't understand. Until you've run a murder investigation involving a bigwig philanthropist, you can't understand. But I appreciate your help. Finding the murder scene and the weapon gives us something more to go on. Let's talk about something else." She smelled good. He reached over and touched the gold cross that hung from a thin chain around her neck, his finger brushing against her warm skin. "Does this mean something to you or is it just pretty jewelry?"

Her gaze danced away from his. "Actually, it means a lot to me. I'm a Christian." Defensiveness fought with defiance in her tone.

Another check in the nice column. Ray smiled. "Good. Me, too."

She shook her head, her face rueful. "I told my mother you're too good to be true."

She'd talked to her mother about him. He felt an intense stab of remorse. It was just a reception. "Except for being set in my ways, stubborn, and opinionated?"

"I imagine those traits develop with age." She gave him a sideways grin. "You seem so calm most of the time. I guess you're like a bomb waiting to go off."

"I do tend to hold it in until I explode." Her remark suddenly registered. "Are you saying I'm old?"

She slipped her hand into the crook of his arm, still grinning. He straightened, and they started toward the door. "You must be at least thirty-five, thirty-six. Why aren't you married?"

Teresa was probably ten years younger than he was and not a very good judge of age, considering he'd hit forty several months earlier. "You ever heard of that book — something like *A Series of Unfortunate Events?*"

"*Lemony Snicket* — I have two nieces and a nephew."

"Well, it's like that." He let go of her arm and opened the door.

She stepped in ahead of him. The home was packed to the gills with people. Some Ray recognized as perennial benefactors. Others looked like staff and graduates of the home, which took in pregnant teenagers with no place to go, gave them shelter, spiritual guidance, and helped them make decisions about the futures of their babies. Ray had helped build a series of cottages where the mothers-to-be lived until they gave birth. It had been a project close to his heart.

"I'll get us some punch." Teresa smiled up at him.

She did have a nice smile. Too nice.

Ray watched her wade through the crowd and then let his gaze sweep the room. Alex Luna from Homicide should be there, as well as a couple of guys from traffic who'd been on his construction team. He spotted

Alex in the corner talking to Araiza from Burglary and Theft, along with his favorite paramedic, Greg Miller, so he headed that direction. Alex looked up and grinned.

"*¿Que pasó,* Mr. Grace? Greg was just telling me what a pain in the rear you are as a patient. Heard you conked out at the park the other day. I'm surprised to see you here — not your kind of thing, is it?"

"Well — "

"Heard you drew the Doyle case — good luck on that one." It was tough to get a word in edgewise when Alex got started. Ray didn't feel like talking about his head anyway, or the Doyle case.

"How's it going, Greg?" he asked when Alex ran down, distracted by some remark Araiza made.

"Busy as usual. Was that Teresa Saenz you came in with?" Greg had an envious look on his face. "How'd you swing that, dude? She's a pretty lady. And nice."

Before Ray could answer, Alex broke in. "You came with the park police chick? I saw Susana a minute ago. I thought you guys were together."

"Susana? Who's Susana." Teresa walked up, carrying two glasses. She handed one to Ray, looking expectantly from him to Alex.

"Uh, all y'all know each other, right?" Ray

205

spoke before Alex could answer. While they exchanged pleasantries, Ray scanned the crowd, looking for Susana.

He spotted her. Draped on another man's arm.

It took forever to squeeze through the crowd to the spot where they stood talking.

"Susana." Ray tapped her on the shoulder. She'd changed perfumes. This new one was citrus. Apparently, it went with her new life and her new friend.

She glanced back, her gaze cool. She had her hand on the arm of a yuppy-looking guy. "Ray."

They stared at each other. "What are you — " they both started to talk at the same time.

"You first."

"No, you." Susana insisted, red spots blossoming on her cheeks. She wore a black dress covered with sparkling sequins. Her hair hung loose and curly around her face. Stunning.

"I didn't know you'd be here." The words sounded lame, even to him. He glanced at the man with her. He was very young. At that moment, he put one hand on Susana's lower back. The possessive gesture fueled a rush of blood to Ray's face.

"We do some counseling sessions here as

206

part of our class work. They were nice enough to invite us." She gestured to the man. "This is Chad Lowenstein, one of my classmates. Chad, this is Detective Ray Johnson. He used to be my brother's partner."

She'd reduced their relationship to one past-tense sentence. Ray shook the man's hand, sized him up, and watched him do the same. "I thought maybe you were tutoring. Or babysitting."

Lowenstein sucked in a breath.

"No." Her eyes blazed. "Chad is my date. We're here for fun."

"I didn't know you allowed yourself to have fun." Ray locked gazes with Lowenstein.

"Of course I do. I have fun all the time." Susana shrugged the man's hand from her back and took a step toward Ray, her tone defiant. "My life isn't about murder and mayhem. I have fun a lot."

"Sure you do. Best get to it."

"I plan to; I don't need your permission." She whirled and marched away, her shiny, black dress disappearing into a sea of colorful clothes.

"What's wrong with you, man? What'd she ever do to you?" Lowenstein rushed after her.

"What did she ever do to me?"

The crowd swallowed them up. Ray refused to let that question go unanswered. He plunged after them.

"Is she in there?" Ray pushed past Lowenstein who stood next to the women's restroom, his face set in angry lines. Not waiting for an answer, Ray shoved open the door. "Susana, Susana, get out here. Now."

She stood in the middle of an anteroom that held a sofa and two easy chairs. Her tearstained face reflected in a mirror that ran the length of one wall.

"You can't come in here!"

Dropping the cane, he slammed the door shut and locked it. A second later, he was kissing her. Susana didn't struggle. She leaned into him, her response unmistakable, making it impossible for him to stop.

The seconds stretched to minutes before Susana finally broke away, pushing against his chest. "We're in the women's bathroom." Her voice was unsteady.

"Technically, we're in the foyer. It's not totally inappropriate — yet. Still, it's not exactly the romantic spot I was hoping for." He managed a weak laugh. He grabbed her wrists and pulled her toward him again.

"Chad's outside." Tears clung to her eyelashes.

He wanted to kiss them away. "Are you two . . . dating?"

"He's a friend, and he asked me to come along this evening. And you're here with someone else." She sounded hurt.

"Do you care?"

She flushed. "You tell me who she is, and I'll let you know."

"Teresa's a park police officer, and we're working the Doyle case together. It's a tough case, and she's been a huge help. She found the crime scene today, leading us to the murder weapon."

Susana wrapped her arms across her chest. "So you rewarded her with a date? Do you get all your girlfriends that way?"

A dizzying rush of relief overcame the anger that swept through Ray. She did care. "No and you know it." He lifted one hand and touched her cheek. Her expression softened, but her hand closed over his, trying to push it away. He let it drop. "How'd you know I was here with someone?"

"I saw you come in." She ducked her head like a child. "I was telling Chad I wanted to leave when you — "

"So that's why you were acting like that."

"Like what?"

"You know what."

"Shut up." She raised her face.

He leaned down.

"Susana, are you all right in there?" Chad pounded on the door. "The door is stuck. Are you okay?"

They stepped apart, leaving a gaping distance between them.

"What are we doing, Ray?" She looked disappointed and relieved at the same time.

"Dinner. Dinner. Maybe even a movie."

"What?"

"Just dinner, Susana. A simple date. Give me a chance."

"I'm here with someone. So are you." She stared at him, the emotion flashing in her crimson face.

"I know that. I know that." His fists clenched so hard his fingers hurt. "You go back to your date, and I'll go back to mine. But we are going to have dinner. Can you handle that?"

"Yes."

"Good." He started to turn.

She grabbed the sleeve of his shirt, tugged him down, and kissed him, in control this time. When he opened his eyes, she wasn't smiling. "That doesn't mean we have this worked out. Chemistry isn't our problem. We both know that."

"I love you, Susana."

She stood very still, a myriad of emotions

chasing one another across her face. Fear
stood out.

She didn't say it back.

CHAPTER FIFTEEN

Ray shoved his front door shut with the cane, limped into the kitchen, and dropped a pile of mail on the counter. He teetered for a second, putting both hands on the cool tile, trying to overcome an overwhelming sense of despair mixed with shame. Susana had ignored his declaration, and he had hurt another human being in the process. Teresa had handled his explanation better than he deserved, but her feelings had been apparent when he'd asked her to take a walk with him. Hands jammed in her pockets, she'd walked fast, studying the ground in the front of them as he told her his story.

"You accepted my invitation to make your girlfriend jealous?" She halted in the middle of the sidewalk, forcing him to stop and face her.

"No! No, it wasn't like that. I didn't know she was going to be here."

"Right. So why'd you even come to the

reception with me if you're already attached?"

"I wasn't attached. At least, I wasn't sure if I was attached." How could he explain the complicated dance he and Susana were doing, when he didn't even understand it himself? "Your invitation caught me by surprise. I said okay without thinking it through."

"Well, I won't be asking again." She reached up and rubbed a spot on his cheek with her thumb. "Your friend has good taste in lipstick. If you get tired of chasing Miss Hard-to-Get, call me. Just don't wait too long."

She'd marched off, her long braid swinging behind her,

Hands dangling at his sides, Ray watched her go. "Teresa, wait. What about the Doyle case?"

She hadn't answered.

Still picturing her hurt face, he dropped his keys on the kitchen counter next to the mail.

The brown envelope on the counter caught his gaze. The one from the seminary. Still waiting to be opened. The evening's events didn't seem to make him a likely candidate for seminary. Rebellion raged through him. He tore off the top of the envelope in a quick motion, like ripping a bandage from an infected wound. An application, course descriptions, paperwork. Hesitancy tore at him. The school had a non-residency program would allow him to take courses and keep working. He'd ordered the materials just to take a look. No commitments. Yet his stomach stewed at the thought.

Leaving law enforcement would knock down a huge barrier between him and Susana. Was that a good reason to become a minister? To make the woman he loved feel safe? He already knew the answer to that question. He started toward the bedroom, the envelope still clutched in his hand. He needed to take a shower and change, get clean, so he could sit down and have a long talk with God.

His cell phone rang.

"Ray." A single slurred word, yet it spoke volumes.

"What's wrong, Deborah?" His partner had said she had big plans for the evening but, as usual, she hadn't elaborated, and he hadn't asked.

"I decided to find out if you put your money where your mouth is, Bible Boy." She sounded as if she had marbles in her mouth.

"What do you need?" He was too tired for sparring.

"Help."

Despite breaking the speed limit, it took Ray almost fifteen minutes to get to the biker bar on Loop 1604 where Deborah claimed to be embroiled in a disagreement with a guy who now had the keys to her truck — which had her weapon in the glove compartment.

"He says he'll give my keys back if I'll go home with him. My gun is in the truck so I can't really defend myself unless I get the keys back." The slur had gotten worse as she talked.

The thought of his drunken partner pulling a gun on some guy in a bar made him punch the gas pedal harder as he careened down the exit ramp. They didn't need this. Not right now. Not with the head honchos breathing down Samuel's neck and Joey Doyle's killer still wandering around. Deborah knew that. So what was her problem? He'd told her to stay in the bar, close to the bartender, and not to go into the parking lot alone. Whether she was sober enough to obey seemed doubtful.

Her Dodge Ram was still in the lot. Ray recognized it from the strands of Mardi

Gras beads hanging from the rearview mirror, along with the SAPD parking pass. Inside the dump, it took his eyes a minute to adjust to the darkness. Patrons stood three deep at the bar in typical Saturday night fashion. A three-piece band massacred a rock cover from the sixties. The first hit of cigarette smoke filled his lungs, making him cough.

Deborah stood at the end of the bar arguing with a man, tall, muscle shirt, a lot of hair. Ray couldn't hear what they were saying, but he got the picture when Deborah jabbed at the man's chest with the long nail of her index finger. The man grabbed her fingers, raised them to his mouth, and kissed them before bending them back until Deborah grimaced.

Ray shoved his way through the crowd, using his cane to part the way until he was close enough to hear the fight. The song neared the end, and the music began to fade away.

"Give me a kiss, and I'll let go." The guy twisted Deborah's arm behind her back and leaned down, his face inches from hers.

"Not in your lifetime, grease ball." She struggled against him. Her other hand come up, and Ray heard the dull thwack as she made contact with the man's cheek.

"You — " The guy dropped her arm and grabbed her around the throat with both hands.

"SAPD. Drop those hands! Now!" Ray let the cane clatter to the floor, flashing his badge with one hand as he ripped his weapon from his holster with the other. "Let her go."

The music ceased. Conversations halted. The crowd at the bar melted away, leaving Ray alone three feet from Deborah's would-be suitor. "Police officer. I said let her go."

A scowl consuming his face, the man shoved Deborah so hard she stumbled and fell to her knees, her hands clutching her throat. She coughed, an ugly hacking sound.

"Sorry, man, I didn't know she was your thing." The words slurred even more than Deborah's had.

"What took you so long, cowboy?" Deborah staggered to her feet and let one hand fly, catching the guy square in the face. "Don't ever lay a hand on me again, buddy, or I swear I will kill you."

The man lunged forward. Ray hurled himself between them, aware that half a dozen guys had advanced from the crowd. A lot of leather and tattoos. Bandanas and stud earrings.

"Deborah, shut your mouth." His weapon held high, he grabbed her arm and shoved her behind him, keeping his body between her and the gang closing in. He lowered the Glock so the barrel was even with the chest of the nearest man. "Look guys, all y'all can stay here, have a good time, and go home at the end of the night with a story to tell the old lady. Or I can call for backup, and y'all can spend the night in jail for drunk and disorderly. What's it gonna be?"

The silence stretched.

Deborah tried to shrug away from him. "You — "

"Shut up." He prayed she'd listen for once in her life.

"She wanted it, man. We were gonna have a nice little date." Deborah's buddy flung a key ring at Ray. He caught it in midair. "She ain't worth it."

The man pulled a torn package of cigarettes from his pocket and took his time lighting one, dropping the match at Ray's feet before turning to face the bar. "Barkeep, set me and my buddies up with shots and Shiners."

"I don't date bar scum." Deborah tried to escape past Ray. He strong-armed her with his free hand and forced her toward the door, keeping his gaze on the gang congregating at the bar, grabbing bottles of beer as fast as the bartender popped the caps. He kept his gun up and crouched long enough to grab his cane. Then he rushed her out the door into the parking lot. The music blared again before the door banged shut.

"Are you crazy or just drunk?" Adrenaline punched through him as he holstered his weapon and dragged her toward her truck. He sucked in air, trying to breath evenly. "Maybe you have a death wish?"

"I'm not crazy. Don't call me crazy! And don't touch me." She jerked away from him, her elbow catching him in the chest. "Give me my keys. Just give me my keys, and I won't bother you anymore. Ever."

"In your dreams. That's just what Samuel needs. One of his detectives on the Doyle case getting a DUI in the middle of the investigation. Or killing somebody. You're coming with me." He grabbed her arm again.

She whirled and faced him. "I said don't touch — "

The look on her face gave him only a split second of warning. He tried to jerk back, but it was too late. She heaved and vomited all over his Ropers, splattering the bottom of his slacks.

"Oh, man!" The sickening stench of tequila mixed with beer and what appeared to be pepperoni pizza filled his nostrils. His stomach lurched. He scrambled back. Bending over, she heaved again, hands propped on her knees.

One hand over his nose, he guided her toward the back of the Bronco, ignoring the booming laugh of a guy lounging on a Harley a few feet away.

Leaving her to finish her business, Ray headed for her truck to retrieve her gun and badge, counting to ten four times as he did. By the time he returned to the Bronco, she had stopped puking and was wiping her mouth with a tissue.

"Is that it?" He bit out the words, unlocked the Bronco and stowed her things under the front seat.

"I think so." Her voice was a hoarse croak. "Man, I must be getting old. I never throw up."

"Could it be the quantity?" Ray let his frustration flow over the words. Deborah had made detective at a young age, but at the rate she was going, she wouldn't need her pension.

"Never made a difference before." She straightened, one arm still over her stomach. Her face was puke green in the neon light of the bar sign. "Give me my keys."

220

"I'm driving you home."

"I don't need a babysitter." She swayed and leaned against the side of the Bronco.

"Apparently you do. Get in." If she didn't do it now, he'd give into the impulse to shove her kicking and screaming headfirst into the back end. The image of her hogtied and strapped to the bumper floated by. Even better. He pushed her into the passenger seat. She flopped back, her head banging against the headrest as soon as he shut her door. By the time he opened his door, her eyes were closed.

Gritting his teeth to keep from tearing into her, he rolled the window down, hoping the dank breeze would blow away the stench. He started the Bronco and headed east on 1604. He didn't need this — not in the middle of the biggest case of their careers. And Samuel's. If Samuel found out, Deborah would be out on her butt so fast she wouldn't know which end was up.

"Ray?" Her voice was hoarse.

"What?"

"I really never throw up."

"Believe me, I'm not planning to tell anyone." He glanced over for a second. She was slumped down in the seat, one hand over her eyes. "But you gotta promise me you'll get control of your drinking. We have a case to solve, and we can't do it if I have to pick up after you in the middle of the night."

"Doesn't this job ever get to you?" The hand slid down so it covered her mouth, muffling her words. "Bodies covered with flies. Families screaming at each other, blaming each other. Kids crying for their daddies."

"Sometimes." Deborah was young for this kind of burnout, but Ray understood it all too well. The tearstained face of a five-year-old bobbed in front of him. *Why am I a poor boy, Mommy?* "Alcohol only makes it worse."

"How would you know? I guess I'm lucky to have a good Christian boy for a partner." The words were more slurred than ever.

Ray's concern ballooned. Had she taken something besides alcohol? Mixed her drugs? "Deborah — "

"Hey, I mean that in a nice way. You have something to believe in."

So drunk, she'd puked on his boots. And now she wanted to talk theology. He grasped for words, trying to set aside his anger and disgust. He'd spent more than his share of nights hugging the porcelain throne. *If you're testing me, God, you're doing a great job.* "It's not a matter of luck. God wants to help you. All you have to do is ask. He's like family, you know, always around when you need Him."

"Family!" She hurled the word at him. "Family, I don't need. I'm fine on my own, believe me."

"So I can see. You're filling a void in your life with alcohol and men and who knows what else."

"I don't do drugs, if that is what you're implying." Deborah struggled to sit up.

"I hope not. You're my partner. I need to be able to count on you. Get a handle on your drinking. If you don't, I'll have no choice but to tell Samuel."

He waited for her to lacerate him with a response. She didn't answer, and he glanced over at her again. Her head was back, her arms slack over her stomach. She'd passed out. "Great. Just great."

They were at her apartment complex ten minutes later. It was gated. "Deborah. Deborah, wake up. I need the gate code." He shook her arm.

She didn't stir, so he pulled over and put the Bronco in park. "Deborah, wake up, I need the gate code." He shook a little harder.

"Get your hands off me." She was suddenly and violently awake, shoving him back, her fingernails raking his face. "Get off me. Get off me."

"Ouch! Stop it! Deborah! I just need the gate code." He recoiled as she flailed at him. "It's me, Ray."

The blows ceased. Deborah shoved her body against the door, her breathing coming in tortured gasps. Her eyes gleamed with fear before she looked away. "Ten-twenty-two, it's ten-twenty-two."

"What's the apartment number?"

"Two-thirty-A." Monosyllabic responses to his questions allowed him to find his way through the maze of buildings to her apartment. When he eased open the passenger door and leaned in to help her out, tears trickled down her cheeks. She was crying without making a sound.

"Come on, I'll help you upstairs." He put an arm around her shoulder. She stiffened, but she didn't resist.

Limping, dragging her nearly inert body, it took him almost five minutes to conquer a flight of stairs. Soaked in sweat, he leaned her against the wall while he fumbled through her keys, trying to find the right one.

Once inside, she collapsed on the couch, eyes closed, her back to him, arms wrapped around her middle. He found a sheet and threw it over her. She didn't stir.

"I'll come by after church tomorrow. We'll pick up your truck before we go to the station."

She didn't answer. Her breathing had already slowed, but her face was still wet. He glanced around the apartment. It was Spartan, walls bare. A glider rocker sat next to a book shelf stuffed full of books — mostly forensic science and law enforcement manuals. He found a notepad on the kitchen counter, wrote her a note repeating the offer, and placed it on the coffee table before closing the door and stumbling back down the stairs in a fog of exhaustion.

Samuel couldn't find out about this. If he did, Deborah could lose her job. She was a thorn in Ray's side, but she was a good detective. Ray tried to sort jumbled thoughts. It was paramount that Deborah get her act together so they could solve the Doyle case, but their careers weren't nearly as important as her drinking problem and whatever was driving it. He should be more concerned about her life — especially the eternal one — than her job. He should turn her in — not just because her drinking endangered both of them in the life or death situations they frequently faced, but because she needed to get help. He knew that, but

the cop in him said he should protect his
own. Partners always did.

Cop or Christian. No contest. Right?

CHAPTER SIXTEEN

"Hey, Sis."

"Danny boy." Susana dropped her hairbrush on the dresser to concentrate on the phone call. She had only a few minutes left to get ready for church, but a chat with her brother was too good a treat to pass up. Only two years her senior, he'd always been easier to talk to than Samuel. They'd both die for her, but Daniel would tell her a joke first. "Where're you, back in town?"

"No. I'm still in Brownsville, but hopefully I'll back by the end of the week. I wish I was there to go to church with you and the boys — and everybody."

Susana knew he was thinking of his wife and the kids. "Have you talked to Nicole?"

Silence reigned for a second. "Yeah, I called to tell her I had to cancel the counseling session this week."

He wasn't helping his own cause one bit. "Daniel — "

"Don't start. I already got the riot act from Samuel, who seemed unusually tense, by the way."

"Samuel unusually tense? How could you tell?" Susana giggled.

Daniel's laugh rumbled over the line. "Right. What was I thinking? How's Marco? I hear he's got a nice cast."

"He's okay, thank goodness. He took quite a tumble."

"And Ray. How's he?"

If Daniel knew about Marco's fall, he knew about the rest. "I'm not Ray's keeper."

Her brother's sigh was heavy. "No, but you care about him. The more you try to push him away, the more obvious it becomes. Have a little faith. After everything you and Ray have been through, he's still hanging in there, waiting for you. Don't you think God has answered your prayers?"

Susana let her brother's words hang in the air while she tried to figure out how much to tell him. "Last night, he told me he loves me."

"Now we're getting somewhere. What'd you say?"

Shame coursed through Susana. She pictured Ray's face as he said those dangerous words. His determined, almost belligerent tone had told her he was expecting

228

rejection, yet hoping she'd reciprocate. She'd done neither. "Nothing."

"Sis! It takes a lot of guts for a guy to come out and say that. Don't be a coward. You want Ray in your life on a permanent basis. I know it. You know it. Get on with it. Don't leave a good man dangling in the breeze."

The words were like a slap in the face. Sure, Daniel would take Ray's side. Nicole had left Susana's brother dangling in that very breeze for over a year now. "I'm not the one hiding in Brownsville while my marriage crumbles."

"Low blow, which for the moment I'll ignore, since we're talking about you and not me." Daniel's words came fast and furious. "You're going to see him at church this morning. Ball's in your court, ten seconds left on the clock. Don't throw it away."

Susana hated sports analogies. "Do you want to talk to Benny?"

"Don't be mad, Suzy Q." Her brother's voice was softer now. He sounded tired. "I just want one of us to be happy."

"I know. Come home soon, okay?"

"Okay."

Susana found her foster nephew searching for his shoes under Marco's bed, while Marco, still half-dressed, laid on it. She gave them the five-minute warning and handed Benny the phone. Wandering out to the living room, she let her brother's advice spin circles in her head. He didn't know the half of it. Would he be pushing them together if he knew Ray had locked her in a bathroom and kissed her?

Those kisses had rocked her down to her toes. Not that she had a lot of experience. The only other man she'd ever kissed was Javier. She'd been sixteen the first time he'd kissed her on the front porch of her parents' house. He'd grinned at her, knowing her mother was waiting on the other side of door, and said, "Guess that makes you my girl."

So pleased with himself. If he'd known — if she had known — would they have been so eager to jump off that cliff?

Biting her lower lip to keep from chewing her fingernails, Susana picked up Javier's framed photo from the fireplace mantel. What would Javier say? His face grinning at her, she could almost hear his deep, teasing voice. "Girl, you only live once."

"Oh, Javier." She touched her fingers to her lips and pressed them against the cool glass of the frame. "Easy for you to say. You bailed out early."

She set the frame on the mantel and

turned resolutely. If she were going to ask Ray on a date, she was going to need a different outfit.

Deborah's eyes were super-glued shut. She needed a crowbar to pry her tongue from the roof of her mouth. She rolled onto her back. Then onto the hardwood floor. Ouch. The pain registered even in the midst of the mother of all hangovers. For some reason, she'd slept on the couch. Oh. Yeah.

A moan escaped her lips before she could press them together. She made it a rule never to complain about hangovers. Today was Sunday. She would have the day to recover. She lay on the floor, staring at the ceiling, listening to the silence, waiting for the vertigo to pass. Her cell phone jangled. A second later, her pager joined in with an unbearably shrill beeping sound. She threw herself forward, grabbed her bag, and dumped the contents on the floor.

"Stop, please stop." She snagged the phone and slapped it to her ear.

"What?"

"Detective Smith, this is Detective McCombs. I understand you have the Doyle case."

"Yeah. So?"

"A horticulturist who worked at the park

where Doyle's body just turned up dead."

Deborah stood up. Too suddenly. Her head whirled, and she sat back down. "Vicky Barrera?"

"Yep."

"Where?"

"In a park, where else?"

She grabbed her keys from the coffee table where Ray had left them. Except she had no truck. Her gaze fell to the note next to them. *I can take you to pick up your truck in the afternoon. Call me if you make other arrangements.* His handwriting was like a little kid's, block print, neat and careful. He'd still be at church. Church. Her stomach flopped.

"McCombs, you got somebody who can give me a ride to my vehicle?"

"Yeah, I imagine we got somebody who can do that — give me an address."

"Make it snappy." She'd get her truck back and get the jump on this body. At least now her partner would be too busy to worry about her drinking habits.

The polite clearing of a throat brought Ray out of his bleary-eyed study of Mark 16:14-18. His Sunday school class started in five minutes, and he wasn't ready. Pastor James stood at the doorway to the patio where Ray sat on a bench, trying to ignore the noisy chatter of half a dozen kids enjoying the playground.

"You've been avoiding me." Pastor James stepped onto the rubber strips of playscape fill and ambled toward Ray, carrying two Styrofoam cups of coffee.

"Good sermon this morning. I always liked the story of Elijah and Elisha." Ray took one of the cups and moved over so the pastor could sit down.

"Thank you. Don't change the subject. You got the material, didn't you?" James stretched his long, skinny legs out next to Ray's. Ray savored his coffee, watching a small boy clamber up the steps to the slide and whish down the other side. Had he ever been that carefree? "Don't worry, you won't go to hell for ignoring me. God, yes, but not me."

"Okay, yeah, I got the application."

"And?" James's gaze was kind, but didn't give Ray much room to maneuver.

"I don't know. I'm not there. I've got stuff that's getting in the way."

"Your love life?"

"What love life?" Ray snorted and then remembered who he was addressing. James was his friend, but he was still his pastor. "I mean, that's the whole problem. I told you how Susana feels about my job."

"Susana would like you to change careers, and you don't think that's the right reason to become a minister?"

Ray glanced down at the Bible in his hands. "I know it's not. Until I met her, I was absolutely convinced it was my calling. Now, when it would make it easy with her, suddenly I'm not so sure. It's crazy."

James shrugged, sipped his coffee, swallowed. "Did you ever consider maybe this isn't about you? Maybe it's about Susana. Her faith. God wants her to take a leap of faith. Maybe he's asking you to wait. Not to give it up. But to wait to answer this calling."

Ray gave a half laugh, as dawning comprehension spread through him. He found himself nodding, even as apprehension tightened his gut.

James smiled. "I know. You could lose her. Trying to force her to trust Him. Remember what Paul said to the Philippians. 'Forget what is behind and strain toward what is ahead. I press on toward the goal to win the prize for which God has called me heavenward in Christ Jesus.' Don't lose sight of the prize, Ray."

Ray's hand shook as he lifted the coffee cup to his lips and then back down again without drinking. "So I could lose her. That's my test."

"Could be." James's voice was soft. "She's come a long way since her husband died. She believes she's trusting God, but she doesn't quite trust you. Give her time. You want to run when she's just learning to walk. Let her go at her own pace, and she'll catch up."

Ray couldn't contain the groan. "I'm too old to stand still for very long. Now I know why I was avoiding you. Don't you have another sermon to give?"

James stood and stretched, a grin on his face. "So you admit it. You were avoiding the preacher. *Tsk, tsk.*"

Ray contemplated the other issue he should be dealing with and wasn't. Deborah's drinking problem. What would James say about his unwillingness to rat out his partner? Not now. James had a sermon to give and Ray had a lesson on the Great Commission to discuss. "Go away. I've got a class to lead."

James tossed his cup in the trashcan and started for the door. "By the way, I know you weren't really avoiding me."

Ray studied his Bible, not wanting to look at his pastor.

"Go find her. Ask her out. Don't wait.

Your class will be thrilled for you."

Ray felt a little sick to his stomach, but he stood and went back into the building. He found Susana about to enter the classroom across from his. She'd always been careful to pick a Sunday school class other than the one he led. She looked gorgeous in a dark green skirt and blouse. He leaned in to take a breath of her fragrance. Spicy citrus.

"Susana — "

"Ray — "

"You first." She didn't quite meet his gaze.

"No, ladies first."

Her cheeks were pink, and one hand fluttered to the top button on her blouse. "Last night you said something about dinner. I thought maybe we could start with lunch today, after Sunday school."

He'd said more than something about dinner. He'd said he loved her. One thing at a time. "I'd like to have lunch with you, but I was kind of thinking of something more — I mean just the two of us." Ray shifted from one foot to the other. He should have just said yes. Lunch was a start and Marco and Benny would like going with them, too. His plan for Susana and him to spend time talking alone would have to wait.

"Piper invited Marco and Benny to her house for hot dogs, homemade ice cream, and a trip to the neighborhood pool."

"Oh. Oh, great. That's great."

"Is that a yes?"

"Of course — " Ray's pager went off just as his cell phone began to ring.

CHAPTER SEVENTEEN

Ray pulled into the circle drive in front of the Botanical Garden Carriage House entrance and parked. He had both boots on the ground before the key was out of the ignition. Another body in another park. They'd interviewed Vicky Barrera yesterday, and now she was dead. He tried to focus on the case, pushing away the memory of Susana's face when he'd asked for a rain check on lunch. Susana hadn't looked mad. She'd looked resigned. His job would always stand between them.

Ray shoved through the wooden double doors and past the officer who let crime scene investigators in and kept visitors out. The second set of doors opened onto a stone walkway that wound through the rose garden. The sweet scent of roses bombarded him. Roses always reminded him of his wife. He held his breath as he trudged past.

Deborah squatted next to one of the ME's

weekend guys, Anson Hopkins, in the shade of the bald cypress, pine, and hickory trees that edged a pond. She looked like death warmed over, but not as bad as the woman sprawled on the ground. Ray glanced at Vicky Barrera. Twenty-four hours earlier, she'd been alive and angry. His gaze traveled to the pond. Turtles sunned peacefully on a log. Cattails choked the shores, and a couple of mallards honked at a flashy red cardinal. Another beautiful place scarred by the violence of his job.

Barrera's face was peaceful, too, except for the ugly bullet hole in her forehead. She had landed, arms and legs jumbled at odd angles, on her back. With her head lolling to one side and her eyes open, she almost looked as if she were staring at the pond. Her bare foot touched the water when it lapped up against the shore. She was still wearing the ratty robe she'd worn during the interview. Same gray sweats, except now they were stained with her blood. A wood duck trundled close to the body, his honking reminding Ray of Barrera blowing her nose in her living room the day before.

No preamble was necessary. "Any ideas on the cause of death?"

"I'll let you know. The most obvious possibility is the GSW to the head." Hopkins paused long enough to wipe sweat from his face with the sleeve of his shirt. "From the lack of blood, I'd say she was shot some-place else and then dumped here."

"We just talked to her yesterday after-noon."

"Well, at least that gives you some param-eters for time of death." Hopkins grinned. Ray knew what he was thinking. Everyone always wanted the ME to provide that criti-cal information and, of course, he couldn't. "She's still in full rigor mortis."

Ray contemplated the timeline. Maybe the killer had been nearby, maybe even watch-ing them interview Barrera. Maybe he'd killed her because she'd been in contact with the police. Ray's stomach clenched with anger.

"The killer left us a present." Deborah leaned forward and pointed.

Ray followed her line of sight. The tip of a finger peeked from the woman's robe pocket. Hopkins reached out with a small set of forceps and gently grasped the finger and slid it out.

The ME rotated the finger from side to side as if admiring the jewelry. "Your dead guy's from the park? We'll run the tests and confirm for you."

Ray closed his eyes for a split second. The

slim gold band was loose on the blackened, decaying finger. Melody Doyle wouldn't get that ring back for a very long time. It would sit in a box in the evidence room, collecting dust until a killer was brought to justice.

"So. Does that mean Barrera killed Joey and chopped off the finger?" Deborah stood, wiping her hands on her jeans. "Or did Melody Doyle find out about the affair and hire someone to kill her — kill them both?"

"Nice theories. Too bad we don't have any evidence to go with them."

"Okay. Fact. Joey Doyle was having an affair with Vicky Barrera. Fact. They are both dead. Fact. Joey Doyle's ring finger is in Barrera's robe pocket. Fact. Melody Doyle is still alive and she stands to collect Joey Doyle's insurance money."

"All true. So how does Melody Doyle find a contract killer? Call information? Look in the Yellow Pages? She's a rich wife who spends most of her time at the gym or the hairstylist."

"You just feel sorry for her because she's pretty and you like her."

Deborah's voice reeked with sarcasm. Ray ignored it. Hangovers tended to make people cranky. "Vicky Barrera knew something about Joey Doyle's murder. That was obvious. Too bad she didn't tell us what she knew." Ray studied the woman's corpse. "Maybe if she had, she'd be alive now. How did the killer get her here?"

"A couple of padlocks were clipped at the service entrance. It's to the back of the main entrance, where the supply sheds are. It looks like the guy trundled her up here in a wheelbarrow from the nursery. The techs are shooting everything now."

"Don't they have security here?"

"Yes, but the city contracted it out instead of using park police. The rent-a-cop on duty last night says he didn't see a thing. 'Course it's hard to see through your eyelids."

"You think he was sleeping?"

"It seems likely. He says he never left the place, but he didn't see or hear a thing."

Together they walked the path that Deborah indicated, looking at the broken branches, disturbed dirt, overturned pots, and broken locks.

"Why here?" Ray asked the question foremost in his mind. "First the wilderness park, now the garden. Does this guy have something against parks, against the city?"

Deborah shook her head. "You got me. You think the killer is making a statement? A serial killer?"

"Different MOs. She's a horticulturist.

242

She spends a lot of time in parks. Joey was a hiker. He spent a lot of time in parks. The location is secondary. They were having an affair." Ray stopped, not really sure he wanted to go down that road. "Revenge? Melody Doyle finds out about the affair? But that doesn't add up. She didn't shoot Barrera between the eyes and then cart her body over here. Or plant her husband's severed finger in a pocket."

Deborah tapped her notebook with her pen. "I stayed around the station for a while yesterday after you left."

"Not long enough, apparently."

"If you were a gentleman you wouldn't refer to last night." Deborah's skin turned a dusty rose color. They stared at each other for a second. "Send me your cleaning bill."

"The last thing I want is your money." Ray wanted to say more, but now wasn't the time or the place.

"I'm trying to tell you that one of the guys was following up on the Doyle interviews for me." Deborah's tone said she was done talking about last night. "He talked to the stylist at the hair salon where Melody gets her hair done."

"Yeah?"

"Her appointment was at ten in the morning."

"And?"

"She exercised at the gym from eight-thirty to nine-thirty, got her hair done at ten, and, after that, her whereabouts are unknown."

"I thought she had a Junior League luncheon meeting."

"No one remembers seeing her there. It's a bunch of women and they would have noticed if Melody Doyle was there. They keep track of these things. She RSVP'd that she was coming, but never checked in and paid for her lunch. They bill people who do that. She was a no-show."

"Her alibi doesn't hold water."

"Nope." Deborah rubbed her temple.

Ray hoped her head hurt. A lot. A constant reminder of what excessive drinking meant. He leaned against the fence, inhaling the smell of fresh dirt and mulch mixed with manure, staring at rows of potted plants waiting to be transplanted.

"Get a couple of officers started here, interviewing all the staff. Round up a couple of guys and start canvassing Barrera's neighborhood. We need to go back to her house — see if that's where she was killed. If it was, maybe the killer left us something we can use. Tear her house apart. We need to know if she had contact with Joey Doyle the day he died."

"Fine. What're you going to do?"

Ray ignored her question. Samuel, still in the suit he'd worn to church, his face grim, was coming up the path toward them. "What's up, boss?"

Samuel grimaced, his gaze traveling past Deborah to Ray. He didn't acknowledge her presence. "Got a call from Alvarez. And Reinhardt at the parks department."

"Figures."

"This one related to the Doyle case?"

"The victim was having an affair with Joey Doyle. The severed finger in her pocket presumably belonged to him."

Samuel rubbed his face with one hand, his eyes hard. "Suspects?"

"A houseful."

His lips thinned. He tugged at his moustache. "You think one of the Doyles did this?"

"If mean, possessive, jealous or arrogant were factors, yes. His wife knew he was unfaithful. Maybe she got tired of it. Or maybe his other mistress found out he was two-timing her, too, and got rid of the competition."

"The mayor is having a meltdown and so is the city manager." Samuel sounded as if he might be close to having one himself.

Not his usual MO. Something besides this case was bugging him. Unfortunately, the case had to take precedence over his friend's well-being. "Two murders in two city facilities. They want officers posted at both places until we've apprehended someone. They're talking about closing down all the parks in case it's a psychotic serial killer who likes to take trophies on the loose. Is this a serial killer?"

"No. The MOs are different. Stab wound. Gunshot wound. The two victims were having an affair. And, of course, the severed ring finger suggests a crime of passion. However, the woman was killed elsewhere, her body dumped here. Someone with physical strength did this. It can't be convenience, breaking in here in the middle of the night. It could be a statement."

"A statement about what?" Samuel mopped his face with a handkerchief.

"We're on it, Samuel."

"Take everyone you need. This is first priority. No vacation leave until we crack it."

"Yes sir."

"I'll be at the station after I drop Piper and the kids off. I'd like an oral report every four hours. Written reports at the end of each day."

Ray had to swallow his first response. Taking time to do reports meant less time actually investigating, but Samuel knew that. "Got it."

Samuel looked as though he were going to say something else. Before he could, an EU investigator strode toward them, a pistol hanging from a pencil. "It was tossed into a bush, but still pretty much in plain sight."

"Yes!" Deborah's pumped her fist like a basketball player celebrating a three-pointer. "Are there prints? I assume the number has been filed off."

"No prints. Wiped clean. Serial number is still there, though."

Ray contemplated a cloudless sky. Left in plain sight. A registered gun. Somebody was really sloppy or wanted to get caught. Or wanted someone else to get caught.

"Well, that's a start." Samuel didn't smile. The same thoughts were probably going through his head. It was too easy. "I'm going. Like I said, keep me posted — every four hours."

"Every four hours?" Deborah waited until Samuel was out of earshot. "Is he nuts?"

"No, just under siege by a bunch of bureaucrats and politicians. Go, find someone who saw something."

"What're you going to do?"

"I'm going back to the station to find out who that gun belonged to."

"What about Melody Doyle?"

"She's next, but we have to find the paper trail. We need to subpoena her financial and cell phone records."

"And talk to Candy Romano?" Deborah stuffed her notebook in her bag and pulled out a pack of cigarettes.

"I suppose." Ray didn't think the chubby-faced young receptionist had done this. Or killed Joey. The facts of the crime said it had to have been a man. And Candy Romano had everything to lose with Joey's death. Melody Doyle would keep her husband's money and standing — if she could put up with the rest of the family. "Yeah, interview her again."

"You get the grieving widow. I'll take the grieving mistress." Deborah lit her cigarette, inhaling deeply. Ray took a step back, trying to avoid the stench. "Meet you back at the station to compare notes."

Deep in thought, Ray stalked through the Carriage House. Melody Doyle might have lied about where she was the day her husband died. What else had she lied about? Once again, Ray was faced with the question: Did being a liar make her a murderer? No, but it sure did make her look guilty.

And she knew her husband had been unfaithful. Motive.

In fact, Melody Doyle had managed to shove Kevin Doyle aside as Ray's number one suspect. He wouldn't have thought that possible.

CHAPTER EIGHTEEN

The gun recovered at the botanical garden was registered to Joey Doyle, part of a matching set, his and hers. Ray studied the grieving widow's face. Melody Doyle wasn't that stupid. Someone wanted to set her up. Apparently everyone living in the Doyle residence, along with their employees, had access to the gun collection in the living room. "Mrs. Doyle, you told me you attended a Junior League luncheon the day your husband died."

"That's right." Melody's hand shook as she raised a glass of amber-colored liquid to her mouth.

Ray could almost smell the alcohol. It was early in the day for a cocktail.

"You came all the way out here to ask me that? You could have called."

"The thing is, no one remembers seeing you there."

"There were at least seventy-five women

250

at the Supreme Cuisine, all talking at the same time. How could anyone tell if I was there or not? Obviously, you've never had the joy of attending one of those lunches." Her incredulous tone matched the spark of anger in her red-rimmed eyes. "Who've you been talking to? Don't you know they all would love to make trouble for the Doyles?"

"So, you maintain you were at the luncheon?"

"They served chicken parmesan and spinach salad."

"Yet you didn't check in or pay for your meal."

"I was late. They'd already shut down check-in, and I didn't want to cause a commotion while *Madam* President was talking." Bitterness coated her words. "I'll send them a check if they're squawking because I didn't pay up for an overpriced rubber-chicken meal."

"Mrs. Doyle, did you ever handle the gun your husband purchased for you?"

Melody slid both hands through tangled hair, her face pinched with exhaustion. "The Doyles believe in their right to bear arms. Rich people are pretty paranoid. Joey wanted me to know how to protect myself."

"Is that a yes?"

"Yes." She soaked the syllable with fury.

"When was the last time you saw the gun?"

"I have no idea. I just noticed it was gone a few days ago."

"Why were you looking for it?"

"Actually, I was going through my things — " her voice dropped to a stage whisper — "planning to move out after the funeral."

"Move out?" Cynthia Doyle stood in the doorway. The woman must have a stealth mode. "The police think you had something to do with your husband's murder, they found your gun who knows where, and you're thinking about moving out? You're an idiot, Melody."

"Mrs. Doyle, I'd prefer to talk with Melody alone, if you don't mind."

"I do mind, Detective. I've called our lawyer. He's on his way. Unless you have an arrest warrant, this interview is over. I'm not going to let this nitwit incriminate herself. She's the mother of my son's children, and I intend to keep what's left of his family together. You can leave now."

Ray stood at the same time as Melody Doyle. He wasn't done by a long shot. If he needed a warrant, he'd get one and haul Melody down to the station for a formal interview.

Maybe it wouldn't come to that. "Before I

252

go, Melody, there's something else I need to know." Ray hated to do it. Her husband was dead. "Did you know your husband was having a relationship with another woman?"

Melody halted, her back to him. Her head dropped, then snapped up. She spun around. "I knew it. I knew it. I knew he had somebody. The jerk." Tears spilled down her face. "Who was she?"

"You've never heard the name Vicky Barrera?"

"No. No. Should I have?" She dashed the back of her sleeve across her eyes, leaving her face and the white cotton streaked with mascara.

"She worked as a horticulturist at the park where your husband's body was found."

"Melody, he's leaving now." Cynthia Doyle took two steps into the room. "I want him out of the house, now."

"No!" Melody turned and glared at her mother-in-law. "Not yet." She sank back into the chair. "So you think she killed Joey?"

"Where were you yesterday about five o'clock?"

"You first."

The grieving widow was replaced by the scorned wife. Ray settled back into his chair, contemplating how much to tell her. "Vicky

Barrera is dead. There are two theories. One, she was killed because she was having an affair with your husband. Two, she knew or saw something that got her killed."

Cynthia Doyle eased onto the couch next to her daughter-in-law, her face white.

Melody stared at Ray, her mouth open. "She's dead and you think I killed her?"

"Your gun was found at the scene. Where were you yesterday afternoon, about five o'clock?" Ray didn't take his gaze from Melody's face.

"I was here. Here, all day. People kept coming and coming. Bringing food, flowers, talking, talking until I wanted to scream." She grabbed her glass and gulped down the rest of her drink. "I was here."

"And you, Mrs. Doyle?"

Cynthia Doyle gave him a withering glance. "Right here, next to her. Greeting my guests."

"I'd like a list of names of those people." Ray waited a beat, then dropped the next bomb. "What about Candy Romano? Melody, did you know her?"

"The receptionist at the I-10 dealership?" Melody look puzzled. "What about her?"

"Did you know your husband gave her money to pay her family's bills?"

"Well, that was — " Melody stopped. "No.

No. She's a baby. Joey wasn't that — "

"That's enough. My son's dead. He can't even defend himself." Cynthia Doyle stood, her face mottled red with rage. "Get out."

"One more thing. One more thing and we're through." Ray steeled himself. "The missing finger. The wedding ring — "

Melody gave a strangled sob.

Ray plunged onward. "They were in the pocket of Ms. Barrera's robe."

Melody's hands went to her face. Tears trickled between her fingers and ran down the back of her hands.

"Melody, do you know anything about how it got there?"

"No, no, no." Each word got louder and more hysterical. "I want that ring back. I want it back."

"The ring is evidence. It will be safeguarded until it can be used in the case. I promise you we'll help the DA make that case. Do you understand? Whoever it is, we'll find out."

Ray stood. He wanted to offer her some comfort, but there was none. He strode through the door into a foyer as big as his living room, Mrs. Doyle close on his heels. He glanced back. Melody sat hunched over, her head down, hands still covering her face. Her body rocked back and forth.

"Melody . . . ?"

"Get out." Mrs. Doyle threw up one hand as if to shove him, then let it drop. "Don't come back without an arrest warrant."

She shut the door in his face.

"Have you ever been to the Doyle mansion?" Deborah watched the emotions play across Candy Romano's face. The woman looked more sad than anything else.

"Never. Of course not. They don't invite the help up there." No bitterness.

"Did Joey Doyle give you a gun? Maybe ask you to hold it for him? Maybe you asked him for a gun — for protection?"

"Are you crazy? What would I do with a gun? I couldn't take it home. I have a younger brother who's twelve and a sister who's ten. And it's illegal to keep guns in your car." Candy's voice trailed away. It was also illegal to shoot and kill people.

Deborah leaned forward on the sagging couch where she sat in the tiny living room of the Romano apartment. She could hear rap music pounding through the thin walls of a nearby bedroom. Candy's mother, her face set in disapproving lines, had sent both of the younger kids to their room after Deborah had introduced herself. Then the older woman had disappeared into a diminutive kitchen.

"We have a theory. Would you like to hear it?"

Candy nodded without speaking.

"We theorize that for some reason Joey gave you a gun. He was planning something. Possibly something illegal, maybe involving drugs. He wanted you to be able to protect yourself if anything happened to him. After Joey died, you were upset. You think either Vicky did it, because he wouldn't get a divorce, or Melody did it, because she found out about you and Vicky. So you decide to take revenge. You kill Vicky and frame Melody with the gun Joey gave you. How am I doing?"

"You're absolutely nuts." Candy sniffed, her eyes reddening. "I loved Joey, but I'm not a murderer. I didn't even know about this Vicky person. I don't believe Joey was with another woman. He wouldn't do that to me."

She stopped, her face staining beet red.

"I guess there's a lot about Joey you didn't know, Ms. Romano."

"Maybe, but I do know he never did anything illegal. He didn't do drugs and he didn't sell them. He was clean. He hiked for his health."

"Where were you yesterday afternoon

about five o'clock?"

"At the movies with my little brother and sister. My mom went, too. Ask her."

"I will."

Deborah strolled across the parking lot in the blazing sun a few minutes later. Candy's mother had confirmed her alibi, the lines in her face shifting from disapproval to fear as she presented four ticket stubs with date and time on them. She and her daughter looked so much alike.

Joey had hiked for his health. That really hadn't worked out for him, had it?

CHAPTER NINETEEN

Ray smoothed the front of his shirt. He'd changed in the PD gym locker room, his hands all thumbs. He should be at the office, comparing notes with Deborah on the Doyle and Romano interviews. Instead he was sitting across from Susana at the Cajun Café, trying to decide what to order. He'd been caught off guard when she'd called and asked if he wanted to give dinner a shot. Absolutely. He could spare a couple hours — for her. Then the doubts had set in. Maybe she needed to tell him something she didn't want Marco to hear. His declaration at the reception hung out there, waiting to be acknowledged.

He glanced at her, catching her gaze. She quickly looked down, the honey brown skin of her neck darkening above the collar of her sleeveless blouse.

"What are you thinking about?"

She didn't look up from the menu, but

her cheeks glowed. "About the first time you kissed me."

"I'm sorry. I got ahead of myself that night." The memory from the previous year was etched in his mind — especially the part where she'd told him to leave the hospital after Samuel had survived surgery to remove a bullet from his shoulder.

"Truthfully, I never regretted that kiss." Her head came up, her gaze meeting his. "Those few seconds stand out now like some sort of reprieve in the middle of a disaster. I shouldn't have been so . . . so mean." In her own way, she was asking to be forgiven.

"It'd been so long since I kissed anyone, it's a wonder you didn't kick me out because the kiss was a disaster."

She stared at him for a second, then laughed. "Well, that's the thing. How could I regret a kiss that good? I thought maybe I'd imagined it, until last night. You're pretty good at it for a guy who allegedly hasn't practiced in a while."

"I would say the same thing about you, but then I couldn't claim we need to practice."

"Gee, practice. Now that's just an awful thought, isn't it?" They both laughed.

"When do we start?" Ray wanted to throw

down his napkin and bolt for the door, dragging her with him.

"Whoa, slow down. I'm starving. Food first."

Ray ripped his gaze off her and focused on the menu. He reached for his iced tea and almost spilled it. Somehow he had to figure out how to go slow, even when everything inside him strained to hurdle over obstacles to the part where they lived happily ever after.

The next hour fled by in conversation that roamed from her classes at UTSA to his new puppy to the boys' basketball games. They were eating mocha mint ice cream when Susana paused, the spoon half way to her mouth. "There's something I should tell you."

Here it came. She would let him down easy.

"I met Melody Doyle. And Cynthia Doyle. Sort of."

"What?" This was about the case. She wanted to talk about the case?

"They were at an art show fund-raiser for the women's shelter. They were having an argument — " Susana stopped.

"An argument about what?"

Her face wore a faraway look. "I didn't think anything about it at the time. I was trying to figure out how I knew Melody Doyle. Something about her seemed familiar."

"What? And what were they arguing about?" It didn't surprise Ray that Melody and Cynthia Doyle would argue, only that they did it in public. It didn't strike him as Cynthia Doyle's MO.

"I don't know what they were arguing about, but I just realized why she seemed familiar."

"You know where you saw her?"

"No. I'd never met her before. I talked to her. It was her voice that was familiar. She called the hotline."

"Melody Doyle called the hotline and got you?" Ray couldn't keep the incredulity from his voice.

Susana looked at him, startled. "No. I mean forget that part. The calls are confidential. I shouldn't have said anything. Besides, I don't really know it was her. Her voice just sounded familiar."

"Susana, if she told you something that would help in this investigation — " Ray stopped while the waitress cleared their dessert bowls and dropped the bill on the table. He automatically smiled at the woman as he reached for it. "Thanks."

"I'm not even sure it was her," Susana

jumped in, "and even if I were — I couldn't tell you a thing."

"Are the calls recorded?"

"No."

"Well, what about the day at the fund-raiser — that's not confidential." He stacked the money on top of the bill, allowing enough for a generous tip, and slid both into the leather jacket.

"No, it's not." Susana chewed her bottom lip. "She told me not to ever live with my in-laws. She said . . . she said it was mur-der."

Ray nodded. "Having met her in-laws, I can see why she would say that."

"She smelled like alcohol, and her eyes were all red. Her hands were shaking. She was a mess."

"When was this?"

"The day after you and the boys found her husband's body at the bottom of a ravine. You hadn't ID'd him yet. She knew he was missing, but she didn't know he was dead, yet — murdered."

So maybe Susana's future profession as a counselor would open a door for their relationship. Maybe she'd see the possibility of them being a team some day. Maybe. "Interesting how our vocations intersected there, isn't it?"

"Yes, it is." She tossed her napkin on her table. "How's your Bible study?"

He tried to figure out whether she was changing the subject. "It's okay. I wish I had more time to devote to it. The case — " He stopped. "You know with my job, I can't do as much study as I would like to in order to prepare, but I think everyone's getting something out of it."

"Piper mentioned . . ." Susana set her purse on her lap; both hands gripped the short strap. "Piper says you're thinking about getting a degree in theology . . . becoming a minister. Is that true?"

"Yes, I'm thinking about it."

She stared at him.

He didn't tell her about the brown envelope lying on the nightstand under his Bible. Or how much she figured into the equation. "But I'm not there yet."

She nodded. "Will you let me know when you make a decision?"

Ray tried to comprehend. Was she saying they couldn't be together any other way? "You'll be the first to know."

They fell quiet. She had to be contemplating what a mistake it had been to have dinner with him.

She smiled. "So, it's really early. Piper promised to keep the boys occupied until I call her. What did you have in mind for the rest of the evening?"

He relaxed and took a breath. "What would you like to do?"

"I have lots of DVDs at my house. We could get in at least one movie before it gets too late. I've got popcorn, too."

"I get to pick the movie?" The case could wait a couple more hours. He'd be awake all night anyway.

"I suppose I could let you do that."

"In return I could take you out to eat again — later this week."

"Another date?"

"The first of many more." He held her gaze. She didn't flinch. "Assistant Chief Guerrero is retiring. They're having a banquet Friday night."

"I'd love to go."

Ray had to fight to keep from grinning like an idiot. One step at a time. Now he just had to get his hands on two banquet tickets.

They were in the Bronco, headed for Susana's house when his cell phone rang. Deborah. She better not need a ride home again. Not tonight.

"We've got a standoff at the Doyle residence." His partner talked fast. "Apparently Melody got into it with her in-laws. She's got the kids on a balcony, and she's got a gun. She's threatening to kill herself or anyone who gets too close. The only person she'll talk to is you."

"On my way." Ray disconnected and jammed his foot on the accelerator.

Susana jerked back against the seat.

This was his fault. He'd confirmed Melody's worst fears about her husband and insinuated she might have had something to do with his death. He should have seen this coming. "I don't have time to take you home first. Sorry."

"What is it?" Her voice was soft, sad. They couldn't have one date without his job bleeding into it. How could they have a life together?

"Melody Doyle's trying to kill herself. Apparently she wants to take a few people down with her when she goes."

"It's time to mess with the cop's mind. Send him a message."

Lalo studied his boss's face. The guy was serious. He thought his money made Lalo his servant. "I'm uncomfortable with this assignment. I'm not a messenger. I kill for you, that's what I do."

The boss poured two fingers of Bacardi in a glass of ice and added a splash of Coke.

"Not this time. Just scare him. Get him to back off."

Lalo shook his head. "He doesn't strike me as the type. Big macho man thinks he's going save the world. Better to put a bullet in his head, remove him permanently."

"He's a cop. I'm not interested in capital murder. Just send him a message — for now." The boss slurped from his glass and set it with a clink on the desk.

"*Está bueno.* Let me see what I can arrange."

Keeping his face blank, he turned to leave. He would do his best to send this message, but if the cop ended up dead in the process . . . well he would consider it a message delivered. This was what he did. The boss knew that when he hired him.

"Hernandez."

"*Sí, señor?*"

"Don't use the BMW. Take one of the other cars. He's seen the BMW."

"Oh, yes, I must use the BMW." Lalo was careful to keep his irritation out of his voice. Amateurs. They always wanted to tell him how to do his job.

"What?" The boss man took another sip of his drink, his irritation plain on his face.

"I must use the BMW." Lalo explained slowly as if to a small child. "He must know

267

I am watching him, getting close. That I can take him out whenever I choose to do it. That is the message. *¿Entiende?*"

The boss shrugged. "Do it your way. You get caught, don't expect anything from me."

Lalo suppressed the laugh that gurgled low in his throat. He never expected anything from the boss. Not that he needed anything from him, except payment.

Taking his leave, Lalo strolled to the car, punching a number into his cell phone as he walked. *"¿Primo?"*

"Lalo. *¿Como estás?*"

"You available for a small job?" He'd worked a few minor assignments with his cousin — third cousin really — in the past. The man had a slight problem. He sucked whatever money he made up his nose and couldn't keep a job because of it. Lalo sent work his way now and then, in case he needed a favor from him, like now.

"*Pues, sí,* for you, Lalo, I am always available." He sounded eager.

"*Bueno.* I need you to get me some fresh plates. And I need you to be my driver. Be available in the morning."

"Where're we going?"

"To deliver a message."

CHAPTER TWENTY

"Stay here." Ray shoved the Bronco into park in front of the Doyle mansion, opened the door, and ran as fast as his limp would allow.

A door slammed behind him. He didn't have time to argue with Susana. He'd wasted twelve minutes on the trip. A SWAT van was already on the scene, along with half a dozen PD units, lights flashing. An officer with a rifle in his hand leaned against a vehicle as he peered through the scope.

Ray's gaze followed the barrel. The back of a woman on a second floor balcony. Melody.

The crowd of uniformed officers, paramedics, and family members parted as he limped up the front steps. Cynthia Doyle attempted to stop Ray, but Kevin Doyle restrained her. Ray brushed past both of them without acknowledging a barrage of angry words. Martin Elliott, SWAT team commander, stood at the top of the winding staircase, deep in conversation with Armando Juarez, one of the department's negotiators. Armando wiped a pair of gold-rimmed glasses with a handkerchief, his forehead wrinkled in concentration.

"What's the story?" Ray negotiated the stairs, the pain in his ankle flaring. The sound of footsteps followed him. He glanced back at Susana. "Go back outside — please."

"I'm a trauma counselor." She had that stubborn look on her face.

"Ms. Doyle is asking for you." Armando handed Ray an armored vest, his gaze traveling to Susana. "Who's this?"

"This is Susana Acosta. She's spoken with Melody on the crisis hotline." He dropped the cane and struggled into the vest, debating what to tell the negotiator about Susana's connection to Melody. It was tenuous at best — and confidential. Still, the two women had connected. "Did you talk to Melody?"

Armando nodded at Susana, but returned immediately to Ray. "Yes, Ms. Doyle and I had a conversation. She claims she's scared and needs protection. She says you're the only one who can help her."

"There are a dozen or more armed police

270

officers on the premises. They could've easily escorted her out."

"She took a shot at her brother-in-law. He's pressing charges. She'll be arrested, and she knows it. She insists her in-laws are setting her up for her husband's murder." Juarez shook his head, his lips pursed in a frown. "The Doyles claim she's delusional, a state brought on by the stress of her husband's death. The mother-in-law says she believes Ms. Doyle has taken some prescription medicine. She apparently has prescriptions for various things — an antidepressant, a sleep aid, something for her nerves. Mrs. Doyle Sr. couldn't be specific. She also said Ms. Doyle made a pitcher of margaritas and took it with her into the room earlier this evening."

"Drugs and alcohol, but we don't know how much of what." Any attempt at rational dialogue was liable to be stymied by the sheer incapacitation of Melody's faculties. Juarez didn't know any of the actors in this little drama, but Ray did. He was more inclined to take Melody's word than Cynthia's, but he trusted neither of them. "Did she threaten to harm the kids?"

"After she took the potshot at her brother-in-law, she dragged the children into her room and then out to the balcony. Now she's threatening to kill herself. She says she's dead anyway, and she would rather kill the kids and herself rather than continue living with the Doyles."

"I don't have any experience with this, Armando. Are you sure putting me in there is the best option — "

"Let me talk to her," Susana broke in. "She'll recognize my voice. She'll remember me. Wouldn't a woman be better?"

Armando gave her a speculative look. "What did Ms. Doyle tell you when she called the hotline?"

Susana looked uncomfortable. "That's privileged information, but I can tell you she seemed suicidal and very upset with certain individuals in her life."

"Are you a trained counselor, Ms. Acosta?"

"I'm getting my masters in counseling. The hotline is part of my practicum."

Juarez was already walking away, leaving Susana with her hands on her hips. He glanced back at Ray. "Let's go, cowboy. She says you're the only one she'll talk to. We go with you, or a sharpshooter will take her out. She's already tried to kill Kevin Doyle, and we can't be sure she won't harm the kids. The sharpshooter's got a clear shot."

"No." Susana's hand gripped Ray's arm.

"That's not an option. She wouldn't hurt her own children. Tell them to back off."

Juarez looked back. "It's up to you, Detective Johnson. Are you ready to give it a shot?"

Ray nodded, ignoring Susana's sharp intake of air. "You had to use the word shot."

"It's the balcony straight ahead after you enter the sitting area. Tell her you're coming in first; she'll be able to see you. I'd rather not find out if her aim is improving."

Ray squeezed Susana's hand before pushing it away. "Go downstairs."

"Be careful," she called after him.

"Wait outside." He didn't look back.

He moved through the louvered doors that served as the entrance to Melody's suite. His shirt, wet with sweat, clung to his back. "Melody, it's me, Ray Johnson. I'm coming in."

"Leave your gun at the door."

Ray couldn't see her yet, but he could hear the fear and desperation in her voice.

"You come in with a gun, I'll shoot you."

Ray laid his weapon on the carpet inside the door and gave it a shove. "It's on the floor, Melody. Do you see it?"

"You can come in, but don't get too close. I *will* shoot you." The quaver in her voice was at odds with the threat. Ray edged into the sitting room. He could see her standing on the balcony, her back to the railing. The exotic beauty had disappeared. This woman's dark hair was tangled and matted, her makeup smeared. Her arms wrapped around her chest so the muzzle of the gun rested just below her chin. She gently rocked side-to-side. She reached down, picked up a margarita glass, and took several gulps.

The boy Ray had met on Friday was sprawled on the balcony floor next to a little girl, running a large dump truck loaded with pretzels across the cement. The girl, dressed in a pink nightgown, clutched a doll in one arm and munched on a Pop Tart or strudel.

She sang off-key between bites, "*Uno, dos y tres, cuatro, cinco, seis, siete, ocho, nueve, diez.* See, Mommy, see I can count to ten in Spanish. Did you hear me, Mommy, did you hear me?"

"Yes, I heard you, Samantha. That's very good. Did you learn that from *Sesame Street?*" Melody smiled, but her eyes were the saddest eyes he'd ever seen.

"*Sí, Mama, sí.*" The little girl clapped her hands together and food flew through the air. She giggled and started feeding the doll.

"We need to talk, Melody." Ray took

another step toward the balcony.

"These people are crazy. They killed Joey, and they are so pleased that you're trying to blame it on me. All that talk about you coming back with an arrest warrant — they were thrilled at the idea. They want me to be their scapegoat."

The words were slurred. He wondered if she would pass out before she could do herself or the kids any harm. *Please, God.*

"Who killed your husband? And why?" He worked to keep his tone conversational. "Tell me what happened, so I can help you."

"You can't help. You're just a city cop. They're the Doyles." She uttered the last name as if her in-laws were royalty. "They can do whatever they want, and no one can do anything about it."

"Who do you think killed your husband? Tell me, and I promise I will do everything I can to bring that person to justice."

She laughed, half-hiccup, half-sob. "You're a nice man, Detective Johnson. You're like my Joey. He was a nice person. You would've liked him. They'll eat you alive just like they did Joey. I knew my husband had affairs." The hysteria in her voice climbed. "I knew, but if I wanted to kill him for that, I would have done it a long time ago. Why would I kill him now? Why?"

"I know that, Melody. Why don't you come over here and sit down and tell me what happened. I promise I'll help you."

Again a sob. "I'm standing on the balcony with my two kids, a gun in my hand. I took a shot at my brother-in-law. No way they'll let me keep them now. They'll take my babies. They had my husband killed. Now they'll put me away. I can't let that happen, don't you understand?"

"The sooner you come inside and help me figure this out, the better it'll be for you. Don't give them anything else to work with." Sweat ran down his forehead and his neck. He could feel the tension in her body like it was his own. "Don't give them the satisfaction of getting away with this. Don't let them win."

"Don't you see, they already won. They got Joey. Now they'll get me. I know what they're doing. They know he told me."

"Told you what? What are they doing?"

"Not here. I can't tell you here. They'll know I told you, and they'll kill me."

"Which one of them, Melody, and why?" His desperation mingled with hers.

"I just want you to promise me one thing, Detective." Her voice was firmer now. She had made a decision. "I want you to promise me my parents will get the kids. I don't want the Doyles raising them. I put it in writing. It's on the piece of paper on the table. I told my lawyer, and now I'm telling you."

"Melody, you'll raise your children." He tried to reach her by the sheer strength of his voice. "You'll raise them. We'll work this out, and you'll be their mom."

The hand with the gun moved up slowly. "Melody, don't do this. If you don't trust me, if you don't trust the system, trust God. He will judge whoever is persecuting you. His punishment will be severe."

The gun stopped for a second. She gazed at him with huge eyes, her face etched with lines of despair and maybe a little hope.

"Let me help you, Melody." He took a few quick steps forward, covering the ground to the balcony with two long strides.

She was within reach.

"No! Stay away!" Her shrieks sliced the air into ribbons. The gun aimed at his chest loomed enormous.

Ray saw the barrel, saw her finger on the trigger, watched her squeeze it, heard the shot.

CHAPTER
TWENTY-ONE

Bullets pinged over Ray's head. He hurled himself to the ground and rolled away, his hand stretching toward the Glock just beyond his reach.

An instant later, the door blew open. Officers tumbled in. He smacked up against the wall. Children screamed, a high-pitched sound Ray would hear in his dreams forever. The moment stretched, then snapped. Silence descended. Movement ceased. He rolled to his feet and staggered toward the balcony. Melody lay crumpled in a heap.

"No!" Ray dropped to his knees next to her. He touched her neck. No pulse. Blood pooled under her head, her eyes stared at him, but he knew she saw nothing. He crouched next to her body, his head down, ignoring the sound of people rushing toward him.

"Are you hit?" Deborah squatted next to him, her weapon still drawn. "Ray, are you

278

hit? Answer me!"

"No, I'm not hit! What were you guys doing rushing in here?"

"Saving your butt. The sniper took his shot. You know the drill. We had no choice. She practically committed suicide by opening fire on you."

If he hadn't moved too quickly, she might not have died. It was his fault; he shouldn't have moved so fast. "How could they take her out, knowing the kids were right here? What if he'd hit one of them?"

"The kids were below the line of the balcony. They were never in danger from our guy. He knows what he's doing. You know that."

"Get everybody back, now!" He corralled his emotions, rocked back on his heels, and stood to get away from her. She looked up at him in surprise for a second and then nodded.

Ethan and Samantha huddled together in the corner. Samantha's screams had subsided, her sobs muffled in the stomach of the doll clutched to her face. Ethan still held his truck, but he stared at it as though he didn't know what to do with it.

"Ethan?" Ray positioned himself between the children and their mother's body, trying to shake the image of Melody Doyle sitting in the dining room, looking at him with those big eyes and wanting to know if a five-year-old understood about death. "Ethan, are you okay?"

"Mommy fell down." The boy's voice quivered. He wiped his nose on his pajama sleeve. "She went bang, bang and then, she fell down. Who are you?"

"I'm Ray. I'm a police officer. Are you hurt?"

"I want my mommy."

"I'm sorry, Ethan." Ray's throat tried to close up. "I can't — you can't talk to her."

His face puzzled, the boy struggled to see around Ray. "Mommy has an ouchy."

Ray glanced at Deborah, standing over him. She shrugged and picked up Samantha, wrapping her arms around the sobbing girl, doll and all, gently murmuring soothing words as she carried her from the balcony. He did the same with Ethan, shielding him so he couldn't see Mommy's ouchy. The boy clung to Ray, his head buried in his shirt. They waded through the crush of people and down the stairs. Ray tried not to make eye contact.

"Detective. Give him to me." Cynthia Doyle lunged at for Ethan. "Give me my grandson. Now. You've done enough damage here."

Ray tightened his arms around Ethan, who burrowed deeper into the shirt, his face hidden. "The damage was done long before I got here." He didn't try to hide his contempt. He struggled to keep his voice down. "What did you do to her? What did you threaten her with? What did she know that you were trying to hide?"

"You're out of line, Detective." Voice icy, she eyed him over Ethan's head, but her hands dropped. "You're supposed to be finding out who killed my son. Not harassing us. Now give me my grandson, and get out of my house."

"Your daughter-in-law made some serious accusations. I plan to investigate them." He shoved past her, his arms still tight around Ethan. "In the meantime, she left explicit instructions that she wanted her parents to become the guardians of her children. I'm contacting them right now."

"What?" Mrs. Doyle clattered down the steps after Ray.

He kept going. "She put it in writing, she notified her lawyer, and she also told me."

"We'll fight it."

"You do that." Ray pushed through the front door and out on to the porch, looking for Susana. She stood beside an ambulance, one arm wrapped around Sarah Doyle's

281

shoulder.

Her gaze connected with Ray's. Her face crumpled, then smoothed. She patted Sarah on the back, turned, and held out her arms. "Let me help you."

Fifteen minutes later Ethan leaned, his body limp, against Susana's shoulder, his face blank, while Greg Miller examined him. Samantha, her thumb stuck in her mouth, had been passed over to her Aunt Sarah, the only one of the bunch whom Ray would trust with any child. Deborah and Juarez were en route to break the news to Melody's parents, hoping they would get there before the media live trucks. Ray should have been the one, but he hadn't argued with Juarez when the psychologist had said he would handle it.

"Give yourself a minute, Detective." The negotiator's tone hadn't allow for argument. "We'll discuss Ms. Doyle's wishes with them as soon as they're able to cope."

It was going to take Ray more than a moment. He felt lightheaded, and the muscles in his arms and legs shook with spasms.

"Physically, kiddo here is A-okay." The paramedic patted Ethan's curly, brown hair. Ethan didn't respond. Miller gave Ray a wry smile. "I'll leave the emotional damage assessment to the experts. How about the

282

detective? He's not looking so hot."

"I'm fine." Ray ignored the concerned look Susana shot him and sat down on the bumper next to Greg. "Are you the only paramedic in town or something — how come I always get you?"

Without answering, Greg rummaged around in a small cooler in the back of the ambulance and produced a carton of juice. "Drink this. Doctor's orders."

"You're not a doctor." Ray drank it anyway. The cool liquid helped him swallow the emotion that threatened to spill out.

"Ray!" Samuel strode toward him, his face half-hidden under a baseball cap. His long-legged gait slowed. "Susana? What are you doing here?"

Ray plunged in before Susana had a chance. "She was with me when I got the call."

He stood and walked away, forcing Samuel to follow. Neither Ethan nor Susana needed to hear this conversation.

"What happened?" Samuel clipped each word.

Ray gave him the rundown, including his doubts about the need to take out Melody Doyle.

"According to Juarez she got off three rounds before she went down. If she'd been

283

a better shot, you'd be dead. They had no choice. They did the right thing."

Ray shook his head. "It was my fault. I was in over my head. I shouldn't have tried to get closer. I screwed up, and it cost Melody her life."

"Don't second-guess yourself. Melody Doyle called the play, not you. When she went out on that balcony with a gun, she named the game." Samuel's face smoothed into sympathetic lines. "You're not the bad guy in this; don't forget that."

Ray's phone rang before he could respond.

"Get that. I'll find someone to take Susana home." Samuel's face darkened again. "She could have done without this."

He turned and walked away, leaving Ray trying to focus on what Deborah was saying on the other end of the line.

"We've broken the news. Melody's brother will drive his father over to pick up the kids. The family lawyer is meeting them there. It'll take them fifteen minutes. Will you be there to make sure no one stands in their way?"

"I wouldn't miss it for the world." Ray patted the piece of paper he'd stuck in his pocket before leaving Melody's suite. He watched as Samuel grasped Susana's forearm and drew her away from the ambulance. She glanced toward Ray, her face etched with regret. She gave him a small wave and allowed herself to be led away.

Ray ached with the desire to follow her.

"Mr. Policeman." He felt a tug on his sleeve. "Mr. Policeman."

"Yeah, Ethan." He squatted next to the boy. "How're you doing?"

"Can you help me find my daddy?"

CHAPTER
TWENTY-TWO

The sun popped out from behind a cloud. The sudden light blinding him, Ray climbed into the Bronco in the station parking lot. The night had passed in a blur of stifled emotions; daybreak had brought no relief. Ethan and Samantha were with Melody's parents. The techs were done with the scene. Melody Doyle's body had been transported to the morgue. His report was typed. Still, he couldn't decompress. He couldn't close his eyes without seeing her face and hearing the kids' screams. He should go home, take a shower, and change clothes. Maybe then, he could start to put this thing together in some form that made sense.

He put the key in the ignition and pulled from the parking space. Fifteen minutes later, he found himself sitting in front of Susana's house. He turned off the engine and rolled down the windows. The air was thick and humid in the early morning heat. Cicadas chorused, their song mingled with the cooing of mourning doves and the occasional barking of a dog down the street. Sounds steeped in normalcy, rooted deep in childhood memories of happier times.

He took a deep breath and let it out, listening to the whoosh of the air. Most people took that for granted. Inhaling and exhaling. Having watched someone die changed that. Sounds were amplified, yet survivors strained to hear them again, to be reassured by them.

The screen door opened, and Susana walked out in bare feet. In a yellow sundress, her hair loose, she looked like a young girl. She bent over to pick up the newspaper, straightened, and looked around. She studied the Bronco. "You want to come in, Ray?" she called.

The offer surprised him, and he found he couldn't respond.

After a moment, she walked over and leaned in the passenger window. "Are you all right?"

When he still didn't answer, she pulled the door open and slid onto the seat next to him, close. "Ray?"

"He didn't cry."

"Who didn't cry?"

"Ethan. He didn't cry."

She shook her head, her face sad. "Shock, I imagine. He'll cry plenty later."

He cleared his throat. "I'm sorry about last night."

"I don't know how you guys do it. I've always known what Samuel faces at work, but to see it up close and personal like that. It explains a lot of things about the way my brother is."

"Your brother would have done a better job than I did."

"You did what you could, Ray. I know you're beating yourself up. Don't. We all think things should work out in the end, but sometimes they just don't." She sighed. "At least, I learned one thing."

"What's that?"

"I made the right career choice. I helped people last night: Sarah. Ethan. The poor maid. She was devastated. Mostly they talked, and I comforted, but it felt right."

They were both silent then, listening to the sounds of a neighborhood waking up.

"Why don't you come in? I'll fix you some coffee. Decaf — you look like you really need to sleep." She touched his face with a cool, soft hand.

He swallowed hard, gritting his teeth until his jaw hurt. He kept his gaze fixed on the street in front of him.

"Have you eaten? I've got bacon and eggs. Marco and Benny are in there, watching some show about dolphins. You could watch with them while I fix you something. Or you could take a nap on the couch."

"All this didn't scare you away — from me?"

"I'll be honest with you, Ray; it scared me a lot." She stopped.

Ray allowed himself a quick glance at her face. Fear and sadness danced together there. He shifted his gaze to the windshield and waited for her to finish the thought.

"I'd like to be as brave as you are, but I'm not sure I can, or that I want to go through this again and again. Right now, I just want to be here for you."

"I'm not all that brave."

She moved closer and put her hand in his. Without thinking, he lifted it to his lips and kissed it. She smiled at him, her eyes sympathetic, inviting him to talk.

"You remember all the things I told you when you were angry at God about Javier dying, all the verses I quoted you when you first moved back here."

"Of course. You were a good friend when I really needed one."

"I must have sounded pretty arrogant,

289

thinking I knew what God's plan was for you or for anybody. For the life of me, I have no clue what his plan was last night."

"No, you sounded like you'd given these things a lot of thought." Her voice was confident. "Like you had suffered like I was suffering. You sounded like you knew you could rely on God to get you through, and you expected me to do the same. Just like we have to do now."

"Thing is." He stopped, not wanting to voice the thought spinning in his head. "Thing is, I'm the one who told her about the affairs. I sent her over the edge, out onto that balcony. I was so busy trying to peg a murderer, I didn't stop to assess the impact on her emotionally."

"No. Melody knew her husband was having an affair. He had a history of doing this to her. Don't forget, I talked to Melody on the phone. I talked to her at the fund-raiser. She might not have had the name, but she already knew. Her husband's death, her in-laws — a combination of events and circumstances pushed Melody over the edge."

Maybe, but he should have found the words to bring Melody back in.

"Ray, listen to me." Susana leaned in, her hand tightening around his. "You're not the Lone Ranger. Rest a while."

"Maybe I just want to wallow a little first."
She was right. God was in control. Not him.

"Allowed." She didn't smile.

They sat there for a while, not talking.
The sun climbed, the air warmed. He let
his thumb rub across the soft skin on the
back of her hand, her scent enveloping him
as he entwined his fingers with hers.

"Mom!" Marco shoved open the screen
door, a telephone in one hand. "Mom, it's
Tía Lily — hey, Ray, aren't you gonna come
in?"

Ray exhaled.

Susana squeezed his hand and let go. "I'll
head him off at the pass. You go home and
get some sleep."

He tried to muster a smile. "I think I'm
headed back to the station."

"You need to go home. Grab a couple
hours sleep, take a shower, get some fresh
clothes. You'll be a new man." The corners
of her mouth lifted slightly. "Not that
there's anything wrong with the old one,
but it'll do you a world of good."

Melody Doyle would still be dead. "Can I
call you later?"

"I'll be mad if you don't."

She leaned over and kissed him. He let
her soft touch envelop him as her arms
wrapped around his neck in a quick hug.

291

When she backed away and slid across the seat to get out, he gripped the steering wheel to keep from snatching her back.

"Hang in there, Ray Johnson," she said through the window. Then she turned and sauntered up the sidewalk toward Marco. "Ray's gotta head out, *m'ijo*. He'll call you this afternoon, okay?"

Marco looked uncertain, but he waved. Ray waved back. *Hang in there, Ray Johnson.* Susana's words sang in his head like the refrain of a song. He started the engine, rolled up the windows, and turned on the AC. Lukewarm air hissed through the vents, doing nothing to cool his damp body.

Rolling away from the curb, he glanced in the rearview mirror. Susana and Marco stood on the sidewalk, still waving. A flash of silver forced his gaze from them. He slammed on the brake and twisted to look back. A BMW hurtled down the street, bearing down on the Bronco. The passenger side window was down and a man, dark and wearing sunglasses leaned out. He balanced the long barrel of a weapon on the door-frame.

Ray's hand shot toward his Glock.

The frenzied staccato of automatic weapon fire filled the air.

CHAPTER
TWENTY-THREE

Susana and Marco were out in the open.

Ray threw himself sideways, trying to slide, but his legs tangled under the steering wheel column. He had to get to them.

Popping sounds peppered the air as lead met glass and metal. The window shattered. Glass showered down and sprayed his face. He ducked his head. Time took on a nightmarish quality. He shoved himself at the passenger door. His body continued to function, even as his mind zeroed in on that one single pinpoint of thought.

They were out in the open.

He fumbled for the handle, prepared to dive headfirst to the ground. As quickly as it had started, the gunfire died. Tires screeched. An engine raced and backfired. Silence descended, then Susana screamed.

"Ray! Ray!" She screamed his name again and again.

He pulled himself up and slid out, bringing a shower of broken glass with him. Susana knelt, her arms wrapped around Marco. Her son slumped to the ground, his arms flung over his head, his tight, high whimpers building. The child couldn't endure any more tragedy. Ray wasn't sure he could either.

"Are you hit? Are you hit?" He covered the ground between them in long stumbling strides, dropped to his knees, and hugged them. Shudders shook their bodies. "Marco, are you okay?"

Marco jerked away, trying to rise. "What if they come back? We gotta hide, we gotta get inside. They're coming back."

"It was a drive-by, Marco. They're not coming back. It's over. It's all over." Ray ran his gaze over the boy. No blood. Just the icy pallor of shock. He turned to Susana and slid his hands over her face and her hair, not believing she was unscathed. He grabbed her again and pulled her into his chest. Her heart pounded against his. "Thank God, you're okay. Thank God, you're not hit."

"He wasn't shooting at us." She sounded angry. "He was shooting at you. I thought . . . I saw you fall over. I thought . . ."

She struggled against him, but he tightened his grip. Even if she didn't need him, he needed her.

"Let me go. I can't do this. It's too much. Let me go."

"You're fine. Marco's fine. Just lean against me a second." He used one hand to pull his cell phone from his belt, punched in nine-one-one, made the report. If a patrol unit was in the vicinity, maybe they could pick up the BMW before it left the area.

Susana pulled away from him, wrapping her arms around Marco again, her head down, her chest heaving.

"Marco? Aunt Susana!" Benny stood in the doorway, holding open the screen door. "What was that noise? It sounded like firecrackers. What are you guys doing? Why are you on the ground?"

Susana turned a tearstained face to Ray. He could read it all in her eyes. Anger. Resignation. He opened his mouth to argue, but no words came out.

"Go back inside, honey. Marco and I are coming in." The emotion in her voice was gone. She leaned down and picked up the phone Marco had dropped, punching a button to end the monotonous beeping. "I need to call Lily and let her know what's going on. If she could hear any of that, she's going crazy."

"She's probably on her way over." Ray stood and grabbed Susana's elbow to pull her up.

She immediately pulled away. Marco scrambled to his feet and slid under his mother's arm.

"Susana — "

She shook her head, her eyes bleak.

Ray let his hand drop. "I'll call Samuel."

"Yes. You'd better do that." She eased back a step, her arm tight around Marco's shoulder. "You have blood on your forehead. I'll keep the boys inside."

Together, she and Marco tottered away, leaning against each other as if they were too tired to stand.

"Susana, please don't . . ." She glanced back and then turned and kept walking. He touched his forehead, his fingers came back wet. It didn't hurt, not nearly as much as the look on her face.

Five minutes after the paramedics got there, skidding tires and burning rubber heralded Samuel's arrival. Without a word, he disappeared into the house and then reappeared several minutes later with a plastic tumbler of iced water.

He sat down on the curb next to Ray and handed it to him. "Paramedic get you patched up?"

"Yeah." Ray felt the exhaustion roll over him in waves. He took the glass and lifted it to his mouth. He couldn't raise his head to look at his friend. Lily, her face fierce with anger and fear, had arrived at the same time as the ambulance. After one look at his face, she'd darted inside. Deborah had been the last to arrive. She stood talking to an Evidence Unit investigator as he dug a round from an AK-47 from a tree in Susana's front yard. They had recovered dozens of rounds from the Bronco and the ground around it. Others, they'd dug out of the front of the house.

A shudder ran through Ray. "Are they okay?"

"Lily's fixing her some tea. She's cold — shock, I guess. Benny's keeping Marco company."

"I should see them. Talk to her." He tried to push off the curb with one hand. His legs felt like rubber, and his ankle was on fire.

"No."

Ray studied Samuel's face. It was kind, but his eyes were the eyes of a brother, not a friend. "Samuel, I would never — "

"You could never have imagined this would happen. But it did. You let her walk into the violence at the Doyle house last night. Then, you brought violence to her doorstep this morning."

Ray swallowed hard. "Nobody feels worse about it than I do."

"Doesn't change anything." Samuel's eyes were dark and hard.

"So she and I — we're, I mean, you're saying — "

"I'm not saying anything. She's a grown woman. She'll make her own decisions. I want the sorry excuse for a human being who fired dozens of rounds from an AK-47 at you and my sister and my nephew. I want him behind bars. Instead of sitting here mooning over her, get going. You can't be around her if this is going to happen. So, stop it."

"How exactly would you do that?" Hands shaking, Ray set the glass on the curb, spilling the liquid into the grass.

"You're a cop. Figure it out. Melody Doyle's gun killed Vicky Barrera. Now, Melody's dead. She wasn't following you around, and she wasn't shooting at you in front of my sister's house." Tension made Samuel's deep voice drop. "If this person wanted you dead, you'd be dead right now, Susana and Marco, too. So, who's trying to scare you? Who wants you to back off?

Figure that out, and you'll figure out this case."

"Right."

"I've already put a BOLO out on the BMW. We'll see what the crime lab has to say about the ammo." Samuel had switched to boss-mode somewhere in the middle of the tirade. "Go home, get some sleep, and we'll re-group in the morning."

Feeling like he'd been punched, Ray took a deep breath and let it out. Samuel was right. "I'd like to say good-bye."

Samuel stood and took a few steps. He stopped between Ray and the front door. "I'll tell them for you."

"Right." Ray forced himself toward the battered Bronco, ignoring Deborah's stare. She hadn't said much when she'd arrived, except to ask if he was all right. Everybody kept asking that. He'd gotten a faint whiff of stale whiskey on her. Who knew where she'd gone after the fiasco at the Doyle mansion. A good partner would have made sure she was okay.

She furiously chewed gum and kept her distance. He pulled open his door and swept glass from the seat. As he eased in, he heard it crunch under his boots. He put his hand on the key, still in the ignition. Anger ripped through him. *Don't I get to be happy, God, or*

is that too much to ask? If there was a message in all this, he didn't know what it was.
Become a minister or lose her? Get out of
the murder business? That couldn't be right.
Somebody had to stop this monster. Why
did it have to be an either/or?

God, what do you want from me?

He pounded on the steering wheel until
his hand ached. He could see Samuel standing in the yard, watching. Deborah stared.
He didn't care. They could look all they
wanted.

A killer could mess with him, but not the
people he loved. Not and get away with it.

CHAPTER TWENTY-FOUR

The red light was blinking on Ray's answering machine when he laid his holster on the kitchen counter. He considered ignoring it, but the thought that Susana might have left him a message during the time it took him to drive from her house to the ranch made him reach for the button. The thought of what she might say made him jerk back his hand. He was caught: unable to go forward, knowing he couldn't go back.

"Get it together, Johnson."

His voice echoed in the empty house. He laughed, the sound harsh. He needed caffeine before he got cleaned up and went back to the station. He needed to finish what a killer started. He jabbed the button.

"Detective Johnson, it's Melody Doyle."

His hand froze. Her voice was so familiar now, with the valley girl cadence she had affected that made her seem younger than she was. He sat down on the stool at the counter, muscle spasms making his legs quiver.

"I heard them talking. I know what they're doing." She sobbed. A TV blared in the background. Cartoons with a laugh track were out of sync with her panicked voice. "You've got to stop them. Milt's in danger. I tried to talk to him, but he didn't believe me. You've got to stop them. Please. I need to talk to you, face-to-face, about what they're doing at the dealerships. Please call me. Call me."

The message had been left while he was eating dinner with Susana. He'd turned his cell phone off for just that brief hour. If he'd been working, instead of socializing, things might have turned out differently. After playing it twice, he popped the tape from the machine, replacing it with another. He dropped it on the table next to his gear and headed for a shower, replaying Melody's message again and again in his head.

Why was Milton Doyle in danger? What were they doing at the dealerships? What did Joey's death have to do with the dealerships? What was Joey's big scheme? The Doyles' youngest son had bragged to Melody. He'd bragged to Candy. He'd bragged to Vicky. Now two of the three women were dead.

That didn't sound like great odds for Candy Romano.

"Detective, as you can see I'm fine."

Milton Doyle didn't look fine. Ray saw the ravages of grief and alcohol on his puffy face and in his bloodshot eyes. His voice had lost its boom. The amber in his tall glass wasn't tea. He sipped, his hands shaking so badly the ice cubes clinked together. He set it down and sank into the same leather recliner he'd sat in the first day Ray had met him. This time Doyle seemed shriveled, his skinny legs protruding from golf shorts, his wrinkled arms skin and bone. Cynthia Doyle had vehemently protested against letting Deborah and Ray in the house, but Milton had brushed her aside and led them into the living room as if his wife hadn't been screaming at him. As if she hadn't even been there.

"I know this is a difficult time, Mr. Doyle, but I'm following up on a message I received from Melody."

Ray ignored the glacial stare Mrs. Doyle tossed his way. She perched on a leather chair and crossed her arms.

"The voice beyond the grave." Doyle laughed, no mirth in the sound. "You been hitting the sauce, boy?"

"Obviously, she left the message before her death." Ray schooled his irritation from his voice as he eyed Milton's drink. For the first time in years, it looked good to him. He could almost smell it.

"And she says I'm in danger. From whom?"

"She didn't say."

"Tough luck for me." Doyle laughed again and took another slug. At this rate, he'd be drunk as a skunk before they could get a straight answer out of him. Lucky him.

"Are you having any problems with your dealerships, sir?"

Deborah framed the question in the silence left by Ray's wandering thoughts. His partner had already been at the station when he'd arrived. She hadn't brought up the scene at Susana's. Neither had he.

Doyle choked.

Mrs. Doyle tapped long fingernails on the glass table next to her chair, the rhythm grating on Ray's frayed nerves as he waited for her husband to recover. "The dealerships? What do they have to do with it? The dealerships are fine."

Doyle coughed some more.

Ray waited until the man caught his breath. "Melody made it sound like there was a problem. You're not aware of any issues — financial or otherwise?"

"Obviously not." Doyle motioned at the lavishly furnished room. "Does it look like I've got financial problems, Detective? Next month I'm announcing the opening of another dealership in Fort Worth. And a million-dollar endowment at UT Health Science Center. And I'll still have enough left to go out for dinner at San Francisco Steakhouse afterward."

"You haven't received any threats, sir?"

"None."

"No ugly letters or telephone calls of any kind?"

"No."

"No arguments with family members?" Ray thought he saw the tiniest bit of hesitation.

"None."

"We'd appreciate it if anything comes up — anything out of the ordinary whatsoever — if you'd give us a call, sir."

"I've been taking care of myself for more than sixty years, son. And I've got a wife and kids who make sure of it. I don't think I'll need the help of San Antonio's finest." Sarcasm dripped from the last three words.

"Sorry to have bothered you, sir."

Setting down his drink, Doyle stood, weaving a bit. He slapped the back of his chair. "No bother, Detective. Tomorrow while I bury my son, you should go find the man who killed him. Put a murderer away where I can't get to him. Otherwise, you'll be arresting me."

"Look, Martinez, you've had five days. What have you accomplished? Two dead bodies, a suicide by cop, and a drive-by shooting that's probably related." Fiddling with a letter opener, Lieutenant Alvarez leaned back in his swivel chair.

Nothing good could come from a call to come into the boss's office late in the evening. Samuel knew that going in. He was just waiting for the punch line. The memory of the look on Piper's face as she'd rolled over with her back to him danced in front of him — resignation mixed with despair. He hadn't been able to ignore the cell phone ringing on the nightstand.

"You haven't made any progress at all."

"Lieutenant, we're getting close." Samuel tugged at his collar. "Melody Doyle left a message on Detective Johnson's answering machine. We think Joey Doyle knew something about the dealerships that led to his death. Milton Doyle may be in danger. The detectives talked to him this morning. We're going through all their financial records and all her cell phone records."

"Not close enough. The Doyles's lawyer called the mayor at home about an hour ago to let him know they're filing suit tomorrow against the city, the city manager, the chief, you, and Detective Johnson."

"You're kidding." Samuel's fists clenched. The pounding in his head kicked up another notch. This scenario was *deja vu.* "They didn't say a word to the detectives."

"They won't tell the underlings — they want to fling it the face of the big guns." Alvarez's face twisted with bitterness.

Samuel felt a fleeting stab of sympathy. The assistant chief probably reamed Alvarez, and he was just passing it on to Samuel.

"They're claiming criminal negligence. They're seeking ten mil in damages. They're also suing the Ericksons for custody of the grandkids."

Samuel fought back ballooning anger. It wasn't the first time he'd been sued. Only last time, he'd been the shooter. The city had settled, taking away his sense of having done the right thing. "What now?"

"Your team's off the case. I'm assigning it to Treviño and Lindstrom. They'll report directly to me."

"What?" Samuel stood, fury coursing

through him. "You can't — "

"I can. There's no way you can conduct an investigation when you're being sued by the complainants, who might also be suspects. Legal doesn't want you having any further contact with them."

Samuel stared at his boss, trying to find something to say that wouldn't get him fired. "Detectives Johnson and Smith have invested every second of every day for the last five days in this case. They're close, extremely close to cracking it. That's why someone shot at Johnson and my sister with an AK-47 this morning. There's no way he'll back off now. It's personal. The perpetrator has made it that way."

Alvarez stared back. "You keep your guys under control, Martinez, or you could end up without a job."

The effort to keep from throwing himself across the desk and smashing a fist into the man's face made it hard for Samuel to answer. "Maybe that wouldn't be such a bad thing. This job sucks."

"Yeah, but it's the only thing you know how to do, isn't it?"

Once upon a time, Samuel had considered that a good thing. A long time ago. He strode from Alvarez's office without answering. He was trying to figure out how to tell

Ray without getting into a fistfight with his closest friend.

"You should go home, get some sleep."

Ray looked up from Melody Doyle's cell phone records to see Samuel standing in the conference room doorway. Ray was going through the records trying to find a clue, a hint, anything that would give him an inkling who had scared Melody so much.

"You're one to talk. I thought you'd gone home for the night." Ray tried to read his friend's face. It was inscrutable as usual. "I saw Alvarez's car in the lot. Did he call you back in?"

"Where's Smith?" Samuel took two steps into the room and shut the door.

"She went to pick up some sandwiches." A tremor of concern ran through Ray. "What? Are we getting canned?"

Samuel didn't smile. "Worse actually. I wanted you to hear it from me first. Before the media get a hold of it."

"What?" Ray had a sudden desire to be back at his ranch, fishing at the pond.

"The Doyles are filing a wrongful death suit against the department, the city, against you and against me personally. They claim we were criminally negligent in Melody Doyle's death."

"They were the ones who pushed her out on that balcony." Ray stood up, his fists clenched, his heart pounding, trying not to articulate the thought that had been eating at him for the last twenty-four hours. Maybe they were right. Maybe it was his fault. "Who do they think they are?"

"They're the Doyles." Samuel leaned down and propped himself up with both hands on the table, stretching as if his back and shoulders hurt. "That's not all."

"That's not enough?"

"Nope. They're also going to sue the Ericksons for custody of the grandchildren."

"So now they're making two little kids pawns in their ego trip power plays." Ray wanted to take a swing at someone. Unfortunately, the only person in the room was his boss.

"Yep. You'll get phone calls, You'll get accosted on the street by the media. Let it go. You don't want to tangle with these people through sound bites. Keep your mouth shut."

"I know better than that, Samuel."

"It would be tempting to shoot your mouth off. You can't do it. Not on this one."

"How much are they suing us for?"

"Ten million dollars."

Ray nearly swallowed his gum. "Ten million dollars. They're rich. We're middle class working stiffs and they think we have ten million dollars?"

"No, they think the city's got ten million."

"They didn't name Deborah?"

"Nope. Just you and me as your supervisor."

"I always knew you'd be sorry you got promoted over me."

Samuel eased into a chair. He looked as exhausted as Ray felt. "It gets worse. Alvarez is taking us off the case. He's giving it to Treviño and Lindstrom. They'll report directly to him. They've asked for a briefing first thing in the morning."

Ray grasped for words. He'd nearly been gunned down on this case. Susana and Marco could have been killed. He refused to let it go. "No."

"Ray."

"No, I'm not giving it up." He slammed his fist down on the table. Surely, Samuel didn't think this was fair. "It's not happening."

"Yes, you are, and yes, it is." Samuel popped up, his face a few inches from Ray's. "We can't investigate people who are suing us. Legal's already weighed in."

"You agree." Incredulity swept through Ray. "You think it's right?"

Samuel eyes still blazed with anger. "No, I don't think it's right. Alvarez didn't give me a choice. We're off the case."

Ray stood and turned his back on Samuel, forcing himself to put as much space as possible between them. This wasn't Samuel's fault. Officially, they might be off the case. Unofficially, no way. "Are you going to tell Deborah?"

Samuel's gaze dropped to the floor. His response was slow. "You can do it."

"You're her supervisor."

"You're her partner."

"What is going on, Samuel? You've been acting weird about Deborah ever since — " He stopped. Ever since she'd asked Samuel to lunch. "Is something going on? Something with Deborah?"

"What kind of question's that? What're you inferring?" Samuel's voice rose to a near-shout. Ray had never seen him set off so quickly. He stormed from the room before Ray could answer.

What was that all about? They were being sued, they'd lost the case, the woman he loved wouldn't answer the phone, and his best friend was losing his marbles. Yeah, that pretty much summed it up. Ray ripped an arm across the table, sweeping papers and folders, office supplies, and a telephone into the air. The telephone crashed to the floor as papers flew in every direction.

He'd had enough. He sank back into the chair. Everything was falling apart. Every time he called Susana, her machine picked up. Her car wasn't in the driveway when he drove by on the way back from the Doyles. He'd called Lily's, thinking she might be staying there. Lily had been evasive, offered to take a message, volunteered nothing. Samuel had been equally vague about his sister's location and her state of mind. *God, I'm asking you again. Don't I get to be happy?*

"What happened here?" Deborah stood in the doorway, her eyebrows raised. "Just so you know: you make a mess; you clean it up."

"The only mess I want to clean up is the one caused by a murderer." Ray stared at her. "And that's what I plan to do."

CHAPTER
TWENTY-FIVE

"Don't give them anything."

Deborah's voice was low as she grabbed Ray's arm, forcing him to come to a halt outside the conference room. Detectives Oscar Treviño and Mallory Lindstrom were already inside, waiting for their first briefing on the Joey Doyle case. The twelve-hour interval since Ray had told his partner they were off the case obviously had done nothing to dampen Deborah's anger. He didn't blame her. A young mother had lost her life, and a killer had attempted to gun down Susana and Marco. He didn't intend to walk away from this fight either.

"We don't have a lot to give them." Ray shrugged away. Five days of dead ends and teeth-grinding frustration. It might actually feel good to dump the whole thing in their laps and walk away. Only the image of horror on Susana and Marco's faces in the aftermath of the drive-by kept him from acting on the impulse.

Deborah gave him a tight grin and held up a folder. "I was under the impression you were in this for the long haul. I've got a couple things up my sleeve if you're interested. Or if you want to roll over and play dead you can. I'll take it on my own. It's up to you."

"No." Ray ripped the folder from her hand. "What'd you get?"

"The report came back on the wine bottle we found at the scene. The big fat latent fingerprint belonged to none other than Sarah Doyle's boyfriend, Tommy Wheeler."

"And?" Ray peeked in the conference room. Oscar and Mallory were getting antsy.

"The tox report is back on Joey Doyle. He was completely clean, no drugs or alcohol. Kevin and Elaine were full of it when they said he was using — at least the day he died. And the attorneys won't be able to argue that Tommy had a drink with Joey someplace else. Joey wasn't drinking. Tommy had to have been at the scene."

"What about the knife?"

"Wiped clean, of course."

"So why did Kevin and Elaine want to make Joey look bad, like a partier who did drugs and drank to excess?" He stared at Deborah, trying to pull all the loose ends together in one neat package. He was running out of time. What were they hiding at those dealerships that Joey had planned to expose? "Maybe they wanted to get rid of Joey and Daddy in order to take over the dealerships."

"They're going to get the dealerships anyway. With Milton's heart trouble, it's not that far off. And Joey didn't seem to be a threat, really. We need to have another talk with Tommy Wheeler. He was there. I know he was." Deborah's eyes glittered. She was on the trail, and she could smell blood.

"We've got to stay in this — somehow." Ray wasn't giving up now. They were too close.

Deborah tugged the folder from Ray's hand. "We feed them a little. Push them toward Sarah Doyle. Then we go looking for Tommy."

Ray bit his lip. It was tempting. He snagged the folder back. Surprise and disappointment danced across Deborah's face. He spoke before she could. "My first priority is to solve this case. Joey and Melody Doyle deserve that. Their kids deserve that. I'll take all the help I can get. We tell Oscar and Mallory, and let the cards fall where they may. They're decent people. We work this as a team, we'll solve it faster."

Deborah shook her head. "I should have known. No matter what happens — even a guy going after you with an AK-47 — you can't change your stripes. At least I can I count on that."

She gave him the first genuine smile he'd ever seen from her. It made her look younger and less jaded. "Oscar's an okay guy, but he's lazy. He might let us help just to save himself some legwork, if nothing else."

"Let's give it a shot." Ray strove for a friendly face as he led the way into the conference room.

"I know you guys are hot about having to give up this case, but you don't need to keep us waiting forever. Let's get this over with." Oscar looked as if he were trying to appear happy with his new assignment. He failed miserably.

Ray knew the detective well enough to know he was a smart guy who recognized the downside of being handed a hot potato case that had the mayor and chief of police hopping up and down trying to keep the town's biggest philanthropist happy. Mallory Lindstrom always looked as if she'd just lost her best friend. Today her face said she knew exactly what they were getting into and it wasn't good. "So where are you with this? Fill us in."

"We got lots of theories. Very little supporting evidence." Ray dropped into a chair across from Oscar. "I think Milton Doyle is lying through his teeth. Melody Doyle saw or heard something that led her to believe her husband was killed over a business deal involving the dealerships and Milton Doyle was going to be next."

"They sell cars, for crying out loud." Oscar didn't sound convinced.

"A lot of money is involved. A lavish lifestyle is at stake."

"The Country Club and a couple Cadillacs are worth killing two people for?" Oscar stood and strode over to the dry erase board where the murder victims' pictures hung over a timeline Ray had drawn. The detective stared at it, then trudged back to the table. "There's got to be more to it."

"You might start with Sarah Doyle, see what she says about her boyfriend's relationship with her brother." Deborah looked as if it pained her to speak the words. "Tommy Wheeler's the boyfriend's name. I made contact with his ex-wife. He claimed she was his alibi."

"And . . ." Ray gave her a hard stare. She rolled her eyes at him and folded her arms, forcing Ray to continue the story. "And

when Sarah Doyle found out her boyfriend's alibi was his ex-wife, she kicked him out. We're not sure where he is now. We have evidence Tommy was at the park the day Joey died." He shoved the report across the table at Oscar. "Deborah's been kicking around a theory that Tommy might be trying to worm his way into the family business."

"He works at some camera shop, right?" Treviño pawed through the paperwork in front of him, a confused look on his face.

"Yeah, but he hasn't been at work in almost a week." Deborah's obvious reluctance to share seemed lost on Treviño. "Wheeler claims he was with his ex-wife when Joey Doyle was killed. She's been out of town so we've had trouble verifying his alibi. I talked to the ex-wife's neighbor this morning, and it turns out Patty Wheeler left an emergency number with her. The neighbor was kind enough to share it with me, and Mrs. Wheeler just happened to be in her hotel room when I called."

"So, was Wheeler telling the truth about being at her house that day?" Treviño kept his gaze on the tox report as he asked the question. Ray couldn't tell if he was impressed with the information Deborah had dug up. He should be. His partner was a bulldog.

"Well, partly. She says they ate an early lunch at the Alamo Café, her and Wheeler and a couple of pals. Afterward, Wheeler did follow her home and 'take a nap' at her house but she says he left about twelve-thirty."

"So he had time to meet Joey Doyle at the park, take a hike with him, stab him, throw him over a cliff and head to the camera shop." Ray leaned back in his chair and ran his hands through his hair. Deborah had opened a whole new can of worms. He might have to go fishing.

"Plenty of time."

"Time to visit with Sarah and Tommy again." Ray tested the waters.

"Uh, we'll be doing that." Oscar looked apologetic. "It's our case now, remember?"

"We know all the players. You're gonna need us." Deborah gave the detective that dazzling smile Ray had seen her turn on other men. It didn't reach her eyes, but they never seemed to notice. They usually looked as if they'd been hit by a two-ton truck. "As consultants. This case could make or break your careers. Come on, Oscar, you need us."

Oscar exchanged glances with Mallory. Ray could almost see the same silent communication going on between them that he and Samuel had once had as partners. The key word was *once.*

"We'll check out Sarah Doyle. Maybe they kissed and made up. We also get the ex-wife's house. That's the obvious place for him to go if the breakup stuck. You guys have done a lot of work on this and to be honest, I don't mind keeping you in the loop. Alvarez was wrong to fold under pressure and take you off the case. So. Nose around where Wheeler worked, maybe look up some of his friends. Just keep it on the q.t. and stay away from the Doyles. Alvarez finds out, my butt is in a sling."

"Our butts." Lindstrom didn't look happy, but then she never did.

"Thanks." Ray meant it.

"Hey, us frontline guys have to stick together."

Ray and Deborah stood at the same time.

"No problem. We'll let you know if we find out anything." He hoped Trevino and Lindstrom would extend the same courtesy.

As soon as the other two detectives left, Deborah chuckled softly. "Nice dance you did there, partner. I've got an old address for Tommy. Actually, for a roommate of his. That qualifies as looking up an old friend, right? His wife said he bunked with the guy before he hooked up with Sarah. She thinks he'd probably go back there if Sarah kicked him out of the mansion."

Twenty minutes later, they were parked in front of a duplex in a neighborhood about five miles from the University of Texas at San Antonio. The area had seen better days — it was mostly student rental housing that needed fresh paint and a lot of yard work.

"That's Wheeler's Taurus in the driveway." Deborah snapped her gum in glee as she checked the license plate against the file in her hand. "Excellent. Maybe we're about to catch a break here."

Deborah took the lead, knocking on the door while Ray hobbled around the dusty car, leaning on his cane. It didn't look like the vehicle had been moved in a while. The tinted windows hid the interior.

"If you're looking for Tommy, he's not here." Ray turned to study the guy who came through the door and stopped on the concrete stoop. He was skinny, white, mid-twenties, and he kept hitching up a pair of jean shorts to almost cover his red boxers. He wore no shirt, and his eyes had that glassy look that said he'd had a few drinks.

"But this is his car, right? Does he live here?" Deborah held out her badge.

He took his time looking at it, then nodded, his expression wary. "Yeah, I guess. I

322

mean I live here. I'm Chris Sampson. I let him crash after his girlfriend cut him loose. Why you want Tommy?"

"We just want to talk to him." Ray hobbled up the steps to join him. "Any idea where we can find him?"

"He ain't been around in a while. I don't know where he is or when he's coming back." The guy scratched his belly. Ray had the urge to take a step back. Given the guy's lack of hygiene, he could have fleas. "He don't even have any stuff here. I think it's still in the car."

"So why leave the car here?"

"He said I could use it if I let him crash here. As usual, Tommy doesn't have no money. 'Course the car, it don't start. The battery's dead. Not much of a deal for me."

"Tommy talk to you much, tell you what was going on with him?"

Sampson shrugged and sat down on the stoop, his legs sticking out. The bottom of his feet were black with dirt. "Sure, he liked to brag a lot about the rich chick he dated. Said she was kind of a dog to look at, but loaded to the max. He'd get a few drinks in him and start telling me how he was going to come into some money himself, and then he was gonna cut her — "

"Did he say where the money was coming

from?" Ray tried hard to keep his disgust off his face. If Tommy Wheeler was the murderer, Ray would take pleasure in putting the guy away.

"Naw. I don't think so. If he did, I wasn't listening. He talks a lot; I mostly tune him out. His daddy is third cousin to my mom; that's the only reason I let him in. He's family, you know. Kind of."

"So, Tommy's not here, but his car is." Deborah sauntered around the car, her tone casual. "So, it's kind of your car."

"Sort of. I got the keys." Sampson sounded overly satisfied for being in possession of a car that didn't start.

Ray recognized the look on his partner's face. "No, Deborah. Don't even think about it."

"Hey, the car practically belongs to the guy. He can give us permission to search it."

"Uh-huh. We screw this up with an illegal search, and we might never nail the guy who — " Ray stopped. The guy who nearly killed Susana and Marco. The guy who might have destroyed any chance Ray had for a relationship with the woman he loved.

"Can we take a peek?" Deborah ignored Ray and broke out the big-gun smile again. Ray could almost see the guy morph into a puddle at her feet.

"Sure, yeah, like whatever you need, man." Sampson dug the key from the pocket of his filthy shorts. Deborah took it when Ray didn't respond. "Ain't nothing in there but dirty clothes anyway. Y'all want a beer?"

Ray declined the offer before Deborah could answer. She laughed as Sampson disappeared into the house. "Party pooper. I was going to say no. I don't drink on the job — much."

"I'm glad you find that so funny." Ray crossed his arms, an uneasy feeling in his gut as Deborah unlocked the Taurus.

Turned out Sampson knew what he was talking about. They didn't have to touch anything, because there was nothing to touch. No bloody clothes. No weapons. Just a pile of stinking takeout boxes from a Chinese restaurant, a mound of stale cigarette butts, and a disgusting amount of dirty clothes that reeked of mold and body odor.

Ray wiped sweat from his face, stepped away from the car, and watched Deborah slam the door in disgust. "So what now?"

"Maybe Oscar and Mallory had better luck with Sarah." Deborah dusted her hands on her slacks and pulled cigarettes from her pocket. "Or the ex-wife's place. I guess we go back to the station, hunt them down."

"Yeah." Ray leaned against the Crown Vic, contemplating. Samuel probably wondered where they were. He'd probably already assigned them another case. The reprieve wouldn't last much longer. "We need to get back anyway. Samuel will get suspicious."

"Naw. He's probably too busy looking for someone to blame for his supreme unhappiness."

"What do you know . . ." An annoying kernel of truth presented itself in Deborah's cavalier assessment of his friend's state of mind. "Give the guy a break. He's under a lot of pressure."

Deborah flicked her cigarette butt onto the street and opened her door. "Not anymore."

CHAPTER
TWENTY-SIX

Ray didn't try to make conversation on the thirty-minute drive back to the station. Deborah seemed lost in thought, and he was trying to figure out how to approach Susana to see if she still planned to go to Assistant Chief Guerrero's retirement banquet with him. If she didn't answer the phone, and no one would tell him where she was, he didn't see much hope for that second date. Deborah rushed ahead of him into the building and disappeared. If she followed her usual MO, she'd reappear at her desk in ten or fifteen minutes. He didn't ask and she didn't tell.

He plopped down in his chair. A second later his phone rang, jangling already-stretched nerves.

"Ray, I can't go to the retirement banquet with you Friday night."

The split second of relief Ray had felt hearing Susana's voice disappeared as the message registered. No need to wonder any longer. She was bailing — and not just for the banquet. An already-knotted gut tightened. He tried to concentrate on convincing Susana not to throw away the fledgling start they'd made.

"Can I ask why not?" He kept his voice soft, trying to rekindle the connection between them.

"I can't. I'm sorry — I'll pay you for my ticket — " Her voice faltered. "Marco's already lost one parent."

"Susana, I don't want your money. Don't do this. Please." He struggled for words that would convince her. "I'll do everything in my power to keep you safe."

"You wouldn't have to do that if you weren't a cop."

"This is what I do." Anger blew through him. She didn't play fair.

"Exactly."

"Well, if you don't think I'm worth it — that we're worth it, I guess that's that." A glance from Deborah as she slid into the seat at her desk across from his said his voice had risen. The room had quieted. He reached for a calmer tone. "I thought we were past this."

"It might be worth it, if it were just me, but it's not. Get on with your life, Ray."

She sounded so sure. The sick feeling in his stomach boiled into sudden, overwhelming anger at her, at the situation, at everything. "I never took you for a coward."

"A coward? After everything I've been through. You're just thinking of you. Think about Marco. About everything he's been through."

"I am. He needs a dad."

"His dad is dead."

"And I can never be the great Javier. I know that. I'm not trying to be him. I just — "

"Don't ever talk about Javier — you don't know anything about him." Her fury clawed at him through the line.

"I know that. But I don't want to marry Javier." He stood, yelling into the phone. "I want to marry you."

Deborah stared at a stack of papers in front of her. All sound in the room ceased.

"I can't go to the banquet." Susana's voice was small now, full of unshed tears. "Ask Teresa Saenz. She's a cop. She likes you. She's perfect for you. Have a good life, Ray."

Ray listened to the dial tone. "Fine, I will. No problem."

He glanced at Deborah who stared back, the expression on her face unfathomable. "Don't you have work to do?"

Everyone started moving again. Conversations resumed. Fine, he would get on with his life. He sank into his chair and tossed around papers until he found Teresa's cell phone number. With a finger shaking with anger, he stabbed the buttons before he could talk himself out of it.

"Officer Saenz."

"Teresa, it's Ray. I know it's short notice, but I happen to have an extra ticket to Jaime Guerrero's retirement banquet tomorrow night. Would you be interested in going with me?"

A pause stretched.

"Teresa?"

"Look, Ray, I'm really sorry, but I already have a date for tomorrow night. When you were busy with Susana at the reception, Greg Miller asked me for my number. I gave it to him. I'm really sorry."

Lightheaded with embarrassment, Ray covered his eyes with one hand, shutting out the light. "Don't apologize. You have every right to accept an invitation from someone else."

"I wouldn't have said yes to you anyway. You're in love with another woman. Despite what I said the other night, I'd be crazy to risk that kind of heartache."

"Right. You're right. I wasn't thinking."

"Not about me, you weren't." Her tone was kind. "I hope you work it out with her. You deserve to be happy."

"Doesn't everyone?"

"Good-bye, Ray."

He dropped the phone, shoved back his chair, and got up. He needed some air. "Cover for me. I'll be back."

Deborah nodded, a hint of sympathy on her face.

Twenty minutes of limping around downtown, sweating, did nothing to improve his mood. He stomped across the lobby, headed for the CID.

"Detective! Johnson! Hey!"

Ray looked up. Janet Hutchens, a notebook in one hand and a huge iced tea mug in the other, hustled toward him. She wore a neon green dress and pink flip-flops. He never knew whether to trust Janet, as a journalist or otherwise. She approached her job the same way he did his — with ferocious dedication. Too often that put them on a collision course.

"What do you want?" He glanced at his watch, ignoring her smile.

"After all we've been through together, you could be a little nicer to me, ya know. I'm not so bad."

The sincerity in her voice made him

cringe. She obviously didn't know he wasn't on the Doyle case anymore. "All media requests go to the PIO. You know that."

"This is me, Ray. We have a history. Come on. I finagled a copy of the supplemental on a drive-by shooting less than twelve hours after Melody Doyle was picked off by a SWAT sharpshooter. A guy in a BMW tried to gun you down in front of Susana Martinez-Acosta's house. Why so hush-hush on this? Is it because Susana Acosta is Samuel Martinez's sister?"

She looked like a hound dog that'd picked up a scent.

"Leave her out of this, do you understand?" Ray leaned into her space, his rage boiling over. "Leave her out of this. If I see her name in print, I swear to you, I will hunt you down and run you out of this town."

"Are you threatening me?" Hutchens planted her feet, her chin up. A couple of people in the lobby stopped and stared.

A uniformed cop he didn't recognize eased their direction. "We got a problem here?"

Ray flashed his badge. "No. No problem, bro. This lady was just leaving."

The cop drifted back across the lobby, but Hutchins didn't budge. "You can't intimidate me with threats."

"You can take it however you want, Hutchens. Back off."

"You're losing it." Hutchens's tone was soft, but she was relentless. She reached out and put one hand on his arm. Her long fingernails matched the color of her dress. "It's no wonder. You're under a lot of pressure. My colleague at the courthouse picked up a copy of the Doyles' criminal negligence suit. How do you feel about them suing you, knowing they hold you responsible for their daughter-in-law's death?"

"That's a stupid question. How do you think I feel?" Ray jerked away from her. "The Doyles drove her out on that balcony—"

"Detective Johnson." Ray swiveled. The door to the CID stood open. The stony look on Samuel's face was clear evidence he'd heard the exchange. "I'd like to see you in my office. Now. Hutchens, you want comment, call the PIO. I'd appreciate it if you went through channels on this one."

Hutchens glanced from Samuel to Ray and back, her lips pursed. "Sure, Sarge. I'll get back to you on this." She gave Ray a small wave and strolled away, leaving him to face Samuel.

Samuel waited until Ray stepped into the office to speak. "Are you crazy? Didn't I just tell you not to talk to the media? Do you want to be unemployed?"

Ray's gaze collided with Samuel's. All he could see was supervisor, not friend. "No, sir."

"Then get it together."

CHAPTER TWENTY-SEVEN

"Just a couple of hours. For me." Piper's voice on the phone had taken on a wheedling tone that made her sound more like her nine-year-old daughter than a mother of three. "You already paid for the ticket. Joaquin and Lily are sitting at our table."

Ray resisted the temptation to give into his best friend's wife. He shifted the phone from one ear to the other as he ducked under the crime scene tape and walked away from the evidence investigators working a murder scene. Witnesses said a guy had stabbed his drinking buddy to death in a fight over a six-pack and a dime baggie. Some cops would call it a misdemeanor murder, as if people who fought over stupid things got what they deserved. Ray could never take that attitude, but today he did feel as if he were drowning in human waste.

Samuel had assigned him — and Deborah *in absentia* since she had called in sick —

the new case with a minimum of eye contact, dismissing Ray from his office as if he were a stranger. Maybe Samuel thought if he kept them busy, it would keep them out of the Doyle case. Fat chance.

Piper's words finally registered. "Joaquin and Lily are coming?"

"Yes. Susana is babysitting. She's been staying with them, you know."

Piper had been attempting to convince him to come stag to the retirement banquet since the previous day. Knowing Piper, she was not only meddling in his relationship with Susana, but also his friendship with Samuel. If Samuel were as tense at home as he was at the station, she had to know something was up.

"Come on, Ray, it'll be fun . . . and informative."

"I don't know. I've got a new case and, to be honest, I'm not up for company right now." Even as he said the words, Ray wavered. She was dangling a carrot stick in his face. Lily would be an excellent source of information on her sister's state of mind. At least, he knew for sure where Susana had been staying. Now that Janet Hutchens's story had been in the newspaper, she'd probably have to stay tucked away there even longer. Ray had made the situation worse by opening his big mouth. "Well, maybe, just for dinner."

"Excellent. See you there." Piper sounded jubilant. The woman loved using her powers of persuasion.

Two hours later, Ray squared his shoulders and limped into La Villita Assembly Hall. He'd left the cane at home, determined to walk freely. The place was already crowded with off-duty law enforcement officers, their spouses, and their guests. Assistant Chief Jaime Guerrero was popular with the brass and the rank and file. Everyone had shown up to help him celebrate a long and decorated career.

A jazz trio warmed up with elevator music as Ray waded through the crowd. Several colleagues greeted him, forcing him to stop and chat. It took several minutes to finally arrive at the table. Relieved, he dropped into a chair across from Samuel and Piper.

Samuel's glance slid over Ray and away, his expression oblique. "Did you try calling Susana?"

"No. You're the one who told me to stay away from her." He couldn't keep the bitterness from his voice. When it came to Susana, Samuel's messages were always mixed. Ray knew his friend was caught between wanting his sister to be happy and wanting her to be safe. "Did Alvarez say anything to you about Hutchens's article?"

"Yeah, he reamed me and threatened to fire you. I told him Hutchens ambushed you, and the quotes were taken out of context."

Samuel had come precariously close to lying for him. "I don't expect you to protect me, Samuel, if it means trouble for you."

Samuel's shrug was eloquent, his expression fierce. "Just keep your mouth shut from now on. You realize, don't you, that the article in the paper fueled the TV coverage? Alvarez got three or four calls from TV stations wanting to know if we have a serial killer who drives a silver BMW roaming the streets looking for victims he can dump in city parks."

"That's a ridiculous exaggeration to — " Before he could finish Piper broke in.

"No. No shoptalk. Tonight, we'll eat and chat and act civilized. No murder talk." She gave them both her severe schoolteacher look. "Understood?"

"Understood." Ray replied, in unison with Samuel. It would be a relief not to talk about work. Samuel couldn't know that he was still working the Doyle case to the detriment of the drinking buddy murder.

"There's Joaquin and Lily." Piper waved.

Ray turned. Lily would stand out in any crowd. Almost six feet tall, voluptuous, with dark, straight, shoulder-length hair. Striking, yet completely different from Susana.

Until she started talking. "Ray, nice to see you again." She sank into the chair Joaquin had pulled out. "I guess we should've brought our Kevlar." Pure Susana.

"Oh, man, here we go. Give the dude a break." Joaquin shook hands with Ray, an apologetic look on his craggy, scarred face. The SAPD gang unit detective wasn't much taller than his wife, but he still had the body of the professional boxer. Ray had played some basketball with him. Running into Joaquin was like slamming head-on into a bulldozer. "I tried to tame her in the van coming over here, but you know how the Martinez women are."

He did, indeed. "It's okay. She can't say anything to me I haven't already told myself."

Lily's gaze held his for a long second. "Sorry." She didn't sound sorry.

"No need. I'm here because your sister-in-law wouldn't leave me alone."

"Ah, the Piper factor."

They all laughed as Piper dipped her head in mock acknowledgement of their awe at her ability to persuade.

Ray took a swig of iced tea, glad the focus had shifted away from him. Joaquin launched into a story about the kids' latest antics, giving Ray a chance to pose a question to Lily. "How's she doing?"

"So you came here to pump me about my sister?" Lily's brows lifted over beautiful, brown eyes that reminded him of Susana's.

He struggled for a second. "Well, yeah."

She shrugged. "She's my sister. I'm not going to be much help to you."

"Come on, Lily. I just want to know if she's all right." He took another drink, trying to rinse the sour taste from his mouth as he remembered the sound of gunfire, the squeal of tires, and the shatter of glass.

"Do you have any idea what it's like to be talking to your eight-year-old nephew and hear gunfire, hear the phone smash to the ground, hear him screaming?" The skin stretched tight around Lily's mouth.

"I don't have to imagine. I was there."

"But they're not your family."

"No need to rub it in."

Lily's expression softened. "She probably would have gone home today, if it weren't for that article in the paper." Her tone was only a slightly accusing. "Autumn came over from the hotline. They talked through some things. Sis's calmer."

"What about Marco?"

"He doesn't want her to leave the house. They've gone back to two sessions a week with his therapist."

All his fault, Ray squirmed with guilt.

"How bad do you want to work things out with her?" Something in Lily's voice made him look up again.

"More than you can imagine."

She smiled, her face so much like her older sister's. "Whatever it takes?"

"Whatever it takes."

"You know where we live." She turned to Piper. Seconds later, the two women were deep into a discussion of some book they were both reading.

"How's the case coming?" Joaquin slid into the chair next to Ray. "Anything new?"

Ray glanced at Piper. She was chatting with Lily, her face animated. Samuel was busy shredding a dinner roll in his plate, his look preoccupied.

"Didn't you hear? They dumped us. Lindstrom and Treviño caught the case. Alvarez even short-circuited Samuel. They'll report directly to the lieutenant."

"I've been out in the field for days dealing with a couple gangs trying to exterminate each other." Joaquin shook his head. "That's cold, man. It's just wrong."

Ray leaned in a little, keeping his voice down. "We're working with Treviño under the radar. He can't find Tommy Wheeler, our primary suspect. We've been through every scrap of paper — "

"Well, isn't this a surprise!"

Deborah. Ray hadn't even noticed her approach. She looked like a Hollywood celebrity in a tight, white, flashy dress that was short at the bottom and plunged at the top. A young traffic cop whom Ray had seen around the station trailed behind her looking bewildered.

"What a nice family you have here, Sergeant." The last word had a slight slur.

"I thought you were sick." Samuel beat Ray to the punch, his voice flat.

"Oh, I was feeling better, and I didn't want to waste the ticket." Her tone was blithe as her gaze shifted back to Ray. "It's a nice to see you rebounding so quickly, partner. Couldn't have one sister, so you're coming on to the other. Detective Santos must love that."

Joaquin make a sound like a hiss and leaned forward as if to stand.

Ray grabbed his arm. "Easy. Deborah, maybe you should have your date take you home so you can sober up."

"What? You afraid I'm going to call you

again, make you chauffer me around?" Deborah's voice was full of spite. "Don't worry, if I want you to tuck me in again I'll call you. I've got your number, Ray." She turned and teetered away on three-inch stiletto heels that could pass for lethal weapons.

Her date stood there, his mouth gaping, as she brushed passed him. After a second, he muttered, "Nice meeting you all," and trotted after her.

"What was that all about?" Piper asked, staring after Deborah.

"I have no idea." Samuel's gaze focused on his plate again.

"I could hazard a guess." Lily switched chairs, so she was sitting next to her husband. Joaquin took her hand, their fingers entwining.

Ray's chest ached with a pressure that built steadily. "You know, I don't care what it was about." He stood up. "If you'll excuse me, I think I'll call it a night."

"Ray, you haven't eaten. Don't go." Piper shook her head, her tone beseeching. "Don't let her spoil the evening."

"Let him go." Lily reached out and gave Ray's hand a quick squeeze. "I'm praying for you two."

Ray headed for the door. He'd done his praying.

Now it was time for confrontation.

Samuel shoved the baked chicken around on his plate with his fork. His appetite had withered.

"What was that all about with Detective Smith?" Piper asked. She pushed her plate away and sat back.

They were alone. Joaquin had dragged Lily off to say hello to Alex Luna and his date. Samuel dropped his fork and picked up a packet of artificial sweetener for his iced tea, trying to look as if it took all his concentration.

"Cough it up, Sarge." She stomped on his toes with her heel.

"Ouch! What did you do that for?" He dropped the packet and glared.

"What's the deal between Ray and Detective Smith? I thought he had gotten used to having her as a partner."

"They're fine. Just mad at me because they think I didn't fight hard enough for the Doyle case." Trying to avoid eye contact, he went back to doctoring his tea.

"Detective Smith was drunk, not sick." Piper sounded peeved now. "And Ray is not fine with her. Or anybody. He looks terrible."

"Whatever problems they have, they need

344

to work them out."

Samuel folded and refolded his napkin, picturing the look on Deborah's face. It reminded him of his face in the mirror during the days after he'd shot and killed the gang banger kid by mistake. What was supposed to be a simple warrant serving would haunt him for the rest of his life. Something haunted Deborah. He couldn't figure out why he felt the need to banish those ghosts for her. Or why the sight of her in that tight white dress made his heart careen out of kilter.

"Samuel. Samuel! Pay attention." Piper's heel miraculously missed his toes this time. "Has Ray tried talking to her?"

"Yes, he's tried talking to her, but she just makes fun of him, calls him Bible Boy and Jesus freak." He recognized that kind of fear.

"That's just her fear talking, Samuel, you should know that." The irritation in Piper's voice kicked up a notch. "Have you tried talking to her?"

"No." And he couldn't risk it either. Somebody else would have to do it. Like Ray. "She's Ray's partner. He'll handle it."

"Well, that's a real Christian attitude. I've never known you to not take care of your people, Samuel." She looked disappointed in him. He'd have to live with it. "I'm going to go to the restroom. Would you ask the waiter if we can have some decaf, please. When I get back we'll start working on our strategy to help Detective Smith."

"We?"

She'd already turned her back. He watched her walk across the room. A half-pint pit bull. She had no idea she might be the one who got chewed up and spit out.

Deborah followed two detectives from narcotics into the restroom. Her hopes for a couple minutes alone were dashed by their boisterous exchange as one leaned against the counter while the other dug in her purse and produced a tube of lipstick.

"Hey, Smith." Gardner, the one in the form-fitting green sequined dress that made her look like a mermaid, spoke first. Deborah's last name came out in a long slur. "I guess losing the Doyle case and all, you're looking for some comfort tonight. Too bad your lover boy brought his wife. I will say this for you, you got guts, girl."

"What are you talking about?" Deborah tossed the contents around in her purse until she found her cigarettes. Took her time lighting one. They hadn't really lost the Doyle case. Treviño and that sourpuss Lindstrom would never solve it without her —

and Johnson, of course. She didn't care who got the credit, as long as the creep who tried to gun down her partner and his girlfriend was off the street.

Carmen de la Fuente, who looked like a penguin in her too tight female version of a tuxedo, gave Deborah a disgusted look as she pointed to the no-smoking sign. She went back to reapplying her lipstick. "We couldn't believe you went right up to Martinez's table with his wife sitting there. She must be totally clueless."

"Like I said, what are you talking about?" Deborah took a long drag and blew smoke their direction.

She'd met Sarge's wife at an SA Police Association picnic. She seemed nice enough. Deborah leaned against the wall, trying to find her equilibrium. She shouldn't have had that last martini — or the one before it. She closed her eyes. Saw little Samantha Doyle's tearstained face, her pink nightgown, felt the girl's sweet breath on her face as she used her body to shield her from the sight of her mother lying dead in a pool of her own blood. Deborah jerked her eyes open.

"Everybody knows you hopped into the sack with Martinez. How else did you get promoted to detective so fast? How was he?

He's so uptight; he's gotta let off steam somehow."

"Shut your trap." Samantha's image fled as Deborah fought the desire to slap the smirk from the other woman's face. "You've been dealing in trash so long, you wouldn't know a decent man if you saw him."

"Oh, sounds like you actually like the guy." De La Fuente did a pirouette to face Deborah. The vice detective perched a hip on the counter and giggled. "You did do the dirty with that gorgeous hunk of rock out there. Wow. A little afternoon delight so the wife wouldn't find out?"

Gardner snickered as she powdered her nose. "Here's my take. I figure since you already got the promotion, you've moved on. Johnson looks like he comes from decent stock. Surely you've convinced him by now to drop the Christian act. Come on, tell us all the juicy details."

"None of your business." She shoved between the two women and dropped her cigarette in the sink.

Let them think what they wanted. Even if she told them the truth, they wouldn't believe her. She wasn't interested in a physical relationship with any man — let alone a married one.

A toilet flushed. A stall door opened. Piper

Martinez stepped out.

"Mrs. Martinez." Deborah felt her face go hot even as the rest of her body froze in a paralysis of guilt and shame under the scrutiny of those piercing blue eyes. For what? She hadn't done anything. De La Fuente and Gardner eased away from the counter, smirks on their faces as if they expected some kind of show.

Martinez's wife stepped between them and turned the water on. Pinched, red spots glowed on both cheeks, but she didn't say a word. She took her time washing her hands, drying them, and dropping the paper towel in the trash.

Deborah wanted the woman to scream, yell, or slap someone. Anything. Yet, she persisted in saying nothing. As if the three women deserved none of her energy. Only her contempt. She simply shoved open the door and disappeared without looking back.

Deborah stared in the mirror, a wave of revulsion flooding her. She needed a drink. Shoving past the other two women, she careened out of the bathroom, but she couldn't move fast enough.

Not nearly fast enough to shake the horrendous feeling she'd just participated in destroying something sacred. Something

that couldn't be retrieved. Something she
would never deserve to have.

CHAPTER
TWENTY-EIGHT

Finally. Samuel spotted Piper trudging across the ballroom floor after a good ten minutes in the restroom. What could possibly take that long? He was tired — of the retirement banquet and his job. He wanted to take his wife home, take a shower, and sleep for a month. But the social butterfly in Piper loved these parties.

He stood and pulled her chair out so she could sit down. "I was contemplating coming in there to fish you out."

She didn't smile at his small joke. She grabbed a glass of water and gulped it down. Her face was flushed.

"Piper, what's the matter? Are you all right?" He leaned over and touched her forehead with the back of his hand. "Is that flu bug back?"

"It's just a headache. Really. I'll take some aspirin, and it'll be fine." She fumbled in her purse without looking at him.

"*Mi amor,* let's go home. You look feverish again, and I'm tired." He let his gaze roam across the room in search of Joaquin and Lily. They were nowhere in sight. "I'll call Joaquin and tell him we're leaving."

He leaned down to pull out her chair again. Stopped. Let one finger touch a tear that trailed down the side of her face. "You're crying?"

She didn't respond, just stared up at him with a hurt expression on her face. Like he'd hurt her.

"Come on." He hustled her from the ballroom and through the walkway to the parking lot. After she slid into the truck, he made a quick call to Joaquin and then climbed in beside her, still trying to figure out what could have happened to upset her so much.

"What's going on?" He glanced at her and then back at the road as he headed for the highway.

"I'm sorry." She gave a small sob, pawed through her purse again, and pulled out a tissue. "I can't tell you right now."

"Piper, tell me." Someone had hurt her. He would do something about it.

"Not in the truck." Her voice steadied. "I want to be able to look you in the eye."

Look him in the eye. She thought he'd done

352

something, she wanted to ask him about it, and she was afraid of the answer. "Someone was talking. Someone said something about me. You overheard."

"Samuel, please." Piper's hand went to the door handle. "Please slow down. It'll wait until we get home. I'd like to get there in one piece."

He forced himself to ease up on the accelerator. The needle on the speedometer slowly inched back down. "Fine, we'll wait until we get to the house, but then we'll talk."

The house was dark when they pulled up. The girls were spending the night at his mother's. Nathaniel should still be at work. Samuel was thankful. He didn't want to have this conversation in front of his kids. He unlocked the door, swerved through a welcoming committee of cats and a dog waiting in the foyer, and led the way to the kitchen. He flipped on lights as he went.

"You never got your coffee," he said, suddenly unsure how to begin. "I'll make some. Do you want to change, or do you want to tell me what's going on first?"

"Samuel, I . . ." She stopped. A tear slid down her cheek. She eased into a chair at the kitchen table, bent down, and scooped up Sable.

Samuel could hear the cat's purr across the room. He turned and grabbed a bag of Costa Rican blend from the counter. Inhaled and exhaled. He turned back around. "Tell me."

"I was in the bathroom. Some women came in; they didn't know I was there. They talked . . ." She stroked Sable's head, then let him slide from her lap as she looked up at Samuel. "Then I heard Detective Smith. They asked her about you. And Ray. I should have come out right away, but it all happened so fast, and I was just sort of frozen there behind the stall door." Her voice trailed away.

Samuel heard a sound like a growl. Then he realized it had come from him.

Piper stared at him. "They said they couldn't believe Deborah had gone up to our table. That it was really brazen since everyone knew you and she were . . . that Deborah got the promotion because . . . you know . . . you . . . it was payment . . . She didn't deny it."

He slammed the bag on the counter so hard it broke, sending ground coffee cascading down the side of the cabinet.

"Idiotas." His fist crashed down, and then he swept the entire mess onto the floor, taking a set of canisters with it. The sound of

breaking ceramic reverberated. Rambo barked. Samuel turned to see the dog standing in front of his wife, on alert. Piper's face was white, still. *"Lo siento, mi amor."*

"You're sorry?" Piper patted Rambo's massive shoulder and the dog eased back on his haunches. Piper's gaze never left Samuel's face. "Why? Because they were right. Or because I heard their moronic, totally false gossip? I need to know which it is."

He took a step toward her. "Don't you trust me?"

"Yes, but they said I was clueless. They said things like 'afternoon delight' and 'hot' and things that made me feel sick."

"It's just talk, Piper." Samuel stepped over Rambo and pulled his wife into his arms in a tight hug. "The kind of talk that goes around when people spend a lot of time working together in a business that deals in the dregs of humanity day after day."

"You knew about this." She jerked away, her face wet with tears. "You knew what was being said about Detective Smith and her promotion and you didn't tell me? You didn't do anything?"

Samuel grabbed her hands and tried to bring her back. "Yes, I knew. Deborah asked me to lunch one day, and Ray happened to overhear. He had heard people saying things . . . things like you heard. What do you think I should have done? Fired her because people talk?"

She tugged her hands free. "She really is after you?"

"No, it was just a misunderstanding."

The look in Piper's eyes reminded Samuel of why her students and her children never messed with her. "She asked you to lunch . . . I'm thinking she asked you the day you came home and made soup for me. Am I right?"

"Let it go."

"Right? Why don't you want to talk about it? Do you have something on your conscience?"

Samuel backed away. He went to the pantry, grabbed the broom, and started sweeping up the mess. After a few seconds, her hand clamped down on his. "Look at me."

Reluctantly, he pulled his gaze from the floor.

"I thought we had stopped hiding things from each other." Her hand tightened. "I'm not going through this again. Talk now, or leave and don't come back."

"You're making mountains out of mole-hills." This wasn't like before, when he'd killed the kid, a mistake that had sent him hurtling into a pit of depression that had taken years to escape. She wanted to know everything that went on in his head? Fine. Samuel forced himself to look into the face of the woman he loved more than life itself and tell the truth. "It's not lust exactly, but I do feel something for her."

"What? What do you feel for her?"

"She has a hurt." He stumbled over the words, unable to verbalize the connection that not even he understood. "I recognize it."

Piper swallowed. He saw the moment she comprehended. Apprehension flooded her face, burying the anger. She nodded. "And?"

He wanted to stop. "Something about it. I want to fix it. It's so strong, it's almost . . . physical."

She dropped her hand and took a step back. "Did you try?"

"No, but I wanted to." He waited, meeting her gaze.

"Do me a favor?" Her tone was soft, no accusation, no anger.

He nodded, fear mixing with sick relief in a vicious swirl. It was out there now, they could move on, get past it.

"Let Ray take care of her."

"I plan to."

She turned away, the next words almost a whisper. "I'd appreciate it if you'd leave."

The words were slow to register. And then they hit him full force. "What do you mean?" He lunged forward and dragged her back. "Leave?"

"Let go of me. I don't want you touching me." She shrugged away from him, even as he let his hand drop, stunned. For twenty years she'd welcomed his touch. Now, in the passage of a split second, she shunned it. "I told you I wanted to know what was going on. It's not fair to punish you for telling me the truth. I know that."

"But?" He waited, barely breathing, as his life shattered around him.

"The idea that you would feel that way about another woman — you can't imagine how it hurts me. It's absolutely the last thing I expected from you."

"Nothing happened. *Nada.*" He fought fury — at himself for opening up to Piper, and at her, for refusing to understand. "I came home and made *caldo* for you instead."

"The point is you really wanted to be somewhere else, and it wasn't soup you wanted to be making. You feel horribly guilty. I can see it in your eyes and hear it your voice. You wanted her. You still want her."

"Not as much as I want you."

"I'm every bit as human as you are, unfortunately. Go away. God is going to expect me to forgive you. I don't want to. I put up with so much from you, Samuel: your emotional distance, your silence, your disappearing acts, the way you choose work over family, time and time again. I shouldn't be expected to put up with this, too. I won't."

"I'm off the Doyle case now; it's going to be better. I'll be home more." No he wouldn't.

"Our married life has been a series of Doyle cases. How many of them do you think there've been — fifty, a hundred, three hundred, a thousand?" Tears made tracks down her face, but Piper's voice was hard and bitter. He'd never heard that tone from her before. "All those people who are dead get more of your time than the living whom you claim to love."

It was as if a dam had broken and the waters of resentment rushed over Samuel. "Is that why you gravitate toward Detective Smith? She closes her eyes and sees the same thing you do — blood and brain matter spattered on walls? I can't compete with that. I'm a seventh grade reading teacher. No sick adrenaline rush in that, is there?"

"That's not true. *Te amo,* Piper, I love you because you don't live in that world."

"But you do." She scrubbed at her face with the back of her sleeve.

"No, I live here with you and the kids."

"What's Jana's boyfriend's name?"

"She's thirteen. She better not — " He stopped as triumph sparked and died in Piper's face.

"Jana turned fourteen two weeks ago. You know the names of the Doyle children, don't you? The name of the guy who was dating Sarah Doyle. Well, your daughter wants your permission to go to the movies with a boy named Michael Cruz. You haven't been home long enough for her to ask you."

Anger blew through him, mixed with a despair that was physical. "I get home when I can. I'm home now. This is my house. They're my kids. I won't let you take that away."

"Our house. Our kids. I won't stay here with you. Do you want me to uproot them? If I leave, they go with me. If you go, they'll hardly notice." The searing honesty in her words was worse than any blows he'd ever experienced. "They won't notice if you're

360

not here for a while."

She turned and disappeared through the doorway.

"But not forever." Samuel knew she couldn't hear him anymore, and he wasn't sure if it was a statement or a question.

Swallowing emotion that shamed him as much as the conversation had, he stumbled up the stairs and dug his overnight bag from the linen closet. Then he sat on the edge of the couch in the family room, his hands clutched in Rambo's fur until the light went out in their bedroom. He slipped into the master bathroom and quietly dumped his toiletries in the bag.

Leaving the door cracked so the light illuminated the bedroom, he grabbed a few things from the drawers and the closet. He could see the outline of her form huddled under the sheet, her head turned away. Her breathing was ragged. He wanted to touch her, to try to make it up to her, but she had sent him away.

When Samuel stood at the truck, his keys in his hand, he finally allowed himself to face the question. Go where? Lily's house was only half a block away. No. The girls were at his mother's house. He couldn't go there. He didn't want to answer questions tonight, tomorrow would be soon enough.

Half an hour later he sat on a double bed in the Holiday Inn Express in a silent room, the sense of unreality so staggering he considered inflicting pain on himself in order to see if he were dreaming.

He didn't bother to undress. He lay down on the bed and stared at the ceiling, the TV remote clutched in one hand. The figures that danced across the muted screen had nothing to do with the movie that played in his head. Piper's face the first time he met her. He'd made a great impression by giving her a speeding ticket. Piper on their wedding day. Then the night their newborn son had died. And the days when Nathaniel, Jana, and Emma were born. And on and on. One milestone after another knitting two people together into a lifetime of shared joy and pain.

God, what just happened?

He'd done what Piper had asked him to do. He'd let her in. And the response had been exactly as he'd feared. She had loathed what she found inside him so much she might never forgive him. He had to face that bleak fact. God would forgive him, but could he live with himself if Piper didn't?

The bald truth stared him in the face. No, he couldn't.

CHAPTER
TWENTY-NINE

Lalo Hernandez whistled tunelessly as he waited, ensconced in the dark in his BMW, listening to *cumbias* on the radio. The parking lot of the movie theater was packed. Saturday night, and nothing else to do in San Antonio. He'd parked two slots down from her car. The pretty receptionist had met a pack of girls in front of the theater, tittering and ogling the guys like teenagers. She was pretty, but she was a little girl. Not a woman like his Sylvia.

He glanced at his watch. Any time now. Any time. The boss had decided that Candy Romano was another loose end. The news stories about a serial killer roaming the streets in a BMW looking for victims to dump in city parks had not been as amusing to *el señor* as they had been to Lalo. Bad publicity meant the cops turned up the heat. The boss didn't like the added attention to his business.

The cops had talked to Candy twice. There wouldn't be a third time. Lalo didn't care why the boss wanted her gone. It really didn't matter. It gave Lalo something to do. He had followed her around, waiting for the perfect moment. Otherwise, boredom would have consumed him.

There she was. She weaved her way through the crowd pouring from the theater. She laughed and waved good-bye to her *co-madres.* Lalo slid the car into gear. She pulled from her parking spot. He waited a minute or two longer, just another minute, then pulled out behind her, keeping a careful distance from the green Neon. Green little car. Looked like an insect.

She got on the highway, he followed. She drove like a woman. Speed up, slow down. Talk on her cell. Check her makeup in the mirror. Come on, *chica.* Get on with it. The drive was quick. He knew now where she was going. Her family lived in a townhouse in a megaplex of townhouses and apartments. Lady luck was with him. The slots in front of her place were empty. The parking lot deserted. He whistled some more as he gently eased the BMW into the slot on the other side of the lot, up against the townhouses that faced hers. He waited, staring at the rearview mirror. She was smiling as she stepped from the car. Must have been a silly movie. Maybe she saw a comedy.

He slipped from the BMW, careful to shut the door without making a sound. He padded across the asphalt, waiting until he was a few feet from her to speak. "Candy. Candy, wait."

She froze. Not turning to face him. "Who's there?"

"Candy. *Dulce.* You have a very pretty name, *chica.* Very pretty."

Slowly, she turned. "Who are you?"

He took a step closer. "Mr. Doyle sent me to pick you up."

"Mr. Doyle?" She stared, her look puzzled. "Kevin Doyle? You work for Mr. Kevin Doyle."

"Something like that."

"I see. What does Mr. Doyle want with me on a Saturday night?" She took a half step back, her hand in her purse.

Lalo took two steps forward. "I believe he wants to discuss your work schedule. He's called a staff meeting to discuss some changes. There may be a promotion in it for you. If you go along with everything that's asked of you."

"Why didn't he call me?"

"Didn't you turn your cell phone off during the movie?"

"Oh, yeah, I did . . . how did you know I'd been to the movies?" She bit her lower lip, looking as if she'd rather believe him than believe the nightmare unfolding around her. Her hand came out of the purse with fingers wrapped around keys. "It's late . . . too late for a meeting. Why not Monday morning, first thing?" Her voice was a whisper now.

"*¿Quién sabe?* Who knows why management does anything?" He shook his head, giving her his saddest smile as he pulled the gun from his suit coat pocket and pointed it at her. Her strangled moan sent a shiver of anticipation through him. "I just do what they ask me, *Dulce*."

Lalo took another step forward and grasped her arm. "If you scream, I kill you now. One shot between the eyes. I'll be gone before anyone finds you. Come with me. It's better if you cooperate."

She glanced around wildly, then tried to jerk away. He smiled. The parking lot was empty. Dark. She was alone with him. He felt a flush of pleasure. He let his gloved fingers bite into her arm, saw her flinch.

Her mouth gaped. "Let go. Please, let go."

"Don't worry, *chiquita,* it's okay. *Todo está bien.* I'll give you a ride in my BMW. Is beautiful car, isn't it? You be quiet for me,

366

and I give you a ride." He jabbed harder with the barrel of the gun, sticking it deep into her chubby stomach. *"¿Sí, querida?"*

She swallowed, her eyes wide. "Yes."

"Good." He nudged her forward, using the gun to control her movements until he had the car door open. "In you go. Nice leather seats, eh, you like, no?"

She nodded, a tear rolling down her cheek. She was one of those women whose faces got all red and blotchy when she cried. Not a pretty sight. He patted her face. *"Don't cry, Dulce."* The gun barrel tight against her nose, he fastened her seatbelt for her, making sure it was snug. He gave her a smile, locked her door, and loped around to the other side.

"Mister, mister, please don't hurt me. I don't know what you want with me, but I don't know anything. Joey didn't tell me anything." The fact that she knew this was about Joey said she did know something. She was a smart girl. Too bad. She started to whimper, the sound annoying him. This was why he had no children. Sylvia had wanted them, but eventually she'd come around to his way of thinking. Every dollar he made, he lavished on her.

"So you say. My boss, he thinks differently." He patted her arm. "Crying makes your face ugly."

He didn't enjoy prolonging the agony for young ladies. For her, he would do it quickly. He would save his time and energy for the man who had been in the park with Joey Doyle.

And the cop, of course. He wouldn't forget the cop.

CHAPTER
THIRTY

Ray shifted from one foot to the other on the steps in front of the Santos house, not sure how to begin. The hours of driving around after the banquet hadn't produced any magic words.

"Hi, could we talk for a second?" Now, that was eloquent. "I need to ask you something."

Susana clutched a paperback book in one hand, her index finger marking her spot. She stood in the doorway of Lily and Joaquin's house and looked up at him, no welcome in eyes red with fatigue. "It's really late. The kids are asleep. You can't come in."

"It won't take very long, I promise."

"It won't change anything." She side-stepped him, padded down the sidewalk on bare feet, and sat on the curb. She folded down the corner of a page and laid the book in the grass, then hugged her knees to her chest. "It's not fair to you, but I have to think about Marco. I can't spend the night at my sister's house like a scared rabbit every time you get a new case."

"They took us off the Doyle case." He sat down next to her. He wanted to take her hand, but he didn't. They'd lost so much ground.

"I heard. That really doesn't change anything, does it?"

"It's true. There'll always be another case." He touched her arm. She leaned away. "Here's my question. If you could go back, knowing what you know now, would you not marry Javier? Would you give up those sixteen years of living with him and loving him and having Marco if you knew he was going to die and leave you alone?"

"Not fair." She shot up and fled to a tangled honeysuckle vine that had wrapped itself around a trellis against the house. Her fingers touched the delicate blooms.

Ray got up and followed. He touched her arm and inhaled her scent mixed with the honeysuckle's. When she turned, he let his hand move to her cheek, tracing the tiny lines around her mouth, and then creep into her hair. Soft and scented like jasmine. His fingers tightened involuntarily. She felt so good, and she was slipping away. "I would never give up the time I had with Laura. You wouldn't pass on Javier, either. It was too precious. And so is the time we have."

"Ray — "

He didn't let her finish. He slipped his arms around her waist and lifted her up, kissing her, a long lingering kiss that felt more like an ending than a beginning. Then, he lowered her back to the ground. "Don't say anything. I'm not giving up on us. I'm going to find out who took those shots at us and put him away. And while I do, I'm just asking you to pray about us. To ask God what his plan is for us. Trust Him for the answers, if you can't trust me."

"Are you still considering changing professions?"

He could feel the heat of her palms through his shirt as they rested on his chest. So much hinged on his answer.

He grabbed her hands and held on. "The point is you have to trust God. Don't make your trust contingent on some future move you think will make you and Marco safe."

"So you're waiting for me to trust God instead of doing the one thing that would pave the way for us to be together." Her tone was incredulous. Disappointed. She shook her head. "I'm not willing to risk going through this kind of pain again. Or put

Marco through it. We wouldn't survive. Not a second time."

The finality of that statement ripped through him. He stepped back. "See, that's the difference between you and me, Susana. I know it's worth it — you're worth it. Whatever time God gives us together, I want it. Short or long, I'll take it."

He forced himself to turn and walk away. Prayed she would call him back. The expanse of dark night reverberated with her silence.

Susana pounded on her pillow again. Rolled over on the narrow twin bed and stared at the ceiling in little Olivia's bedroom. Lily had decorated it with stars that glowed in the dark. The tiny house was bursting at the seams with too many guests. Maybe Susana should just take Marco and go home when Lily and Joaquin returned from their date night. It would be easier to sleep in her own bed. As if the feel of Ray's mouth on hers and his hands tangled in her hair wouldn't follow her home. Or the hurt in his voice and the love in his eyes. She sat up and put her feet on the floor.

"Mom?"

She sighed and twisted around to peer at her son standing in the doorway. "What's the matter? Is Benny keeping you awake with his snoring?"

Benny's snoring was a running joke. The two were camping out in the backyard in Joaquin's tent. "No. I just wanted to see if you were asleep." His voice had that anxious quality it seemed to have all the time now. "Where were you going?"

"To get a glass of milk. Do you want one? And then you need to get some sleep. It's late."

"I can't sleep. I was looking for cartoons on TV and they were talking about the man we found in the park on the news."

Susana's stomach rocked. She'd tried to protect Marco from the media coverage of the Doyle case, but she'd been in the shower when the ten o'clock news came on.

"Come sit down next to me, sweetie." She patted the bed and waited until he sat down. His legs swung back and forth, feet banging on the box spring. "What did they say?"

"That the guy who killed him might be the one in the silver car, the one that shot us." His face reflected his fear. Susana put an arm around him and felt the shiver that ran through his body. "He might be a serial killer. He might kill more people before they catch him. I think we should go back to Ray's right away. We can stay there like we did before."

"Honey, we're safe here. Joaquin is a police officer." She was glad Marco didn't know Ray had been on the porch a few hours earlier. "The man in the BMW was shooting at Ray, not us. We're safe here."

"How do you know? Did they catch the bad guy and ask him?"

"No, but — "

"I want Ray." Marco's sigh filled the darkness.

She gave him a tight hug. "I know, sweetie, but we don't always get what we want. I'm sorry. We're safer here."

"Ray loves us." The words were muffled as Marco hid his face against her shoulder. "I don't want to stop seeing him just because you do."

Marco couldn't continue to see Ray. Eventually a man like him would find someone else. Would his future wife want the son of an ex-girlfriend hanging around? Marco would only end up hurt.

"We'll see what happens after they catch the man who killed Mr. Doyle. You can't hike or play basketball until you get your cast off, anyway. And Ray has his own injuries to heal."

"Ray is the best police officer of all." He

jerked away from her. "It's stupid not to let him."

He slid from the bed and ran. Susana wanted to go after him, but she didn't have the words to stop the breaking of her own heart, let alone his.

Someone sat in the dark on Ray's front porch swing.

It swayed. Ray eased his weapon from the glove compartment and tried to decipher the shadows. Deborah jerked from the swing and meandered toward the steps, her white dress reflected in the floodlight that threw flickering shadows on the sidewalk. He let out his breath slowly, stuck the Glock back in its holster, and got out. Her truck wasn't in the driveway. How did she get here and, more importantly, how was she getting home?

"Ray, honey, is that you?" She was doing that sultry southern belle routine.

He limped up the porch steps past her. "What're you doing here, is a better question."

She took a swipe at his arm, missed, and sat down on the step. "Whoops! I think I fell." She giggled. "Ray, I can't get up."

"How'd you get here?" He ignored her outstretched hand. "Where's your truck?"

"I'm having fun. You should try it some-time." Pouting, she pulled a cigarette from a crumpled package and tried to light it. "My date turned out to be a dud so I made him drive me out here. I told him it was a secluded lover's lane. When we got here, I admitted it was Ray Johnson's place, and he almost lost his supper."

"I hope you have money, because I'm call-ing you a taxi."

"Oops." She grinned and took another drag from her cigarette. "Left my purse in Deadly Dud's car. No money, no credit cards, no keys to the apartment. I won't be able to get in."

Ray wanted to curse. Instead, he sat down in the rocking chair next to the swing and tried to think. He breathed in the humid night air and listened for God's instruction. All he could hear was Dog scratching at the front door, whining to come outside and play. Not now, buddy. Deborah would lose her job if she didn't get her life straightened out. She was a mess and, for some reason, she had come to him. *That's the best you've got, God? Come on. I don't think I can handle this. She needs someone who knows how to deal with her kind of problems.*

He sat there a second longer, but the refrain in his ears was the same. *She came to you.* He got up and walked over to sit down beside her. "Any idea why you had your dud bring you here?"

"It seemed like a safe place." She sounded almost sober. "You're safe."

That simple statement caught Ray up short. "I'm safe? You mean not a threat — to you?"

"You're a man, and you don't want anything from me."

She would definitely regret this conversation in the morning. "You need to go home. It's safe there, isn't it? No men bothering you there?"

"Too many bad dreams."

That he could understand. "Yeah. I've been having a few myself lately. Melody Doyle?"

"Just one of many." She shook her head, her long hair sliding back behind her shoulders. "I can't believe the Doyles. They've got so much. More money than they could ever spend. Big house, nice cars. All they do is fight. People like them who have everything and mess it up — they make me sick."

"Yeah." But Deborah had started drinking long before the Doyle case. "You ever ask yourself why you drink so much?"

"Nope."

"Maybe you should." Ray remembered

the warm, fuzzy feeling, the ability to lie down and lose consciousness without having to think about the casket slipping into that gaping hole.

"I know why I drink." She reversed course. "And thanks for bringing it up. I had almost forgotten this!"

With a flourish, she picked up a bottle wrapped in a paper bag. She unscrewed the lid, took a noisy gulp, and wiped her mouth on the back of her hand, a satisfied look on her face. "Dudley sprang for it on the way out here. He's really a nice boy, just naïve. You want some?"

Ray took the bottle from her and set it on the sidewalk. "Tell me why you drink."

"To forget. To feel better." The words were coated with sarcasm. Her bitter smile didn't reach her eyes. "To have fun."

"What're you trying to forget?"

"Don't analyze me." Sudden anger burned through the words. "You don't know me."

"That's why I'm asking." Ray kept his voice even as he swatted at a swarm of mosquitoes. "I'm trying to understand what's going on with you. It must be pretty bad for you to risk losing your job like this."

"Whaddya mean?"

"You called me and said you'd use your gun on a guy in a bar. You come to work

378

hung over. You're late half the time. You spend half the day smoking in the bathroom. Then you got drunk in front of your boss and your boss's boss."

"Oh, that." She leaned forward and rested her head on her forearms. Her eyes were closed. For a second, he thought she'd gone to sleep. "There's something I have to tell you."

"Yeah. What's that?"

"Something happened at the banquet. I ran into Mrs. Martinez in the restroom."

Ray's exhaustion fled. He jerked to attention. "Ran into her? What do you mean?"

"She was in a stall. She heard some things De La Fuente and Gardner from vice were saying about Sarge . . . and me. About you and me, too."

"Deborah, what things?" Sick fear crawled through his gut. Ray grabbed her arm and shook it. "Sit up, Deborah. Talk."

She jerked away and stood, swaying. "Look, don't take it out on me. I didn't say anything. I didn't do anything. I never did anything to Sergeant Martinez. It's just garbage. Garbage . . ."

Her voice broke, and she sat down abruptly. "I wouldn't. I couldn't."

Ray worked to steady his pulse as he tried to imagine Piper's reaction to what she had heard. "Did you tell De La Fuente and Gardner they were full of it?"

"No." Deborah's voice shook. "I didn't know she was in the stall, or I would have."

"Samuel loves Piper."

"I know that, but sometimes he looks at me funny . . . like he's trying to figure out something. But he could never want me — I'm damaged goods." Deborah faced him for the first time, her blue eyes dark with anger and pain. "You could never want me, either."

"You're my partner. I never even considered it." And she'd done nothing but ridicule his faith from the day they'd been assigned together.

"Yeah, because you're too good for me. You Christians are so high and mighty."

Ray searched for words that would convince her. "You're a beautiful, intelligent woman. A man will fall for you so hard some day, he'll love you forever."

Deborah shook her head. "No. No man is going to love someone who slept with her mother's boyfriend when she was twelve."

That was it. The key. Ray sucked in air. "Deborah, are you telling me you were molested?"

"Dad did a disappearing act. Mom got a boyfriend. Bill." The emotion had drained from her voice. "Bill would come over to the house when she was at work. He'd be waiting there for me when I got home from school. He said if I told anyone he'd make me watch him kill my mom, then he'd kill me. When he was done . . . he would kiss me on the lips and tell me that all the boys at school would love me because I was experienced."

"I'm sorry, Deborah." Ray's response felt stunning in its inadequacy. "What did you do?"

"I'll spare you the gory details. My mother figured it out, but not until he'd gotten his fill. I'm not sure who she blamed more — me or him. She got rid of him by threatening to go to the police, but she didn't turn him in. She was too ashamed. She told me to never talk about it. I didn't, because no one would want me if they found out."

Deborah stumbled forward on her knees, grabbed the bottle from the sidewalk, lifted it to her lips, drank deeply. Then she coughed so hard he was afraid she'd be sick.

"And now you're trying to drown the memories with alcohol." Ray tugged the bottle from her hand and poured the rest in the bushes. Then, he helped her back onto the step. "I've tried it. It doesn't work."

Deborah turned reddened eyes toward

him. "Bible Boy, you don't have to make it up — "

"Shut up and listen. I was married."

"You were married." Now she sounded shocked. "You're kidding."

"You don't have to sound so surprised. I'm not so bad."

"Didn't mean that." She fumbled for another cigarette, lit it. "You never talk about it."

"Nothing to talk about. I was married. And then she died." Ray tossed the empty bottle on the grass. "I spent a lot of time after that pickling myself. And doing stuff — half of which I probably don't even re-member."

Ray contemplated the things he did re-member. None of the memories were good.

"Same here." Deborah's voice dropped to a whisper. "I didn't used to drink so much. I thought becoming a cop would help. It didn't."

They sat silently then, listening to the cicadas and the toads harmonize. Mooch's bright eyes glowed in the dark as she streaked across the yard and bounded onto the porch. The puppy's whining at the front door became a howl.

"What's wrong with the animals?" Ray got up and jerked open the front door. The cat slipped in as the puppy darted out on the porch, halted, ears straight up, then raced down the steps and out into the yard. "Hey, get back here. Now."

The dog circled back, stopped in front of Deborah, and gave an ear-splitting howl. "What has gotten into you?" Ray followed him out to the end of the short sidewalk. Uneasiness stirred as he stared into the darkness, trying to make out the shape of the barn. Had something — or someone — moved? Or was it a trick of his imagination?

"Where are you going?" Deborah called. "We were talking here."

"I thought I saw something out by the barn." He grabbed the puppy and stuck him under one arm, scratching between his ears as he carried him back. "Sorry, buddy." D-Dog squirmed and yipped. "Yeah, you're ferocious. It's probably a coyote, and he'll eat you alive."

"I didn't hear anything." Deborah used the nub of her burning cigarette to light another before tossing the old one on the ground. "For a country boy, you sure are jumpy."

Ray sat back down, propped the puppy up on his outstretched legs, and groped for words to help his partner. "Deborah, you've got to find a way to accept your past and move on."

Deborah stroked the puppy's head. "What's his name?"

"I don't know yet. I've been calling him D-Dog." He was ashamed to admit it.

Her body rocked as she murmured words so low he couldn't hear them. She glanced up at him. "Rocky."

His puppy had a name. Her shaking hand slid beside Ray's along Rocky's back. "Where was God when Bill was raping me?"

"I don't have all the answers, Deborah." How he wished he did. "When I was in college, my parents died in a car accident. I had no other family. I was alone for years. Finally, I met Laura. Life was good. A year after we got married, we found out she had cancer. So, believe me, I get the shake-fist-at-sky thing."

"But you still believe." Her tone was incredulous. "What kind of God does that to a good person like you?"

The same God who helped him use the life insurance money to buy this place and put his life back together, piece by broken piece. "I just know if it weren't for Him I'd be in a gutter somewhere right now or worse. I feel his presence all the time. I'm not alone."

"But I was just a kid. An innocent kid."

Deborah took Rocky from Ray and buried her head in the dog's fur. He squirmed and then rested on her knees. "Why did this stuff happen to us?"

"I asked that question over and over." Especially in the dark hung-over aftermaths. "All I know is that I can sit here and talk to you about this because I understand suffering. I walked through the valley and came out the other side a stronger, better person. So will you."

"I want to be able to go to sleep at night without thinking about his weight suffocating me." Her sobs were muffled.

Ray put one hand on her shoulder, rubbed. "If you're not ready for church yet, there's a therapist at the station."

She stiffened and pulled away, letting go of Rocky. He jumped down and circled back, before hopping into Ray's lap. "No touching and no therapy."

Ray dropped his hand. *No touching.* That simple statement made him want to weep for a pain so staggering it had left Deborah cut off from human comfort. "You need help."

"What I don't need is a psych report in my folder."

"You're going to throw away your career if you don't come to terms with this. A clean

385

folder won't mean much then."

She didn't answer and, after a moment, he leaned forward and smoothed back her hair so he could see her face. Her eyes were closed again. "Deborah?"

He shook her arm. "Deborah, get up. Come in the house. You can sleep on the couch."

She didn't move. Ray let Rocky in, then half-carried, half-dragged her into the house. She slid onto the couch without offering resistance. He grabbed a quilt and dropped it over her. He stood studying her sleeping form. "This is a habit you'll have to break, my friend."

Numb with weariness, he started down the hallway to the bedroom.

"Ray." Her voice was a whisper.

He stopped. "Yeah?"

"I'm sorry about Mrs. Martinez."

"I know." He forced himself forward, shoulders bowed under the weight of the knowledge that sorry wasn't always enough.

CHAPTER
THIRTY-ONE

"Miss Susana. Wake up. Wake up!"

Susana jerked awake, instantly terrified by the fear in Benny's voice. Early morning sun streaming through the window blinded her, but she felt him tug her arm. "What, Benny, what is it? Are you okay?"

Benny shook his head. "He made me promise. He said I had to wait until it was light." His voice rose to a hysterical pitch. "I knew it was wrong, but he made me swear. Please, don't send me back. Please, don't tell Mr. Daniel. Please."

He sobbed, his arms wrapped around his thin chest.

"Benny, it's okay. We're not sending you anywhere. I promise." Susana shoved back the sheets and slid from the bed. "What are you talking about? Is it Marco?"

When Benny didn't answer, she grabbed his arms. "Look at me. Did something happen to Marco?" Benny cringed as if expecting a blow. Horrified, Susana wrapped him in a quick hug, then touched his chin, forcing him to look up. "Please, Benny, I'm not mad at you. I won't hurt you. Just tell me where Marco is."

"He got stuff from your purse." He punctuated the words with hiccupping sobs. "Money and your cell phone."

She flew across the bedroom. Her purse lay open, the contents strewn about the desk. Her billfold was empty. Marco had taken money. And her debit card. A horrifying sense of dread rippled through her. She leaned over, propped her hands on her knees, and tried to breathe. Marco had taken money and left the house. And gone where? "Benny, where'd he go?"

"To Mr. Ray's ranch. He was going to call a taxi with your phone. He said Mr. Ray would make it safe for you, like he did before when the bad guy was after you." Benny suddenly sat on the floor as if his legs wouldn't hold him.

How could an eight-year-old boy get safely from a San Antonio suburb to a ranch on the other side of Helotes in the middle of the night? A worse thought plunged through Susana like a finely-honed sword. If Marco had made it to the ranch, Ray would have called her immediately — unless the shooter in the BMW had shown up at the ranch and found both Ray and Marco there.

Her knees buckled as horrifying images sprang to mind. She forced herself upright, raced to the phone in the kitchen, and punched in her cell number. It rang and rang. *Come on, Marco, pick up. Pick up.* It rang once, then voicemail kicked in. She disconnected with a jab of a shaking finger. What was Ray's number? Terror blocked it.

She dashed back into the bedroom, smacked into the chair, nearly fell, rebounded. Her address book was in the mess that had been the contents of her purse. Her hand closed around it. Ray Johnson. Ray Johnson. The number came to her, even as she flipped through the pages.

Back to the kitchen. Again, no answer. Susana waited with barely contained impatience until Ray's recording finished and the all-important beep sounded. "Ray, pick up, please, pick up. Is Marco there? Call me the second you get this message. Sooner, if Marco shows up at your place."

She called Samuel. Voicemail. It wasn't like Samuel not to answer his phone. Maybe he'd gotten called to a scene. She left a message and slapped the phone down. Benny stood in the middle of the kitchen, tears streaming down his pinched face. Susana didn't have time to comfort him. "I've got to look for him, Benny. You stay here."

"I'm going, too." Before she could stop him, Benny charged from the room.

It took two minutes for her to change into jeans and a T-shirt. She pounded on Lily's bedroom door. Joaquin opened it a second later, stifling a yawn. The sleep in his eyes fled as she explained. He wrapped his arms across his massive chest, his expression immediately opaque. Instantaneous cop mode. "No one's answering at Ray's?"

"No. And Marco doesn't answer my cell."

Lily shrugged on a robe. "Maybe they're asleep. Maybe Ray didn't want to wake you up, so he just let Marco spend the night," she said, tightening the belt. "They probably stayed up all night talking."

Susana tried to rein in mounting panic. Too many scenarios pressed against her. Too many terrifying possibilities. "No. Ray would have called me right away if he knew Marco was there. Maybe Marco got out there and Ray wasn't home." She didn't voice her worst fears. Saying them aloud might make them real. "Maybe Ray got called in to work. I'm headed out there to see for myself."

Joaquin grabbed a rumpled T-shirt from the chair next to the bed. "I'll get dressed.

Let me drive."

"No. Find Samuel. He's not answering his cell. I need Samuel." Susana swallowed back a sob and tried to keep her voice steady. "If anybody in Missing Persons owes you a favor, ask them to be on standby. I'll call you as soon as I get to the ranch. I may need you to start checking with taxicab companies . . . and emergency rooms."

Joaquin looked doubtful. "You sure you can drive?"

"I'm fine. Just find Samuel."

"Okay. Drive very carefully. It won't do any good to get yourself killed on the way out there."

Benny dashed into the room and collided with Joaquin. The boy's dirty shirt was buttoned wrong, and his feet were bare. "I'm going to look for Marco."

"No. You stay here with Lily and Joaquin."

"He's my friend. I lost him. I have to find him."

The stubborn look on his face and the tears in his eyes broke her heart. She took his small hand in hers and squeezed tight. "Let's go then."

Marco had been out there alone for hours.

"Hey, hey, quit it!" A rough, wet tongue slathered Ray's face. He breathed in funky puppy breath. He forced himself from murky dreams of gunfire and screaming babies, opened his eyes, and shoved the puppy from his chest. Rocky barked twice, jumped back up, and licked his face again. "Yeah, yeah, I love you, too, but stop it."

A pounding noise registered. Sudden adrenaline pulsed through him. The noise was coming from the front of the house. Ray rolled, sat up, grabbed his weapon from the nightstand, and stood. Paused, listening. It was pounding on the door.

Rocky woofed twice, jumped from the bed, and raced from the room. Ray laid the gun back down, rubbed his face with both hands, trying to get the sleep out of his eyes. The pounding accelerated, as did the barking.

"I'm coming." He dragged himself down the hallway, realizing as he went that he was still wearing his dress pants and shirt.

"Ray, Ray. Open the door. Please!" Susana, her voice muffled, was outside his door. She sounded as if she'd been crying.

He pulled the door open. She stood there, hand still raised. Benny was with her. But not Marco. Rocky launched himself onto the porch, and Benny scooped him up in his arms.

"Why didn't you answer the phone?

Where's Marco? Is he here?" Susana had to shout over Rocky's delirious barking.

"What? What are you doing here?" He wanted to understand. Despite everything, she was here, and his sleep-deprived brain couldn't quite grasp why.

"Hey, do you mind? Not so loud!" Deborah's voice floated out to them. "I'm trying to sleep."

The look on Susana's face would be etched on Ray's brain forever. He grabbed her arm before she could turn. "It's not what you think."

She pulled away. "I have to find Marco. Benny thinks he came here looking for you. He saw the story on the news about the Doyle case and freaked. He thought you could keep us safe."

The sarcasm in those words slit him to the bone. She might believe Ray could keep her safe physically, but she would never trust him now to keep her safe emotionally.

"What's going on?" Deborah staggered into the foyer. She wore Ray's favorite Houston Astros T-shirt. Her long legs and feet bare. The shirt was just long enough to touch the top of her thighs. "It's gotta be the crack of dawn. First, I had to disconnect the telephone. Now, we got pounding on the door. All this racket makes it hard for a person to sleep."

"I have to find Marco." Susana bolted down the porch steps.

Rocky wiggled from Benny's arms, plopped to the ground, and shot across the yard toward the barn.

"The puppy knows he's here. He can smell him." Benny took off, his short legs pumping.

Susana veered away from the car and followed.

Ray stumbled after them, barefoot, hampered by the pain in his ankle. "Wait. I'll help. Have you called the police?"

"You are the police. That's why Marco came here. The innocence of a child, right? He doesn't realize we wouldn't be in danger if you hadn't involved us in the Doyle case in the first place." Susana's bitterness raked over him. "I left Samuel a voicemail. He'll call as soon as he checks his messages. Don't worry about it. We'll find him."

"I can help. What if he did somehow get here during the night? If he saw — saw what you just saw, he may've decided not to come in, after all." Ray tried not think how the scene last night would have played to an audience of one young boy who badly wanted to believe he and his mother would spend the rest of their lives with Ray. "I thought I heard a noise. The animals went crazy. Let's just take a quick look around before I make calls. We'll get Missing Persons involved, okay?"

"Joaquin's already calling someone he knows." Susana walked faster, then broke into a trot, outdistancing Benny.

Ray limped as fast as he could, but he couldn't keep up. "Nothing happened. She was here when I got home last night. Her date dropped her off. She didn't have her purse or her keys. She was drunk, so I let her sleep on the couch."

Susana grabbed the barn door and heaved it open. "Who you spend the night with doesn't concern me. Only finding Marco."

"We didn't spend — nothing happened." Ray hopped on one foot, so he could try to pick off stickers piercing the tender skin on the bottom of his other foot.

"Marco. Marco." Susana screamed the name. It echoed. Then silence.

"Marco, please, if you're in here, please come out. I promise I won't be mad."

"Marco, it's me, Benny. I waited, like you told me to. I waited until it got light." Benny's voice was tiny in the big barn.

"Mom? Benny?" The anxious note in Marco's voice bounced against the rafters.

Benny darted across the barn to an empty

horse stall and squeezed through the gate, Susana right behind him. When she spoke, her voice shook. "Marco. Oh, son, are you okay?"

Marco huddled in the corner of the stall under a horse blanket. His face was dirty, and he had straw in his hair. Otherwise, he looked perfect. Ray leaned against the stall gate and sucked in air in greedy gulps.

Marco's voice was rusty with sleep. "I took a taxi. I — I wanted — but then — I slept here."

"A taxi driver agreed to give a little boy a ride at eleven thirty at night?" Susana glanced back at Ray, the fury in her face so intense he wanted to take a step back.

"I told him my parents were divorced and I had a fight with my mom so I was going to my dad's house." Marco stumbled over the word *dad,* his tone painfully defiant. "He said whatever, as long as I had the money to pay. When we got to the beginning of the dirt road, I told him I wanted to surprise my . . . my dad. He said, whatever, and drove off."

Susana dropped to her knees next to the boy. Her hands went to his face, her fingers wiping away the smudges. Wordlessly, Benny sat down on the ground. Ray wanted to join them on the ground, take them all in his arms. He gripped the rough wooden bar of the stall until his hands hurt.

"Why didn't you answer when I called you?" Susana clipped every word with controlled anger.

"The battery's dead."

She gave one sob, pulled Marco to her, and smothered him in a hug. "Don't you ever do that to me again. Do you understand? Never again."

Marco stared over his mother's shoulder at Ray, his dark eyes bleak and accusing. "I won't. I'm never coming here again, ever."

Susana grabbed Marco's hand and pulled him to his feet as she stood.

"Wait, let me explain." Ray started after them.

Susana hustled the boys through the barn door and out into the brightly lit morning.

"Wait — "

"Ray, Treviño's on the line." Deborah stood on the porch, still in his shirt and not much else, waving a cell phone. "You remember Joey Doyle's main squeeze, Candy Romano? She went to the movies last night and never came home."

CHAPTER
THIRTY-TWO

Abduction was an ugly word. Ray stood in the middle of the apartment complex parking lot and closed his eyes. Heat radiated from the asphalt. Sweat trickled down his temples. Candy Romano's face, blotchy and red from crying, swam in front of him. It had been dark and a little cooler when she'd come home from the movies. Maybe she'd been laughing. Maybe still thinking about the flick she'd seen. Not thinking about dangerous people who lurked in shadows. The laughter had disappeared. A choking, breathless fear had followed. That kind of fear ought to leave a residue. He jerked his eyes open. The parking lot was empty, a silent, unwilling witness to her horror.

Oscar Treviño trudged over to Ray. The detective shoved his hair from his eyes and turned his back to the sudden, hot wind. "We've canvassed every townhouse and apartment on this side of the complex.

Nobody saw or heard anything. It's like Candy Romano just disappeared. Maybe she was in this with someone else, and they decided to cut and run."

"Did she take any bags? Is there any evidence that she split?" Ray's gut reaction said abduction. No evidence of that either.

Oscar shook his head. "Nope. *Nada.*"

Deborah's pickup truck careened into the lot, forcing them to take a step back. She pulled in too fast, screeched to a stop, and didn't bother to straighten the vehicle.

She hopped out. "Well, what's the deal? Did you find a body?"

Like nothing had happened. Ray exhaled. She seemed determined to be oblivious to the train wreck she'd left in her wake at the ranch. They'd made the drive to her apartment in silence. She'd descended from the Bronco with a blithe, "See you at the scene," like they'd been out to dinner or gone to the movies.

"No. No body. Car's parked and locked. No sign of struggle. No nothing." Oscar leaned against Deborah's truck, his forehead wrinkled. Ray waited, giving the detective time to collect his thoughts. Oscar had begrudgingly admitted he needed Ray and Deborah's insight to try to find Romano. They'd interviewed her twice. Deborah had been in her apartment and talked to her mother. They should have some feel for her demeanor. They were still in the game, at least marginally.

That was the good news. The bad news was Susana and Marco would probably never speak to him again. At least, he had work to do. He didn't want to sit around his house, reliving the look on Marco's face as he'd stumbled from the barn and climbed into Susana's car without giving Ray a chance to explain.

He glanced at Deborah. She gave an impatient shrug. The previous evening's events were plastered across her face — bloodshot eyes, pasty skin, brutal purple slashes under her eyes. She'd been no help in assuaging the situation. She claimed she'd awakened during the night uncomfortable in her dress, so she'd grabbed his shirt from his drawer. That was it. A simple explanation for his huge blunder.

No point in thinking about it now. Solving the Doyle case would be the first step in getting Susana and Marco back. Determined, Ray shut out his seething feelings and focused on Oscar. His wrinkled clothes, scruffy five o'clock shadow, and red-rimmed eyes told Ray he hadn't seen the inside of his own home in quite a while.

"Candy Romano's mother is upstairs in the apartment," Oscar said. "She spent the night at her sister's. That's why she didn't know until this morning that Candy hadn't come home. She's worked herself up to some pretty good hysterics. I'm letting Mallory deal with her."

As if on cue, Lindstrom came out of the second-story apartment above them and clomped down the stairs, her lips pursed as if she'd been sucking on a lemon. She waited until she was at the bottom of the steps to speak. "The mother says her daughter has been getting weird phone calls. She wouldn't tell her mother what they were about. She suddenly started talking about looking for another job — out of state. We looked at the notes from your interview with her at the dealership after Joey Doyle died. Could she have been involved in Doyle's death? Maybe an accomplice?"

"I didn't think so at the time." Ray let his gaze skip to Deborah again. His partner seemed absorbed in sipping from a tall Starbucks cup. "Candy admitted that she was involved with Joey, but she said he never gave her any details on the big scheme he was supposedly hatching. She seemed devastated by his death. And didn't like Kevin Doyle at all. I felt she was genuinely upset about Joey's death. She described in detail the last meal they had together, talked about how he'd given her money, so they didn't lose the family car, said he was a kind man."

Oscar began to pace from parking space to parking space, stepping over the painted lines like a kid who didn't want to break his mother's back. "I think Mallory and I should go back out and talk to Kevin and Elaine. Last time, Kevin indicated he planned to hire a replacement for Candy and then fire her for 'inappropriate behavior on the job.' He seemed anxious not to deal with her anymore."

"Hired help who had an affair with his married brother — his reaction isn't too surprising, really." Not that Kevin Doyle had cared about his sister-in-law's feelings. Only how it would look if people found out.

"Was the old man there when you inter-viewed them?" Deborah seemed relaxed, too relaxed. Hair of the dog? Anger burned through Ray. Surely not.

"Nope. They said he's spending all his time golfing — trying to get over his grief or something." Mallory unlocked the Crown Vic parked next to Ray's Bronco, then talked to them over the roof. "Man, that poor girl had no idea what she was getting herself into, sleeping with a Doyle . . . Or did she? Gold digger?"

"I didn't think so." Ray could usually trust his gut, but lately he'd begun to wonder. "What would make a receptionist worth kidnapping or killing?"

"We don't know she's been kidnapped. Maybe it's totally unrelated. It could be a mugging and sex assault that went bad. Her body could still show up out in the county," Lindstrom theorized. "She was alone in a parking lot on a Saturday night. There are predators everywhere."

"What about Tommy Wheeler?" Ray knew he was grasping at straws. "Maybe there's a connection between him and Candy that we don't know about. Have you checked to see if they know each other outside the Doyle circle? Or had any luck finding him?"

"None," Oscar said. "As far as we know, there's no connection between the two of them beyond the fact that they both saw Joey Doyle the day he died."

"Wheeler is hiding, not missing," Deborah asserted.

"Agreed." Ray ticked off the facts in his mind. Joey Doyle had lunch with Candy. Then he went hiking with Tommy Wheeler. Now Joey was dead, and so was the other person who had been at the scene — Vicky Barrera. Now Candy was missing. That left

Wheeler as the lone witness to the events of that day. "We need to find them both — Wheeler because he's involved in Joey's death, and Romano because her disappearance has to be related somehow."

"No, *we* need to find them." Mallory opened the car door. "We can take it from here."

"You could use our help." Ray held the detective's gaze. "That's why you called us out here, isn't it?"

Her smirk said it hadn't been her idea. "Only to review your notes and pick your small brains. I suppose you think you could have solved this by now." She laughed, a high, brittle sound. "You guys had beans when we took over."

"You bet your butt, we could've solved it." Deborah whipped around the Crown Vic. She was in Mallory's space so fast, Ray didn't have time to react. "You're the one with the pea-sized brain."

"Deborah!" Ray shot forward and got between the two detectives before contact was made. "Back off. We're all on the same team here."

"Yeah, you know, Johnson, you need to get your partner under control. Maybe drop her off at AA." Oscar snatched the keys from Mallory and urged her into the car. "I think we can take it from here. Go solve your misdemeanor murder, why don't you? It's more your size."

Ray let go of Deborah and she stumbled away. He wanted to shake her. "What is your problem? Are you drunk again?" He headed for the Bronco.

"No, I'm not drunk. And you're my problem. You and Martinez and every other guy on the planet." Deborah's voice rose and then tapered off.

He halted, turned, and marched back so he could get in her face. "No. We're the good guys, Deborah. And if you haven't figured it out by now, you've got the pea brain."

He hobbled to the truck and got in, fighting the anger that blazed through him.

Deborah kept digging the hole deeper for both of them.

Shiloh Hills Golf Course was somewhat pedestrian for Lalo Hernandez's taste. Set on the outer fringes of the hill country northwest of San Antonio, it seemed to have delusions of grandeur. It did have one thing going for it. The course was a long way from Milton Doyle's house at King's Row Estates. The boss said *Señor* Milt like to knock back a few martinis with lunch after a full morning of golf. The drive home would give Lalo plenty of opportunity to set his plan in motion.

Knowing that, he didn't mind hanging out in the BMW, waiting. Boss said they needed the old guy as insurance. Didn't say for what. Lalo didn't ask. He'd set aside his plans for the other gentleman who had been at the park. He would come back to him later. The old man wouldn't take much time — especially since he wasn't allowed to go for the kill.

The unsatisfied feeling he'd had after leaving the cop hiding, still alive, in his SUV, resurfaced. Ridiculous to send a hired gun to do these half jobs, but he was getting paid the same, so he accepted the task. In some ways, it was a greater challenge. Live people were so much more trouble than dead people were. He gave a small groan of pleasure as he remembered the girl's soft red hair, white skin. So sweet. Young and tender.

It was almost three o'clock before Lalo saw Doyle stumbling to the gold Mercedes convertible. Superb car. Almost as superb as the BMW. Lalo waited patiently. He wanted to pick just the right moment. He needed to get him before he got on the highway, but there was time. Traffic wasn't bad. The sun was shining. It was a perfect day for a kidnapping.

Doyle drove sedately. Waste of a fine machine on an old man. Or maybe it was because he was inebriated. Lalo didn't care. No need to chase him. He picked his moment. Picked his spot and simply let the BMW drift across the centerline as he passed the Mercedes. He caught Doyle's startled look, huge eyes, as he jerked the steering wheel to the right. The Mercedes bucked, hit the dirt shoulder. Doyle tried to correct, but Lalo didn't let him. He hugged the right lane, forcing Doyle from the road, where the Mercedes skidded into an empty field and came to an abrupt halt, engine still humming.

Lalo pulled on to the shoulder, parked the BMW, and hiked back to the Mercedes. Doyle was still in the car, slumped over the steering wheel. The airbags had deployed and Doyle had a bloody nose. Otherwise, he seemed in one piece. "*Señor* Doyle? Are you all right?"

Doyle stared up at him, his features slack, eyes dazed. "Who are you?"

"You crashed your car. I saw it all. I am a witness. I will call Triple A. You sit in my car while I call for help. *¿Sí?*" He opened the door, handed the old man a handkerchief, and helped him out. "Keep your head back until bleeding stops, and I will make calls."

He led him to the BMW and opened the door. At the last second, the car's make must have registered through the alcoholic haze.

Doyle tried to pull back. "Hey."

Lalo gave the old man a hard shove, but not too hard, so he plopped down in the seat. Lalo felt a delicious sense of accomplishment. He pulled his weapon from his jacket and watched *Señor* Doyle's face turn a deeper shade of red. "Don't worry, *señor.* I take good care of you."

CHAPTER
THIRTY-THREE

The approaching rumble of an engine had a familiar sound. Ray looked up from unlocking the Bronco. Samuel's truck pulled in next to him in the station parking lot. Ray chewed on his lip. Might as well get this confrontation done. He'd known Samuel would track him down sooner or later. He would know all about Marco's night at the ranch — and about Deborah's.

Samuel shoved open his door and slid out. "Ray." Fury in one syllable.

"What's going on?" Ray leaned against the Bronco and waited.

His former partner looked bad. His face was gray with fatigue, his eyes were bloodshot over sunken cheeks, and dark stubble stained his chin. For the first time since Ray had met Samuel, the man looked his age. Ray didn't have to ask how Piper had taken the fiasco at the retirement banquet — he could see it in his friend's face.

Before he could probe, Samuel lit into him. "Susana's at my house, and she's a mess. Marco's in Emma's bedroom, refusing to come out. Benny's paralyzed with fear that Daniel will send him back into the foster care system. I understand Marco spent last night in your barn, while Deborah spent the night half-naked in your house."

Ray stared at his friend's face. He could see the pulse pounding in Samuel's temple over his clenched jaw. "Susana never gave me a chance to explain — "

"I trusted you not to hurt her," Samuel broke in. "You took a woman to your bed while my nephew watched. He was so traumatized by what he saw that he hid in your barn all night."

"Be very careful, Samuel, that you don't say something you can't take back." Ray fought to keep his tone even. Every muscle in his body knotted with the effort to restrain himself. He was one second away from a fistfight with his best friend. "How long have you known me? Putting aside Susana, professional ethics, and our friendship, do you really think I'm just pretending to follow Christ's teachings?"

Samuel sucked in air. Ray refused to look away. Seconds tore by.

410

Samuel crossed his arms, his face stony. "So what happened?"

"It was a stupid, stupid thing. I handled it all wrong," Ray shook his head. He chose his words carefully. The temptation to skewer his partner was strong, but still wrong. He had to tell Samuel — as a boss and as a friend — the simple truth. He couldn't shield Deborah anymore. If she didn't get help, she would kill herself or someone else.

He watched Samuel's face for signs of softening as he ran through the series of events of the previous evening. "That was it. Nothing happened. We talked, and I let her sleep it off on the couch. And I had no idea Marco was out there watching. Rocky — the puppy — went crazy and Mooch hid, but I never went out there to see what it was, something I regret now."

"You couldn't have known Marco would show up like that." Samuel sagged against his truck. The anger had fled leaving his face etched with weariness. "If Deborah admits to the drinking problem voluntarily, we can get her help through the Employee Assistance Program. She doesn't have to lose her job, but she has to be willing to stop."

"She admitted it to me, probably because she was so drunk. Whether she'll admit it to you or anyone else when she's sober . . . I kind of doubt it." Ray tried to figure out how much to tell Samuel. Deborah had trusted her partner with her secret, not her boss. "She needs therapy. She won't stop drinking until she deals with some underlying problems that go back to her childhood. I've got to get her to see a therapist."

"I'm her supervisor." Samuel's tone was curt, but something about his expression — almost as if he were in pain — made Ray want to probe, but Samuel pressed forward. "I'll insist that she take steps to solve the problem. She'll be required to see the department shrink for evaluation. If she doesn't, I'll insist on medical leave. I . . . I'll deal with her Monday morning. Tell her I want to see her first thing."

"Take it easy on Deborah. It's not her fault — "

"Not her fault? Come on, Ray. How long have you known? How long have you been covering for her?"

Ray let his gaze drop. "Not that long."

"Long enough. She's probably been driving drunk. Drinking on the job. Carrying a gun and drinking. And you knew it. If she'd hurt someone, you would've had to carry that guilt with you for the rest of your life. I understand wanting to shield a friend — "

"A partner, Samuel. She's my partner. I would've done the same for you."

"And you would've been wrong. You have enough book learning to know that. It's called enabling. You cover for her, she never hits rock bottom. She never has to face the consequences. As long as you do that, she keeps drinking. You're not doing her a favor."

"Right." Samuel was right. "But you would've thought twice about turning in a partner, turning me in for something like this. I know you. You're a cop. That's what we do."

Samuel was silent, his dark eyes staring at something in the distance that Ray couldn't see. "Yeah. And I would've been wrong. Deal with this thing with Susana before it gets any worse." The keys jangled in his hand but he didn't move. His gaze met Ray's, and he quickly stuffed the keys in his pocket.

"Look, Deborah mentioned something else." Ray tried to reach out. "She told me what happened in the restroom with Piper. Is she all right?"

"You'll have to ask her." Samuel's face twisted with bitterness. "She kicked me out."

Ray took a step forward. "Samuel — "

413

Samuel threw up a hand. "Don't. What are you doing here, anyway?"

"I wondered the same about you."

Samuel shrugged. "The hotel was — "

"Hotel? Samuel, at least stay at the ranch." Ray wanted to pound on something. He wanted to drive his friend home and lock him in a room with Piper until they worked it out. "I've got an extra room."

Samuel shook his head. "I heard about Candy Romano."

"Yeah. Oscar asked us to go over our interviews with them again."

"So, that's why you're here."

"Well." He couldn't lie. "Well, we did that this morning. I was just looking through some records." He'd been giving Oscar and Mallory time to cool off. They'd gone to talk to the Doyles again. Ray planned to go home, take a shower, and come back to wait for them so he could try to smooth things over with them. Covering for Deborah — again.

"Go home. Stay there. I don't want to see you here again until Monday morning. You look done-in. Get some sleep." Samuel turned and strode toward the station.

Ray could hardly tell his boss he looked just as bad. He climbed into the Bronco. He'd go home and come back later — when

Samuel was gone.

But first he had a phone call to make. When he couldn't see Samuel in the rearview mirror anymore, he pulled out his cell and punched in the number. It rang and rang. Finally someone picked up. Piper's voice was soft as if she'd been asleep.

"Did I wake you?" He fumbled for words now that she was on the line. "It's Ray."

"No . . . I was just . . . resting my eyes." All her usual over-the-top energy was absent.

"Look, Deborah told me what happened at the banquet — "

"You don't want to get in the middle of this." Sudden, bitter anger.

"You know Samuel would never cheat on you. He loves you too much."

The silence crackled. "I'm sure you're familiar with Matthew 5:27-29. Looking at another person . . . that way . . . is committing adultery."

"Yes, but — "

"He didn't have to take her to a motel to cheat on me — " Her voice quavered, and she hesitated. "It's not right for me to talk to you about this."

"Then talk to Pastor James."

"Another man." The heavy bitterness made her voice almost unrecognizable.

"A man of God."

"I would have said Samuel was a man of God, too."

"He is. Samuel's the most honorable man I know." Ray sought to find words of reconciliation. "If you can't talk to James, at least talk to Susana or Lily."

"No. Not his family."

"They love you like a sister." Ray fumbled for the words. "So do I."

The sigh lingered over the line. "I love you, too."

She hung up.

When you were a cop, love wasn't always enough.

CHAPTER
THIRTY-FOUR

Lalo Hernandez sauntered into the bar and
peered around. The dim, smoky room stank
of urine and stale beer. Lalo frowned. He
didn't like going home to Sylvia smelling
like *una cantina.* He would make this his
last job for the day. The old man had been
too easy. Maybe this guy would be a more
interesting. After a few seconds, he spotted
his prey at the bar.

"Buy you a drink, *Señor* Wheeler?" He slid
on to a stool next to the other man and
proffered a package of cigarettes.

Wheeler's bloodshot eyes studied him
before he snagged one. "Do I know you,
pal?"

"No, but you are going to want to know
me."

Wheeler fumbled with his lighter. It wavered before it hit its intended target.
"Why's that?"

"I am paying." Lalo slapped money on the

bar and summoned the bartender. "I have heard you are a business man in need of cash. And I have a business proposition for you."

"Gin and tonic, heavy on the gin."

Wheeler sounded like he'd already had more than a few drinks. Enough that any sense of self-preservation would have drowned. Easy prey.

"You look familiar. Have I met you before?"

"No. You don't know me, *compadre.* My name is Pedro Montemayor. Your friend, Chris, recommended you to me and told me where to find you." After Lalo had worked his magic on him for several minutes. Pain opened many doors. "He said you are a man who appreciates the finer things in life."

"Chris said that? Huh. I always thought he didn't get me. Yeah, I like the finer things." Wheeler turned his gaze to the muted TV bolted to a stand over the bar. A Dirty Harry movie was showing.

"Ever consider getting into the procurement and dispersal of recreational drugs?" Lalo lit a cigarette. The first hit of fine tobacco soothed his impatient soul. Slow and easy.

"You aren't a cop, are you?" A concerned

look leaked across Wheeler's slack face. He slugged back his drink and smacked the glass on the bar. "I may be drunk, but I'm not stupid."

"I am not a cop. If you are not interested, I have plenty of other potential partners."

"What are you peddling?"

"Take a ride with me, and I will show you."

"I don't know." Wheeler wiped beads of sweat from his upper lip with the back of his sleeve. "I don't know you."

"Fine." Lalo dropped a ten on the bar. "Have another drink on me. I'll save my free samples for someone who is interested, if you are too paranoid to trust me."

"Wait." Wheeler slid from the barstool, staggered, and nearly fell.

Hiding his disgust, Lalo grabbed his arm. "*Compa',* you need a little help. I have just the help you need."

"Yeah, great. That'd be great. Something to pep me up would be nice."

Lalo propelled the man out the door and into the parking lot. The BMW sparkled between two junk heaps that were obviously owned by college students with no money.

Wheeler jerked away from Lalo and meandered toward the car. "Nice wheels."

"Thank you. It is a 325i, five-speed automatic with four-wheel anti-lock brakes, air-bags, CD player, DVD, 16-inch alloy wheels. It is so smooth, it is mechanical magic. Go into business with me, and you'll be able to afford one of your own. Let's take a ride." He held the door open.

Wheeler sank onto the seat and laid his head back, eyes closed.

Piece of cake.

A siren blared. No. That shrill sound was something else. The phone. The phone rang, insistent and inexorable. Ray dragged himself from a semi-sleep, punctuated by the usual gunfire and screaming. He took a swipe at the coffee table, missed the phone, and knocked an empty glass on the floor. The second time he connected with the phone and stuck it to his ear. He squinted at his watch. Two A.M.

"Ray, it's Teresa. Sorry to wake you." Suddenly Ray was wide awake. Teresa didn't give him time to respond. "I thought you might want to know, we found one of your suspects in the Doyle case, Tommy Wheeler."

"You found him." Ray knew he sounded stupid. Too little sleep. Too much surprise at hearing her voice on the other end of the line.

"Well, some of my Park Police colleagues did. They did a sweep of Duncan Park for curfew violators, and they found him lying in the grass. Looked like a drug overdose, but my favorite paramedic Greg Miller says he thinks the scumbag will make it. I just thought you might like to know."

"Absolutely. Thanks for calling me. I mean . . ." He stopped. It was awkward, considering how their one and only date had ended with him kissing Susana.

"Don't worry about it, Ray. I met Greg because of you. Everything happens for a reason." She hung up.

Pushing aside the whys and wherefores of Teresa and Greg Miller, Ray jabbed Deborah's number into his cell phone as he loped down the hallway to the bedroom to change. He explained as quickly as he could.

Deborah sounded wide awake. "He better not die on us before we have a chance to interview him."

"We need to get to him first. I'll meet you there. Hurry." He disconnected.

They were back in the game, at least until Treviño and Lindstrom got wind of it.

Ray broke the speed limit the entire thirty miles to the hospital. Wheeler had been moved to a room on the third floor. The steady blip of a monitor provided the only noise. Wheeler's features were slack, his only movement the rise and fall of his chest. The nurse had described it as "sleeping it off." The guy was very lucky.

"Mr. Wheeler. Tommy." Deborah put her hand on the man's arm. She'd made it to the hospital at the same time as Ray. Her eyes were bloodshot and sunken with fatigue, but she looked sober. When Ray eased in next to her, he didn't smell alcohol. Maybe the scene yesterday had gotten through to her — at least for a little bit.

Wheeler grabbed Deborah's wrist. He opened his eyes. Ray saw unfettered fear. "What? Who are you?"

"Easy, Mr. Wheeler. We've met. I'm Detective Smith. This is Detective Johnson. Remember, we interviewed you with Sarah Doyle."

Wheeler groaned. "How could I forget? The ignominious end of another relationship played out on a stage for an audience of two."

"Mr. Wheeler, the doctors say you overdosed on high-grade heroin." Ray jumped in. "Are you a habitual drug user?"

"The doctors are full of it." Wheeler squirmed and lifted his head. "Sit me up, will you?"

Ray hit the button to raise the bed.

"I never OD'd. I don't shoot up. I don't do needles."

"Right. Whatever you say." Ray pulled his handcuffs from his belt, slapped one side on Wheeler's wrist and the other to the railing of the bed, and pulled a Miranda card from his pocket. He recited the familiar words. "If you understand these rights, I need you to initial the bottom line."

"No way!" Wheeler tried to pull away, thrashed, and grunted in anger.

The door burst open. Treviño burst through it, Lindstrom right behind him.

"What do you think you're doing?" Treviño came to a halt in front of the bed, his face red with anger.

Wheeler jerked away from Ray and grabbed at an intercom button at the side of his bed. "I want a phone. I want to call my lawyer."

"I'm arresting this man on the charge of murdering Joey Doyle." Ray ignored Wheeler's demand. "We need to post an officer outside his door, and the second his doctor releases him, haul him downtown, magistrate him, and throw him in jail where he belongs."

"No. No." Wheeler's face went from white to red with exertion as he rolled from side to side. "I didn't kill Joey Doyle, but I know who did. The guy who drugged me. I met him at a bar. He was buying drinks. Paying. I thought he just wanted to be the big shot. Fine by me. Then he offered to let me sample some product. Said he was looking for business partners. I took a ride with him. That's all I remember. Had to be him."

"Not another word. Absolutely not another word." A man who looked like Wheeler's twin stood in the doorway. The room was getting crowded. Ray glanced at Treviño. He looked as angry as the new arrival. This was not a friendly group.

"Ted, am I glad to see you!" Wheeler crowed. "How'd you know I was here?"

The man, obviously a Wheeler relative, strode forward. "Apparently, you got me down as next of kin on a card they found in your billfold."

Wheeler smirked at Ray. "This is my brother, Ted. He's an attorney."

Ray took in the man's cheap, ill-fitting suit, scuffed shoes, and battered briefcase. Business apparently wasn't very good.

"I take it you guys are cops." Ted Wheeler ignored the hand Treviño extended. "Y'all know better. Interrogating a witness without legal counsel present."

"He spoke with us voluntarily." Deborah's face was expressionless as she shook the lawyer's hand. "He didn't ask for a lawyer."

"It takes four of you? Does SAPD have some sudden overabundance of manpower? Wait outside. I wanna talk to my brother."

The four of them jostled into the hallway, Treviño leading the way.

"Who do you people think you are?" Lindstrom's voice got loud. A nurse at the nursing station gave them a severe look. Lindstrom turned her back on the woman and glared at Ray, but her next words were quieter. "We're running this show."

"Yes, you are." Ray put one hand on Deborah's arm, restraining her. She immediately shrugged it off. He'd spent fifteen minutes the previous afternoon apologizing to the other detective. Deborah better not blow it now. "But we've dealt with this guy. We've got a relationship with him. He'll talk to us. Even though he's lawyered up, he's scared to death of something or someone. He's gonna want to talk. Let us do this."

Lindstrom and Treviño had another one of those silent partner conversations that involved eyebrows, smirks, and shrugs. "You start it, we'll finish it."

"Deal." Ray charged into the room before Lindstrom could change her mind.

Ted Wheeler stood by Tommy's bed, arms crossed, face disapproving. "My brother —

my client — has some things to say after you remove the handcuffs."

Ray nodded, but he took his time removing the cuffs.

The lawyer shifted on his feet, re-crossed his arms. "But first, we want some assurances. And he wants protection."

"We didn't just ride in on the turnip truck." Deborah gave the lawyer her best East Texas accent. "You know it depends on what your client has to deal, and we won't know that until he starts talking."

"Believe me, Detective, he has plenty to deal, but he's holding his cards until we know you'll make it worth his while."

"Did you kill Joey Doyle?" Ray watched Wheeler's face, trying to gauge his truthfulness.

"No." Wheeler threw a paper cup of water across the room as if to punctuate his point. The cup hit the wall and splattered. The drama king. "No."

"Do you know who did?"

"Maybe." His gaze slide from Deborah, past Ray, and back to his brother. "I want protection."

"Give us what you got, and we'll tell the DA you were cooperative." Ray leaned against the wall, feigning relaxation. "It's their call."

"Not enough. He doesn't get prosecuted for anything," Ted Wheeler broke in.

"Nothing? We don't even know yet what he did. Besides obstruct an investigation by failing to divulge pertinent information."

"He's divulging now."

The room was so quiet Ray could hear the ticking of the clock over the door. "You tell us what happened to Joey Doyle in that park, and we'll go to bat for you. That's the best I can do."

"But they'll listen to you." The guy sounded scared. "They'll listen to you, right? You have to protect me. They'll kill me if they find out I told you anything. I'm a dead man."

"What happened up there?" Ray swallowed his contempt.

"We were just hanging, the way we always did. We had found this little, hidden spot where we could party. It was cool because you weren't supposed to get off the trail, and we were off the trail, and no one knew. I got him to go up there because they wanted me to find out what he knew. I was supposed to get him drunk so he'd talk. That was all. Thing is, I didn't know that he had stopped drinking. Completely. No drugs. No booze. Who knew?"

"What happened then?"

427

"Well, first, that park nature lady dropped by. Joey argued with her. That was a drag."

"Vicky Barrera was there?"

"For a while, man. He basically told her to get lost. She was crying and carrying on. Didn't want to break up. Said she didn't mean it. He didn't have to get a divorce. That was the thing about Joey. The chicks really dug him. I could never figure that out. Married, kids, and they still kept coming after him."

"So Vicky left?"

"Well, as far as I know, she did, only see — I saw her — look, just let me tell this in order, okay? I was nervous so I smoked — just a little dope — and then I had some wine. I kept thinking he would see how relaxed I was and want some of it, too. Only he didn't. I was getting pretty wasted, you know. I was just kicking back, enjoying the scene because, like you know, I had been working so hard, been under a lot of pressure with school and work and Sarah always hassling me to do better. That woman — "

"What happened on the hill?"

"Right." Wheeler swallowed hard. "You got a cigarette? I really could use a smoke."

Ray shook his head and pointed to the No Smoking sign on the wall.

"Vicky Barrera charged in there and

428

started flapping her jaw about Joey leaving his wife. He said, no way, and got up to take a leak. He said he was going hiking. That she should leave, and I should go home. He got over to the side of the clearing, and that's when I realized that there was something there, in the trees. I thought, man, this is some good stuff. I'm hallucinating.

"Then Joey was kind of like pulled into the brush, sucked in, and he was yelling. He was saying, let me go, you won't get away with this. My dad will kill you. Stuff like that. Then I heard this kind of gasp and, then, nothing. He stopped talking. Man, I got up and ran. I'm not kidding. I just threw myself back down the hill. I thought whoever it was would come after me. Vicky Barrera was right behind me, and she was totally freaking, man. She was screaming and crying. Said the guy had stabbed Joey. She fell a couple times, and I had to help her up. She knew her way around, and she found one of those karst-things, you know like caves, where the water goes down in the aquifer. We hid in there. We ran in there, and we stayed for a long time. We were afraid to move. She kept saying we had to go back and find him, help him."

"Did you — go back?"

Wheeler rubbed his hands together and

then cracked his knuckles. "I wasn't in favor, but she told me I'd better stay with her, or she'd tell the police I did it. She was a crazy woman."

"So you went back?"

"We waited almost half an hour. I had to take a whiz so bad, I was floating. But we finally went. Only he wasn't there any more."

"Wasn't there?"

"No. He wasn't there. Vicky was all relieved. She figured he'd been able to get out, get help. She kept saying he must be okay. He's not here so he must be okay. I guess she was just telling herself. I saw the blood, man, no way he was okay."

"So you're saying some guy was in the bushes, and he whacked your buddy, and Vicky Barrera saw him do it?" Deborah snorted.

"That's exactly what I'm saying. That's what happened."

"What did you do then?" Ray shook his head slightly at Deborah as he asked the question. No breaking the rhythm here. The guy was talking. Let him talk.

"We got out of there. She kept trying to call Joey on his cell phone but there was no answer. She said she'd try to contact him at work."

"You didn't try to contact her afterward?"

"No. No way. I didn't plan to admit I was there. I figured she didn't either."

"How much weed did you smoke?"

"I was feeling good," Wheeler admitted. "But it's not like I was tripping."

"Who asked you to find out what Joey knew?"

Wheeler hesitated. "Kevin Doyle."

"Why involve you? What do you know?"

"I don't know anything, really. But I owed him money and I didn't have it, so he said I could do him a favor instead. He said Joey was really getting on his nerves, going around, telling people he was going to take over the business. He knew we had hung out together, and he wanted me to find out what Joey was up to. That's all."

"That's all? He didn't ask you to do anything else?"

"I swear. We just talked." Sweat dripped down Wheeler's face. The neck of his hospital gown was wet. "Man, I think I'm gonna throw up. I could really use a cigarette."

"So what did the guy look like?"

"What guy? Oh, that guy. I didn't really see him."

"Tall, short, Hispanic, African-American, fat, skinny? Come on!"

"I didn't see him."

"So Kevin Doyle asks you to spy on Joey. You go up to the park with him. Some guy stabs him. You run away. That's your story. You couldn't be a little more creative?" Deborah sounded as if she was suppressing a laugh.

"I told you. I didn't OD. The guy at the bar said he had some recreational drugs. I got in the car with him — sweet, silver BMW. Gorgeous car."

Adrenaline shot through Ray. He pictured the silver BMW swerving down the street in front of Susana's house. The ping of the bullets. The shattering of glass. Susana's screams. "You got in a silver BMW. What did this guy look like? You got a good look at him, right? Did he give you a name?"

"Pedro something. He said he knew my old roommate, Chris. I got in the car. I remember going for a ride. But not much else. I was totally wasted." Wheeler laid his head back. "I've got a bad headache. Can't they give me something for it? Painkillers or something?"

"We're sending a sketch artist over. I want you to describe the man who gave you the drugs. We need to ID the BMW driver — fast."

Wheeler started to protest.

Ray grabbed the front of his hospital

432

gown, leaned in. "Shut up. You withheld information on a murder. Now two more people are dead, and a woman is missing. You're in this up to your neck, bud. You want to cut a deal with the DA, you better cooperate."

Ray started for the door. He could hear the others behind him. This guy knew who drove the BMW. That's all Ray needed to know.

"Hey, what about my protection? I need protection. These guys are killers." Wheeler's shouts followed them down the hallway.

Ray jabbed at the elevator button. Treviño was right behind him, already on the phone. He disconnected with a frown that said bad news.

"How fast can we get a sketch artist over here?"

"The contract guy we usually use is out of pocket until after lunch. We really can't do anything until we ID the BMW guy. And that's if we are able to get a hit on Wheeler's description."

Frustration rocked Ray as the elevator eased to a halt on the first floor. They finally had a break, but things still weren't moving fast enough. He held the door, letting Deborah and Mallory exit first. "And even that is predicated on whether we believe Wheeler's story."

"Tell me you don't." Deborah gave him a disbelieving stare. She shoved through the double doors and sauntered ahead into the parking lot without waiting for an answer.

By the time Ray made it to the Bronco, she was leaning against it, smoking a cigarette.

Treviño stopped in front of his car, tossing his keys in one hand. "You guys interviewed him before — do you think he's telling the truth?"

Ray unlocked the Bronco, still trying to focus on the pieces of the puzzle. If he could just see them all together, he could get it. Something was just beyond his periphery. The BMW. The used car dealership. A guy who killed people and had access to high grade heroin. The pieces were there.

Somehow Kevin Doyle was involved in transporting drugs through the dealerships. That had to be it. Ray didn't dare say those words aloud. Not until he could prove it. Accusing a wealthy philanthropist or his family of drug trafficking without proof was career suicide. He would take a lot of people down with him if he were wrong.

"Ray, are you buying this?" Deborah's voice was impatient.

"Maybe," he said. "I'm thinking."

"The guy admits he was there. He admits doing drugs." Deborah assumed a pose similar to Treviño's. "He knows we can place him at the scene. He made up this whole fairy tale to save his butt."

"Maybe." Ray pictured Melody Doyle. How frightened she had been. How sure she was that something bad had happened to her husband. How sure she had been that the Doyles had been involved in his death. How Joey Doyle had bragged to her and to Candy Romano that something big was going down. How about shutting down a low-producing dealership, affecting drug sales, for instance?

Cars. Used cars. Drugs. What did cars do? They transported someone — or something — from point A to point B. Drug dealers often created traps in vehicles to conceal product when they smuggled it across the border. Why not take it a step further and do it on a mass scale? Who would think of doing it in a dealership load going from one city to another once it was in the country? Nobody.

"Hello. Earth to Ray. You don't believe this creep, do you?" Deborah's voice was incredulous. "He's a druggie who cheats on his girlfriend. He's a loser who mooches off his ex-wife and his friends. He lies about

435

everything."

"Maybe."

"Stop saying maybe, Ray. You're driving me nuts."

"Why would he kill Joey Doyle?"

"Drunks get into fights all the time. They don't need a reason. That's what they do." Deborah's glare dared Ray to say something about her drinking.

"Why cut off the finger and leave it with Vicky Barrera? Why kill Barrera?" Ray let his fingers trace the bullet holes in the Bronco door. "The same person who killed Doyle killed her."

"Maybe he liked Barrera, and she ditched him for Doyle. Or maybe it was to throw us off the scent."

"Where's the evidence? His prints aren't on the knife or the gun. We don't have one stinking piece of physical evidence tying him to Barrera, and we don't have any witnesses."

"It can't hurt to see what the sketch artist comes up with." Treviño turned and opened the door to his car. "We've got to do something. Alvarez is on the warpath. He's getting even more heat. Wheeler was found in a city park. They're talking about closing the parks or having PD take over and patrol them — all two hundred plus."

"Then what?" Lindstrom walked around the car to the passenger side. Her look wasn't any friendlier.

"We can place Wheeler at the first crime scene." Ray tried out a smile on her. She didn't respond. "He's not going anywhere for a couple of days. Ask the DA to pursue charges, maybe we can hold him a couple more days. Danger to himself. Danger to others."

"Maybe." Treviño slid into the car, but left the door open. "We're going to see Wheeler's buddy, Chris, see what he knows about our mystery man in the BMW. Why don't you guys just hang loose until the sketch artist shows up. Keep our friend Wheeler company." He slammed the door and drove away, leaving Deborah and Ray alone.

"Hang loose? Hang loose!" Deborah stomped back and forth between their vehicles. "This is ridiculous. We've interviewed Wheeler's buddy before. He knows us."

Ray worked to let the frustration go. "Oscar's in charge. At least we'll have a sketch to work with."

Deborah still didn't look happy, but she nodded, dropped her cigarette on the asphalt, and mashed it with the heel of her loafer. "Fine. I'll call the sketch artist, tell him to get his laptop and behind over here. You going to the station until he gets here?"

Ray studied the keys in his hand. It was Sunday morning, still early. He had someplace he had to go before going to the station. No matter how tough a case was, he always went to church. In fact, the tougher the case, the more he needed to go. He wondered if there were a way to convince Deborah she needed to be there as well.

"I thought I'd try to make it to church first. You're welcome to come along." He shut out the image of what Susana and Marco's faces would like look if he walked into the sanctuary with Deborah at his side. How much deeper the divide would become. And Samuel. Guilt jolted through Ray. He hadn't told Deborah about the meeting Samuel wanted with her. "Wheeler's not going anywhere."

"Me in church. No, thanks." She lit another cigarette and took a deep drag. "But thanks for the invitation."

There was no sarcasm in her voice. She walked back toward the hospital.

Dilemma solved. Ray knew the relief that drenched his body was a disappointment to God. He shuffled to the Bronco, feeling sick with the shame. If anyone needed to be in church, he did.

CHAPTER
THIRTY-FIVE

Samuel paced between the desks in the CID. His stomach burned from the three cups of coffee he'd consumed after dragging himself from a lumpy bed in a silent hotel room for the third morning in a row. The Night Utility detectives were finishing up paperwork and filtering out while the Monday crew dragged in a few at a time after too much weekend frivolity. It was still too quiet. Ray had passed through earlier, his face lined with fatigue. He'd headed straight for the break room and the coffee pot. Samuel wanted to talk to him, but he couldn't bring himself to do it.

He also wanted to get the meeting with Deborah over. She was late. As usual.

The thought hadn't quite disappeared when Deborah strolled into the room. She slowed when she saw him, then charged toward her desk without speaking.

"In my office."

She veered toward the break room. "As soon as I get some coffee."

"Now."

"Yes, sir." The sarcasm was faint, but clearly present.

Samuel strode into his office without looking back. He knew from the scent of perfume and cigarette smoke, she'd followed. He halted behind his desk.

"Shut the door. Sit."

She did as she was told, her lips pressed in a tight line. Her bloodshot eyes told Samuel what he needed to know. She hadn't laid off, despite everything that had happened over the weekend. No matter how bad it got, she didn't stop drinking because she couldn't.

"Your behavior — "

"Look, Sergeant, you want me to quit. I'll quit. But spare me the lecture." Her eyes sparked with anger as she hurled the words at him.

He fought to keep his face neutral, thinking of what she had cost him through no fault of her own. He'd told Piper he would let Ray handle her. That was before. Before she messed up his sister's life, before her appearance at Ray's house, before she bruised and battered his nephew's image of a man who was essentially his substitute father. Before Piper sent him away. Before he'd realized that Deborah was in a free fall, spinning toward rock bottom. God help him, it was his duty to pick her up when she hit.

"I won't try to get you terminated. I'm not even talking reprimand." He sat down at his desk and picked up his coffee cup. His stomach lurched.

"You're not? Why?" She sounded skeptical, not relieved. Maybe she wanted to be fired. "Ray ratted me out. Don't do me any favors. You won't get anything in return."

Thank God. "I'm not doing you any favors, believe me. By the time I'm done with you, you'll wish you had quit." Samuel blistered her with his gaze, letting her see the fury in his face. "What you do on your own time is your business. However, if you mess up on the job and endanger your partner or others, that's my business. Keep it up, you'll be out on your butt so fast, your head will get there before your feet, no matter what the police association has to say about it."

Her face stained red. "I don't let anything interfere with my work."

"Not even your drinking?"

"I'm a good cop."

"I made an appointment for you to see Mavis Reynolds."

"I don't need a shrink." Hostility radiated from her. Chin up, she crossed her arms. "Ray spoke out of turn."

"Ray didn't violate a confidence. He only told me what I needed to know. You drink too much. This isn't optional. Either you keep the appointment, and it goes on your record as posttraumatic stress, or I put you on medical leave, and you go into rehab. Which would you rather have in your folder?"

She shifted. "Reynolds."

"You go, you answer her questions, you take her advice, or I put you on mandatory medical leave. There will be permanent periodic random drug and alcohol testing. Zero tolerance, Detective. I find out you're drinking, you'll give up your badge and your gun until you can show me a clean bill of health."

"Understood."

"Mavis will keep me posted on whether you show up to your appointments."

"You don't trust me?"

"Alcoholics can't be trusted."

"I'm not an alcoholic." Her voice faltered. She studied her hands in her lap.

Samuel hesitated. He had to drive the point home. "Yes, you are. Face it. Deal with it. We'll help you."

Deborah's head came up, but she couldn't contain the wobble in her voice. "With all due respect, sir, I don't need your help." She stood and put one hand on the door-knob, her expression uncertain. "Look, about the banquet. De La Fuente and Gardner are idiots. I'm sorry if they upset your wife." Her breathing was audible. "Really sorry if it caused any trouble."

"Don't worry about it. You and I know there's nothing to it."

"Right. Of course." She slammed the door behind her so hard the walls reverberated.

Samuel exhaled. He teetered on a tight-rope, knowing he could fall at any second. Help Deborah. Lose Piper. Keep Piper. Watch an officer throw away her career, and maybe even her life.

Find a way to help Deborah and keep his marriage intact. *Lord, I'm sorry. I love Piper. Only her. Please help her to forgive me.*

Deborah stormed across the office, wanting to kill the first person who crossed her path. Ray was at his desk. Convenient, since he was the source of her problem with Martinez. Her partner's gaze met hers.

She prepared to let him have it with both barrels. "You just couldn't keep your mouth shut, could you?"

"I had no choice — "

"I don't believe it." Treviño dropped the phone. "A nine-one-one operator just got a call from the Doyle residence. Milton Doyle's been missing since yesterday afternoon, and they're just now reporting it."

Ray stood. "You need help on this one."

"Yeah, all hands on deck." Deborah chimed in. She stowed her anger until later, when she could stoke it to full fury.

"No." Treviño headed toward the door. The look on his face said he didn't enjoy shutting them out. His case had just gone from bad to worse. "We take Doyle's disappearance. You wanna help, keep moving on Candy Romano's disappearance while we deal with the Doyles. I want to know why they didn't report him missing immediately. They're impossible, totally impossible."

"We haven't found their son's killer; they probably don't think much of our ability to help them on anything else." Ray sank back into his chair. He sounded as if he might have the same opinion himself. "Good luck."

Treviño was already out the door. Deborah walked past Ray's desk and into the break room. She needed caffeine so bad, it was shame she couldn't mainline it. She heard Ray's boots on the tile and turned.

His face twisted. "I had to tell him."

"So much for watching your partner's back, huh?"

"You need help."

"And stabbing me in the back to save your own butt with your girlfriend's brother helps me how?"

"Look, Deborah, I just want — "

"Forget it. Anything new on Romano?"

His face implored her to let him in. She couldn't. He stuck his empty cup on the counter and shoved both fists in his pockets. "No. I'm going to re-interview the women she went to the movies with. If it was a kidnapping, we'd have a ransom demand by now."

"Ransom." Deborah snorted, relieved they were back on safe ground. "Like her family's got money."

"Unless she knows something the kidnappers can use against the Doyles. They want to use her to leverage something. I just wish I knew what." Ray took the pot from her and poured the remainder of the coffee in his mug. His hands shook.

A wave of nausea rolled over her. It wasn't bad enough that her life was messed up, she had messed up his stuff, too.

In the cold light of day, she couldn't begin to imagine why she'd gone to the ranch in the first place. Her drunken words about feeling safe came back to her, and she felt color flood her face. At least he was too much of a gentleman to ever bring up that conversation.

"With Wheeler in the hospital, he can't have played a role in Doyle's disappearance. Doyle probably got drunk playing golf and drove off into a ditch. Or he's holed up somewhere with a mistress." Deborah knew she sounded hard, but it was true. "Wheeler's still involved in this. Somehow."

"Yeah, but I still don't think he killed Joey Doyle or Vicky Barrera." Ray sipped his coffee, his face dark. "And there's a good chance Candy Romano and Milton Doyle are already dead."

"Hey, Smith. We're taking you out for drinks after work," Detective Miles Stone hollered as he walked into the room. "Johnson, didn't you know it's your partner's birthday? We're gonna par-*tay* tonight."

Deborah froze, the coffee mug halfway to her mouth. How did they know? She forced herself to smile. The last thing she wanted was to party with Miles Stone. He was a divorced jerk with wandering hands.

She glanced at Ray. He had a pained look on his face. He probably thought he should have known it was her birthday. How would he? She hadn't said anything. Didn't plan to say anything. She just wanted to get through it. Another milestone unmarked by family or friends. Stone put an arm around her. She shrugged it off with a sharp elbow to his midsection.

He grunted, then grinned. "I'm buying, girl, better be nice to me," he insisted, oblivious her distaste. "You gotta come, Johnson."

"Sorry, guys," Ray didn't meet her gaze. "I don't think there is gonna be an after work. It'll probably be a triple shift. I'll make it up to Deborah later."

That statement brought catcalls and one-liners from a couple guys who had followed Stone into the break room. Deborah watched blush burn all the way up to her partner's hairline. She almost felt sorry for him.

"You know what I mean." He directed the words at her and shoved his way through the guys clustered around the table.

Deborah could almost taste the tequila. It was nine o'clock in the morning. "Look, you guys, I've got work to do. Let's meet tonight around sevenish at the Cadillac Bar. Will that work?"

Stone grinned. "You sure you don't want a sneak preview for lunch — the Mexican

Manhattan for enchiladas and margaritas?"

"Sorry, duty calls. See you around seven."
She tried to move past him.

"You're on, babe. Don't be late." His arm
snaked around her shoulders again, his
breath against her cheek.

She wasn't drunk enough for that. Not
nearly drunk enough. "Later." She ducked
from his embrace and shot after Ray.

Ray was at his desk, wrapping something
in comics from the paper. She started to
approach him, stopped when the civilian
clerk trotted up to her.

"Do you know where Detective Treviño
is?" The clerk waved a sheet of paper in one
hand. "This just came in for him."

"I'll take that." Deborah snatched it from
his hand.

"Hey — "

"Don't worry, I'll make sure he gets it."
Deborah turned her back and started reading. The composite sketch they'd entered
into the database had come back with a
name. Eduardo "Lalo" Hernandez. Contract killer. Last known address: Nuevo
Laredo. A hit man had taken out Joey
Doyle. Taken pot shots at her partner and
his girlfriend.

Deborah sat down hard in her chair.
Instead of making more sense, this case

made less.

"Here." Ray thrust the package at her. "Happy Birthday."

"I don't expect gifts." She had no choice but to take it. The note said. "Try starting with Matthew. Happy Birthday!"

"It's something I want you to have. You need it." He hesitated. "Those guys in there aren't your friends, Deborah."

Irritation burned through her. He had people who cared about him. He didn't understand. "I'm not an idiot. They're the best I can do on short notice, but thanks for the gift."

"You might not be thanking me when you open it." He met her gaze.

"I can read. I know who Matthew is — was."

Ray was trying to help. In his own way, he really did care. She tried to hang on to that thought through a pounding headache and increasingly urgent thirst. After all the problems she'd caused him, he was still trying.

She dropped the package on her desk without unwrapping it. "So, did you work things out with your girlfriend?"

"Don't worry about it."

"I'll take that as a no." She'd messed everything up for him. And he was still trying. She offered him the printout. "We got a hit on the sketch they did from Wheeler description. Eduardo 'Lalo' Hernandez. Get this, paid assassin."

"You're kidding me." Ray sat, looking as stunned as she'd been. "A hit man took out Joey Doyle? Who hires a pro to take out a car dealer?"

"Drug dealers?" It was a shot in the dark. She focused, trying to see a bigger picture that refused to take shape. Her head pounded, and her stomach did a heave-ho. She hadn't been able to keep breakfast down. "Hernandez has connections to the Gulf Cartel. He's a pro, works out of Laredo and Nuevo Laredo. Became a naturalized citizen almost thirty years ago. Been picked up several times, even tried once, but was acquitted when a couple of key witnesses disappeared. Nothing has ever stuck. The guy's like Teflon."

"So what's he doing in San Antonio, picking off people related to Joey Doyle?" Ray ran his hands through his hair, making it stand on end. He looked like a big kid. "We need to get Treviño to show the sketch to the Doyles, see if they recognize him."

"I'll give him a call on his cell, meet up with him somewhere." Deborah grabbed her purse, formulating a plan. She could do this and maybe take Stone up on that lunch offer, after all. Just a little pick-me-up to get her by until the shift ended.

"Just stay off Doyle property, whatever you do."

She nodded. She wasn't in the mood for their high-class garbage anyway. Let the dynamic duo handle them, while she took a quick breather. Martinez's words echoed in her head. *Zero tolerance.* She swallowed. Stealth was her middle name. "Then I'm gonna visit some of my CIs. See what the word is on the street. Any outstanding contracts. I'll check back with you later."

"Right, like your informants hang with contract killers. Tell Treviño to call me as soon as he waves that sketch around in front of the Doyles. If they've know this guy, maybe we can get a line on where he's staying." Ray had a doubtful look on his face.

She shoved away guilt. He couldn't read her mind. And she'd put in full shifts Saturday and Sunday, her alleged days off.

Today was her birthday, after all.

Ray ran his index finger down a long list of vehicles in the inventory records open on his desk. If Joey Doyle knew something was going on at the used car dealership, it would explain why it had been necessary to remove

452

him. If he'd found out about the illicit drug business and refused to go along with it, he was definitely a threat, and the downhill spiral would have begun when Joey shot off his mouth about selling the underperforming dealership.

"Whatddya got?"

Ray glanced up. Deborah. As good as her word. She had come back — almost seven hours later. Her eyes had that sheen, her cheeks were unnaturally red. "Where have you been?"

"I told you — hanging with my CIs."

"Right. What were they serving — margaritas?"

"Don't be such a fuddy-duddy. I was only trying to get on their good sides — as if they had good sides. Whew, one stank to high heaven." She chortled and flopped onto her chair. "Man, I'm tired. I think it's time to call it a day."

"There's still a lot going on, in case you're wondering." Ray couldn't keep the sarcasm out of his voice. "Wheeler's buddy, Chris, is in Christus Santa Rosa hospital with multiple broken bones. A guy looking for Wheeler worked him over. The guy matches Lalo Hernandez's description. Oscar and Mallory drew a blank with the Doyles on the sketch. They deny knowing him or ever having seen him.

"In addition, they talked to every employee on duty at the course where Milton Doyle played yesterday. They all said the same thing. He played golf with his usual foursome. They had drinks in the bar. He got in his car and headed home, just as he always did."

Deborah nodded, but Ray couldn't be sure she'd actually heard.

He plowed ahead. "His car was found parked in a field about five miles from the course. Skid marks indicate he'd been run off the road. No sign of struggle inside the car. A very small amount of blood, nothing lethal."

"Okay, yeah." She nodded again.

"I've been going through the inventory records from Doyle's used car lot on Broadway. I think Wheeler was telling the truth. Periodically, they move cars from this dealership to the ones in Dallas and Fort Worth. I'm not seeing a whole lot of sales here in town. Kevin told us that dealership was doing a healthy business. You sure can't tell it from the way the inventory moves. This is exactly what Tommy Wheeler was talking about. He was telling the truth."

Deborah straightened in her chair, looking more alive. "So Kevin lied. Wheeler told the truth. Kevin wanted him to find out what Joey was up to, because he didn't want Joey bringing attention to his used car dealership. He has something going on the side there. But what?"

Ray debated telling Deborah the details of his drug smuggling theory. If he was wrong, Deborah might be kissing her job good-bye, too. He needed proof. Joey Doyle said he'd show his siblings. He would bring them to their knees. Joey Doyle had found out and planned to expose Kevin and Elaine. Follow this lead, and they would find Milton Doyle. And Candy Romano. Before it was too late.

"Whatever it is, I think it's drug-trade-related." He kept his voice down, even though the room was virtually empty. "We need proof before we go blabbing about it to anyone. I'm going to do some surveillance on the used car lot." He stood.

The look of disappointment on Deborah's face came and went. It was her birthday, and they had work to do and not much time left. Milton Doyle and Candy Romano might already be dead. "We need to see what goes on there after hours. It may be the only way to save Milton Doyle and Candy Romano — if they're still alive."

"We gonna tell Treviño?"

"Not until I can prove it. It's suicide to say anything that will reflect on Milton Doyle's reputation in this town until we're sure. Treviño's got his hands full trying to find him and Candy Romano. When we have something definite, we'll tell him."

Deborah's earlier glow had faded, leaving her skin pasty white. She wiggled in the chair as if trying to stay awake.

Ray wavered. He couldn't depend on her, anyway, not if she'd been drinking. "It's your birthday. We don't really know anything for sure. It's just a hunch. I'll do a little reconnoitering. Stake it out without engaging. Let you know."

"Fine. I can do a shift later." Her chin came up. "You take the first shift. I'll go talk to Tommy Wheeler again."

The Deborah who cared about getting the bad guy was still in there somewhere.

"Good idea. Call me on my cell if you get anything." Ray didn't really expect her to call. "Deborah — "

"What?" She waited, her gaze a challenge.

"If something really is going on over there, I may need your backup tonight. Okay?"

"Yeah, sure, no problem." She gave him a faint grin. "Partners, right?"

CHAPTER
THIRTY-SIX

Lalo parked the old clunker in the hospital lot. He straightened his collar. Wearing disguises was one of his favorite things. Where he came from, priests didn't drive fancy silver BMWs so he'd picked out a nondescript Taurus from the dealership lot. Poor parish priests rode bicycles to work in the neighborhood where he'd grown up, but he felt no need to go that far. Mr. Wheeler would certainly never know the difference.

First, a quick stop at the information desk for the room number. The candy striper didn't even look at his face. Just the collar. A uniformed cop leaned against the corner at the nurses' station, chatting with a *chica bonita*. Oblivious.

Lalo pushed the door open with one finger and peeked in. The boss had been furious when the lawyer tried to coerce the Doyles into exerting influence over the DA. Now it wasn't just the boss's rear Lalo had to cover.

His own was exposed. A syringe of smack that pure should have done the trick. How was he supposed to know the Park Police were so efficient in enforcing a curfew? Just bad luck. That was all. But not today. Today he felt lucky.

Wheeler's eyes were closed. The steady rise and fall of his chest reminded Lalo of the park lady. This would be easy. He laid the Bible on the table next to a tray of half-eaten food, pulled gloves from his pocket, and tugged them on.

One of Wheeler's pillows had worked its way toward the side of the bed. That would suffice. He picked it up. Wheeler's eyes fluttered open. He looked confused by his surroundings. Just like that day in the car. He'd fussed about the needle, but that was all right. Lalo had calmed him down.

Just like he did now. "Quiet, please. Everything's fine."

"You? What are you doing — " His eyes wide with panic, Wheeler looked around as if searching for something.

"Are you looking for this?" Lalo held up Wheeler's call button, then dropped it on a chair out of reach. "You don't need this. Just lie back and relax."

He stuck the pillow over Wheeler's face, climbed up on the bed, and pinned him down with his knees. A few pounds of pressure for a few minutes — all it took to suffocate someone.

"Just relax. Everything is fine. Just fine." He whistled softly.

The arms flailed and the feet jerked.

Then they stopped.

He dismounted and took a deep, invigorating breath. Time to pick up the boss and take him to the work site. The boss wanted him on hand for security purposes. He was a paid assassin, not a bodyguard. Tonight, he would tell the boss this was it. He and Sylvia would move to Vallarta in the next few weeks. Salty ocean breezes, clean white curtains in the windows, clean white sheets on the bed. He could almost smell them.

Samuel helped Emma shove her backpack and sleeping bag into the bed of his pickup truck. They weighed almost as much as the nine-year-old. Emma had been in a hurry to go to Girl Scout camp, but now she was dragging her feet.

She scrunched up her pixie face against the early evening sun as she turned to look at him. "*Papi,* how come Mom isn't coming with us? We always go together."

Samuel glanced back at Piper, standing on the driveway in shorts and a T-shirt, her feet bare. He couldn't decipher the look on her face. "That's when you go up on Sunday afternoon, *m'ija*."

He opened the passenger door, so she could scramble in. Emma had been sick and missed the first few days of camp in Waring. It had taken some convincing, but Piper had finally agreed to let him drive their daughter up for what was left of it. But Piper had refused to come along. "Tonight, your mom has some mom stuff to do, and I want some alone time with my girl."

Emma giggled. Everyone said the dark-haired *chiquita* with honey brown skin looked just like him, but Samuel could see Piper in her smile and hear his wife in the laugh.

"I thought Mommy was your girl."

From the mouths of babes. Samuel left her door open, so Piper could say her good-byes. She brushed past him without speaking. He waited until she closed Emma's door to approach her.

"Thanks for letting me do this."

"I was just surprised you could get away. Surely, some new hot case is occupying your time."

Sarcasm wasn't Piper's forte, but he got her drift. "It doesn't matter. The new case isn't nearly as important . . ." He tried to force out the words, but they died in his throat. "As other things."

Piper studied his shoes. "Emma told me last night that she misses you."

"She knows?"

"They all do. Our behavior at church was a dead giveaway."

"What did you tell her?"

"I told her you were working a really difficult case right now that kept you away, but it wouldn't be for long."

"Did you mean that — it wouldn't be long?"

Tears welled and trickled down her cheeks. She swiped them away. "I'm still working on it. God and I have had some pretty heated arguments." She crossed her arms. "Where're you staying? Are you getting enough to eat? You look . . . rumpled and tired."

"I want to come home."

The look on her face told him he wouldn't get the answer he wanted.

"*Papi,* it's getting later and later." Emma stuck her head out the open truck window. "I've already missed a bunch of days. Are you and Mommy done fighting so we can go now?"

Emma was a bright child. "In a minute, *m'ija.*"

461

Samuel took a step closer to Piper, allowing himself to crowd her space. Much as he wanted to, he didn't touch her. Her hands came up as if to ward him off.

He leaned down so his face was close to hers and spoke softly. "I've talked to God, too, *mi amor*. I asked Him to forgive me. He did. If He can, couldn't you maybe consider it, too?"

He headed for the truck without waiting for her to respond. He thought he heard his name. He stopped, hand on the door. Only silence. When he looked back, she'd already disappeared into the house.

His question hung in the air.

Ray ate another bite of his peanut butter and jelly sandwich. The dealership had been closed for almost an hour. The sales staff had gone home first. Then the admin staff. The lights were still on in the service department. Ray could see movement through the smoky panes in the long garage doors that had been pulled down when the shop closed for the day.

He glanced at his watch. He considered trying Susana again. Despite his earlier resolve, he'd given in and called her twice already — both times her machine had picked up.

Stop thinking about her, and focus.

He needed to get closer without tipping them off that they were watched. He took another bite, chewed, and swallowed as he debated. He punched in Deborah's cell phone number.

"The mobile number you have dialed is unavailable. To leave a voicemail message — "

He disconnected. The Wheeler interview would be long over. The party most likely was in full swing, leaving him on his own.

He stashed the phone in his pocket and glanced up in time to see a silver BMW pull in and park on the street in front of the service shop. Ray hunkered down behind the wheel, his hand on the door.

Lalo Hernandez, their visiting hit man, stepped from the car.

Ray's pulse revved as he relived the seconds when the glint of the barrel in the sunlight registered in the Bronco's side mirror that day. Remembering, he sucked in air and peered out, trying to get a good look at the car's other occupants. A Hispanic man who looked vaguely familiar got out of the front seat. Kevin and Elaine Doyle exited from the back. There was no mistaking the blond hair and arrogant tilt of their heads. What were they doing with a hit man from

Nuevo Laredo?

Ray punched in Deborah's number again. Voicemail. He considered calling Samuel, but the thought of his boss's reaction when he found out Ray was working surveillance by himself and without Treviño's knowledge nixed that idea. Of course, Samuel would react differently if Ray broke the case. He had to have enough to make an arrest, before he let Samual know he'd flown solo.

He needed to get close enough to see what they were up to. Ray slid from the Bronco, eased the door shut, and hobbled toward the back of the dealership. A chain-link fence delineated public from private property. The dealership backed up to a service road that meandered into a neighboring park. Overgrown weeds, broken concrete, and trash made for an attractive scene. The back doors had windows. Jackpot. He stayed low to the ground and close to the building as he slipped up to the window.

Mighty busy for a place that was closed. Three men — Hispanic, late teens, early twenties — worked on cars, lined up side-by-side. All of them had the doors open and various panels removed. Each car had its own worker, the three men seemingly choreographed to the *ranchera* music blaring from a boom box.

One of the men stuffed small, brown, paper bags into the compartments inside the door of one car. On an upside-down cardboard box, someone had laid out foil, plastic wrap and bags. Emergency bag repair. Cocaine. The man finished, then screwed the door panels back in place.

Bingo. Ray smacked a fist into his palm. He had them. The men were building traps to conceal the drugs. First, a minivan. Soccer-mom vehicle moving drugs, pretty typical for drug dealers. Even though the DEA had spread the word that minivans were favorites for smugglers, they still used them. Then, a town car.

Lots of room for medium-sized traps in both of them: Voids in the dashboard, between the body panels, and in the frame of the vehicle. Also, inside the fuel tanks, in the engine compartment, the batteries. The traffickers were getting more and more sophisticated in their attempts to find new niches that law enforcement would miss.

The third car was an older, four door sedan, nondescript, easily forgettable.

The children of the city's biggest philanthropist were drug smugglers. Who would believe that? Nobody. He couldn't believe it, and he was seeing it with his own eyes.

Kevin and Elaine Doyle stood by the

door, talking to the other passenger from the BMW. He looked familiar. Ray racked his brain. The man gestured wildly. He was short and squat, with a lot of bicep, like he'd been a body builder at some point in his life. A gray beard and thick gold chains around his neck were probably his way of shifting the focus from a bald head that shone in the glare of fluorescent lights.

Ray finally dragged the name from the recesses of his brain. Mariano Echeverria. He'd gotten up close and personal with the guy five or six years earlier, back in his uniformed days, when he'd accompanied two narcotics detectives on a knock and talk at a crack house.

Echeverria had made a run for it, and Ray had done the fifty-yard dash before tackling the guy and cuffing him. Echeverria would remember him — they'd been eye-to-eye in the dirt, cigarette butts, and prickly burrs of a vacant lot.

Even though they knew Echeverria had connections with one of the two biggest, warring drug cartels in South Texas, the DA's office had been unable to make the charges stick. Here was a guy who knew where to find a hired killer when he needed one. And could afford one.

He'd obviously done some empire building of his own since his brush with U.S. law — with the help of the Doyle siblings. Ray peered in the window, then ducked down low again so he could dial Deborah's number one more time. He needed her here now. No answer. Where was she? What about Samuel? Now that Ray had something, enough maybe, to apply some pressure on these people. No answer on Samuel's cell phone either. He left a quick message asking Samuel to call him back as soon as possible and disconnected. What now?

He cranked his neck and peered in the window again, trying to flesh out his theory. When Joey started talking about selling the dealership, Kevin and Elaine had gotten antsy. Their hidden revenue stream would be cut off. Not to mention, you didn't mess with a guy like Echeverria. Partners weren't allowed to bow out of the business when things got dicey. If Kevin and Elaine didn't arrange for Joey's demise, Echeverria did. Or maybe he made an example of Joey to keep Kevin and Elaine in line. So what were Milton Doyle and Candy Romano? Bargaining chips?

Echeverria and the Doyles were arguing. Even at this distance, Ray could see it was heated. Kevin Doyle's face contorted with anger. He grabbed Echeverria's arm. Echeverria shook him off. His hand went up as if to strike the other man and then dropped.

Ray didn't plan to go in without backup, but he wanted to know what they were arguing about. He slipped around toward the front, searching the shadows. No one was in the parking lot. These guys weren't stupid, they had to have a lookout. Floor-to-ceiling windows covered the front of the building, leaving him exposed, and the streetlight at the corner flooded the area with light.

Maybe on the other side.

Lalo Hernandez came out of nowhere.

Ray registered the tire iron in one hand, saw the swing coming. He didn't have time to throw up an arm. The thud when it hit the side of his head reverberated in his ears.

Surprise, pain, then nothing.

CHAPTER
THIRTY-SEVEN

Deborah studied Tommy Wheeler's slack face as Tito Sanchez took the dead man's liver temperature. Wheeler lay sprawled on his hospital bed, his bare, hairy legs still tangled in the sheets.

"Well? Any thoughts on COD?"

"You know the drill, Detective." Sanchez delivered the words with icy coolness. A happily married guy, he seemed immune to her charms.

"Come on, Tito, a little speculation."

"We've got petechial hemorrhaging, slight cyanosis, some small contusions on the inner lips, all of which suggest he was smothered." Sanchez touched a pillow at the dead man's feet with a gloved finger. "Deadly weapon? We'll know more when we do the autopsy."

"Great." Deborah didn't try to keep the sarcasm from her voice. The martinis she'd had at the Cadillac Bar made it hard to focus. She'd just planned to have a couple with the guys, before she split for the hospital. Wheeler was dead by the time she'd arrived.

Trying to ignore the guilt that twisted her gut, she strode into the hallway. Treviño was deep in conversation with a candy striper.

He slapped his notebook shut and trotted over. "Girl says the only visitor Wheeler had was a priest."

"A priest." Deborah rolled her eyes. "Did you show her the sketch of Lalo Hernandez?"

"Yep." Treviño gave her a tight grin. "Looks like our hit man got religion. What were you doing here, anyway?"

"Following up a hunch."

"Right, messing in our case again. Where's your partner?"

"Making up with his girlfriend, I guess." Treviño didn't need to know about Ray's after-hours plan. Not yet.

Deborah tugged her phone from the clip on her waist and jabbed in Ray's number. Treviño brushed past her into Wheeler's room. The phone rang and rang. Voicemail. Her irritation skyrocketed. She'd been calling Ray for the last hour. No answer on his cell. Or at the ranch.

It was her birthday. She punched in the

number again. Voicemail. Maybe Ray had left the dealership. Maybe their secret surveillance had been a bust. Maybe he didn't answer the phone because he and Susana really had decided to kiss and make up.

Biting her lip, Deborah called information and asked for Susana's number. Unlisted. She tapped her nail on the back of the phone. Susana's house was much closer than the dealership on Broadway. She wouldn't have to drive all the way over there if she could catch Ray at Susana's. Then she could get back to celebrating. Half a dozen free rounds waited for her.

Deborah stuck her head in the hospital room. "Oscar, I'm off to find Johnson, okay? He's gonna want in on this."

"We've got it covered." Treviño had aged ten years in the last week. Another dead body and another dead end. Joey Doyle's murderer was still out there. "Have a drink for me."

"I'm not — " Deborah shut up and walked away. She'd just slip by and see if Ray's Bronco was parked in front of Susana's. She punched the button to the elevator twice, anxious to get going. She was missing her own party.

Deborah made the drive to Susana's on the fast track. Only missed one stop sign. Nope. His Bronco wasn't parked in Susana's driveway. The lights were on, though. Deborah could see movement through the living room window. It was worth a shot.

Susana opened the door. Surprise filled her face. "Deborah, what are you doing here? Where's Ray?"

"You haven't heard from him, by any chance? I can't raise him on his phone."

"He's not answering his cell?" Surprise gave way to concern on the woman's face.

"Yeah, I thought maybe he was over here, having it out with you."

"No." Susana flushed, and her gaze dropped. "He called a couple times, but I . . . I have company, so I let the machine get it."

"Well, I'm sure he's still on stakeout. I was just trying to save myself a trip there. We've got another body on the Doyle case . . ." She didn't bother to finish the thought. Susana didn't want to hear about this case or any other.

"I thought that case was reassigned."

"We're just doing a little off-duty reconnoitering. Unofficially, if you know what I mean."

"Samuel doesn't know? That's — " An odd look flitted across the woman's face. She leaned toward Deborah and sniffed. "Have you been drinking?"

A sudden thrill of fear careened through Deborah. "What I do on my time is my business."

"But you're still Ray's backup — "

"Sorry, I bothered you. I'll see if I can catch him at the dealership." She started back down the sidewalk, curbing the desire to break into a run. Sarge's stony face when he said the words *zero tolerance* crowded her. Tough. Martinez was out of town.

"Which one of their dealerships is it?"

Deborah forced herself to halt and look back. "The used cars on Broadway."

"Did you find Milton Doyle? It wasn't his body, was it?"

"No. It was his daughter Sarah's ex-boyfriend. We haven't found Candy Romano, either. This case is going nowhere fast, it seems." Deborah clamped her mouth shut. Why was she babbling like this? A combination of alcohol and nerves? Or because Susana knew she had been drinking and her next step would surely be to tell Ray . . . and Sarge.

473

Instead of shutting the door, Susana moved onto the steps, her look hesitant. "Deborah, you know if you want to come in, maybe you could have a cup of coffee, while I try to call Ray." Her voice strained with concern. "You shouldn't be driving. You could tell me what's going on with you. I'm a counselor and I'm a good listener — "

"As I recall, the last time you counseled someone, she committed suicide by cop. Stay out of my business, okay?" Deborah forced herself to walk to her car without another glance back. She didn't want to see Susana's worried face again.

Close call. Too close.

Ray struggled to open his eyes. The pulsating pain forced them closed again. The rough, concrete floor was cold. The smell of burnt oil filled his nostrils. Someone had taped his mouth; rope cut into his wrists and ankles.

The bile in the back of his throat gagged him. He swallowed it back, promising himself he'd never eat a peanut butter and jelly sandwich again. *Please God don't let me choke to death on my own vomit.* He tried to swivel his head, but a bright light sent more pain shooting through it, forcing him to shrink back into the darkness again.

Deborah knew where he was. Unless she was too drunk to remember. Or care. Samuel knew. If he got the message, and if he got back to town in time . . .

God, let me survive this for Susana and Marco's sakes. They need to be able to believe in something again. She needs a second chance. Please Lord, let me be that chance.

Someone was coming. Arguing voices got closer. He recognized Elaine Doyle's clipped style. And Kevin's. The third man's voice sounded vaguely familiar, a hint of Mexico in it.

"You can't kill a cop." Elaine. Her voice was brittle with tension.

Ray peered through a squint. He could see pant legs and shoes, four pairs, three men, one woman.

"He saw the operation. He knows about the cars." Had to be Echeverria.

"He didn't see anything. The idiot bonked him on the head for no reason. We have a right to be here. We own the place." Elaine knew how to think on her feet. "It was stupid to hit him. Now, it's too late to hide what we're doing."

"He was here because he suspects us." Kevin. Smart guy. "He's trying to pin Joey's murder on us. He knows something."

475

"You're lucky Lalo was acting as *halcon*. If he hadn't been watching, the cop would have called for backup and we'd all be in jail by now. You see just how high the stakes are." Echeverria talking. "If you'd reined in your brother when I told you, we wouldn't be standing here."

"You didn't have to have him killed." Elaine actually sounded upset about Joey's death. Or just upset at the problem it had caused?

"You weren't taking care of him. I had no choice. I have obligations to my suppliers. You have obligations to me. Nobody backs out."

"You didn't have to kill him." Elaine repeated the words, but with less force. "And you didn't have to get my dad involved. Tell us where he is. We'll do whatever you want."

"Your dad is involved because the two of you wanted out. If you had understood your commitment, I wouldn't have had to push. You're writing your poor *papi's* death certificate."

"No. No!" Kevin's voice.

He must have gotten too close to Echeverria. Ray heard a whack, a loud inhale, and then felt someone slam to the floor beside him. But he was left looking at Kevin's

476

shoes as someone — Echeverria? — dragged him back up.

"Yes. You want to see your dad alive? You'll complete this shipment on time."

"Yeah. Yeah, I get it." Kevin's voice sounded muffled. "What about Johnson?"

"We'll take a short trip to a place more conducive to dealing with him. I think you should be the one to handle it. You do the cop, and that way you're committed, once and for all. Know what I mean? Once this shipment is out, we'll talk about your dad."

"*Señor,* perhaps it would be best if I handle this." Hernandez? A soft voice with the accent of a native Spanish speaker. "I believe that is what you said. That if it became necessary, I would do the policeman."

"Sorry." Echeverria's laugh was ugly. "Kevin needs to learn his lesson."

"*Está bien, señor.*"

The Doyles knew how to pick them. Hernandez bent over Ray and worked the ropes until they slackened and fell away from his legs. Ray's heart hammered as Hernandez tore the tape from his mouth. He stifled a gasp of pain and stared into Hernandez's face. Ray would never forget it, and he would make sure the man never forgot his.

"On your feet, *señor.*" Hernandez stuck a

gun in Ray's face, grabbed one arm, and dragged him to his feet.

"What happened?" Ray pretended to be disoriented as he struggled to straighten.

Waves of nausea made it an easy act. The pounding in his head increased until he could barely hear over the racket. He took a quick look around. The mechanics had disappeared. The car doors were shut, the evidence out of sight.

"We wanted to ask you the same thing." Echeverria leaned casually against the wall. "One of our guys thought you were an intruder."

Kevin's usual sneer had disappeared. Blood was smeared under his nose. Swelling nearly hid one eye. He looked petrified. "We know you're not an intruder."

"I was on my way over to talk to you about your dad's disappearance. Someone hit me in the head." Ray focused on Kevin, refusing to giving Echeverria control of the situation.

"Shut up." Echeverria muscled into the space between Ray and Kevin. "It's detective now, isn't it, Johnson? Congratulations. It's good to see you again, especially since I have the upper hand this time. Where's your ride?"

"I'm surprised to see you in these parts,

Echeverria. I thought you were back in Rio Bravo with your cartel buddies."

"*N'ombre,* it's too *caliente* down there, with all that turf war." Echeverria gave Ray a tight-lipped sneer. "San Antonio has been very hospitable. Where's your vehicle?"

"It'll be a lot hotter where you going." Ray made eye contact with Echeverria, making sure he understood the message.

Hernandez lunged forward; the nine-millimeter handgun flashed in his hand. The barrel smashed into Ray's face. Pain so intense he couldn't breathe knocked him back. Salty blood ran from his nose into his mouth. Hernandez shoved him. The back of Ray's head bounced against the wall. Spots danced in front of his eyes. The room threatened to go black.

"I think Deputy Dan is ready to show us where his ride is." Echeverria cocked his head toward Ray, a grotesque grin spreading across his face.

Ray forced himself upright as he wiped blood from his chin onto his shirtsleeve.

"Doyle, you follow me in his car. We'll dispose of the vehicle with him."

"You really want to go down for capital murder?" Ray swallowed the pain and worked to keep his voice even. "You stop now, you can probably make a decent deal

479

with the DA. I know you've got information on the South Texas operation they'd love to have. Take me out and you're done."

"Not if we do it right. By the time they find you, *compadre,* Mr. Hernandez and I will be underground again. And believe me, these poor, pitiful *gente* won't be talking."

Hernandez gave him another shove. The barrel of the gun jabbed his side. Echeverria grinned again. Ray wanted to wipe the smirk from his face with his bare hands.

"I'll take Elaine with me just to make sure that we all make our destination together. Lalo's a professional, Kevin. You mess with me, and your sister's dead. You want to see her and your dad again, don't take any detours."

"You trust him?" Hernandez's eyebrows arched. He looked directly at Ray and smiled. "A professional to handle a professional might be more . . . strategic."

"Doyle only has to remember what's at stake. He's already lost a brother; I don't think he'll risk a sister, too." Echeverria sounded determined.

It would be so nice if he'd give in. Ray wanted a shot at Hernandez. The cold hard knot in his chest told him he could take the man on here and now.

Forming an erratic line, they straggled from the building. Echeverria and Hernandez split to the left with Elaine. Kevin kept a gun pressed into the small of Ray's back as they veered right and walked to the Bronco.

"Get in and don't be stupid, okay?"

"You trust this guy, Kevin? He's setting you up to take the fall for my murder. Are you ready for a needle stick?"

"I don't have much choice. I have to do it. Get in."

Ray got a good look at Kevin's face in the streetlight. Naked fear shone in the man's eyes. He kept the gun — Ray's Glock — on Ray, forcing him into the SUV. Kevin loped around the vehicle and slid in the other side before jamming the key in the ignition and turning it.

"You're not a killer and you don't have to do this. I can help you get your dad back. Who do you want to trust — the police or a drug dealer who killed your brother?"

"As soon as this shipment goes out, Echeverria will let Dad go."

"You think your dad will keep quiet?"

"He has to." A sweaty sheen on the Kevin's face said the pressure was getting to him. He smelled bad. "If he doesn't, Echeverria will take my mother next."

"How did you get involved with this guy?"

"I did a real estate deal with a couple of guys in Laredo. Went to a few parties. Echeverria was always around." The words came fast and low. "He always had blow. We partied — hard. There were women. Not the kind of women you bring home to Mom and Dad.

"When he approached me about this deal, I thought he was crazy. After I saw how much money was involved, I was tempted, but I said no. Then he sent me a packet of photos . . . dirty photos. I had to play along or be exposed."

"He blackmailed you, and you let him, instead of going to the police?"

"I couldn't let my dad and mom find out. Or my wife." The weapon in Doyle's hand shook as he raised it toward Ray's head. "Now shut up . . . Please, just shut up."

"You don't want to try to save your dad and put an end to this?"

"I wish I could." The ring of truth in that simple statement was undeniable. "But I don't know where Echeverria has him stashed."

"Echeverria can't take a chance he won't keep his mouth shut. If we can take Hernandez here, he won't have a chance to hurt your dad or your sister." Ray had to convince Doyle. "Right now, all you've got is the drug smuggling. If you agree to testify against Echeverria, the DA will deal. Joey was your only brother, the father of two children. Don't you want to punish Echeverria for that?"

Emotions freewheeled across Kevin's face. Fear mingled with desperation.

"Kevin, he'll kill your dad anyway."

Kevin groaned, a primal sound. He gave a furtive glance out the windshield, and then pulled a pocketknife from his jeans. A second later, Ray's hands were free.

"You better be right about this. Here." He pulled a familiar P12.45 from the pocket of his jacket and thrust it at Ray. His backup piece. "I may not have the guts to kill you now, but if my dad dies, I will."

"Understood."

"I want Hernandez. You get Echeverria."

Ray took a breath and crammed guilt back in a box. He would do whatever was necessary to save lives and ask forgiveness later. "I'm taking Hernandez."

One clean shot would be all he needed.

CHAPTER
THIRTY-EIGHT

Ray didn't answer his cell. Again. Susana laid her phone down and grabbed her iced tea. She took a long drink and used it to swallow her tears. She'd tried to ignore her encounter with Deborah, but she couldn't. Deborah was right. Susana had failed as a counselor, and she'd failed Ray.

Deborah had reeked of alcohol. Ray couldn't depend on Susana any more than he could depend on Deborah. Which was worse? She should've answered the phone when Ray had called. She hated this, half-in, half-out of his life, and she had only herself to blame.

"Susana? You won't get your scrapbook done in there!" Lily had decided Susana needed a hobby, and she'd picked scrap-booking. She'd dragged Autumn away from the crisis center long enough to join them for the evening. The two were carrying on like a couple of teenage girls in the living room.

"Coming. I'm just getting more tea."

"Okay." Lily didn't sound convinced.

Susana snagged the phone again and punched in the number at the ranch. After four rings, Ray's machine kicked in. She hung up and dialed his cell phone. The steady ring served only to irritate her. *Pick up. Pick up. Please pick up.* Nothing but voicemail. "Ray, call me. Please. Deborah stopped by looking for you. She was drunk. Call me."

She dropped the phone on the table, stomped into the living room, and plopped down on the couch, ignoring Autumn's quizzical look. Maybe he'd ended the stake-out and decided to go somewhere for a late dinner. With Teresa Saenz. Maybe he'd taken Susana's advice and gone on with his life. That was the better scenario, really. Then he wouldn't be counting on a drunk partner as sole support.

Through a blur of tears, Susana stared at photos of Javier and Marco on their son's first day of kindergarten. She'd rather know. Know where he was — on a date or at the stakeout. If it was the latter, he needed to know Deborah had been drinking. So how could she be sure he'd gotten the message?

"So, Susana, did you try to get Piper to come over?" Lily didn't look up from the photos she was sorting. "I was hoping we could get her to tell us what's going on between her and Samuel."

"I tried. She sounded like she'd been crying." Susana fought to keep tears from her own voice. "She said she had a cold."

"She doesn't have a cold. She's as stubborn as he is." Lily sighed. "I'd like shake them both. I just wish I knew what the problem was. I keep telling myself they'll be all right. They've had rough patches before, and they always work through them."

Susana kept her gaze on the photo in her hand. Javier and Marco building a mammoth sandcastle on the beach only days before Javier's death. Lily couldn't guarantee Piper and Samuel would be all right. No one could.

"Susana?" Autumn's voice was soft. "What did Deborah want?"

"Nothing." To her dismay, her voice shook. She stood, ran back to the kitchen, snatched up her phone, and punched in Samuel's number. More voicemail. She left a message trying to explain herself as clearly as possible, and disconnected. If Samuel was still in Waring with Emma he was at least forty minutes away. She ran back into the living

486

room to the desk where she kept her purse and keys.

"Lily, can you keep an eye on Marco for me for a little while?" She slung her purse strap over her shoulder and charged toward the front door.

"Sure. Where're you going?"

"To talk to someone."

"Ray?" Lily's eyebrows rose in surprise.

Autumn let out a whoop. "You go, girl!"

Susana slammed the door behind her.

Ray waited. He had the P12 tucked in his lap underneath clasped hands.

Kevin eased the Bronco along the curb directly across the street from the BMW idling in front of the dealership. Echeverria sat in the driver's seat of the silver car, Elaine Doyle next to him. Hernandez walked toward the Bronco.

"All is well?" Hernandez stopped a few feet from the Bronco. He wielded a Mac 10 that made the P12 look like a water pistol. Kevin's lips stretched taut against his teeth, his hands white on the steering wheel. Ray prayed the guy could hold it together a little longer.

The menace in Hernandez's voice matched the look on his face. "You go first. We'll take Mulberry to the highway. Go

487

north. Mr. Doyle, anything happens before we get to the location, I kill your sister. One shot to the forehead. *Es todo.* Then I do your father. Only him, I make suffer, and I make you watch."

Hernandez turned to walk away.

"No!" Kevin shoved open his door and heaved himself from the Bronco, his weapon raised.

"Not yet!" Even as he screamed them, Ray knew the words were futile.

Hernandez was still too close. Kevin fired wildly as he darted around the front of the vehicle, his body cutting a shadow in the headlights. Hernandez whirled and fired. Ray grabbed his weapon and jerked open his door. Too late. Kevin jolted back; his head slammed into the bumper before he slid to the ground.

Ray leaned across the seat and returned fire through the open window. Four shots. That left eight. Hernandez ducked behind a tree, then burst out again, firing steadily. Ray rolled through the open door onto the street, letting the vehicle shield him. Fighting to breathe through the adrenaline rush, he crept to the corner of the bumper and peeked around it.

Kevin lay in a pool of blood, his open eyes staring at the black sky. Ray threw himself on his belly and crawled forward far enough to reach his Glock, lying at the dead man's fingertips. That should give him at least nine more rounds — if Kevin had only gotten off one shot. In the volley of rounds, Ray couldn't be sure.

The next spray of bullets nearly took his head off. He returned fire, getting off four shots before rolling back around the side of the Bronco. He leaned against it and listened to his heart pound. He had more firepower now, but he needed better cover. The main entrance to the park was about fifty yards away.

Stay here and die in a hail of bullets that was quickly making mincemeat of his Bronco. Make a run for it on a bad ankle and take a shot in the back. In the park he might have a chance. Hernandez would surely follow. One on one, Ray's odds were better.

Here we go, God, I'm all yours. He threw himself into a mad dash, firing three times as he streaked through the entrance, past the statue of George Brackenridge. His ankle wrenched, the pain taking what little breath he had left. The last few feet were a jumble of hobble and stumble.

The shadow of huge trees did a bizarre dance in the streetlight as the branches twisted in the wind. His ears strained for sound. His lungs threatened to burst. He slammed into the closest tree and grasped the bark. The rough texture under his fingers assured him he was still alive. He ducked behind it and glanced back. In the glare of the headlights, Echeverria held a gun on Elaine, who bent over Kevin's body. She screamed again and again. Hernandez ran straight at the park entrance.

Ray whirled and ran deeper into the park. Hernandez would love the sport of the hunt, and he had much greater firepower. Darkness and familiarity would work in Ray's favor. He veered onto the first crushed granite trail that intersected with the road.

It was pitch black. His ragged breathing and the thump of his boots against the rocky trail filled an eerie silence. He could make out strange, round shapes in a clearing — the sculpture of a felled tree, cut in chunks. The familiar piece of artwork helped him get his bearings. He was close to the river.

"Mister policeman." Hernandez's whisper carried in the darkness, his sultry accent reminding Ray of long-forgotten trips as a teenager to Matamoros. "Mister policeman, I know you're there. Have pity on an old man. You know how this is going to end. Why prolong the agony and make me chase you around in the dark?"

His soft laugh told Ray Hernandez really didn't mind. It was the chuckle of a grandfather or a dear uncle. He was close, very close.

Ray hunkered behind the largest piece of sculpture.

A crunching sound. He strained to hear. An animal. Dozens of feral cats and stray dogs inhabited the three-hundred-plus acres of park. Yellow eyes shone pale in the dark, so close he could have reached out and touched the face that blended into the night behind them.

He crouched on the balls of his feet, ready. Footsteps crunched on the path.

Straining to see, he held the Glock, barrel up, close to his face as he peered into the darkness. Movement, a dash across the opening from his left to right. He fired once, twice. Pulled back in time to duck the rapid fire of Hernandez's Mac. A grunt and the crunch of shoes on crushed granite gave him a new location, he whipped out and fired again, two more shots. Six left.

"Mister policeman. I tire of this game."

Hernandez's voice was almost on top of Ray. He saw the muzzle flash, threw himself to the ground, rolled twice, and fired four times from flat on his stomach. He heard

Hernandez's gasp, and the unmistakable sound of a body thumping to the ground.

Ray rolled back behind the sculpture and waited; the shadow's darkness a welcome friend.

Hernandez coughed and gasped again.

"Mister policeman." His voice was a faint whisper.

Ray eased forward and peered out. Hernandez lay on the ground a few feet away, not moving.

His Glock still trained on Hernandez, Ray crept forward. The moonlight revealed a Mac on the ground next to Hernandez, who clutched at his chest with both hands. Ray grabbed the weapon. Locked and loaded, a weapon in each hand, he approached. Dark black stains grew on the man's shirt.

He coughed, a grating hoarse sound. "Mister policeman."

Ray dropped to one knee and leaned in, trying to make sure the man had no other weapons. Hernandez whipped out his hand and grabbed Ray's shirt, dragging him down. He jerked back, but Hernandez's grip nearly strangled him.

The old man's face contorted with pain. "Sylvia, *mi mujer, dígale* . . ." Hernandez's hand dropped. His face went slack, eyes still wide, his body limp.

Ray laid the Glock on the ground long enough to put two fingers to Hernandez's neck. No pulse.

Echeverria would take off with Elaine. She and her dad were as good as dead and Candy Romano with them. He picked up the gun and ran.

When he reached the edge of the park, he heard the squealing of tires and saw an unmarked Crown Vic smash into the rear of the BMW.

His partner did love to make an entrance.

Deborah reversed and smashed again. Was she trying to disable the BMW or was she just mad — or worse, drunk? A second later, her door opened, and she tumbled onto the street. Using the door as a shield, she fired through the open window.

Echeverria grabbed Elaine and dragged her into the BMW, keeping up a steady stream of gunfire aimed at Deborah's vehicle. Using the diversion, Ray raced across the road and dived through the Bronco's open door. Echeverria took off. If they got away, it would be too late to save the Doyles or Candy. If he followed, it would divert the heat from Deborah.

Ray turned the key, and the engine snarled to life. He jerked the wheel and snatched a look out the windshield. Deborah had crawled back into the Crown Vic and was trying to start it.

He leaned out the Bronco window. "Call for backup! High-speed chase on 281!"

"Wait." She stumbled from her car, staggered, and fell.

That answered his question.

"Call it in!" He tromped on the accelerator and left her on her knees in the street next to Kevin Doyle's body. He was better off alone, and she was out of danger. With any luck, the chase would draw attention, and he'd pick up some marked units alerted by her call to dispatch.

The BMW raced down Broadway, hitting at least sixty miles an hour in a matter of seconds. The Bronco shuddered and sputtered, no match for a finely-tuned BMW engine. Ray fishtailed behind the other vehicle, ran a red light, narrowly missing an SUV.

Echeverria took a right at Mulberry; Ray stayed with him. The potholes and cracked asphalt in the old street caused the Bronco to shake and shimmy as he wove in and out of traffic, trying not to take out an innocent bystander. A few seconds later they hit 281 and headed north.

The BMW stretched its lead. The Bronco's engine whined, the chassis rocked.

"Come on, come on," Ray chanted as he steadied the vehicle. "Don't give up on me now."

He hit the curve at Olmos Basin doing eighty, jerked left and then right to hurtle between cars that seemed to move like turtles in the middle of a racetrack. Too many curves for this speed. Ray fought to maintain control. *God help me, help me.*

The BMW veered off course and smashed into a retaining wall, spinning in a crazy, sickening whirlwind. Metal scraped cement; sparks crackled in the dark. The vehicle slammed into a minivan, forcing it against the opposite wall.

The BMW, a smashed heap of metal, spun to a stop upside down in Ray's lane, squarely in front of him. He had only a split second to react. He wrenched the wheel to the right to avoid the wreck. The Bronco sideswiped the SUV in the next lane, shoving it onto the shoulder. It was too late. He couldn't stop. The scream of metal on metal. Rubber stripped away, leaving metal against asphalt. The Bronco ripped through the side of the BMW and then went airborne, sailing toward the retaining wall, turning, turning.

Susana. Jesus. Pain devoured him.

■ ■ ■ ■

Susana slowed on Broadway. The dealership had to be on this block. She hadn't been on this side of town in years, not since she'd played in the park as a kid. There it was. No Bronco. A Crown Victoria sat at an awkward angle up against the curb, one tire deflated, the rim smashed. Deborah knelt in front of her car, the headlights illuminating her body.

Understanding struck her. The side of Deborah's car was spattered with dark spots — holes — bullet holes. A man lay in the street several feet from the Crown Vic. He didn't move. Susana jammed her foot on the brake and shoved the gear in park.

She pounded the steering wheel. "No. No. No." Spots danced in front of her eyes. Not again. God would not let this happen to her again.

"It's not Ray," Deborah yelled. She raced toward the Camry, leaned through the window, and grabbed Susana's flailing fists. "Look at me. It's not Ray. Get out. I need your car. Ray went after the BMW. I let him down. I have to help him."

"I'm not getting out."

"Then get over!"

"You're drunk."

Deborah stared at Susana. She didn't bother to deny it. She dashed around the car, jerked open the door, and slid in. "Go. Go! They went north. It's gotta be 281."

Susana stomped the accelerator. The Camry shot forward. Her neck snapped back, and her head smacked the headrest. The park passed in a blur. She shot up the entrance ramp to 281 doing seventy. The traffic in front of her suddenly slowed in a vast red sea of brake lights. She veered onto the shoulder and fought the next curve. Her foot hovered over the brake.

The crumpled wreckage loomed in front of them. A BMW had flipped upside down in the middle lane. A Bronco had smashed against the retaining wall. Ray's Bronco. A minivan and a Tahoe stood upright, parked on the shoulder, hazard lights flashing. Debris littered the highway, decorating skid marks that stretched several hundred yards.

"Stop!" Deborah screamed.

"I'm trying." Susana shrieked. The Camry squealed and swerved. She fought back. The car skidded to a halt a hairsbreadth from the wreck.

"There's a first aid kit under the seat. Bring it." She shoved open the door and ran. Behind her Deborah's voice screamed

497

into her phone, only occasional phrases penetrating Susana's single-minded focus. *Officer down. Ambulances. Traffic control.* Meaningless phrases in the face of the horrible dawning realization that Ray was in that crumpled Bronco.

A man wiped blood from his face with the bottom of his white T-shirt as he talked on his phone a few feet from the Bronco. "I already called 911," he yelled as she sprinted past. "The idiots were racing. He sideswiped me. I had no place to go. I could've been killed."

Susana didn't answer. In her haste, she stumbled and dropped to her knees next to the shattered windshield of the Bronco. She stared at Ray's bloody face, half hidden behind the deflated airbag. His eyes were closed, mouth slack. Bloody. Blood everywhere. A long, jagged cut across his forehead oozed blood. *No. No. No. God. Not again. Please God, not again.*

She pushed at the glass.

"Wait." Deborah handed her a PD windbreaker "Use this."

Susana cleared the glass. "Ray? Ray!" He didn't answer, didn't move. She swallowed a moan and touched his neck.

A pulse. Thready. Still, a pulse. "He's got a pulse. He's got a pulse!"

Deborah reached in and grabbed his seat-belt.

"No." Susana pushed the woman aside. Her training as a firefighter kicked in, squashing the monstrous panic back into its cage. "You know better. Don't move him."

She broke open the first aid kit "I need something clean. A towel, anything. I have to stop the bleeding. Find me something and then check on the others."

Deborah jolted to her feet. A few seconds later she was back with a towel. "Some lady on her way to the gym had this. She says it's clean."

Susana eased through the jagged hole in the windshield and shoved aside the airbag, getting as close to Ray as she could.

"Stay with me, please stay with me, promise me you won't leave me." She pressed the towel to his head. "Ray, don't you dare leave me. I love you."

His arm jerked, fist clenched, then went slack.

"Ray, Ray, can you hear me?" She squeezed his hand. "I'm right here, honey, right here. Help is coming. Just hang on. Hang on."

He mumbled something, but his eyes didn't open. One hand still clutching the bloody towel to his head and the other squeezing his hand, Susana bowed her head. *Jesus, please save him. You gave me another chance to love, and I threw it away. I'm so sorry, Jesus. Please help him hang on. He still has work to do for You. Please.* Susana let prayer be her silent scream for help. *God, I'm counting on you. Abba, Almighty God of mine. Jesus, I cry out to you. Let him live.*

CHAPTER
THIRTY-NINE

They wouldn't let Susana get in the ambulance. A paramedic kept telling her Ray would be okay. His face said otherwise. Deborah dragged her back to the Camry. Susana sped after the ambulance. Deborah spewed a steady stream of obscenities into her phone.

"We've got people at the dealership now." Deborah stuck her phone in her pocket. "They found another body in the park. Looks like Ray shot and killed our suspect."

Susana didn't frame a reply. Ray had done what he had to do to survive. She focused on navigating through traffic snarled from yet another accident. A drive that should have taken ten minutes stretched to twenty. Every second inflicted another laceration on her heart. She gripped the wheel and bit her lower lip until it bled to keep from screaming with impatience.

Vehicles jammed the hospital parking lot.

Down to her last thread of patience, she swerved into a loading zone and bolted from the Camry at a dead run, not looking to see if Deborah followed.

Tears blinded her as. *Let him live. Please, God, let him live. Javier left me this way. Not Ray, too, I'm begging You. Let him live.*

The refrain pounded in her head as she struggled with heavy double doors at the main entrance, as she ran through the corridors, as she slammed her fist on the ER information desk to get the nurse to look up.

Please, God, let him live.

The nurse spoke, her words barely penetrating Susana's panic. Ray was in an examining room.

The refrain beat a steady rhythm in her head as she tottered on shaking legs into the waiting room. Samuel appeared. And other people. Officers. Ray's colleagues. His police family. The only family he had. The paramedic stood in the doorway, his shirt stained with blood. He stared at her, hands slack at his side. His lips moved, but she couldn't hear what he was saying. All she could hear was the refrain.

Let him live.

Samuel towered over her, his hands raised as if he wanted to hug her and didn't quite

502

know how. "Susana. Susana, it'll be okay. The trauma doctors here are the best." Stress etched lines around his mouth, his jawbone jutted against his skin.

The agonized timbre of his voice triggered the memory of him standing next to her, looking into Javier's open grave. Her throat ached with unshed tears. Samuel's hand gripped her elbow so tightly it hurt. The casket disappeared into the hole. The dull thud as errant dirt clods hit the box sickened her. Susana crumpled onto a couch, hands over her mouth, trying to stifle sobs that threatened to turn into hysteria.

"Give us a minute." Samuel spoke to the others. They backed off.

She searched Samuel's face. "Will he make it?"

Samuel's big hand curled around hers. "They're taking him up to surgery. His spleen is ruptured; he's got a fractured skull, a broken collarbone, broken ribs, and a broken leg."

His features blurred through her tears. "But, he'll make it?" She repeated. Samuel would never lie to her.

His lips tightened. "I don't know."

A shudder ripped through Susana. "I can't believe this is happening again."

"Have faith, Sis." Samuel's voice cracked.

"It's all we've got left."

"Okay." She saw a sliver of the agony he was trying to hide; she wasn't the only one in pain. She tried to clamp down her emotions, but her voice still shook. "I guess you got my message?"

A shadow darkened his face. "Yeah. Ray left me one, too. Unfortunately I was too far away to help him. I can't raise Deborah. One of the officers at the scene said the two of you left together. Where is she?"

Struggling for coherency, Susana raced through the events that had ended with Deborah and her in the Camry together. "I assumed she was right behind me. I don't know where she went."

The look on Samuel's face flashed from grim to furious. "I'll deal with her later."

Susana tried to make sense of it all. "Do we know why Ray was chasing them?"

Samuel eased onto the couch next to her and rubbed his face. "The dead BMW driver was Mariano Echeverria, a drug dealer. The detectives working the Doyle case are over at the location now. They've found evidence they were using the inventory at the dealership to transport drugs. There's a dead guy in the park. Lalo Hernandez, a contract killer. They think Ray shot him."

Susana couldn't contain a shiver. "What about Milton Doyle?"

"They found him alive at a cartel outpost in the county. The DEA gave us a line on the location. But not Candy Romano. They're looking for her body, but with Hernandez dead, they may never find it."

"So, all this was about money? Wealthy people wanting more money?"

"Looks that way."

"And how many people are dead?"

"Joey Doyle, Melody Doyle, Vicky Barrera, Tommy Wheeler, Candy Romano, Kevin Doyle." Samuel ticked the body count off on his fingers. "And of course, Hernandez and Echeverria."

"Did Kevin Doyle know they were going to kill Joey?" Susana could hardly grasp the kind of avarice that could invade a person's life so insidiously that it wiped away any vestige of a moral compass.

"Elaine Doyle claims they didn't. But with the main players dead, it's unlikely we'll ever know for sure."

"How long will Ray be in surgery?" Cold fear churned inside her.

Samuel wrapped an arm around her, his voice soft in her ear. "I don't know."

Susana buried her head in her brother's shirt. Her lungs were flat. She couldn't

505

breathe. She wouldn't be able to until she could tell Ray how wrong she had been.

And how much she loved him.

She might never get to say those words.

"Martinez."

Samuel looked up, his arm still around Susana.

Lieutenant Alvarez crooked his head.

Samuel gave his sister one last squeeze, then joined his supervisor in the hallway. Word traveled fast. Dozens of officers including Alex Luna, Joaquin, guys from the homicide unit, and officers from Ray's cadet class lined the corridor, waiting.

"What's the word on Johnson?"

Samuel shook his head. "We won't know until somebody comes out to talk to us."

"He was supposed to be off the case. This is what happens when an officer goes off like some cowboy in a Wild West show." Alvarez rubbed his hand over the stubble on his chin, his bloodshot eyes hooded.

"Look, he nearly got killed in the process, but he got them. Give him that." Samuel stuck clenched fists in his pockets. He hadn't been there to back up his guy. And where had Deborah been?

"Yeah. I talked to Treviño at the scene. He gave Johnson full credit for breaking it wide open." Alvarez pursued his lips. "What about his partner? Smith? Where was she?"

"She has some problems. I'll deal with her."

"I've heard rumors." Alvarez's expression hardened. "If they're true, you should've addressed those problems a long time ago."

"I said, I'll take care of it."

"See that you do." Alvarez turned away. "I'm getting some coffee. Call me when Johnson's out of surgery."

Samuel headed back into the waiting room. Stopped. Piper and Lily sat on either side of Susana, entwined in one of those group hug things women did. Piper looked up at him, her face so sad he couldn't stand it. She nodded toward the door behind him. He looked back.

Deborah stood in the doorway. His gaze met hers. He shook his head. "Wait for me outside." Without a word, she turned and left.

Samuel started toward Piper. She stood, and they met in the middle of the room. She reached for him and he grasped her hand, squeezing so hard, she winced. He loosened his grip, but didn't let go.

"Where are the kids?" It was the first question that came to his mind, followed by a dozen more.

"Autumn's with them."

"Does Marco know?"

Piper shook her head. "He'd want to be here, and we didn't want him to go through this again. We'll tell him once we know — " Her voice died.

"No matter what happens, Ray will be okay." Gently, Samuel cupped her face, wiped away her tears with his thumbs, then asked the question that pressed against his heart. "But will we?"

"When this is over, come home," she whispered.

The chain that locked away his emotions slipped. He cleared his throat before whispering back. "If I had to live without you — "

"Me, too." Piper hugged him and let go before he could react. "Deal with Detective Smith. I'll stay with Susana."

Feeling as if he'd just received a get-of-jail-free card, Samuel strode into the hallway. He glanced both ways. Deborah leaned against a wall, head down, at the far end, away from the other officers.

He walked slowly toward her, corralling his anger. She'd been missing in action for two hours. "Where've you been?"

She looked up. Her eyes were swollen and red. "What are they saying about Ray?"

"He's in surgery. Where've you been?"

"I need to talk to you about that." The slur deepened with each word.

"Talk."

She shifted, her gaze on her shoes. Samuel leaned against the opposite wall and waited.

She sniffed. Sniffed again. He pulled the packet of tissues he'd held for Susana from his pocket and handed them to her.

"Thanks."

More silence.

Then, "I need help."

Finally. "You're ready to stop drinking?"

"I had my last drink at a bar two blocks from here." She looked at him then, her lips trembling. "When I drove up to the primary scene, I thought I was too late. I thought it was his body on the ground. I was too late because I'd stopped for a drink — a couple drinks. I went a little crazy. Smashed the car. I didn't want them to leave. I wanted to kill somebody. Then, he drove off without me because he knew I was . . . I thought he was okay. Then he wasn't. He could die, because I wasn't there for him. I'm his partner. It was . . . it was my birthday."

She ended the rambling explanation as if the last sentence explained everything.

Compassion warred with disgust. Samuel

509

stared at her face, absorbing her desperation. And devastation. "Do you really want to stop?"

She nodded, one hard jerk. She dashed her tears away, then stood up straight, shoulders back. "Yes."

"Give me your weapon, your badge, and your keys."

Deborah's face blanched.

He pushed off the wall and pulled his cell phone from his pocket. "I'll get you into a clinic. I'll take you as soon as Ray's out of surgery."

She shrugged off her shoulder holster and handed it to him. She hesitated over the badge, her gaze going to his face.

"Get sober, stay sober, and there's a chance you'll get it back. Don't, and it's over. I'll see to it." He held out his hand.

She sniffed and laid the badge in his palm. Emotion raged through him as his fingers folded around the metal. He focused on compassion. Nothing more. Nothing less.

"Find a chair and sit in it until I come for you. And don't talk to anybody."

"I won't."

Samuel turned away.

"Sergeant."

"What?" He paused.

"I'm sorry."

"I'm not the one you need to tell."

"I know, but Ray's in surgery."

"Your partner is a forgiving man, but I'm talking about God. Get straight with Him, and the rest will follow." She looked so lost, he wanted to give her hope. "Deborah, I promise you God forgives. I personally know that to be a fact."

She nodded.

Samuel walked toward Piper, every step a step toward getting his life back. He'd almost reached her when a nurse in surgical scrubs dodged past him, racing toward the doors that led to the OR. Her intense expression stung him. He fought the urge to drop to his knees and ask God to intervene in the life or death struggle going on in that room. Ray deserved the chance to get his life back, too. Only God knew if he would.

The doors swung violently, then closed.

CHAPTER
FORTY

The enigmatic look on the surgeon's face told Susana nothing. Her legs trembled as she forced herself to stand. Lily rose next to her and slipped her hand in Susana's.

"Who's Detective Johnson's next of kin?" The doctor's gaze traveled around the waiting room.

"We all are." Susana tugged away from Lily and went to stand in front of the doctor. She felt the weight of Samuel's hand on her shoulder. "Please, just tell us, how is he?"

"Are you his wife?"

Samuel's fingers tightened.

Susana felt her face flush with heat. "Not yet."

"Detective Johnson made it through surgery. He's unconscious. His condition is critical."

Susana swayed.

Samuel's arm came around her and held

her up. "But he's going to pull through, right?" He asked the question she couldn't.

The doctor's eyes seemed kinder. "We're doing everything we can to make sure he does. The next few hours are critical."

Susana broke away from her brother. "I want to be with him."

The doctor shook his head. "I'm sorry, he can't have visitors yet. Besides, he wouldn't know you were there anyway."

He would know. Susana was sure of it. "I need to be as close as possible then."

The doctor nodded. "Follow me."

Susana sat where she could see Ray's bed through the ICU window. People came and went, offering comfort and company. Their words didn't register. Ray's fight to stay alive filled the space around her.

Night fled into a long day followed by another dark stretch when the halls emptied and nurses sat at consoles, the tapping on computer keyboards or the rustling of papers the only sounds that told her some-one shared her vigil.

"You should go home, sleep for a few hours."

Susana shook her head and looked up at Samuel. His bloodshot eyes and two-day old growth of beard made him look more like the criminals he arrested than a career cop. "Are you?"

He shrugged. "I'll get us some more coffee."

She nodded and sank back against the chair. When she couldn't hear his footsteps on the tile anymore, she bowed her head and gripped her hands together like a child saying her nightly prayers. *I see your point, God. When evil is all around, love is the only thing stronger. You offered me the one thing you knew I needed more than anything else and I was too weak to hold out my hand. Forgive me for not trusting you. I want my second chance, if it's not too late. Ray lost his first love, but he didn't give up. He wasn't afraid. He trusted you. He deserves to love again. Let me be his second chance —*

"Ms. Acosta. Ma'am." Susana jolted back and gripped the armrests. A nurse stood over her. Susana's heart flew into overdrive as the possibilities careened through her head. "Detective Johnson's awake. He's asking for you."

Relief made her stagger as she entered his room. His head turned toward her, and he made a small sound, almost a groan. What she could see of his bandaged face was so swollen and bruised that she wouldn't have recognized him if she hadn't known it was him. Careful to avoid the IVs, she squeezed his hand. He squeezed back.

"You're here." His eyes were hazy with painkillers. A sudden grimace told her they weren't entirely doing their job. "I heard you praying for me."

She nodded. He couldn't have heard her, but it didn't matter. "We've all been praying for you. I've been praying I'd get a chance to tell you I love you."

"Did I die and go to heaven?"

"Funny guy." She touched his bruised face, traced the line of his jaw with one finger. "Forgive me for being so pigheaded and such a fraidycat. To quote a very persistent homicide detective, whatever time God gives us together, I want it. Short or long, I'll take it."

"Pigheaded fraidycat — that's the woman I love." He closed his eyes, and his hand went slack in hers. She thought he'd drifted away, but his eyes opened again.

"Are you going to marry me?" he asked, his voice hoarse.

"You haven't asked."

"Just did."

His fingers wrapped around hers in a fierce grip — she couldn't tell if it was pain or emotion.

She squeezed back. "Yes, I'll marry you."

"If I'd known wrecking the Bronco would

be the only way you'd agree, I would have done it sooner." His voice cracked. "I think you better seal the deal."

She bent over and kissed his bruised lips, just a feather of touch, not wanting to cause him more pain.

His good hand came up and brought her head back down. "More."

She obliged.

EPILOGUE

Deborah had a sick feeling in the pit of her stomach. Her deodorant had failed. Wet rings under the arms of her white blouse would be the first thing they noticed about her when she walked into the sanctuary.

Coming here was a mistake. She wanted to race back to her apartment and hide there, like she'd done since she'd finished rehab. Facing the people she'd let down had been even harder than she'd expected. They'd all tried to make it easier for her, but she knew they were watching, waiting, to see if she'd dive headfirst back into a bottle.

Ray's new Dodge Ram sat next to Sarge's old pickup in the church parking lot. Watching Ray pick out his truck — from a truck dealership not owned by the Doyles — had been the most fun she'd had in ages. Deborah could imagine the shock on his face when he saw her walk in. She couldn't bear the thought of everyone staring at her.

A young couple greeted the latecomers who straggled in to the service. Soon they would shut the doors, and it would be too late. Then she could start her truck and go home where she belonged.

"You know, it generally works better if you actually go inside."

The man who walked toward Deborah's truck looked vaguely familiar. He wasn't very tall, kind of wiry, big eyes, dark hair, and a full mouth under a thick moustache. He had a kind face. Three kids trotted ahead of him.

One of them looked back, and the man waved him on. "I'll be right there, Benny. Save me a seat."

Deborah shook her head and put her hand on the key in the ignition. "I was just leaving."

"Wait. Don't go. We're a friendly bunch, I promise." He smiled at her.

Straight, white teeth shone against olive brown skin.

"The thing you have to remember," he said as he put one hand on the doorframe, his tone conspiratorial, "is that everyone in there is a sinner. No exceptions."

She managed an uncomfortable smile. This stranger had no idea how deep, or how far back, her sin went. He appeared to be a church-going, family man. How could he begin to understand her?

Deborah couldn't help herself, she tossed the words out like a challenge. "So what's your sin? Did you buy a lottery ticket? *Tsk-tsk.*"

"Not that simple." His smile slipped. "My wife wants a divorce."

"Wouldn't that be her sin?"

"Well, I think a lot of people in that sanctuary secretly wonder what I did to make her leave me."

"They're judging you? I thought Christians weren't supposed to judge." She couldn't keep the sarcasm out of her voice. That was exactly what she hated about Christians. Always judging.

"Christians are humans. We make mistakes."

Eyes the color of charcoal filled with pain, and suddenly she felt ashamed of her ugly response to his overt act of kindness. He could've ignored her sitting alone in her truck. Instead, he'd reached out. She'd forgotten people like him still existed in a hostile world.

"Well, did you do something to hurt her?" she asked, thinking of her own experiences with men. "Does she have a good reason?"

"Oh, she has reasons, but I've loved her and no one else for sixteen years."

"How could she stand it?" She made a little joke in hopes of glossing over her unfriendliness.

He smiled again. "Apparently, she couldn't. Okay. Your turn. Why are you so afraid to go in there?"

"I'm not afraid." Deborah turned the key and listened to the comforting rumble of the engine. "I'm an alcoholic, not a coward."

"Then come in."

"I can't."

"Sure you can. It's not about them. It's about Him." He gave the door a pat with his hand and tilted his head toward the building. "Come on. I'll walk you in. It's easier not to have to go it alone the first time."

"I don't know." Deborah reached for the key again, and sudden silence made her realize she had turned the engine off. He opened her door, and she stepped into a July sun so brilliant she could barely see. She took a deep breath and banished the fluttering moths doing somersaults in her stomach. *Here I am, God. I may be a drunk, but I'm not a coward. I don't know how to do this. Help me. Please.*

The man held out his arm.

520

She looked at it, then at his face. "Do I know you? I'm positive I've seen you somewhere before."

"I'm sorry. Where're my manners?" He dropped his arm and extended his hand. "I'm Daniel Martinez."

"Sergeant Martinez's brother." She shook his hand. "You look just like him. I'm Deborah Smith."

"Ray Johnson's partner?"

She nodded, waiting for him to step back. His desire to help her would disappear, now that he knew she was the one who'd let her partner down.

"You ready?" He held out his arm again. His gaze showered her with compassion, and her pulse steadied.

"No." She wrapped her hand around the crook of his elbow.

He smiled. "We'll face them together."

ABOUT THE AUTHOR

Although born in the Midwest, **Kelly Irvin** has always suffered from wanderlust. She spent a year and a half in Costa Rica as a college student, before graduating from the University of Kansas with a degree in journalism. She worked as a newspaper reporter along the Texas-Mexico border for several years before moving with her husband, Tim, a professional photographer, to San Antonio. By day, she works as a public relations professional. By night, she's a writer who shines the light in dark corners. She's also the mother of two phenomenal young adults.

The employees of Thorndike Press hope you have enjoyed this Large Print book. All our Thorndike, Wheeler, and Kennebec Large Print titles are designed for easy reading, and all our books are made to last. Other Thorndike Press Large Print books are available at your library, through selected bookstores, or directly from us.

For information about titles, please call:
(800) 223-1244

or visit our Website at:
http://gale.cengage.com/thorndike

To share your comments, please write:
Publisher
Thorndike Press
295 Kennebec Memorial Drive
Waterville, ME 04901